Kimberly G. Giarratano

DEATH OF A DANCING QUEEN

A BILLIE LEVINE NOVEL

DATURA

DATURA BOOKS
An imprint of Watkins Media Ltd

Unit 11, Shepperton House
89 Shepperton Road
London N1 3DF
UK

daturabooks.com
twitter.com/daturabooks
Diamonds are a Girl's Best Friend

A Datura Books paperback original, 2023

Cover by Sarah O'Flaherty
Edited by Eleanor Teasdale and Red Adept Editing
Set in Meridien

ISBN 978 1 91520 242 0
Ebook ISBN 978 1 91520 251 2

Printed and bound in the United Kingdom by TJ Books Limited

9 8 7 6 5 4 3 2 1

Dedication

To the Jewish women who made me:
my mom, Jane, and my grandmas, Elaine and Pearl

CHAPTER ONE
June 6, 1991

Starla Wells lit a cigarette and slipped into the shadows. She pressed a spiked heel against the brick exterior of the building, and her bent knee revealed a slender thigh and a garter belt with a tiny dagger tucked underneath.

The other heel stood in a puddle of rainwater, a souvenir from an earlier thunderstorm so violent it had forced a young family to seek refuge inside the club. The mother had cast an anxious glance around the smoky interior, spotted topless dancers and men bucking their hips, and decided that they'd be safer in a minivan getting pinged by softball-sized hail.

She wasn't wrong.

Starla had danced in too many clubs where too many men thought a striptease also entitled them to things they hadn't paid for. Hence the dagger.

She took a drag off the cig and flicked ash to the wet concrete below. The sky was hidden by haze. What stars muscled through the Manhattan light pollution twinkled dully like the sequins on her skirt.

This was the time she liked best. After a show, still high on adrenaline, she would slink into the alley to be alone, letting the air dry the sweat that ran down her cleavage and cool the heat rising off her collarbones.

Here, she could bathe in the afterglow of a performance without judgments and jealous looks. She was Icarus without wax wings, and she would fly as high as she liked.

Starla fingered the diamond ring that hung from her neck. She reveled in how the jewel glinted under the stage lights, how it blinded the corneas of the elite set: the politicians, the Wall Street bankers, the mobsters. The eight-carat rock was integral to her act. It made her seem expensive even if everyone thought it was fake and made her appear worthy of the bills tossed at her feet. Made Neil Goff look twice.

She was no longer a two-bit stripper from the *Lucky Lous*. She was Starla Wells, the cabaret vixen of the *Malta Club*. She had men lining her pockets and lining up to take her to bed, gangsters and cops. Both sides of the law courted her favor – a far cry from her adolescence.

She smiled softly to herself. *If they could see me now.*

The music from the club pumped through the brick, matching pace with her heartbeat, as if inexplicably mixed in her bloodstream. Mama Ree had just begun her set, soaking up Starla's leftovers. Starla knew that Mama Ree loathed following her, but what didn't kill a girl…She blew out another plume of slate and dropped her leg.

Stubbing out her cigarette on a concrete block, Starla admitted to herself that she couldn't do this gig forever. She was in her thirties, and despite the best plastic surgeon in Bergen County, her body would eventually betray her, and Neil would find a younger tramp to replace her. He didn't have his father's vision. He saw the club as a means to his success, but the club could be a jewel on its own.

With the right direction.

She flicked the butt into an oily puddle and fingered the diamond. That was what this baby was for. She was going to open her own place. Rule the roost. Do things her way. No Neil to boss her around. No bosses at all.

And her girls would be special. Like diamonds themselves.

She had an appointment tomorrow at the jewelers to see what the gem would fetch. She believed that it would be more than enough to buy Neil out. Wouldn't that be something?

Starla glimpsed movement as a dark silhouette ghosted under the piss-yellow light that illuminated the club's dumpster.

Her breath caught, a quick intake of air that surprised even her. She slipped the dagger out of her garter and gripped the hilt. "Who's there?" Her voice sounded weak, so she tried again, deeper and throatier. "Who is *there*?"

The figure emerged fully into the light.

Starla exhaled again, but this time, it mimicked the sound of annoyance. She dropped her arm but kept the dagger at her side. "You have some nerve coming here after what you did to me. We had an arrangement, remember?"

"I made no such deal."

Starla scoffed.

"Give it to me."

"No," Starla growled.

Two steps forward and a hand yanked on the gold chain, snapping the delicate links. The ring fell to the filthy gutter, and Starla cried out. But it was too late. The diamond had been scooped up, and not by her.

Starla lurched forward and brandished the dagger, stabbing the air. "Give it back, or I will cut you." She lunged again, tripping over the concrete block. Her knees hit the pavement first, followed by her palms scraping against asphalt and pebbles.

The dagger skidded across the ground, stopping only when it made contact with the dumpster.

Starla's skin sang. She hissed as she got to her feet and hobbled toward the dagger, realizing too late that it wasn't there when the blade burrowed into her shoulder.

Starla whirled around and stumbled in her heels. Crimson droplets fell at her feet. She pressed a hand to her shoulder, and it came away berry red, the same color as her lipstick.

Starla screamed. But the dagger came down again, slicing the patch of skin left exposed by a too-short top and a too-low skirt.

Blood oozed hot.

She staggered to the brick wall, her hand pressed firmly to her skin, but it was like trying to plug the cracks in a dam.

The dagger slid out like butter and came down again, meeting her breast, meeting a lung, meeting her hip. Starla gasped for air.

It came down again and again and again.

She couldn't see anything but her reflection in the metal as it hacked her into darkness.

CHAPTER TWO
30-ish years later...

Billie Levine was typing the answer into the daily crossword app on her phone – *12 Down, Eighties band times two* (Duran Duran, puh-leaze) – when he walked into *Nagel's Deli* wearing ripped jeans and a nasty shiner. He looked to be around her age, old enough to order a whiskey sour at the *Clam Bar* but not without getting carded first. But based on his sunken cheeks, shaky hands, and bloodshot pinball eyes, booze was not this kid's vice.

He was tall and thin with a crop of dark, wavy hair. His skin was unblemished but flushed. His shirt was missing a button, and there was a patch of light skin on his wrist where a watch would normally rest. Lines cracked with dried blood snaked out from bruised knuckles. His lower lip was puffy and split. His leather jacket was supple but coated in dirt as if he slept wrapped in it like a burrito on a bus station bench. That coat would soon follow the fate of the watch.

Sensing this kid was here for her, Billie glanced his way and signaled to him with the arc of her brows. If this had been a blind date, she would've excused herself to the bathroom and shimmied out through the square window above the toilet.

She probably should have done that anyway.

He approached her booth and hovered, his eyes making contact with the autographed photos of C-list celebrities on the wall. His fingers danced at his side. His leg jangled. He was twitchier than a field mouse in a cat's shadow. "You the private investigator?" he asked.

The kid was making her anxious, although that could've been the five cups of coffee she had consumed before he got there.

"Yes," answered Billie, but it sounded like a question.

He plopped into the seat across from her and immediately reached for the salt shaker, which he twisted in his chapped palms. "I need help."

That was an understatement.

Billie set down her phone and waved Bernice over. The waitress begrudgingly placed another mug on the table and filled it with coffee. "I'll cover him," said Billie.

"Yeah, yeah." Bernice was in her late sixties, with soft bouffant hair that she dyed strawberry blond. The only reason she let Billie conduct business in the corner booth was because she had a crush on Billie's grandfather, who was yukking it up with his cop buddies on the other side of the deli. Billie heard him now:

"And then the perp said if I gave him back his teeth, he would deal me in a slice of the haul. He was a ninety-five year-old bank robber."

Yuk. Yuk. Yuk.

"Never gets stale," said Ken Greenberg as if he hadn't heard the story a thousand times, toasting the air at the Levine kitchen table.

"Photos of you online show an old dude," the kid said to Billie.

She pointed to her grandfather. "You mean that guy?" Then, even more specifically because there were a bunch of old men in the corner, "The one standing up as if conducting an orchestra?"

The kid stretched his neck like a giraffe. Bruises dotted his trachea. "He's pouring scotch into his coffee."

"That's him," Billie said without even glancing over. "William Levine, the original. Technically, this is his PI firm, but he's retired. I handle the cases now. Belinda Levine, but you can call me Billie."

The kid lowered himself back into the booth. She nudged the coffee cup closer to him. "You okay there, buddy?"

"Yeah," he said, not meeting her gaze, clearly lying. He worked his jaw and scratched violently at the skin above his thumb. His teeth were wearing away from the constant grinding. Heroin did that to you, and so did meth. Billie wasn't sure which poison had its hooks into him. Could be both. Either way, this kid wasn't clean. He'd need a fix soon. Real soon.

Billie gestured at the tender skin beneath his eye. "How'd you get that nasty mark?" Then she pointed at his swollen knuckles. "And those?"

He dropped his hands into his lap. "Beef at the bar."

Excuse at the ready. She might've believed him if she thought that booze was this kid's problem. Which she didn't.

His eyes bounced off everything: the red vinyl booths, the grimy tables, the counter, and the glass dessert cases. "I've never been here before."

She stretched back and rested one arm along the top of the booth. "Finest Jewish deli in all of North Jersey." And the only one that would let Billie sit for hours without having to order a twenty-five-dollar pastrami sandwich. The portions were huge, but it still felt to Billie as if she needed to take out a mortgage just to eat dinner. "Try the coleslaw and half sours. They're on me." Actually, they were on the house, but whatever. Bernice didn't care. "What's your name?"

"Tommy Russo."

His Jersey accent was subtle enough to suggest that he might have spent his formative years in an out-of-state boarding school. If she had to guess, the kid came from money. Where that money was now, who knew? She certainly imagined what he did with it.

Billie leaned forward, smoothed down her U2 T-shirt, and crossed her legs, unsticking her Doc Martens from whatever goo they had settled into underneath the table. It was a vintage outfit that she had scrounged together from a thrift store in Sussex County, but something about nineties fashion was badass. And at five feet four inches, with a round baby face, she needed all the edge she could get.

"How did you hear about me?" she asked.

"Nicole Mercier in Student Housing gave me your card."

"You go to Kentwell?"

"Yeah." Then, more quietly, "For now."

Tommy didn't look as if he could stay clean long enough to attend classes, let alone be enrolled in any, but Billie trusted that Nicole wouldn't toss her a helpless drug user to pay the bills.

He added, "Nicole said that you used to go there."

Billie nodded. "Graduated two years ago with a bachelor's in English."

"And this is what you do with it?" Tommy might've been an addict, but apparently, he was lucid enough to raise a judgmental brow at her job choice.

"I like making my own hours," she said dryly. "What did you come to see me about?"

Tommy picked up a napkin and proceeded to shred it. "My girlfriend's missing. Can you find her?"

"Maybe," said Billie. "Did Nic mention that I'm not licensed? My grandfather is, and technically, he's my supervisor..." Her voice trailed off.

Gramps cackled like a drunken sailor.

She could see how bad this looked. "He was in the force for thirty years, investigator for twenty."

Tommy shrugged. "I don't know where else to go. If you can help me, then I don't care about licensing."

Billie nodded as she slid a small notebook and pen out of her leather bag. She opened to a clean page and clicked the pen a few times. "Girlfriend's name?"

"Jasmine Flores. She's a junior at Kentwell."

"So roughly twenty, twenty-one years old?"

"Twenty-one," he said.

"And when was the last time you saw her?"

"Um…four days ago, maybe five."

"Anyone else report her missing?"

"No," he said. "I don't think so."

"Not her parents? Roommate? Teachers?"

He shook his head. Or maybe his head was just shaking uncontrollably, the side effect of whatever he was on.

"Is she also an addict?" she asked.

"No, she doesn't use. Never has."

Billie exhaled and put down her pen. It didn't take a bloodhound to sniff out this shit. "Is it possible that Jasmine is simply taking some time away?" she asked gently.

"For what?"

"Listen, Tommy. You seem like a nice kid, but you need help." Billie shot a glance at the napkin he had torn into confetti. "Maybe Jasmine told you that? Maybe she suggested rehab?"

"What's your point?"

That she had ghosted him faster than a Victorian widow haunting a mansion. "Maybe she wants to break up and doesn't have the heart to tell you."

His hand slapped the table hard, rattling the coffee mugs and spilling precious caffeine. The voices in the deli halted at the outburst. Gramps peeked over, but Billie waved it off. Kid had a temper, but nothing she couldn't handle.

"We love each other," he said insistently. He went back to scratching his hand. "She wouldn't leave me."

"Why haven't her parents reported her missing?" Billie asked.

"They live in Honduras. Jasmine never talks about them." Scratch, scratch.

"Go to the cops?"

"What if they contact ICE or something?"

Red lines bloomed on his skin. She handed him a fresh napkin.

"Is she not documented?" Billie asked.

Tommy blotted his scratches. "She never said, which makes me think she isn't. Y'know? Like she's afraid someone might report her?"

"Do you have any reason to believe that she is on ICE's radar? A few years ago, you would have had cause for concern. But now...I'm not so sure."

Billie wondered if Gramps had a contact in ICE she could ask.

Tommy sighed and rubbed his hands over his face as if he was molding clay. "So maybe not ICE, then. If she's hiding from me, I'll deal with it. I just want to know that she's safe."

"If I find her and she doesn't want further contact with you, are you going to be all right with that?"

"Yeah," he said.

"You sure?"

"Hundo percent."

"You're still gonna have to pay me even if she doesn't want you to know where she is." Billie leaned back and crossed her arms. The kid was a walking advertisement for a halfway house. No way he could pony up the cash for her services. And she didn't work pro bono, not even for charity cases, because honestly, she was one too. She was still paying off college loans and her mom's debts. "I don't work for free," she said.

"How much?"

She rolled her eyes, not even bothering to hide her annoyance. He could only be wasting her time. "It's a $500 retainer. That'll cover my initial time and expenses. Then it's sixty bucks an hour plus costs like food and gas, which I charge per mile. A dollar per mile to be exact." She would see what he needed more – his girlfriend or his fix.

To her surprise, he removed several big bills from his jacket pocket – kid was more flush than she'd thought – and dropped them right onto a pool of spilled coffee. Billie cocked her brow.

"Will that do?" he said smugly.

She stared at the cash. Now it was her turn to decide what

she needed more – money to pay her bills or a sketchy client with a bad drug habit.

Billie's phone lit up with a text from her brother. *Think we have a hole in the roof.*

"It'll do just fine." Sighing, she wiped the cash with a fresh napkin and stuck it into her bra while Tommy signed a client retainer agreement – a dinosaur of legal jargon Gramps had had a lawyer draw up decades ago.

Billie asked him for details – Jasmine's height, weight, eye color, and any identifying tattoos and scars. He swiped through his cell phone – cracked screen – until he came across her photo. He showed her the picture.

"She's short, like you. Five-three at the most. Dark, curly hair. Brown eyes. She's Latina. Her family is –"

"Honduran," Billie finished as she glanced at Jasmine's pretty face. "You said that already." The girl was a looker, no doubt, but there was something in Jasmine's eyes that gave Billie pause. Like she was keeping a secret. Like she was keeping a lot of secrets. "What about her social media accounts?"

"Her Insta is JasmineFlowers12."

"Facebook?"

"Nah."

"Twitter?"

"No."

"TikTok?"

"She scrolls, doesn't post."

"Reddit?"

"Yes," he said with disinterest. "She moderated one for some club she's in. I don't have deets."

Billie continued, "Any places she frequented? Coffee shops? Libraries? Did she gamble on horses?" Billie was kidding about that last question, although people would be surprised at who liked to toss money on thoroughbreds.

Tommy scratched the back of his neck. "She hangs out at the

Ugly Mug coffee shop in Ridgewood. Her friend, Nuri O'Brien, works there. They do a podcast together."

"About what?"

"Jasmine says it's a rip-off of *My Favorite Murder*. I don't really listen to it."

Billie jotted down the name of the podcast. "Got any contact info for this Nuri?"

Tommy shrugged. "Lives in Fellman House. Total weirdo."

Nice.

"Lastly, Jasmine's place of employment. Part-time job?"

"Stripper."

Her hand hovered in mid-air. "Where?"

"Some joint off Route 17."

"You're gonna have to be more specific."

He scrunched his forehead, folding the skin into ripples. Then he snapped his fingers. "Something Club. Italy Club. Sicily Club."

Billie looked up, resigned. "*Malta Club*?"

"That's the one," he said.

Dammit. Of all the places Jasmine could work…

Billie pointed her pen at him. "This is gonna cost you."

"I'm good for it."

She would see about that.

CHAPTER THREE

The next morning, Billie was awakened by a poke to her shoulder. She blinked to see her mother, Shari Levine, hovering over the bed, a pointer finger raised to strike again.

"Stop," Billie said as she pushed herself to her elbows and squinted at her mom's pinched face. She reached for her glasses on the nightstand then scrambled for her cell phone to check the time. Her attic room was still dark. "Ma, what are you doing?" Billie asked groggily.

"Someone stole my credit card," Shari said, still dressed in the same gray sweats she had worn yesterday. She would not stand still, and it made Billie uneasy.

Billie brushed her bangs off her face and adjusted her glasses, trying to see clearly in the dim room. "We took your credit cards, remember? Me and David. You can't have them back." She exhaled slowly, waiting for the blowback. Sometimes, her mom would yell and tantrum like a child.

Billie still hadn't settled into the role of parenting her parent. But it had to be done after Shari had racked up thousands of dollars in debt buying stupid shit online – all impulse buys – and that was already on top of the penalty fees for not paying household bills on time. Gramps had begged a Navy buddy who worked for PSE&G to get the lights turned back on.

When Billie's father had still lived with them, Shari used to organize the family finances with the precision of a vascular surgeon. Now it was left to Billie and her color-coded spreadsheet to keep everything organized. Green for paid, yellow for pending, and red for late. There was a lot of red.

"What do you even need it for?" Billie asked and then instantly regretted it. Her mom might tell her something insane, like she wanted to have a comet named after Grandma, which would be another reminder of how different a person her mom had become.

"To help abused animals. There's this sad thing about it on the box," her mom said.

"You mean a commercial?" Billie swung her legs over the side of the bed and got to her feet. She grabbed her hoodie off the desk chair and slid on a pair of unlaced sneakers. No sense in going back to sleep now.

The doctor had said that her mom would forget words. Loss of language. Paranoia. Difficulty with money and figures. These were all symptoms of early-onset Alzheimer's disease. And they would all get worse in time. Billie gently took her mother's elbow. "Let's brew some coffee, all right?" She yawned.

Shari shrugged her off. "My credit card," she insisted.

"They were all canceled. You can't use them."

"The animals," her mom said again.

"We'll drop some coins in the humane society can when we're at the supermarket. Okay?" Billie went down the steep attic stairs first. Her mom's balance wasn't too good anymore, and if she took a tumble, better she should fall on Billie than seventy year-old hardwood.

On the way to the kitchen, they passed her brother David, who was dressed in mauve scrubs. His stethoscope was still draped around his neck. A badge that read *David Levine, LPN* was clipped crookedly to the pocket. His blond hair stuck up at odd angles. He was twenty-eight years old and still lived in his childhood bedroom, just with more expensive video game consoles.

He needed a shave and sleep. Working twelve-hour overnight shifts was killing him, but he didn't really have a choice. They needed someone home with Shari during the day. Billie tried to schedule as many late nights as she could to alleviate his burden, but some investigation work could only happen during normal business hours.

Like today.

That was why she had decided to revamp Levine Investigations. With her mom being sick, she needed a very flexible work environment. Luckily, Gramps was a pretty easygoing boss.

David cocked his brow. "Morning."

"How was work?" Billie asked.

"Long," he said with a yawn.

Shari went into the living room and plopped down on the sofa to watch television.

"Not too loud," Billie said to her. Then she whispered to her brother, "She woke me up in a frenzy, asking to donate to the ASPCA. Sarah McLachlan must've really gotten to her."

David frowned. "I think she's getting worse. She's been forgetting to shower lately."

Billie wasn't so sure that Shari was getting worse, although she certainly wasn't getting any better.

"We need to see about getting some help," he said, massaging his forehead with the tips of his fingers. "There's a social worker who knows of some places."

"I don't want to put her in a home," Billie said as she tugged on David's sleeve to drag him into the kitchen, out of their mother's earshot. Billie set to filling the coffee maker. "First, it's expensive –"

"Medicaid," David began.

She cut him off. "It may not cover enough." She turned around and leaned against the Formica counter. "We should wait until it's really bad and save up in the meantime."

David gingerly opened the fridge door – the hinge was broken – and took out a can of seltzer. He peeled back the tab on the can, took a sip, and belched. "I just don't think we're doing her any favors. I'm a zombie when I'm home with her. And Gramps is past seventy. He's tired, and it's unfair to ask him to help all the time. Plus she could use the socialization."

"These are all good points you're making, and we'll figure something out." Billie tried to sound both proactive and noncommittal, but she wasn't fooling him. She wasn't even fooling herself.

She simply wasn't ready to have *that* conversation. To Billie, putting her mom in a facility was akin to washing her hands of the whole ordeal. She couldn't do that to her mom even if, at times, it didn't feel as if Shari was still with them.

And there was something else. Something no one ever talked about, especially not Billie. Not aloud anyway.

Early-onset Alzheimer's had a large genetic component. Billie, being female, was likelier to inherit the disease from their maternal line than was David, who had already gotten saddled with bipolar disorder. He had, thankfully, figured out how to manage it after much trial and error. Some errors worse than others.

In thirty years, it could be Billie relegated to the sofa to watch television numbly while her kids whispered behind her back on where to stick her. Except Billie had decided two years ago that she wasn't going to have kids.

If the disease came for her, it was going to stop here.

Unfortunately, that didn't give Billie a lot of time for the living she had always wanted to do. She was twenty-four years old and on a potential crash course to losing her mind at a young age.

She was also broke, and her dreams, like moving to Barcelona to write novels, required loads of cash. Funny how that worked.

"I'm going to sleep for a little bit," said David with a yawn. "Don't drink the whole pot of coffee, okay?"

"It blocks inflammation in the brain," she replied automatically.

David said nothing, but Billie thought she detected a hint of pity in the creases of his mouth.

She hefted the coffee carafe and smiled to show David that there was nothing to feel sorry for. "I'll save you some."

CHAPTER FOUR

Later that morning, after a stop at Starbucks, Billie drove her beat-up Hyundai to Kentwell College and parked it in the visitor lot because alumni were offered zero perks despite most of them still paying off the tuition.

She wore black-rimmed sunglasses and a vintage Paris Blues denim trench coat that wasn't warm enough for the late-autumn temps but that she loved too much to stuff back in the closet.

Billie spotted several students outside the administration building, huddled in puffy coats, their breath huffing over lattes. They laughed raucously, mouths opened so wide Billie spied their tongues, and shoved each other playfully.

Two hulking guys tossed a football. Several yards away, girls in beanies and Patagonia jackets accosted upperclassmen for signatures. "We're petitioning the admin to remove single-use plastic from the dining halls. We also want to introduce composting," they said.

Thanksgiving break was en route. The excitement permeated the air like perfume.

Pausing near an oak tree, Billie called Jasmine Flores's cell phone. Tommy Russo had assured her that he had done this several times already and gotten no response, but label her distrustful. She still wasn't convinced Jasmine hadn't ghosted him. But like Tommy, Billie didn't get a response either.

So she left a voicemail and fudged her identity. "Hi, Jasmine. It's Ashley, and I'm calling from the campus café, wondering if you'd like to perform your podcast on our open-mic night.

I think it will be a huge draw." Appealing to ego usually had a high success rate. "Please call me back." Every collegiate coffee shop had at least one employee named Ashley.

Then Billie headed into the admin building. Student Housing was on the second floor, where her old roommate, Nicole Mercier, had a tiny cubicle in the far back near windows that looked out on the quad. Sunlight, thick like ribbon, streamed in through the glass panes.

Nicole sat behind a desk, dressed in a bright pink sweater that highlighted flawless brown skin. Her hair was pulled taut, making room for a headset, the microphone pointed at full lips coated in Mac Dare You.

"I understand your concerns, Mrs Abdul, but I can't just move your son to the quiet study floor if there's no space for him. A ninety-two average in biology is not heading toward failure." Nicole sighed. "I'll put him on the waitlist for a room transfer, but that's all I can do right now." She caught Billie's bemused expression and rolled her eyes. "The library is open twenty-four hours. It's quiet there all the time. Yes, Mrs Abdul. Please call again if you have further concerns."

Nicole threw off the headset and pushed herself away from the desk. "Helicopter parents. I can't deal with them anymore."

"You forget that your mom *was* one," said Billie.

"My mama was never that bad."

Billie gave her a pointed look.

"Karma's a bitch, yada, yada."

Billie glanced around the empty office. "Where's everyone?"

Nicole flicked her wrist in annoyance, making her bracelets jingle like wind chimes. "Some staff appreciation thing."

"And you didn't want to go? Free food?"

"I'd rather deal with a hundred Mrs Abduls than fight Carol in Student Accounts for the last pumpernickel bagel." Her eyes hardened a bit. "What are you even doing here? I haven't seen you since Labor Day. Not since you dropped off your business cards."

Billie felt the bite of accusation – *you only come by when you need things.* How easily she was proving that point.

"Right," said Billie, pushing down the guilt and reaching for an olive branch at the same time. "I appreciate you referring me to the students. Caring for my mom makes working a nine-to-five a little hard, you know?" Billie tossed down the sick parent card like a reverse uno.

"How is your mom?" asked Nicole as she settled on the edge of her desk, arms crossed, on guard.

"Good days and bad." Mostly bad. "David is a little less optimistic than I am, so…"

"Listen," said Nicole, softening. "When the time comes, I can refer you to this social worker friend of mine. She deals in home placement for patients with dementia."

"Sure," Billie said dismissively. "I'll keep it in mind." Inhaling a big breath, she readied herself for the pitch. "What do you know about Tommy Russo? Is he legit?"

"Oh, he's legit, and he's a mess."

"Is he still enrolled?" Billie plucked a pen off the desk and twirled it around her fingers.

Nicole tugged down her sweater and wobbled her head back and forth as if considering the most tactful way to answer the question. "His money is good until the end of the semester. After that…" She held up her hands as if to say, *he's no longer my problem.* "Listen, I'm only helping him as a favor to my aunt. She works in human resources at Russo Foods."

"Russo Foods?" Billie nearly dropped the pen. "Holy crap. *The* Russo Foods?"

"Yup."

Russo Foods was the Italian equivalent of Goya. Instead of beans and plantain chips, they imported high-end olive oil and San Marzano tomatoes. Billie had recently skimmed a headline about an incident at the Elizabeth seaport involving Russo Foods, but she hadn't bothered reading the article.

Where had she seen that? In Gramps's copy of *The Bergen*

Record? On the North Jersey subreddit? And when did she see that? A week ago? Less than that?

Her stomach sank. Why couldn't she remember?

Nicole snapped her fingers. "You there?"

Billie shook her head as if jolting herself awake. "Yes. Just wondering how I missed the Russo Foods connection. That's all." In her defense, when Billie had googled Tommy's name, all she found was his Instagram page with photos of stereo parts he was trying to sell. But it was just as she had suspected. "He's an heir."

"Not exactly. His uncle is Paul Russo. Tommy's father is some hedge fund guy."

"Still wealthy," Billie pointed out.

"My aunt said that Tommy's parents have washed their hands of him. He's been in and out of rehab a lot, and they have no intention of floating him anymore. Cut him out of the will and everything. Paul tried to set Tommy up with an easy office job, but he bailed on the gig after one week."

"Lost cause?"

"Some people are."

Billie tried to ignore that. "What about Jasmine Flores? Don't you think it's weird that no one has officially reported her missing?"

Nicole shrugged. "I doubt she's really gone. Probably just hiding out from Tommy until he takes the hint. But I checked with her professors, and she hasn't been in class since Monday."

"He should've gone to the police," Billie said.

"Tommy doesn't seem like the kind of guy who plays nice with officers."

"True." After a moment's thought, she asked, "Do you know Jasmine's immigration status?"

Nicole shook her head. "Above my pay grade. Maybe she's in DACA, maybe not. A lot of our classmen got cut off from the program when Trump ended it. Besides, New Jersey doesn't prohibit undocumented students from enrolling in college.

You said that she is legally employed? To work lawfully, she needs to be documented."

"She dances at the *Malta Club*," said Billie. "'Lawful' is not exactly the adjective I would use in this case." Billie had an idea. She lowered her eyes, hoping to look properly humbled before a big ask. "Can I get into her dorm room?"

"Billie –"

"Think of it as a welfare check. I see that she's all right, case closed, and it's the easiest five hundred bucks I've ever made. If you give me access, then I'm not breaking any laws."

"I can get fired," Nicole said.

"We're making sure she's okay. No one is going to fire you for that."

Nicole bit her lip, probably second-guessing their six-year-long friendship, if they could even call it that anymore. "You know what? If our entire relationship is transactional–"

"It isn't," Billie cut in.

"Then I want something too," Nicole finished. "There's this guy in a neighboring office who wants a date, but I'm not ready to go to dinner with him until he checks out. After everything that happened with my ex, I'm not taking chances. Last thing I need is another psycho stalker. You got me?"

"I got you. Text me his details, and I'll run a background check."

Nicole nodded, and Billie thought she was in like Flynn until Nicole said, "Maybe we should get Chief Mancini involved. You said yourself that Tommy should've gone to the police."

"Yeah, the Bergen County Detectives Bureau. Not Mancini. Not campus police."

"I don't know…"

Billie groaned. She and the chief did not have a copacetic history. "Mancini gets a pension and health insurance. We'll get him involved, but me first."

Nicole huffed, gave it some more thought, and yanked open the top drawer of her desk. She handed Billie a plastic card.

"This belongs to maintenance. It can get you into the building *only*, not her room. You can ask the students on her floor if they've seen her." Then, more seriously, she added, "Don't get caught with it."

"I won't," Billie said automatically. "What is her room number?"

"Billie," warned Nicole.

"It's just a question. So I can talk to her next-door neighbors."

Nicole returned to her desk and typed Jasmine's name into the computer. "Fellman 315."'

"Thanks, and I'll be discreet."

Nicole scoffed. "No one's calling campus security on your white ass."

"Let's hope not," said Billie.

The elevator dinged. A flurry of voices meandered through the cavernous space. Nicole sighed.

"I guess the staff has felt appreciated," Billie said, walking backward. "I'll see myself out."

"Don't forget to return the key card," Nicole hissed just as Billie slipped into the stairwell, the door closing solidly behind her.

CHAPTER FIVE

Fellman House was located on the far side of campus, sandwiched between the state-of-the-art library with its fancy club chairs and coffee shop and the Soviet-era humanities building slated for demolition next spring. It was a squat four-story building that had never seen a remodel or update, for which Billie was grateful.

She hustled up the concrete stairs. A girl dressed in black stubbed out her cigarette on the statue of a lion. Her eyes lingered on Billie.

"Number one rule of the business is to always look like you belong," Gramps had told her once.

Billie confidently tapped her keycard over the electronic reader until it flashed green. The mechanism clicked, and the door unlocked. Voila. She was in.

Aside from a new mural painted in the lobby, Fellman looked no different than when Billie had lived here. The bulletin board even had the same faded yellow border, now peeling at the edges.

Billie avoided the elevator and took the stairs because she was impatient and in need of exercise.

Room 315 was halfway down the hall, past the trash chute and custodial closet. Ariana Grande and the Rolling Stones emanated from different places and melded into a disorienting mashup. Billie passed a guy with headphones on who was sitting at his desk and vigorously tapping a pen against a notebook. Popcorn churned inside his microwave, emitting an odor that was one burned kernel away from becoming toxic fumes. Billie gagged on the stench and knocked on the doorframe.

He glanced at her and slid his headphones down to his neck. "Yeah?"

She handed him a business card. "Have you seen Jasmine Flores? I'm checking into her whereabouts."

He inspected the card before handing it back to her. "Nope." He gave it more consideration. "I might've seen her last Sunday."

"That long ago?"

"It's not unusual."

"Why not?"

The guy shrugged. "She's one of those super-busy types. Not around a lot. Always doing a club or activity."

"What about the boyfriend? Tommy?"

He rolled his eyes. "I avoid that guy. He tried to sell me broken subwoofers once." He shook his head. "Don't get that 'ship."

"No?"

"She can do a lot better."

No doubt.

"Thanks," said Billie, and she left him to his popcorn.

Knocking on doors was never a waste of time, but she'd be more efficient if she simply could see inside the girl's room.

She checked both ends of the hallway, making sure it was clear, before removing her lock-pick kit from her bag. Good thing the building hadn't been upgraded with fancy keypad technology.

This, she knew, was not kosher and definitely was not sanctioned by Gramps. She had asked him once to teach her how to pick locks, but he'd refused. "Listen, you don't need to be Houdini," he'd told her.

So instead, her ex-boyfriend, Aaron Goff, had showed her. Aaron had been skirting the law since he was in diapers. "It's easy," he said. "You insert the tension wrench into the bottom keyhole and apply very slight pressure. Then you put the pick into the top lock and then scrub the rake back and forth." He tried to make it sound sexual, but it was a smart lesson.

Also he had been good with his hands.

She smiled and let herself into Jasmine's room. The door locked behind her.

She now stood in a coveted single room. A frilly bed made up with a lavender comforter and thick pillows was pushed up against a large window that faced the student parking lot. A laptop and stacks of books covered the desk surface. A red rug peeked out from underneath a well-organized array of index cards.

Billie stepped gingerly around the rug and opened up the desk drawer. There was nothing inside but pens, highlighters, and a pay stub for the *Malta Club*.

There would be no avoiding *that*.

She examined the corkboard above Jasmine's desk. It was covered in various newspaper clippings with grisly headlines that would make even the most seasoned detective grimace. Some articles appeared printed from the internet, and others looked photocopied from the newspaper themselves, likely microfiche from the reference section of the library. The dates ran the gamut from decades ago to last week.

A badge that read *Jasmine, Safety Brigade Officer* hung from a pushpin next to a business card for a Felicia Jann-Smith who ran the Gilded Spine Agency. Whatever that was.

A copy of Jasmine's course load – mostly criminology classes – was tacked up next to a black-and-white photo of a striking woman with long, dark hair and thick bangs above big, pale eyes. She had a long, straight nose – a goyish nose, Billie's grandma would've said – and full lips. Her makeup was flashy but flawless. She wore a miniskirt and sparkly tank top, a diamond ring on a chain nestled in her cleavage, and a bangle sat on her wrist. Who was this woman? A murder victim? A family member? A family member who had been murdered?

Billie snapped a photo of the entire corkboard.

She continued to case the room, ghosting her finger over the spines of the books on the desk. Black Dahlia. Jack the Ripper. Whitey Bulger.

And *I'll Be Gone in the Dark* by Michelle McNamara.

Research for Jasmine's podcast or class assignments?

Why not both?

A knock on the door startled Billie. A female voice called out, "Jaz? You in there?"

Shit.

"Open up, will ya? You're freaking me out."

Double shit. Billie had promised Nicole that she would be stealthy. Stealthy people did not get pinched within minutes of breaking into a room. That was probably not one of Gramps's explicit rules, but it should've been.

Billie opened the door, and the girl jumped back. She was the chick from outside, dressed all in black, who had used the concrete lion as an ashtray. Her hair was white blond and cut jaggedly to her chin. Her eyes were that shade of hazel that looked green in some lights, yellow in others. Right then, they looked like suspicious muddy slits.

She pressed against the door molding to peek inside the room. "Who are you? Where's Jasmine?"

"I'm an investigator," Billie said, pushing back. "I'm conducting a welfare check."

"An investigator? Like with the police?" She turned abruptly and began making her way down the hall.

Rule Number 2: the PI asks the questions.

"Do you have something to hide?" Billie called to the girl's retreating back while stepping into the hallway and shutting the door behind her.

The girl stopped, turned slowly, and hardened her stance. "I don't trust cops. They're not on our side."

"I'm on the side of finding Jasmine Flores," said Billie, growing impatient. "What's your name?"

Her eyes clicked back and forth like a pendulum for several moments. Then, finally, she answered, "Nuri O'Brien. Jasmine's best friend."

Perfect. This was just the girl Billie needed to talk to. "Her boyfriend, Tommy, is worried about her."

"Oh, I'm sure he is," Nuri said sarcastically and crossed her arms. A tattoo on her wrist peeked out from her sleeve. Billie glimpsed a bright-green clover with MGSE written in a Gaelic-style font.

She pointed to the girl's arm. "What do those letters stand for?"

Nuri furrowed her brow, glanced down at her skin, and softened. "It stands for Murder Girls Suspect Everyone. It's our catchphrase for the podcast we host. We call ourselves the Murder Girls, and because we're naturally into true crime, we have a tendency to suspect everyone."

"Like *My Favorite Murder*," Billie said. "Karen and Georgia."

Nuri frowned. "Yeah, like that, I guess, except we're our own thing too. In fact, we're the number-one minority-led collegiate podcast in the tristate area."

Billie didn't like making blanket assumptions, but she had to ask, "Are *you* from a marginalized group?"

"No, but Jasmine is, so we qualify, and it raises our visibility." Nuri sounded almost insulted by the question. Was she offended on her behalf or Jasmine's?

Never mind. Billie didn't have time for this. "Have you seen Jasmine recently? If she's hiding out from Tommy, you can tell me. I won't tell him. I just want to make sure she's safe."

Nuri shook her head. "She said she would be flaky for a while because she has a lot on her plate. But we're still supposed to record the podcast tomorrow, and I've been getting freaked out because she won't answer my texts. That's not like her. We have a strict schedule, and fans are counting on us."

"Right," Billie said with a smirk. "Because you're the number-one minority-led collegiate podcast in the tristate area."

Nuri didn't laugh.

"Did you record an episode last Saturday?" Billie asked.

"Yeah," said Nuri.

"And everything seemed fine and normal?"

"Totally. I covered a dismembered killing in Maine, and Jasmine tackled a stabbing in Florida in the late nineties. Typical stuff."

"Right," Billie said. *Typical.* Then, "You mentioned that she had a lot on her plate. Did she say with what?"

"Trying to get Tommy into rehab. She said it would be a struggle because he's, like, a major dickhead. Also she's got issues with Tommy's uncle."

"What kind of issues?"

"Money, I think. Rehab ain't free. Also she thinks he hates her because she's brown."

"Does he hate her for that reason?"

"I think Paul Russo is just suspicious of Jasmine. I mean, why would she date a guy like Tommy? His uncle would think it's because of their money."

"Is that why she dated him?"

"Tommy blew a lot of money on drugs, so probably not." Nuri ran her hands through her short hair, making it stick up far enough to expose her black roots. "But if he hurt her or one of his Percy Street friends did, I swear –"

"Percy Street?"

"The Percy Street Garage is where he goes to score," said Nuri. "A lot of lowlifes hang out there."

That they do. The garage was a known junkie hangout. "Did he get into it with any of them?" Billie asked, remembering Tommy's battered face and bruised knuckles.

Nuri shrugged. "I try not to ask because then it sounds like I'm judging. Jasmine gets defensive if I even hint that they should break up. She says she's not ready yet. She's worried Tommy will hurt himself if she leaves him."

That didn't seem healthy. "What is Jasmine and Tommy's relationship like?"

"It isn't functional, that's for sure. Jasmine's awesome – so accomplished – but Tommy, he's never himself when he's high or worse, jonesing. Who knows what he would do? A month ago, I caught her trying to conceal a black eye."

"You think Tommy hit her?"

"She swore it wasn't him, but who else would do that?"

"His Percy Street friends," Billie guessed.

"I'm, like, really freaked that something has happened to her."

"It's more likely that Jasmine is hiding out from him and his associates," Billie said. But Nuri didn't look convinced, so she added, "I'll get to the bottom of it. Do you know Tommy's dorm room?"

Nuri exhaled. "First floor. 110."

Billie started heading toward the stairwell, anxious to grill Tommy about black eyes and parking decks, when she thought of something else. "Where are her parents?"

"Huh?"

"Jasmine's parents?"

Nuri shook her head as if waking herself up from a deep sleep. "I don't know. Central America."

"Does Jasmine have a US passport?" asked Billie.

"I don't know," Nuri replied, and she sounded on the verge of tears. "Why is that important?"

"Just a question."

Nuri blinked several times, her face dawning with a realization. "You think she went to visit her folks?"

Not exactly. Maybe Tommy was onto something. Jasmine could've been targeted and sent to an ICE detention center, especially if she wasn't under DACA's protection and was working unlawfully. But saying that aloud might freak out Nuri even more, so instead, she smiled reassuringly. "It's quite possible that she decided to go on a last-minute trip."

Nuri dropped her shoulders. "I hope you're right."

Billie headed toward the stairwell.

"But not tell me?" Nuri added.

"Maybe it was an emergency," Billie said as she turned around.

"Maybe she didn't have a chance, and when she got down to Honduras, there was bad cell service or she lost her phone."

Nuri bobbed her head several times as if that was a totally believable reason and not just bullshit that Billie made up on the fly.

"There's something else," said Nuri. "Last week, maybe ten days ago, a black car was parked outside the coffee shop where I work."

"Make? Model?"

"Nondescript. Town car. Buick? I don't know."

"Did you see the driver?"

She shook her head. "The windows were tinted. Like illegally tinted." Then she bit her lip. "But it was weird, you know? It just sat in the lot. It didn't leave until Tommy came and picked up Jasmine."

"That is weird," Billie said, adding it to her notes. Weird but hopefully easy to figure out. She handed Nuri a business card. "Call me if Jasmine turns up."

Nuri nodded. "I will." Then she read the card, squinting. "You're a private investigator?" Her face relaxed. "Don't know why I thought you were police." She waved a hand over Billie's face. "You obviously don't look like a cop."

"Plenty of women are in law enforcement," she countered.

"Most of the Jewish girls on campus are like, marketing majors and stuff."

Billie frowned.

Nuri flicked the business card. "Sorry, I saw the name, Levine, and I just figured –" She added quickly, "I meant it as a compliment. Takes a lot of smarts to get a business degree. They'll never be poor a day in their life." Laughing awkwardly, she added, "Not like me."

"Why would they work?" Billie stared at Nuri as she tucked her notebook away. "When they could just marry a doctor."

Billie turned around, rolled her eyes, and headed toward the stairwell.

CHAPTER SIX

Billie headed to the first floor and knocked on Tommy's door. No answer.

She pressed her ear to the thick metal, trying to discern any noise that might prove someone was inside but hiding out.

She heard nothing.

She sent him a text, requesting a chat. He didn't respond to that either.

Billie decided to wait him out. She retreated to the lounge by the elevator and dropped onto a beat-up sofa. There she had a perfect view of the soda machine and lobby entrance. When Tommy returned, she would spot him immediately.

To kill time, she took out her cell phone and scrolled through Jasmine's Instagram account. Her preliminary search had revealed a slew of hazy photos of Jasmine and Tommy, their arms draped around each other, their gazes cloudy and unfocused, their mouths pink, raw, but smiling. Cigarettes burned in ashtrays. Pilsner glasses littered coffee tables. They looked like two college kids in love. No different than any other twenty-something couple. No different than Billie and Aaron once upon a time.

Billie's finger flicked up the screen. Jasmine's account slowly segued into memes about serial killers and promotion for her Murder Girls podcast merchandise, but even that slowed to a blip. One photo showed Jasmine standing next to a Black girl, her arm draped over her shoulder, in front of an old-school chalkboard that read SLEUTH SQUAD in crisp print.

Who was this girl? She continued to scroll. She found her again, standing tall in the center of a big group of women wearing Safety Brigade badges.

The Safety Brigade was a group of students who escorted other students, mostly women, around campus for protection. Safety in numbers and all that. Billie had been a member for a year.

She found the girl a third time in a photo taken inside Jasmine's room. The girl was wearing headphones. The caption read, "Me and Tasha brainstorming."

Meanwhile, Tommy barely registered in any of the later pics. It was simply Jasmine and her friends.

As Billie sank further into the cushions, she imagined Jasmine revising her relationship status to *It's complicated* then *Single*.

This all seemed so pointless. Jasmine was clearly shaking Tommy off. But why ignore the best friend? Unless Jasmine was no longer interested in sharing a podcast mic with Nuri "All Jews are accountants" O'Brien. Billie felt confident that Jasmine would soon emerge from her cocoon after she overcame whatever nervous breakdown she was having.

Billie wouldn't want Jasmine's life – the girl was clearly overbooked and overwhelmed – and that was saying something since Billie's life mostly sucked.

She was tempted to end Tommy's contract, except she was being paid, and money gave everything purpose. Besides, this was her job now. If Billie wanted to eat or put gas in her car, she needed to work these cases as if her life depended on them.

Just then, a man crossed her path. He was tall, with shorn dark hair and a clipped beard to match. He wore denim – not designer – clothes, work boots, and a scowl. He was youngish, although the facial hair made it hard to pinpoint his age.

He definitely wasn't a student. So who was he? Someone's boyfriend? Someone's weed dealer?

The guy adjusted his sleeves, and Billie spotted the tattoo – a cross above a row of skulls.

She recognized the tattoo immediately. It was the identifying symbol for the Torn Crosses, a neo-Nazi skinhead gang known for trafficking heroin and meth – and, sometimes, women. Their numbers had been declining for years, but they were still listed as an operating hate group. They were dangerous. Hella dangerous.

They were also the Goff crime family's biggest headache.

The last thing a Jewish girl needed was to deal with Nazis.

What business did he have here? A Torn Cross in a Kentwell dormitory? Only time any of them would ever see academia. Most of the members didn't make it past fifth grade, which was how they got sucked into lives of extreme hate in the first place.

How did he even get inside the building?

She waited until he rounded the corner before scrambling from the worn sofa cushion. She followed him for a minute and then ducked into the trash chute vestibule. Peeking around, she watched as he hit Tommy's door with a fist.

The hallway became eerily quiet, like when forest creatures disappear before a wildfire.

Tommy Russo had not said anything about associating with Nazis.

The guy pounded on the door again. "Open up, shithead. I know you're in there."

She guessed they weren't friendly.

The guy rattled the handle and pressed his hand to the door as if trying to test its thickness, but that was useless. The dorm doors were made of reinforced steel. He bent down and examined the lock, his brow furrowing.

Seriously, dude, you're wasting your time.

He removed a gun from the waistband of his pants, and Billie's eyes went wide. She slid her cell phone out to text Nicole. She needed to get an alert out to the student body – put the campus on lockdown. Then he hit the doorknob with the butt of his gun, and the handle came off in chunks.

How the fuck?

The door swung open. A scrawny guy stood on the other side, his eyes bugging out, his mouth opening and closing like a fish. Tommy's roommate, Billie presumed. "What the hell, man?"

Quickly, he was yanked onto his toes by the collar of his shirt.

"Tell your junkie boyfriend to stop hiding from us. We always collect. Colfer isn't playing." He dropped the roommate roughly and shoved him away.

The poor kid stumbled backward and fell on his ass and elbows.

Billie ducked back into the trash chute, but it was too late. She was made. He passed by, casting Billie a cursory glance before he sized her up and laughed.

She didn't find him funny. No Torn Cross member had ever made her chuckle except when they got nabbed in an FBI sting. She found that hilarious.

She did, however, wonder what he intended to collect on. And what would happen if Tommy couldn't pay up? Because Colfer Dryden, leader of the Torn Crosses, was notorious for disappearing his enemies. His ideologies were a joke, but rival gangs and the FBI took him seriously.

Billie realized then that she had been hoping that Jasmine had simply skipped out on Tommy – after all, she had good reason. But if he was mixed up with skinheads, maybe Jasmine had become collateral damage.

When Billie went outside, she passed students enjoying the sunshine. Nothing but smiles and laughter and friendly jabs to the arm. She wondered if they knew how good they had it, living in their protective collegiate bubble.

Billie wondered how protective that bubble was for Jasmine.

CHAPTER SEVEN

Later that afternoon, Billie pulled her crumbling car into the *Malta Club* parking lot. It was early enough that the neon sign of a martini glass with legs in place of a skewered olive hadn't been turned on yet. Although the placard outside boasted a $9.99 wing buffet that had started an hour before, she had no intention of staying to eat.

One Yelp reviewer had said that if the *Hustler Club* ate a giant kosher meal and burped up a strip joint, it would be the *Malta Club*. Billie thought that was both specific and oddly accurate.

The *Malta Club* was owned and operated by Neil Goff, head of the last remaining Jewish crime syndicate in the Northeast, if not the entire US. It wasn't a distinguished role. Jewish mobsters were dinosaurs, their extinction on the horizon, and Neil was clutching his power as if he was dangling off a cliff.

He was also Aaron's dad.

The Goffs had emigrated from Odessa at the height of the pogroms and made a name for themselves bootlegging during Prohibition before moving on to smuggling black-market goods during World War II. In their heyday, the Goffs had been so powerful it was said that even Bugsy Siegel owed them a favor. Eventually, like the Italians, the Goffs turned to racketeering until too many of their men ended up in East Jersey State Prison, including Sol Goff, the original "Goffather." He'd been a king for a little while until he got sent up.

Last Billie had heard, the Goffs were dabbling in diamonds and cryptocurrency.

That had been Aaron's idea. A last-ditch effort at relevancy. Except their criminal empire was nothing more than a strip-club front for money laundering, so small it wasn't even a blip on the FBI's radar. The feds needed to focus their resources on the big players: the Russians, the Brazilians, and the Chinese.

Traffic had just started to ease on Route 17 when Billie got out of her car. The sky was that shade of cobalt blue that briefly made her forget it was early November.

She closed her eyes for a split second and sighed, but she couldn't go home now; this was what she had signed up for. Or what she had signed Tommy Russo up for when he scribbled his name on the client retainer contract.

She went inside.

Her eyes struggled to adjust to the club's dark interior. A brunette with a nose piercing was wiping down the bar and singing along to Lady Gaga while a redheaded dancer was wrapping her legs around the fireman's pole on the raised platform. She wore a black G-string, heels, and nothing else and was performing for an audience of one – a middle-aged man with a Santa-sized gut whose dollar bills were clutched between thick, wing sauce–stained fingers.

Behind her, a drag performer in a pink wig and false eyelashes was raising a microphone to accommodate her six-two frame. She glanced up the minute the door closed behind Billie and hollered, "Belinda Levine, is that you?"

Billie smiled. "Yes, Mama Ree."

Descending the stage in platform heels, Mama Ree enveloped Billie in a hug. Then she pushed her away for inspection. "Let me take a good look at you. You do somethin' different with your hair? Highlights?"

Without thinking, Billie pushed the bangs from her face. "Same dirty blond, just shorter."

"You look damn fine, girl. How long has it been?"

"Two years." Billie had come here the night she graduated college to break up with Aaron and drown her sorrows in mojitos. Mama Ree had been kind enough to hold her hair back while she hurled up her guts behind the dumpster.

Billie chuffed herself up like a rooster. "I'm working as a PI now." She dug her cell phone out of her coat pocket and swiped through the texts. She held up the photo Tommy Russo had sent her when she had asked for Jasmine's most recent picture. "I'm searching for this girl."

Mama Ree squinted through her spidery lashes and then pulled a pair of reading glasses out of her cleavage. She perched them on the tip of her nose. "My seniority keeps me from hobnobbing with the dancers." Mama Ree was *Malta Club* royalty, having worked the drag circuit for years in the eighties before Neil discovered her floundering in some dive on the Lower East Side. He then made her an offer she couldn't refuse – her own show with no pesky club owner telling her what to do – and she had been Neil's artistic director ever since. "You sure she's missing?"

"According to the boyfriend," said Billie.

"Strung-out child?"

"Yup." Billie glanced around, suddenly anxious that Aaron might be lurking in the shadows, but last she'd heard, he was in Israel.

"He's not here," said Mama Ree with a quirk of her eyebrow.

"I wasn't –"

"Uh huh."

Billie exhaled then smiled. No sense in refuting the obvious. "If you didn't know Jasmine, who *did*?"

Mama Ree called to a dancer adjusting her breasts in the corner. "Shonda, come here, darlin.'" Then she whispered, "They got into it a few times."

Shonda sighed but did what Mama Ree had asked because no one went against Mama Ree. Shonda wore a neon-orange bikini and nothing else. Her brown skin was powdered in glitter. Her black hair lay in long, thin braids down her back.

Billie held up Jasmine's photo. "What do you know about this girl?"

Shonda cast a glance at Mama Ree, who nodded encouragingly.

"Pfft. Tonta," Shonda said with an eye roll. Spanish for dummy.

"Me or Jasmine?" asked Billie.

Shonda mimicked shooting a pistol at Jasmine's photo. "*La Hondureña.*"

"How so?"

"I listened to her true-crime podcast." She made air quotes around the last part. "Girl was careless."

"Okay," Billie said, drawing out the word like a piece of taffy. "Can you elaborate?"

Again, Shonda shot a nervous glance at Mama Ree. Nothing was said or unsaid without Mama's permission. Mama Ree gestured for Shonda to get on with it.

Shonda stood with her hands on her hips. "She did a bunch of episodes about Neil Goff."

Fuck. That got Billie's attention. "Anything in particular?"

Shonda shrugged. "Just talking up his alleged high crimes and scandals. It was reckless. I mean, he's her boss. Plus she let that boyfriend hang around. He got into it with Matty."

"Really?" It was Neil's unspoken rule that the dancers did not let their romantic lives intersect with their professional ones. It was bad for business if the customers saw the dancers cozying up to the partners they actually had sex with before hopping onto the laps of men who had no shot of going home with them. "Ruins the fantasy," Neil had said.

"Anyway, she'll stay missing if she knows what's good for her," said Shonda.

"Shonda!" Mama Ree snapped.

"What? It's not like everyone doesn't know."

"Know what?" asked Billie.

"Enough," Mama Ree said with annoyance. Then to Billie, she said, "You need to talk to Matty. Let him answer the rest of your questions."

"All right." Malta girls knew that if they wanted to keep their jobs (and their heads), they had to also shut their mouths about club business.

Billie smiled despite the acidity churning in her stomach. She was a pro, so she could do this. She and Matty went way back. Besides, Aaron wasn't here. He wasn't even in the country. And even if he was, they were done.

Billie had taken a guillotine to that relationship.

"You can go to his office. You know the way, sugar." Mama Ree winked at Billie and then kissed both of her cheeks.

"Thanks," said Billie before heading toward the inky curtains that hid the dressing rooms.

"Don't be a stranger," Mama Ree called as she futzed with the mic stand.

"I won't," Billie lied, and then she caught it – the side eye. Mama Ree was holding back.

The partition fell behind her.

CHAPTER EIGHT

Matty's office was down a dark hallway and past the staff restrooms. On the walls hung framed photos of the Malta's more prestigious visitors. Unlike *Nagel*'s, which only got C-listers to eat there, the club had attracted the likes of movie stars and singers and a few members of the *Sopranos* cast, who had scribbled *Bada Bing* on their headshots in gold Sharpie, which was the most Jersey thing Billie had ever seen. There were even a few pictures of Bergen County's finest, their arms draped around Neil Goff as if he was their best friend. In one of those photos, Billie spotted Gramps's buddy, Ken Greenberg, who had been retired from the force for close to thirty years.

But the photos, like the celebrities in them, had aged. The Malta wasn't what it used to be.

She paused outside Matty's open door and watched him for a second as he hummed Sinatra's "My Way" and entered data into a spreadsheet.

On second thought, *that* might have been the most Jersey thing ever.

His office, a glorified storage closet, was crammed with a desk, a file cabinet, stacked boxes, and feminine hygiene products.

Matty's hair had gotten shorter, the dark frizz tamed into sophisticated waves, the dimple in his chin a little more pronounced. His lashes were nearly as long as Mama Ree's, only he had been born with his. He was wearing a gray T-shirt that showed off chest hair. He filled it out well.

A bruise, faint and yellow, was fading from beneath his right eye. A workplace hazard. A customer might order one too many from the bar, think his money entitled him to more than a lap dance, and take a swing at Matty, who emerged from the office to handle the matter. It happened all the time. Rarely was Matty's skin pristine.

Billie rapped a rhythm on the molding.

His head jerked up, and that furrow between his eyes disappeared. "Billie." He said it softly, almost wistfully, as if her name had been on his tongue when he exhaled.

"Hey." She gave a slight wave.

He turned down the volume on the speakers and rose from his chair. No hug from him. No kiss. None of that familial shit.

Matthew Goff was Aaron's brother and Neil Goff's firstborn. Neil had made Matty manager of the *Malta Club* years ago when Aaron had proved to be too reckless to manage his time, let alone a money-laundering front.

"What are you doing here?" he asked, surprised.

"I don't know if you're aware, but I took over Levine Investigations, and I'm working a missing person case."

"How Veronica Mars of you."

"Low-hanging fruit," she said. "Jasmine Flores is MIA, and I need whatever info you can spare."

Matty sat back down at his desk and jiggled the computer mouse. He tapped a few keys, and the printer rolled out a piece of paper. "This better not come back to bite me in the ass." He handed her Jasmine's employment record. The club was mostly a cash business, seeing as its sole purpose was to scrub dirty money, but some things needed to appear legit for Uncle Sam.

"Better me than the Bergen County Detectives Bureau."

Jasmine Flores's address was listed as Fellman House at Kentwell College. Her number was a cell phone with a Philly area code, and the first emergency contact listed was Tasha Nichols, the second Nuri O'Brien. "She has a Social Security number."

"So?"

"Means she's documented and eligible to work." It also meant that Tommy's reasoning for wanting to keep the police out of the loop wasn't quite valid. Unless Tommy wasn't aware of this.

How many secrets did Tommy and Jasmine keep from each other?

"What do you know about the boyfriend?" Billie asked.

Matty shrugged and went back to his spreadsheet. "A junkie lowlife who came in once. He watched the floor and never tipped. Told her the rules. That was the last I saw of him." Matty wiped an eyelash off the tender skin beneath his eye. "I canned her ass a few weeks ago."

"Why?"

"She stole cash from the bar register when Tamara had her back turned."

So that must've been what Shonda was alluding to.

Billie folded Jasmine's personnel record into quarters and slid it into her coat pocket. Stealing from the Goffs was the stupidest thing a girl could do, not that she had ever been dumb enough to try. "How much did she take?"

"A few C-notes."

Twenty years ago, Jasmine would've gotten smacked around for that. But with Matty in charge, a firing and a threat were enough. Even Neil wouldn't get himself dirty over a few hundred bucks. He'd just send a goon to take care of her.

Matty reached out to gently touch Billie's hand and then must've thought better of it. He casually dropped his arm onto the chair. "How's your mom doing?"

She wished everyone would stop asking her that. "Fine."

"And David?"

"He got his job back at the nursing home in Bogota, and he's taking his meds."

Matty nodded his head several times. "That's great. Really great." But it was spoken with the false bravado of a man whose heart had been shattered and stapled back together.

One might have said that the Levines and the Goffs had a long history of exploiting each other's devotion, intentionally and otherwise.

"They would've been assholes not to take him back," Matty added. "He's so good with patients."

Good with patients, less so with boyfriends.

Billie pointed behind her, toward the back door where the exit sign's glow cast the hallway in crimson shadows. "I better go and see if I can sniff this girl out. Thanks for your help." She turned to leave.

"Billie?"

"Yeah?"

"Not sure if you're aware, but Aaron's back in town."

Billie schooled her face into her own mask of bravado even as her stomach plummeted to her socks. "Really? Israel didn't pan out like he'd hoped?"

"He got into trouble," he said. "He can tell you about it."

"That's all right," she said coolly. "I can't imagine we'll run into each other." Jersey was a big state.

"Tell your brother that I'm glad he's well." Matty pressed his lips firmly together as if trying to keep whatever else he wanted to say from escaping his mouth.

"I will." Billie smiled and gave Matty a playful salute before making a beeline for the exit, desperate to get the hell out of there.

CHAPTER NINE

Billie returned home to black smoke streaming from the kitchen window and the fire alarm screeching like a deranged bird.

She fumbled for her house keys to unlock the front door but found it was already ajar. Darting inside, Billie screamed for her mother. She whipped her head around wildly, trying to locate her mom, as gray air swirled inside the living room, seeking an escape.

"Ma! Where are you?"

"Kitchen!" she hollered.

Billie ran into the back of the house, where Shari was swatting acrid smoke with an oven mitt. The kitchen window was wide open, and the blackened carcass of what Billie could only assume was poultry sizzled in the stainless steel sink.

She coughed and fanned the air in front of her face. "Christ, Ma. What were you doing?"

"Making supper," Shari said, flustered. "I forgot that it was in the oven."

Billie pulled the cord on the ceiling fan until it spun like helicopter blades. "It's three o'clock in the afternoon. And you're *not* supposed to be cooking."

"Don't tell me what I can't do," Shari snapped. "I always make dinner. I'm the only one who ever does."

Yeah, when Billie was a kid. Now it was Billie's turn to get pissy. "Where's David?"

"I don't know. He went somewhere."

"He *went* somewhere? He's supposed to be watching – I mean, hanging out with you."

Billie ran around the first floor of the house, pulling up windows, swapping out smoke for fresh autumn air. "Put on a sweater, Ma!" she called to her. Then, more kindly, she added, "Please."

Grabbing her cell phone, Billie dialed her brother. It went to voicemail, so she called again and again and again until he picked up.

"Where are you?" she asked impatiently.

"Stop & Shop," David replied. A beeping sound like that of a price scanner could be heard in the background.

"Mommy almost burned down the house. She used the oven."

"Oh, God." He sighed. "She was napping, so I figured I could grab a few things for dinner before she woke up."

Billie went back outside and sat down on the cement stoop to catch her breath and air out her clothes.

Mrs Rodriguez, whom Gramps called the yenta of Teaneck, was pushing her granddaughter in a stroller when she stopped to take in the sight of the Levine house. "Everyone all right in there?"

"We're fine," said Billie with an exaggerated smile. "Kitchen mishap."

"Should you be leaving her alone?" she asked.

"What's she want?" asked David.

"Nothing." Billie pressed the phone to her chest to mute the call. "We're on it. No need to worry."

"I can get you the card for Safe Horizons," Mrs Rodriguez continued. "It's where we put my aunt when she got dementia."

Billie gritted her teeth. "We've got it handled." She hated it when well-meaning people tried to compare an elderly relative's disease progression to that of her fifty-eight year-old mom. It was not the same, not by a long shot.

There was a *fwoop* sound. Something landed on the side

lawn, so Billie went around the house to inspect. Blackened chicken cutlets lay in the grass. "Like I said, kitchen mishap."

Mrs Rodriguez grunted.

Her granddaughter swung her chubby legs against the stroller and whined to leave. The old lady shrugged but then went on her way, shaking her head in disbelief.

David sighed and thanked the cashier for his change. "I'll be home in five minutes." He disconnected the call.

Billie was hovering over the burnt chicken when Gramps sauntered home, whistling a jaunty tune and jostling coins in his pocket.

"What's going on here?" It was said in the carefree manner of a man who had spent the last few hours drinking his lunch at the *Clam Bar*, which, despite its moniker, did not serve seafood.

"Mom used the oven."

"Oh." Then, more seriously, he asked, "Where was David?"

"Supermarket," she said, exhausted.

Gramps squeezed her shoulder. "You want me to do the shopping next time?"

It was a thoughtful gesture, and if she was going to put off sending her mom to a facility, she needed his help. "Sure. Thanks."

Sighing, Billie pinched the bridge of her nose. The shrubs on the side of the house were in dire need of pruning, and the grass begged to be reseeded. They hadn't had a spring crop of tulips in years, and she couldn't remember the last time anyone had painted the shutters.

Plus there was that roof issue.

This was all the stuff Billie's father used to handle before he ran off with David's high school art teacher on the same day Billie threw her mortar board in the air.

Just then, David pulled his clunker, a 2005 Cutlass, into the driveway and cut the engine. He ran around the car, pushing his hand through his bedhead, and opened the passenger's-side door. He attempted to haul six heavy bags of groceries into the house.

"You wanna hand with those?" Gramps offered.

"I got it." David hoisted his arms.

"I'm not an invalid, you know," Gramps shot back.

"He can do it." Billie kicked a pebble into the street. "Can I pick your brain about work?"

Gramps's green eyes lit up as he rubbed his hands over his gray scruff. He needed a shave. "Always."

"I've got a missing person case. Young girl. Dancer at Malta."

Gramps closed his eyes for a second and grimaced. "Oy vey, Billie. You can't be getting involved with the Goffs."

Billie ignored that. Too late now. "She's been gone for four days, maybe longer."

"Girl got a boyfriend?"

"Yes."

"All right, he did it."

"She's not dead. At least, I hope not."

Gramps gave her that look, the one that said, *Don't be a moron.* "It's always the lover."

"Always?"

"Ninety-nine percent of the time. And if not him, then someone connected to him."

Like a Torn Cross gang member?

"Why hire me then?" she asked.

He shrugged. "Take the heat off himself."

A large-engine plane, headed to Teterboro Airport, roared overhead. So much for that new flight plan.

"Tail the boyfriend," said Gramps. "You want me to come with you? It could be fun, like old times."

"I never went with you on stakeouts," she pointed out.

"Well, you were too young then." Gramps glanced at the house. Remnants of smoke still trailed from the window. "Maybe I should unretire."

Billie scoffed, and he frowned.

"We need to get you a gun permit," he said.

"Uh uh. No guns."

"The Taser then."

"I have pepper spray."

That got a laugh out of him.

"Stay away from the *Malta Club*." Gramps pointed an arthritic finger at her. "Capisce?" He patted her head like he used to do when she was a kid. "Time for a nightcap." It was still the afternoon. He trudged up the stoop, his knees creaking under his old-man weight, and into the house.

Billie's grandpa had once been notorious for hitting the pavement. All the local cops used to say so. "That Billy Levine. He can sniff out cheating husbands like a German Shepherd." Now, unfortunately, he was only good for hitting the bottle.

CHAPTER TEN

Billie wiped steam off the bathroom mirror. She had just come back from a run in Overpeck Park, sweaty and smelly, to jump into the shower.

The grime was still swirling down the drain.

A few years ago, she had read a study that said people who ran more than fifteen miles per week had a forty percent lower risk of dying from Alzheimer's disease. The study wasn't clear on whether it applied to early-onset Alzheimer's, but Billie figured that it couldn't hurt. So that was what she did. Rain or shine, heat or cold, snow or sleet, she ran.

David said she couldn't live her life this way, always sampling the snake oil because it might outwit her genes, but she thought that was easy for him to say. He likely wouldn't inherit the disease, being male and all.

Dr Cohen, one of Neil Goff's old classmates who had examined Mom as a favor despite Gramps's protests, had been forthright about the diagnosis. "The only question remains is whether this is sporadic or familial."

"How can we tell?" Billie asked.

"We'd need to know if her parents or grandparents also had it," he said.

Billie didn't know her maternal grandparents. Her mother had been raised by an aunt who died when Shari was a teenager. But what did she die from? A car accident? Billie looked at Gramps, who was leaning against the bookshelves. He just shrugged. "I don't know, kiddo."

"Aren't there, like, only a few hundred families who have this?" David asked.

The doctor nodded. "That's one very specific gene mutation. In those cases, if you inherit the gene, you're a hundred percent likely to get it. If you inherit a different gene strand, your chances can drop to fifty percent."

Billie's stomach turned sour. "Silver lining."

Dr Cohen caught Billie's downturned mouth and watery eyes. "You can get tested if you think that will help you."

"That's not necessary, Doc," Gramps said gruffly.

Dr Cohen smiled weakly. "Let's hope it's sporadic." He didn't elaborate, but Billie caught his meaning.

"Because we're at risk for inheriting it, too," she said.

He reached across and gently patted her hand as a kindness. *There, there.* But it only made her feel worse, like she was someone to be pitied.

"What does this mean for our mom now?" David asked.

Dr Cohen cleared his throat. "We look at medication and vitamin protocols. Diet. Even exercise. She'll need to be looked after. No more late-night shopping." He grinned at that last bit, as if inserting humor into the room might cut through its tension.

The Levines were pros at using humor as a defense mechanism. This doc didn't have the talent.

"She's a nurse, right?" he said.

David nodded. "She works ICU at Hackensack, but she's on a leave of absence."

"She's young enough to apply for disability and Medicaid," he said. "But she can't return to nursing."

Disability wouldn't cover the property taxes.

"We can ask Dad for money," Billie suggested to David, but Gramps scoffed loudly.

Craig Levine was shacking up with a woman half mom's age and twice as blond in a trailer community outside Sedona – pardon, an *artist colony* outside Sedona. If he had money, it couldn't be much, and he wouldn't part with it.

So there went Billie's postgraduation plans of Barcelona and flamenco lessons.

And shortly after the diagnosis, David hit a manic period. It took a while to get him back on track.

And that was when Aaron had high-tailed it to Israel. He had invited Billie to come with him, but she had broken his heart instead.

Anyway, it wasn't as if he was going to live on a kibbutz. He had put together a crew for a heist. He'd left to make money.

Aaron Goff had always been a kid from the neighborhood before he was her first kiss – her first everything – but he had also been a delinquent and his father's protégé. Even then, when he was feeling her up in the catering-hall kitchen at Becky Goldman's sweet-sixteen party, he'd been scheming about how to lift the frozen seafood, which was worth thousands of dollars, to fence using his *own* connections.

"My dad doesn't control me," he'd told Billie a few weeks later as he slipped her a Franklin. "No one does."

She held the hundred dollar bill between pinched knuckles. "What am I supposed to do with this?"

His brows shot up.

"Gramps will want to know where I got it."

"So don't tell him."

It was always easy for Aaron to lie – to his father, his teachers, the cops – because of his good looks and charm. He resembled his brother Matty, had the same ash-brown hair and hazel eyes, but he'd inherited an arrogance from some ancestor who had cheated death one too many times. Witty and intelligent, Aaron was valued for tossing big bills into the Hebrew school tzedakah box as if they were nickels found in couch cushions.

He was ridiculous and confident and gorgeous, and Billie had fallen hard for him.

Gramps, on the other hand, hated the Goffs for a multitude of reasons, the most prominent being that they were criminals.

Billie supposed it was reason enough.

"They're the mob, Shari," he had stressed to Billie's mother when Neil offered to float them the dues for synagogue so Billie could have her bat mitzvah. "Would you take blood money from the Gambinos?"

"If it means I don't have to work overtime this week, then probably," she had said.

"It's bad enough that Belinda has a crush on that boy," Gramps whispered loudly.

Shari rolled her eyes. "They're kids."

"You were a kid when you started dating Craig."

"Doesn't mean she'll marry him. The infatuation won't last. This isn't anything you need to worry about."

And it wasn't. Her mom was right. Billie's relationship with Aaron lasted a lot longer than some marriages, but it was still a dumpster fire jonesing for a match.

The truth was that being saddled with debt and a brain on an ill-fated course for catastrophic erosion made it awfully selfish to chain herself to another person.

She ran a comb through her wet hair and tightened the towel around her body. She climbed the stairs into her stuffy attic room and flopped onto the bed.

David had left the utility bill on her bedspread to add to the red column.

Gramps called up to her. "Hey, kiddo, you wanna order pizza? My treat!"

"Sure!" she called down.

Then her phone buzzed with a text from the handsome Detective Esteban Morales, inviting her out for a drink at the Wagon.

She didn't drink – couldn't risk losing the brain cells she had left – but she appreciated the invitation. He was cute and emotionally unavailable. He was perfect.

"On second thought," she called down to Gramps, "I'm going out."

CHAPTER ELEVEN

The *Wagon*, an Irish bar on Cedar Lane within spitting distance of the Levine backyard, catered to the sports crowd. Flags of various European soccer clubs hung from the sloped ceiling while World Cup paraphernalia covered every inch of the wood-paneled walls.

U2 blasted from speakers mounted in the corners.

The pub boasted decent wing specials and stouts, but it was its Irish whiskey that attracted Esteban Morales and his colleagues from the Bergen County Detectives Bureau.

That and the numerous televisions glowing with soccer matches from all over the world.

Billie was pretty sure the owner was actually a Turkish guy from Clifton.

Morales sat at the bar and sipped a Jameson. He threw his hands up at the TV screen when the Colombian goalkeeper let a penalty shot slip through the net. He grumbled in Spanish and twisted on the barstool, only to catch Billie's eye as she watched him from the entranceway.

Morales was eight years her senior, with dark hair and dimples embedded in olive skin. He was a good cop, known as a Boy Scout among his co-workers, but sometimes, he'd stretch the rules for Billie.

They had met one afternoon after Shari had taken an unannounced walk to the bank to withdraw money for a stranger who had emailed her, begging for help. She had grown flustered and belligerent when the teller flagged her account.

Morales had been standing behind her with a deposit slip and noted her condition. He offered to call someone, found Billie's name in her mother's cell phone, and waited with Shari while Billie hauled her ass from a final exam at Kentwell.

Since then, he had frequently invited her out for drinks but never to dinner. Billie learned that he was still hung up on an ex-wife.

Morales winked at her. "I knew you'd come."

Billie shrank back, feigning offense. She was *not* that easy.

Morales patted the seat next to him. "What do you want? I'm buying."

One of his detective cronies, a gray-haired behemoth of a man, called to her. "Well, if it isn't Billy Levine's grandkid. What's your old, old man up to these days? Still a gumshoe?"

"Supervisory," she said. "I'm working under him."

He paused with his pint glass midway to his mouth and laughed. "Good one."

Morales dismissed him. "She's not kidding, Malley." He grabbed her shoulder playfully. "Billie's a PI."

Malley considered this. "What's a typical caseload look like? Insurance fraud and cheating lovers?"

Billie shrugged. "One hopes." Although she wished she had gotten cases like that. They seemed far more cut and dried than whatever she was dealing with now.

"Maybe something to consider postretirement," Malley said before tilting his double chin at her. "You licensed?"

"Too young," she said with a shake of her head. "And I don't have all the requisite hours."

"You should consider doing work for an investigative firm. A former flame of mine owns a company. That'll get your numbers up."

It would, but she couldn't be reliable. She didn't say that, of course. "I'll think about it."

Malley screamed at the television.

Billie pointed to the flatscreen above the bar. "Didn't this match already happen?"

"Colombia wins two-one." Morales smiled as he sipped from his highball. "So how is the private-dick business?"

Billie settled into the barstool and ordered a seltzer with a spritz of citrus. "I'm working a case, and I didn't have to chase anyone for payment. Small victories."

"Can you talk about it?"

The bartender set her soda on a cocktail napkin and slid it across the shiny surface. She plucked off the orange slice and removed it from its peel before popping it into her mouth. "Missing person."

"And the bureau gave up?"

"They weren't notified. No one reported her gone except for the boyfriend, and he came straight to me."

"That's weird," he said with raised brows. "Parents?"

"No one knows where they are."

Morales shook his head. "Still, the boyfriend should file a report with BCDB. No offense, Billie, but there's only so far you'll get with this."

That might be – cops could access databases and request search warrants that she couldn't – but she had one advantage: this was her only case. And she could devote herself fully to it while the bureau juggled everything from murder to kidnapping to drunk-driving accidents on Route 4. Not to mention the myriad of *other* missing person cases piled on their desk.

"It's not a crime to be missing. Plenty of people don't want to be found," she pointed out.

"Is she at least twenty-one?" asked Morales.

"Yeah," she replied. "Barely."

"Get the boyfriend to come in, unless you think he has something to do with the disappearance."

"I'm not drawing conclusions yet. The boyfriend's an addict. I think she's just hiding out until he forgets about her." Wishful thinking, but she was going to hold onto that.

"What do the kids call that these days?" Malley snapped his fingers. "Ghosting."

Billie nodded at him. "Way to be hip to the vernacular."

Morales pursed his lips. It was clear he wasn't buying into Billie's hunch. "Perhaps she ghosted him, perhaps not. Any history of abuse?"

Billie remembered what Nuri O'Brien had said about the black eye. Then there was her whole Instagram account, which was severely lacking in recent photos of the happy couple. "I don't know. Maybe."

"In my experience, drug addiction and violence team up. Be prepared."

She said nothing. They were both quiet for a moment, their interest stolen by an hours-old soccer game.

Then Morales leaned into her and whispered, "After you finish your drink, you wanna get outta here? Go to my place?"

Billie was tempted to scratch that itch, but she shouldn't be gone too long. Otherwise, she would be the worst daughter this side of the George Washington Bridge. Granted, her mother had swallowed a trazodone before bed, which usually kept her knocked out for most of the night, but Billie needed to be local just in case.

"Rain check?" she asked.

"I hope it storms soon." Morales feigned disappointment, but then he grinned. He knew Billie's life was complicated, same as his. Which made everything so simple. No one had time or mental room to catch feelings.

He shifted on the barstool to unclip his cell phone from his belt. He pressed it to his ear and walked out the door. Billie heard him say, "Morales."

"Work never ceases," Malley said with a shake of his head.

"You're off the clock," she noted.

He shrugged. "Why do you think I've been divorced twice?"

"You're a real cop-show cliché, aren't you?" said Billie.

He smiled as he sipped his beer.

Morales returned and jerked his chin at his partner before taking a seat at the bar. "We're helping Richards with a case tomorrow. All hands on deck for this one."

"Oh yeah?" said Malley. "Is it like the time we had a black bear wander into Overpeck Park? Took hours to aid animal control with the capture. My ass crack was slick with sweat. Chafe city."

"There's an image," said Billie.

"No," said Morales, but his lips quirked up with a smile. He shook it off. "Dead body. But we need to track down the girl's parents. I might have to translate."

Billie's pulse jumped. "Say that again. Who's the girl?"

Morales squinted at her. "I can't release details, Billie."

"Give me specific generalities."

"College kid. Early twenties. Latina."

Bergen County was filled with young Latinas, but what were the chances? "Are her parents from Honduras?"

He exhaled slowly. "Shit, Billie, is that *your* missing person case?"

"Jasmine Flores. Kentwell student."

"That's her. Cops found her driver's license. Friend is going to come in and ID the body."

Billie fired off questions as fast as her brain could shoot them. "Where specifically was she found? Was there evidence of foul play at the scene? Do they have a time of death?"

"Whoa, whoa." Morales pumped the brakes with his hands. "You know I can't tell you any of that."

"Just tell me where they found her. It's gonna be in tomorrow's *Bergen Record* anyway."

He rubbed the back of his neck and leaned in close. "Tow company was called to pick up an abandoned Honda Accord from the Percy Street Garage. It smelled bad, so they popped the trunk–"

"Oh, God," Billie whispered.

"Looks like blunt-force trauma," he added.

Percy Street Garage? Shit. That was where Tommy went to score.

"I don't know anything else," Morales said. "This isn't my case. We just gotta assist Richards."

Billie chugged the rest of her seltzer and wiped the back of her hand across her mouth. Her throat burned from the carbonation.

"Are you all right?"

"Yeah, of course." Truthfully, she had hoped that the girl was just squatting in some dorm room to avoid her crappy boyfriend, not lying in a freezer drawer in the Bergen County Medical Examiner's Office.

What if Morales was unknowingly right? What if Tommy's addiction had pushed Jasmine into the path of an Amtrak train in the form of the Torn Crosses?

He stood up and dropped a few bills on the bar. "If I'm going home alone, then I should leave now. I got an early day tomorrow." He glanced at Billie, eyes soft, as if she was a puppy he'd accidentally kicked. "You're sure you're okay?"

"I'm fine," she said, her voice all sharp edges.

"You're done with this, you know? Whatever happens now, it's up to us. Got it?"

She said nothing.

"Billie?"

"You're going to lean hard into Tommy, aren't you?" She looked at him. "The boyfriend."

"You know how it goes. Why? You don't think he's good for it?"

The girl had been found murdered in his favorite scoring location.

"If he had hurt her, why would he hire me?" It was the same question she had posed to her grandpa. The situation didn't make sense to her, especially because Tommy looked like a kid who would use any cash on hand to buy drugs, not a PI.

She motioned to the bartender. "Add cranberry juice to this. I wanna pretend."

Morales whipped his suit jacket off the chair and sighed. "Your client knew the girl would be discovered eventually. With you in the picture, he looks like the concerned lover and not a killer."

Gramps had hinted at something similar.

Billie clutched her glass with both hands. "It doesn't feel like that."

"You said he's an addict."

David was an addict – recovering, sure – but still. If one of his boyfriends had ended up dead, would the police automatically assume he had something to do with it simply because he had abused drugs in his youth?

"I'll catch ya later, okay?" Morales said with expectant brows.

"Totally," she replied, but she couldn't look at him. Instead, she fired off a text message to Tommy.

Get a lawyer, she wrote.

He replied, *My uncle Paul already did but I need your help he said he'll pay whatever you want please.*

Whatever she wanted? Didn't Billie have an obligation to uncover a killer? For Jasmine? For all the dancers of the *Malta Club* that were treated like objects and nothing more? And for Tommy, who might have been a victim of his own addiction and bad circumstances?

Billie hadn't realized that Morales was still there, watching her. "Billie?"

She glanced up at him and lied, "Message received. I won't touch this."

CHAPTER TWELVE

Paul Russo lived in a two-story nouveau-Tuscan home in Closter, New Jersey, where the property taxes cost more than Billie had earned in the last two years.

A cursory Google search revealed that Paul had made the Forbes list for Top Ten Richest Men in New Jersey. He was married to Roxane Russo, née Donovan, who used to chair several charities, including those that benefited Hackensack Medical and the Rutgers Geology Museum.

Roxane and Paul Russo had no children. They did, however, have several squish-nosed purebred dogs that came charging at Billie, barking incessantly, as she pulled her Hyundai up their stone-paved driveway. She cut the engine and watched as the dogs sprang from crouches, snapping like hungry alligators.

A dog whistle must've gotten their attention, because they bolted from their attack as quickly as they had arrived.

Billie took a deep breath and got out of the car.

The Russo house had a gorgeous stucco exterior and wrought-iron balconies, a three-car garage, and two chimneys. The windows were taller than her great-uncle Mel, who had been an anomaly in the Levines' short-statured family tree.

When she rang the bell, a melody played. The dogs barked again, and someone yelled at them to shut the hell up.

A tall man with bone-white hair and Grecian features opened the door with a tense grin. He wore pressed slacks, a crisp white shirt, and a sweater vest. He looked like he belonged in a J. Crew catalog. "You must be Belinda. I'm Paul. We're so happy to see you."

He led Billie through a glorious foyer with gleaming marble floors and a dramatic staircase to a stunning living room with vaulted ceilings, brocaded furniture, and large oil canvases on pristine walls. The rabid dogs were nowhere to be found.

"Can I get you water, tea, coffee?" he asked.

Billie bet he owned one of those fancy Italian machines that made a bitchin' latte. She'd have skinned one of those dogs for a cup of fresh Costa Rican coffee. But her grandma's voice rang inside her head, telling her not to put anyone out. "I'm good," she said.

He raised a silver brow in protest.

"Really," she said. "And you can call me Billie."

"But Belinda is so much prettier."

Billie smiled politely at this little "compliment." It wasn't the first time a man had found her nickname an affront to his masculinity, and it certainly wouldn't be the last.

Paul gestured for her to take a seat on the couch across from Tommy, who sat listlessly, eyes rimmed in red, in a tufted leather club chair. He looked as if he was in need of a good night's sleep. And yet he seemed better than when Billie had last seen him – less twitchy.

"Uncle's got me on buprenorphine to help with the withdrawal," said Tommy as if reading Billie's mind.

"That's good."

"Feel like shit," he added.

That was to be expected.

A Black woman in blue scrubs passed the room, carrying a pile of towels. Billie cocked her brow, thinking she was the manicurist or esthetician. Didn't rich people have them on staff?

No one offered up an explanation.

Tommy sat up and rubbed vigorously at his face. He was wearing dress pants and a light cashmere sweater, clean, expensive labels that did little to brighten his sallow appearance. "The police–"

"They had him in that interrogation room for an hour before I finally got my lawyer over there," Paul interrupted, glancing sympathetically at his nephew. "He knows better than to let them talk to him without counsel."

"I was too out of it to think straight," said Tommy. "Cops say Jasmine was hit over the head with a pipe." He gestured to his forehead to illustrate the point.

"A pipe?"

"A metal pipe," he said. "Percy Street Garage is littered with crap like that."

He would know.

Billie took out her notebook and pen to jot down notes. "Did they give you a time of death?"

"Tuesday morning," he said. "They didn't say the exact hour or anything."

Billie wrote that down.

Paul gestured to her pen. "Old school. Everything is on the phone nowadays."

Writing things down helped Billie remember details better than typing them into her cell. Something about the scribbling motion forged tighter connections in her brain, or so she had read.

"Moving on," she said. "Do you have an alibi for where you were Tuesday morning?"

Tommy swallowed hard. "I don't know."

"What do you mean you don't know?"

"Like I said, I was pretty out of it in the days leading up to her disappearance." Billie noted how Tommy kept choosing his words carefully, as if "out of it" was the result of pulling all-nighters cramming for exams and not shooting up in a grimy parking deck. If her experiences with David were anything to go by, hiding behind euphemisms only frustrated those trying to help him.

"The police will want to know where you were," she explained. "If you can't establish an alibi, they will establish one for you – say, in a parking garage with your girlfriend."

"I *was* in the parking garage," Tommy said. "With my roommate Glenn Peters, but we went Monday night. I usually go there on Tuesdays, but not last week."

Billie wrote down Glenn's name. "Where were you on Tuesday morning?"

"I don't remember," he said. "I woke up in my car, pretty loose."

"Why didn't you go to Percy Street on Tuesday like usual?"

"Glenn wanted to go on Monday," he said. "I only go when he goes. Safer."

"That's why I asked you to come in today," said Paul in a businesslike tone. "We need you to establish his alibi, because I can't have Tommy giving the police jumbled answers only to correct them later when he remembers. It only makes him look bad, and I can't send him out to talk to his friends because–"

"He'll score," Billie finished.

Tommy slumped lower in the chair and chewed his thumbnail.

Paul cleared his throat. "We got him on the opioid-disorder meds, and I can't risk it. I'm willing to take a chance on you because I need you to work quickly. Thomas is a good kid. He's just sick."

Funny. That was the same thing the doctor had said about David when he had been in the psych ward, days after he had nearly overdosed on sleeping meds he had stolen from a friend. Oftentimes, drug addiction was a symptom of mental illness; other times, the addiction itself was the disease. Many times, it was both.

"Did Tommy mention that while I'm not licensed, my grandfather is, and I work under him?"

"William Levine," Paul said. "Our paths never crossed, but I am familiar with his work. He has a rep as being a smart investigator. I'm hoping his granddaughter takes after him, just maybe without the alcohol."

Gramps's reputation was still solidly intact.

Billie cleared her throat. "I don't drink anyway." Then, to steer the ship away from the iceberg that was her life, she said, "What do you think Jasmine was doing at Percy Street?"

Tommy stared at his hands, which were red and chapped. "Probably looking for me. She used to do that sometimes."

"And when she couldn't find you there, maybe she ran into a Torn Cross gang member?" asked Billie.

That got everyone quiet. Paul stared at Tommy. Tommy stared at his hands. Billie stared at them both with uncomfortable satisfaction. She liked being right; she just wished it didn't have to involve a dead college kid and her person-of-interest boyfriend.

"Christ, you didn't." Paul's chin dropped to his chest. Billie sensed a war waging inside that man's head. "You never learn, do you?"

"If I'm taking this job, I want honesty," she said. "I saw him outside your dorm room. What did you get yourself into?"

"I owe him money."

"How much?"

"A grand."

"For what?"

"What do you think?" Tommy said defensively.

"That Torn Cross gang member, the one I saw outside your room, could've gone to the garage to shake you down, and when you weren't there, he went after Jasmine instead."

Tommy's eyes welled.

"I can sort it out," said Paul quickly. When Billie cocked a questioning brow, he said, "Some of the Russo Foods dock workers know people who know Torn Cross members. It won't be hard to cancel the debt. I'm not proud of the association, but it's a reality in my business."

"Italian food imports?"

"Anything that comes off the dock is at risk to gangs," he said simply.

"I guess do what you gotta do, but Tommy should just lie low. Otherwise, what happened to Jasmine will happen to him." There was something else. "Nuri O'Brien mentioned that she saw Jasmine trying to cover up a black eye with makeup. Do you know anything about that?"

"O'Brien, you say?" asked Paul.

"Jasmine's bitch of a best friend," Tommy grumbled. "I had asked Jasmine about it, and she wouldn't tell me how she got hurt. Said something about opening up a door in her face."

Billie stared at him for a beat.

"Thomas wouldn't put his hands on a woman," Paul said, sensing her distrust. "I can assure you. Russo men do not do that."

"I wouldn't," Tommy interjected, pleading. "I would never hit her."

"People can get real angry when they can't get high," she pointed out.

"That hasn't been my problem," Tommy mumbled.

"Could the Torn Cross guy have hit her?" she asked. "As a warning?"

"I don't know."

He sounded so sincere. She wasn't entirely sure she trusted Tommy, but he was a kid, lost in a hell of his own making, and she felt for him.

Billie opened the flap on her messenger bag and slid out a folder containing the retainer agreement, contract, and business card.

Paul glanced over it and rose from the couch. "I'll get my checkbook."

Billie got up too, antsy to stretch her legs. "May I use your bathroom?"

Paul gestured toward the kitchen. "Before the guest suite. You can't miss it."

She thanked him and headed down a cream-painted hallway with crown molding and artistically done black-and-white photos documenting the house's renovation. She wouldn't have been surprised if Annie Liebowitz had shot them.

Television sounds emanated from a bedroom farther away. Billie heard the familiar voice of Reginald Beckman, her mother's favorite soap opera actor. He played Harold Reilly-Guinness, heir to the Reilly-Guinness empire on *Stormy Weather*. Her mom had been watching that program for decades. Billie passed the bathroom and crept toward the open door.

The woman in scrubs was folding laundry and nodding toward the television, which was the size of a movie projection screen. "That Mr Reilly-Guinness. What's he up to now?"

A woman in her early seventies, with gray hair, sat in a club chair and stared at the television. She was dressed in pressed pants and a plain white blouse. Her hair had been pinned up in an elaborate French twist and secured with a sparkly comb. Her wedding band shone. She wore several gold bangles. She looked like she was headed to brunch, except she wore no makeup. No lipstick. Not even a pair of shoes. In her youth, she clearly had been a stunner.

"He's sleeping with Penny," she said.

That wasn't right. That storyline had ended years ago. Penny had died after falling down a mine shaft, and the baby born from the affair was now twenty-five years old and vying to run the company.

"Miss Roxie, I think he's married to Agatha now."

Roxie? Roxane Russo. The one who had single-handedly secured the Star of India for a museum exhibit?

Something felt off here.

"Penny is stealing Harold right under her nose. She needs to catch them. What's her name?" Roxie stabbed a finger at the television. "The woman!" Her voice rose, her temper bubbling beneath the surface. "Where's the girl? The brown-haired one?"

"You mean Penelope? She died in a mine shaft explosion, remember?"

Billie's mom got like that. When she couldn't remember something, she grew belligerent, as if it was Billie's fault that Shari had dropped a word or misplaced a face and couldn't pick it up.

"Miss Roxie, it's time for your nap," the nurse said, because who else could it be other than a nurse? She wasn't a manicurist here to work on Roxie's nails but a woman sent by an agency to care for her.

"I'm not tired."

Billie backed away.

She went into the bathroom and splashed water onto her face.

Roxane Russo had Alzheimer's too, likely late-onset. Billie was well versed in this now.

This case was already taking a toll. Roxie. The *Malta Club*. Not to mention a skinhead gang that probably had already killed a young woman. There was too much familiarity and not the good kind. What had happened to the cheating lovers and insurance fraud clients that Malley so wistfully mentioned at the *Wagon*? Why couldn't Billie get saddled with one of those for her first big case?

She had just left the bathroom, thinking she would tell Mr Russo that he should hire someone else, when he presented her with the contract and the check.

She glanced down at his penmanship, all sharp lines and edges. And all those zeros.

"You get my nephew out of this and I'll reward you. I promise."

Leaky roof. Overgrown shrubs. Maybe they could hire a day nurse.

How could she say no?

Paul cast his nephew a look. A beat later, Tommy rose from the chair. "I'll walk you to the door."

"We'll be in touch," Billie told Paul and let Tommy escort her through the mansion's labyrinth.

"Thanks for doing this," he said, eyes hollow.

Everyone's advice rang in her ears. *The boyfriend is always good for it.* "It's my job. I'm being paid." *And not by you*, she wanted to add.

"I didn't hurt her."

She wanted to believe him – Tommy needed help – and for some reason, she did.

"But I might be responsible for setting this all in motion."

His drug abuse had led Jasmine into the path of violence, but perhaps that was unfair. *You don't blame victims, Levine.* Tommy was as much a victim of his addiction as Jasmine was.

"That whole thing with Matthew Goff," he said.

"Huh?" *That* wasn't what she'd expected to hear.

He shifted from one foot to the other. "I think he came after her because of me."

"Because of the money she took? A few hundred bucks wouldn't make him risk his neck like that, and Matthew Goff isn't a violent guy."

For a second, Tommy looked confused. Then he said, "Right. No, you're right. That's a silly theory."

"Why would she steal money from the *Malta*?" asked Billie.

"For one of her groups, maybe. Safety Brigade is always fundraising."

That was true. The Safety Brigade ran on volunteers, but the app cost money. So did T-shirts and advertising.

Tommy thrust his hands inside his pockets and nodded.

"Stay clean." She thought there was hope for Tommy, just like there had been for David.

Speaking of whom, he texted her.

Can you make an early day of it? Wanna see a friend before my shift.

She wrote back, *I'll try.*

Please try hard.

Billie scampered down the front steps and across the stone-paved driveway. She fumbled to open her car door, anxious to get the hell out of there. This case had her rattled in a way she wasn't prepared for. Maybe, when this was all over, she would take Detective Malley up on his offer to get her a job with his friend.

She would try to quit early today. Dealing with her mother was sure to be easier than dealing with the Russos.

CHAPTER THIRTEEN

Billie drove back to Kentwell College to interview Tommy's roommate, Glenn Peters. But when she arrived at Fellman House, she was just in time to see the Bergen County Detectives Bureau swarming outside Tommy's dorm room with boxes and evidence bags.

One detective in a navy suit jacket and bushy mustache shoved a paper at the scrawny kid who had gotten yanked off his feet by the Torn Cross gang member.

Billie presumed that was Glenn.

An officer from Campus Police was also there, pretending to look supervisory but mainly looking extraneous.

Glenn sullenly leaned against the wall with his arms crossed over an argyle sweater. At first glance, he did not look like a heroin user. He wore nice jeans and brown Oxford shoes. Nerdy, clean. But now that the opioid epidemic was reaching a crescendo, Billie understood that no one fit the stereotype anymore.

She needed to look beyond clean clothes and an upper-middle-class disdain. Still, she couldn't see it.

The mustachioed detective ushered Glenn into another room and shut the door. That would take some time, and Billie would have to wait them out.

Meanwhile, the hallway began to fill with bodies. Dorm-room doors opened. Wide-eyed juniors stretched their necks for snippets of police conversation.

She took the stairs up to the third floor to see who was

combing through Jasmine's stuff. Maybe she would spy a familiar face who would offer up some intel.

When Billie flung open the stairwell door, she heard the halls buzzing with gossip. Students had filtered into the hallway, their lips pressed against friends' ears. The dorm sounded like it was alive with bees.

"Did you hear? A girl was murdered."

"The police are in her room."

"There's yellow tape."

"They're taking her things."

"Which girl?"

"Jasmine Something."

"The podcast girl! The one into true crime."

"Is this the definition of irony?"

Detective Esteban Morales caught Billie lurking outside and turned his head as if he could pretend he hadn't seen her.

Amateur.

She pushed through a cluster of residents and right up to the yellow tape and peeked inside Jasmine's room. Several techs wearing latex gloves opened and closed various desk drawers.

Detective Malley was inspecting the corkboard with a furrowed brow.

Morales lifted the crime scene tape and joined Billie in the hallway. He led her to an adjacent room that was empty aside from two stripped beds, desks, and dressers. He shut the door.

"You shouldn't be here," he said. "How'd you even get into the building?"

"Not important. So what's going on?"

"I'll tell you what was released to the press," he said, resigned and massaging his temple. "Homicide. Anyone with information is encouraged to come forward." He gave her a look.

"Well, that's what I'm looking for," she said. "Information."

His eyes narrowed. "Are you still working this?"

"I was hired by Tommy's uncle to prove his alibi," she said.

He sighed. "Come on, Levine."

Oh, so we're doing last names now. "He's paying me well, and I'm not so sure Tommy is the prime suspect. Especially now that skinheads are involved."

"What are you talking about?"

She decided to toss Morales intel since it could help her too. "Tommy's roommate was threatened by a Torn Cross gang member. When Tommy didn't answer the door, he attacked the roommate. I saw the tattoo."

Morales's brows rose in a perfect arc. "Describe it."

She rolled her eyes. She knew her skinhead markings. "A ripped cross sitting above a row of skulls."

He rubbed out the tension on the bridge of his nose. "Really?"

Billie pushed in tight – close enough to inhale Morales's cologne. If he wasn't going to play ball, she would play dirty.

He stepped back. "You sure? It's more on trend to wear collared shirts than shaved heads."

"If it quacks like a Nazi," she said.

Morales scoffed at that.

"Despite what I'm telling you, you still think Tommy Russo is good for it? What's the motive here?"

"According to her friend, Jasmine would often go to Percy Street to prevent Tommy from using. They probably got into a fight. He got violent. Hit her over the head with a pipe."

"Did you find the pipe?" she asked.

"Yes. It was clean."

"And you think a drugged-out Tommy Russo was cognizant enough to wipe his prints off the murder weapon?"

"Desperation and panic can be a real surge to the senses."

"Usually, desperation makes people do stupid things," she said.

"Right," he said. "Like murder your girlfriend who is trying to stop you from using."

Touché.

"One of her diamond earrings was also missing," Morales added.

"Really? Then maybe this was a mugging gone wrong. Think about it. It's a known user hangout."

"Richards is looking into all leads."

"Tommy could've stolen those earrings anytime if he needed cash to score," she pointed out.

"According to the uncle," Morales continued, "who has a giant stick up his ass, Jasmine insisted Paul pay for Tommy's rehab. They even secured him a spot in Ringwood. It's possible she went there under the pretense of getting him into the car to take him there, and Tommy freaked."

"She insisted, huh?"

"That's what Russo claimed. He said he would pay for it directly. He didn't want Jasmine as the go-between. Maybe he knew this would be the result."

"Or maybe he didn't trust Jasmine."

"Rich white dude who didn't like a brown girl," said Morales. "Big shock."

"What are you even looking for in her room?" Billie asked.

"There's a list."

"What about the Torn Crosses?" BCDB seemed to be building a case around Tommy rather than evidence.

Morales huffed again. He opened the door and ushered her outside. "Go. And don't talk to anyone," he said, his voice stern.

Billie held her hands up in a placating manner. She could play at being a professional even if she technically wasn't one. "What happened with Jasmine's parents? Did you find them?"

"They flew in this morning. I met with them for a moment. Devastated, of course." Morales lifted the tape and went over to his partner, who was reading the spines of Jasmine's murder books.

"Girl was morbid." Malley gave a sad little shake of his head.

"Said the homicide detective," Billie retorted. She tried to imagine how Jasmine's Honduran parents had managed to scrape enough money together for plane tickets. Unless they weren't poor. "How did her folks get in so fast?"

"I'm not here to be interviewed." Morales huffed then stared down the hallway as if he was considering something.

Billie gave up and walked away. Morales wasn't going to tell her anything else, not without a few drinks in him first. Besides, Glenn Peters should be done with his interview by now.

CHAPTER FOURTEEN

Billie halted at the sight of Glenn sitting against the wall in the stairwell. His hair stood up on end as if he had been running his hands through it repeatedly.

He let out a sigh and glanced at her. Dark circles sat underneath his blue eyes, and his brows quirked so high Billie thought they might try to escape his forehead.

"You come here to gawk at me?" Glenn sounded annoyed and put out, and Billie couldn't really blame him. After all, the cops were combing through his stuff and invading his privacy because of Tommy Russo.

Glenn probably didn't realize it, but he was going to be quite popular among the underclassmen. College kids loved swapping juicy stories around the keg at the next Beta Theta Pi party.

She handed him a business card. "No. I came to ask you a few questions about Tommy."

Glenn gave her a long, examining stare but then got to his feet. He brushed dirt from his knees. "I just got grilled by a detective. I don't really have anything else to add. Besides, I don't know you."

"I don't work for the BCDB. I work for–" She couldn't say Tommy. Glenn would not have a soft spot for him. So instead, she said, "The Safety Brigade. I used to be an officer."

He examined the business card. "And they hired you?"

"Yes," she lied. "I'm trying to find out what happened to Jasmine."

"Tommy happened," he said, his face relaxing.

"How long had she and Tommy been together?" Billie asked.

"A year, maybe. I think Tommy said they met at a Halloween party when they were sophomores."

"So she knew what kind of problems he had?"

Glenn shrugged. "He was a lot cleaner back then. It wasn't so obvious. Makes me wonder why she didn't dump him when he got worse."

"Maybe she loved him," Billie suggested.

That elicited a laugh. "Yeah, right."

Billie removed her notepad from her bag. "I need to ask you something sensitive. Again, I don't work for the BCDB."

Glenn narrowed his gaze, suspicious. "What?"

"Were you with Tommy Russo Monday night? Scoring at the Percy Street Parking Garage?"

Glenn's eyes widened. "How do you know–?"

Billie cut him off. "I'm not here to get you in trouble. I don't care about what you did unless you murdered Jasmine Flores."

Glenn peeked through the square window in the door that looked into the hallway. He pushed off then leaned over the banister to check if anyone was hanging around on the landings. But the area was strangely quiet. Probably because all the residents were huddled in the halls, spying on the cops.

Glenn gritted his teeth. "I'm not an addict."

"And I'm not a cop."

Glenn huffed and shook his head as if he was having a silent argument with himself. Billie wasn't sure who was winning.

"Yes," he said finally. "We did go there to score, but not for me, and I don't let Tommy near my guy."

"Oh, really?" Again, Glenn seemed pretty alert. Like someone who consistently slept well.

"We normally go on Tuesday," he added. "But Tommy said he couldn't go on Tuesday, and my sister–"

"Your sister?"

"She can't get off it, and the last time she went out to get high, she was nearly assaulted. I'm not proud of doing this, but I can't figure out an alternative yet. This way, she's safe."

"Can you get her into treatment?"

"You don't think I've tried? There's a six-week waiting list. She'll be dead before she gets in."

"What about going to the police?"

"Hell no," he said firmly. "I can get kicked out of school. And if Tommy tells them, I'll deny it. They won't believe him anyway."

"But if she was hurt, maybe they can help her."

Glenn scoffed. "When I suggested she file a report, she threatened to run. She didn't want to snitch."

"Snitch on who?"

"The Torn Crosses." Glenn rubbed his neck, where a red bruise still lingered from his altercation with the gang member.

She gestured to it. "Was it the same guy who hurt your sister?"

"Don't think so. Just a different racist asshole. She said that the one who hurt her had a tattoo on his eyelid."

"On his eyelid?"

"Scary mothereffer." He blinked at her. "And my sister's Asian. Adopted. He took one look at her and tried to – he didn't get a chance – a security guard at the mall showed up at the last minute." He shook his head as if trying to disperse the memory. He peeked through the window again. "When do you think they'll be done?"

"Soon," she said. "Why do you take Tommy with you?"

"I don't want to see anyone die, and my dealer is clean. Tommy wanted an introduction, but no one smart will do business with him."

"Why not?" asked Billie. "Isn't his money good?"

"Word is that Tommy got busted by the BCDB with intent to sell when he was a teenager. His parents made a deal with prosecutors that if he gave up the name of his supplier, he'd get off with a sealed record."

"Let me guess," said Billie, not really having to guess. There was only one Torn Cross gang member who was a big get for the BCDB. "Tommy gave them Colfer Dryden."

"Not Colfer. His kid."

Ian Dryden.

"And lived to tell the tale?"

"I heard that the only reason Tommy is alive is because the Torn Crosses aren't finished with him yet."

"Finished how?" she asked.

Glenn didn't answer. He stretched his neck and peered through the window. "What are they looking for anyway?"

"Dunno," she said. "They have a list. I'm not privy to it."

"Listen," Glenn began, "I can't imagine what you must think of me for doing what I do, but my sister wants to get better." He stared at the cement floor, where a glob of gum had dried into the shape of a pistol. "But I can't afford to get her into a decent place, and the ones insurance will pay for don't have room. Meanwhile, Tommy's been to several rehab resorts, and it won't stick."

"A lot of people relapse. Doesn't matter if they get clean in county lockup or a thousand-dollar-a-day rehab."

He frowned. "Is that supposed to make me feel better?"

"No." Billie was no optimist. "I'm sorry about your sister. Like I said, I'm not here to get you in trouble."

Interesting how Jasmine was dead, but Tommy was still alive to score. Had he made another deal with the Torn Crosses that kept him in one piece? Had he sacrificed his girlfriend to stay alive?

But if Jasmine was desperate to get Tommy off drugs and to keep him safe, maybe she had taken a risk with Colfer and Ian Dryden.

Glenn reached for the door handle. "I'm gonna grab my stuff, head to the library. I'll sleep there tonight. I just can't be here anymore."

He pulled open the door with hunched shoulders, carrying the weight of his sister's problems with him.

Billie wondered if she looked similar after spending time with her mother.

"Wait," she said as she flipped through her cell phone, looking for her contacts. "Here's the number for Nicole Mercier in Student Housing. She can find you a place for the night." Billie held out her phone screen to him.

He waved it off. "It's fine. Couches are comfy there." Glenn exited the stairwell.

A voice called her name.

She froze, feeling as if she was momentarily in trouble, but it was Morales. She went over to the banister and looked up.

He called down, "Glad I caught you. Malley is waiting outside to show you mug shots. We're going to ID your white supremacist."

CHAPTER FIFTEEN

Billie sat in the back of a police cruiser, parked on the sidewalk in front of Fellman House, with the door open. Students gave the car a wide berth as if they could catch murder by proximity. Malley squinted at a tablet in bright sunlight and swiped a thick finger across the screen several times, each moment growing more and more frustrated.

"They digitized these mug shots," he said with annoyance. "What was wrong with the book?"

Billie shifted uneasily on the dirty seat cushion. How many perps had sat in the back of this car, covered in piss and vomit? Did anyone ever wipe down the leather with a bleach spray? Next to her sat a box, the kind office workers carried out after they'd been sacked from their job. The lid was on tight, but it wasn't marked as evidence.

"What's in this box?" She jerked her chin at it.

He sighed and adjusted his belt around his big belly. "Just some stuff from the girl's room. It's nothing but notes for her podcast."

"Are you allowed to take stuff if it's not named in the warrant?" she asked.

"It was in plain view," he said. "It's not evidence. Just research."

"About?"

He leaned his forearm on the car and pushed in. "Starla Wells, dancer. Murdered outside the *Malta Club* in 1991. I worked that case. Still open."

"No leads?"

"Leads, sure. Smoking gun? No."

"A stripper was murdered outside a Goff-owned club, and you drew blanks?"

Malley frowned. "She was a cabaret dancer. And Neil Goff is a pro. But I had my suspicions. Ask your grandfather. He worked it too."

"Who hired him to do that?"

Malley grunted. "No one. Pet project."

Billie undid the flap on her messenger bag and retrieved a pair of latex gloves. "May I?"

Malley glanced around the scene. "It's not really anything connected to the Flores case."

"Then it shouldn't be an issue." She looked at him expectantly.

"It's because you're Levine's grandkid that I'm letting you do this. You got two minutes while I try to figure out these mug shots." He made an I'll-be-right-there face before he lumbered under the shadowy canopy of a glorious maple tree that was still clinging to its dead leaves.

Billie snapped on the gloves, turned around, and lifted the lid off the box. Peeking inside, she found a stack of note cards written in girlish handwriting. She gingerly took out the stack and flipped through the cards.

April 1990. Starla Wells performs for the first time at the Malta Club.

She flipped to another.

May 1990. Starla Wells gets kicked out of the Pembroke Hotel *after a drunken altercation.*

And then another – *December 1990. Starla calls 9-1-1 for a black eye.*

And lastly – *June 1991. Starla Wells stabbed to death outside the* Malta Club. *Her diamond pendant is stolen.*

Below the cards were several newspaper articles photocopied from *The Bergen Record*.

The headlines read:

STRIPPER MURDERED OUTSIDE MOB-OWNED MALTA CLUB

*NEIL GOFF QUESTIONED IN CONNECTION WITH THE
MURDER OF EMPLOYEE*

MUGGING GONE WRONG OUTSIDE FAMED GENTLEMEN'S CLUB

Jasmine was researching a crime that had happened outside
the *Malta Club* in 1991, when she hadn't even been born then.
Hell, Billie hadn't even been born then.

Billie wondered if this was a chicken-and-egg situation. Had
Jasmine applied to dance at the *Malta Club* before or after she
found out about Starla Wells?

It sounded as if Malley was finishing his phone call, so she
put everything back into the box and took off her gloves. She
dumped them back into her bag.

"Okay," Malley said with a bit of satisfaction. "I got it." He
handed her the tablet. "Bergen County's overachievers."

She was staring at a group of mug shots of men with shaved
heads, their tattooed faces fitting neatly inside little rectangles
with white backgrounds.

"Tap on the top left and then you can swipe through,"
Malley instructed.

"They all look alike," she noted.

"Check for scars."

She started with the first one and kept going. The thing
about skinheads was that there was no distinguishable style.

Shaved head. Swastika tattoo. Swipe.

Shaved head. Swastika tattoo on the cheek. Swipe.

Shaved head. Swastika tattoo on the neck. Swipe.

This one had a swastika on the upper eyelid. She squinted
at his nameplate. Ian Dryden. That was who had attacked
Glenn's sister.

She kept swiping, searching through a hellish Tinder.

Wait. This one was sorta handsome if she could totally

disregard the fact that he was a racist scumbag. Which she couldn't.

"Him," she told Malley and held up the tablet for his inspection. "This assmunch. Who's he?"

Malley shook his head with annoyance. "Damon Shane. Errand boy mostly. Did five for assault and battery. Paroled last year."

"Great," said Billie, snapping his photo with her cell phone. "Well, he's the dude who scared the piss out of Tommy's roommate. Don't you think he's worth looking into?"

Malley ran a meaty palm over his scruff. "I'll have to call my buddy in the domestic terrorism task force." He looked at her, eyes all soft as if she was some kindergartner. "Honestly, though, the boyfriend is typically the–"

"Guilty one," she finished. "Yeah, yeah. Except you have a freaking skinhead in the mix. Changes things, don't you think?"

"Not really," he said. Then, considering, he said, "Well, maybe. Again, we'll look into it."

"So, Starla Wells."

"So, nothing," said Malley. "It was the case that got away."

"Seems like a mugging gone wrong. Right? Stripper killed. Diamond stolen. A lot like Jasmine actually."

"The cases are not alike," he said. "Trust me."

"What do you mean?"

A gaggle of girls passed the car, murmuring in hushed whispers. Malley straightened up. "It's probably time you head out. This place is gonna be a madhouse soon with press and every college kid with a TikTok and YouTube channel."

Billie shimmied out of the backseat. "I wanna talk more about Starla. You got me curious."

"Another time," he grumbled. "Now, go."

Billie acquiesced if only because she had a more modern and immediate murder to tackle first. She headed down the path that led to the quad. The sunshine made everything feel warm and alive despite police combing through a dead girl's things.

A voice called her name, and she stopped.

Billie whipped around to find Nicole jogging toward her in a Burberry-knockoff trench coat and vintage Dior sunglasses, which she lowered to offer Billie an exasperated stare. She held out her hand.

Billie fished out the keycard and slapped it into Nicole's open palm.

"You were supposed to have returned this yesterday." Nicole glanced around, her dark eyes ping-ponging off everything – brick exterior, students' heads, the paved walkway. She lowered her voice. "The police asked me who had access to her room, and I lied for you."

"How do you know that I broke in?" asked Billie.

"A hunch that you've now verified." She put her hands on her hips. "You put me in a bad position."

"I'm sorry," said Billie earnestly. "I *am*."

"I texted you Calvin's info. Did you run that background check like I asked?" Nicole pursed her lips as if her level of forgiveness would be based on Billie's response.

Billie would fail this test. "Not yet," she said, jutting her chin toward the dorm. "My case got more complicated."

Nicole's eyes darted behind Billie to the towering silhouette of Fellman Hall. "So I heard. I'm sorry about that. Horrible." Then, giving Billie a hard stare, she continued, "That said, you owe me big time."

"I'll take care of it ASAP," said Billie. "I swear."

Nicole softened. "I'm not trying to be a bitch. I realize that this isn't a big deal in the grand scheme of things–" she gestured toward the police presence "–but Calvin keeps hinting about making plans..."

"I will do it," said Billie as she turned around and stared at the building. Even from here, they could see cops milling about in Jasmine's room. "How did Jasmine pay for her tuition?" Billie blurted out.

"I have no idea. Same as everyone? Massive loans."

"Can you find out for me?"

"Maybe. Why?"

Morales had said the parents flew into Jersey the minute they heard of their daughter's death. Therefore, they were not likely to be deported immigrants. Billie assumed they were rich or at least well-off enough to land at Newark Liberty without red tape. So then why was their daughter stripping at the *Malta Club*? It didn't make sense.

Billie shrugged. "Working a hunch, that's all." She didn't want to dissect everything right then and there.

"What we don't know about people could fill an ocean," said Nicole with a sigh and a little shake of her head.

Billie thought about Glenn scoring heroin for his sister. About Tommy, a wealthy heir who couldn't kick his drug habit. And even about herself, still preoccupied with her childhood love.

Nicole was right. People kept massive parts of themselves hidden from view. And yet, with time, everything would eventually float to the surface. Because when people were agitated, their dirt was exposed.

And that was what Billie was banking on.

CHAPTER SIXTEEN

Billie was approaching her Hyundai with her keys sandwiched between her knuckles when her cell phone rang with an unfamiliar number.

"Levine Investigations," she said as she unlocked the driver's-side door.

"Billie?" said a girl's voice. "It's Nuri O'Brien, Jasmine's friend. I need your help." She sounded skittish and nervous, as if one wrong word could make her dissolve into hysterics.

"You all right?" Billie threw her bag into the passenger's seat as she slid in behind the steering wheel. She slammed the door closed and inserted the key into the ignition.

"Can you come to the *Ugly Mug*?" Nuri asked in a tiny voice. "I'm still on shift."

Billie glanced at the clock on the dashboard. She had promised David that she would get home early. "Honestly, this isn't the best–"

"The car is here again."

The engine grumbled as if it was pissed that Billie was trying to get it started. "What car?"

"The black one. The one that had been following Jaz. Although now, I'm wondering if it's following me."

The town car. Right. She should've remembered that. Crap. Why hadn't she remembered that?

Billie glanced at the dashboard clock and did a mental calculation. If she got to the coffee shop within fifteen minutes, that should give David enough time to see his friend before work. "I'll be there in a few." She disconnected the call and reversed out of the spot.

The sun's glare proved so hazardous that traffic was backed up because of it, and Billie arrived at the *Ugly Mug* far later than she had intended.

She pulled into the lot and drove around but didn't spy a black vehicle. No Buick or town car. Nothing suspicious. And, yet she decided to park her Hyundai behind the building as a precaution.

Billie entered the coffee shop just as Nuri glanced up from behind a glass counter topped with pastries. Espresso machines hissed behind her.

Despite its moniker, the *Ugly Mug* was cute and charming, with pastel-painted walls covered in bright canvases and mixed-media art. Overstuffed couches held pillows shaped like various animals. Billie's senses were overloaded by the sheer adorableness of it all.

Nuri wiped her hands on her red apron and came around the counter. "Taking my break," she told a skinny guy pouring an iced coffee. She jerked her chin at Billie and signaled that they should go outside.

Billie followed her around the building to an area by the dumpsters.

Nuri fished a cigarette from her apron and pressed it between pale lips. "All this shit with Jaz has left me anxious as hell." She lit the end of the cigarette and inhaled deeply.

"I don't see the black car," said Billie.

"It left shortly before you got here," Nuri said, tapping ash to the cracked asphalt below. "But I think he was young." She danced on the balls of her feet, no doubt trying to keep warm. She inhaled and blew out a plume of smoke. "I don't know if I'm being paranoid or what. I'm constantly freaked out. My stepdad says I make myself crazy with fear because all I talk about is murder."

"Nothing wrong with being vigilant," said Billie.

"That's what I said. My best friend just died, but he doesn't get that. He thinks I bring this on myself."

Most men did, but they typically were free to roam the streets without having to jab their car keys between their knuckles in case some guy jumped out of the bushes to rape them. "Listen, did Jasmine ever talk to you about Tommy's past?"

Nuri flicked more ash to the ground. "All I know is that his parents are loaded. Probably why he hasn't been kicked out yet. They bribed the college president with a large donation. He'll be gone from school, but his name will be on the new rec center or something."

"I'm talking about his *previous* troubles. The shit he got into when he was younger."

Nuri shrugged. "Jasmine said that Tommy had a juvenile record but that it was sealed because of a deal his parents had made." She sighed. "Like I said, if trouble is the question, money is the answer."

Billie pursed her lips. "You should put that on a mug and sell it."

"I tried. The owner wouldn't let me. He's loathe to listen to any ideas that aren't his own. I probably shouldn't have majored in communications. My mom says I won't get a job after college that isn't slinging coffee. She joked that I should claim I'm one-eighth Cherokee in job interviews so I can get hired."

Billie stared, open-mouthed.

"She was kidding, but it's not like they ask for proof. I need a decent-paying gig just like anyone else." Nuri kicked a rock into the parking lot. She took another puff off the cigarette. "If only our podcast made more money."

Speaking of… "What's the deal about Starla Wells?"

Nuri turned her cheek, letting a breeze carry off the smoke. "It was a story we covered on an episode."

Billie flashed on the books in Jasmine's dorm room. "So all the serial killer stuff–"

"Research. We often read books, watch documentaries, and use articles to talk about the crime."

"Seems like a lot of extra homework for two college girls," Billie pointed out.

Nuri shrugged. "It's interesting, and it doesn't feel like work. Plus people are really into it."

"It requires a lot of time," she pointed out.

"With hopefully a lot of payout. Look at *My Favorite Murder*. The live shows. The fan base. It's huge. We could be that."

"Jasmine called your podcast a rip-off of *My Favorite Murder*," Billie said.

Nuri gave her a look then stubbed out the cigarette on a loose brick. "Jaz didn't say that. Tommy did. Jaz really liked doing the podcast. We spent a lot of money on microphones and software and design services for the merchandise. She wouldn't do that if she wasn't invested."

"Where did you get the money for your equipment?" asked Billie.

Nuri gestured around the building. "Where else? Our paychecks."

"Did your parents or Jasmine's folks help out financially in any way?"

Nuri snorted. "I grew up in a trailer park in Moonachie, so no."

The cafe's backdoor opened, and the skinny guy came out carrying a bag of trash. He hefted it into the dumpster and said, "Five more minutes."

Nuri rolled her eyes but then lit another cigarette.

"So Jasmine was really into true crime, huh?" Billie said, thinking of all her books, the ones Malley had called morbid.

"Definitely. She was majoring in criminology. She wanted to be a writer."

"Like Michelle McNamara?" Billie asked.

Nuri pointed at her with the lit end of the cigarette. "Exactly."

"Who heads up the Safety Brigade now?"

"Tasha Nichols," said Nuri with a swoop of her head. "She's also president of Sleuth Squad."

Billie recalled seeing that name on the chalkboard on Jasmine's Instagram. It wasn't an organization that had existed when she was in college. "Who are they?"

"A bunch of girls who meet at school to discuss cold cases. Most of them are criminology students and psych majors. Fair warning: they are serious about what they do."

"And Jasmine belonged?"

"She was the vice president." Nuri inhaled and flicked ash onto her boot. She smiled. "Tasha is really intense, and she put a lot of pressure on Jasmine with the club. She wanted her to spend all her free time on it, and Jasmine's a busy girl. *Was* a busy girl. I thought it was unfair." She glanced at the clear sky, which was just beginning to darken.

Billie swiped through her cell phone and held up the mug shot of Damon Shane. "Ever see this guy bothering Jasmine?"

Nuri took another drag and squinted at it. "Yeah, I think I saw him following us once after class. He doesn't look like he goes to Kentwell."

"He's not a student," said Billie.

Nuri glanced at the cigarette as if sad to let it go. She stubbed it out. "I should quit. These things are expensive." Sighing, she threaded her fingers behind her head. "I can't do this. My friend just died, and I'm serving coffee." When she glanced at Billie, tears had gathered in her eyes.

"You're doing the best you can," Billie said sympathetically. "Jasmine would get that."

"What do I do if that car comes back?" Nuri asked.

"Just let me know. If you can get a good look at the driver, I'll take care of it."

"You're not scared?" Nuri asked seriously.

The only things that terrified Billie were the ones she couldn't see coming. "Nah," she said confidently. "I'll be prepared."

"Thanks for coming here," said Nuri. "I appreciate it. The girls at school, they all have each other, but I just had Jasmine."

"Good friends are hard to come by," Billie said. "I'm sorry you lost yours."

Nuri smiled sadly before heading inside.

Billie went back to her car.

CHAPTER SEVENTEEN

Billie arrived home to find David pacing the front lawn. He was dressed in his scrubs, but Billie noted a hint of cologne. He'd also shaved, and his hair held a glossy sheen that only pomade could produce.

"I asked you to come home early," he said, not angrily but disappointed. Which was worse.

She checked the time on her watch. To her, it was early. "I was following up on something. Is Gramps home?"

"Yeah," he said as he hurried to his car, his keys out.

"Okay, then, you didn't have to wait for me." Gramps would've handled the overlap.

"I asked you for a favor," he said.

"I was working."

He huffed out a long breath. "I wanted to go hang out with a friend for an hour. And now, with traffic, you've left me with no time."

"Sorry." But she didn't sound apologetic. She tried again, more slowly and deliberately. "I'm sorry."

He wordlessly got into his car.

"David, come on, don't be like that."

He didn't answer her, just dropped into the driver's seat and peeled out of the driveway.

Shit.

She went inside, dumped her bag in the foyer, and walked into the kitchen. She found her grandfather sitting at the table, his reading glasses perched on his nose and *The Bergen Record* splayed out before him. Steam coiled from a cup of coffee.

His buddy, Ken Greenberg, was standing with his head inside the fridge, his tush wagging slightly like Winnie the Pooh with his nose stuck in a honey pot. "You got any rotisserie left?"

It was like stumbling upon two fraternity brothers who had taken up residence in her house.

"No," Billie said, now hungry, now wishing she did have rotisserie.

Ken shut the fridge. The door fell off its hinge.

"Easy unless you're buying us a new one," Billie said as she shoved him out of the way to set it right.

Ken snorted. "On my pension?"

"Your brother has a date," Gramps said formally.

But Billie caught it. The slurring. Now she understood why David wouldn't leave until she had gotten home. The two of them were sloshed.

And the Bad Sister Award goes to Belinda Levine.

Thank you. I couldn't have done it without Alzheimer's and debt.

"Where's Mom?" asked Billie.

"Watching television. Her story is on."

Her story was always on. She watched it on repeat via the app.

Gramps glanced at the newspaper, but Billie could tell he was using it as a prop to appear functioning when he wasn't. No way the newsprint was anything but a blur.

Ken rummaged around the cupboards. "What's for dinner?" he asked.

"You don't live here," she said.

"Hey, be nice," said Gramps. The crockpot lid popped on the counter. "I assume supper is in there."

Ken frowned. "If it's your brother's chili, no thanks."

"Maybe you should've gotten a doggy bag from the *Clam Bar*," Billie told them both. She disappeared down the hall and into the living room, where she joined her mom on the couch.

She plopped down and rested her head on her mother's

shoulder. The television screen glowed with the latest recorded episode of *Stormy Weather*.

That reminded her of Roxie Russo. Billie's stomach pitched.

She gestured to the screen. A woman dressed like a fortune-teller was lighting a cigarette. "Is that Penelope Delacroix? What's her deal now?" She then pointed to an older guy dressed all in denim. "Who's that guy? The hired handyman?"

She used to do this to her mom when she was a kid. After a long day at work, Shari would sink into the couch to watch her soap opera, and Billie would interrupt every three seconds asking about the various storylines.

"Who did Alexandra marry? Is that the kid from the affair? Whatever happened to Lawrence Delacroix? Did he come back from the dead? Did they ever solve Bartholomew's murder?"

At first, Shari would attempt to unravel the complicated threads until she realized that Billie was making fun of the show. She would get exasperated and roll her eyes, but Billie could tell that her mother was amused.

Billie was nothing if not amusing.

"Whatever happened to Mackenzie? Did she get out of prison?" Billie laughed.

But her mom threw up her hands. "I don't know!" she snapped. "Stop with your questions."

Billie stilled. She had forgotten, momentarily, that this was not the same as when she was a kid. "Sorry, Ma. I was just playing."

"I'm trying to watch the show in peace, and you won't leave me alone." Shari got up from the couch. "Can't you kids give me a break? I work all day, and I'm tired. I just want to relax, and you're always needing something."

"Ma, it's all right."

"I know it's all right!" Shari grabbed the remote and tried to turn off the television, but she kept pressing the wrong buttons. Then she threw it across the room. The batteries flew out and rolled across the floor.

Gramps hollered, "What's going on?"

Billie truly felt as if she was twelve again. "Nothing."

Shari cried, "I just want to relax and watch my story."

Billie got on her hands and knees and retrieved the batteries from under the armchair. She popped them back into place and reset the soap opera to the part before she had interrupted. "There you go, Ma." She set the remote down on the coffee table and backed away slowly as if retreating from a wild animal.

Billie tried to remind herself that it wasn't really her mother yelling at her. It was the disease. Her mind was different now, and she couldn't help her frustrations and anger. But even though Billie understood that, she couldn't help grieving for a different version of her mom, the one who might have gotten exasperated with her but laughed it off because she knew Billie was being a smartass.

Was that person still inside her somewhere? Or was she gone forever?

And what would Billie be like when she got the disease? Would she be screaming about entitled college kids and their rich uncles? Would she recognize David? And where would she be? At home? Or somewhere else?

And who would she be? Would she still be her?

Most days, it was all Billie could wonder about.

CHAPTER EIGHTEEN

Billie spent the following morning raking leaves into the gutter for the township to pick up. This allowed her to tick one item off the enormous chore list while David got a few hours of uninterrupted sleep. It was the least she could do, if simply to lessen her guilt. She felt bad that she had screwed up his plans.

Shari came outside in an old coat and stared blankly at her daughter. Billie wondered if her mother was struggling to identify her or her surroundings. Then Shari held out her hand. "You want me to help?"

Billie glanced at the rake as if she had forgotten what she was holding. "Sure."

Shari took it from Billie and began petting the leaves.

The air was cold and sharp, but the day was sunny enough that physical exertion got Billie sweating in minutes. She unwound the scarf from her neck and draped it over her mother's shoulders. "It's cold out."

For a little while, everything felt like it used to, a far cry from yesterday's drama over the soap opera. Perhaps today would be a good day. And by good, she meant uneventful.

"I'm going to make a call," Billie told her mom.

Shari nodded, but Billie couldn't be sure if she was really listening.

Billie removed her glove with her teeth and scrolled through her phone. She dialed the number for the Safety Brigade office.

A girl picked up on the second ring and sighed dramatically. Her voice came out rehearsed and robotic. "Did you know that the Safety Brigade now has an app? You can schedule safety escorts right on your phone. This is Rebecca. Where can we escort you today?"

"I don't need an escort," said Billie. "Can you tell me who was on duty last Tuesday morning?"

"No. Only Tasha Nichols can give out that information."

"Is Tasha there?" Billie asked.

Rebecca huffed into the phone. "She's setting up for the vigil."

"What vigil?" Billie watched her mom stop every so often and stare into the street before going back to her task. She wasn't so much clumping the leaves as tapping the rake to the ground.

Billie put her hand over the phone and called to her mom, "When you get tired, I'll take over."

Shari shook her head slightly. "Okay."

A plane roared overhead, muffling Rebecca's response. "I'm sorry," said Billie. "Can you repeat that?"

Rebecca sounded put out. "I *said* that we're hosting a vigil for Jasmine Flores today on the campus quad."

Billie said to her mom, "Stop if you're tired." Then to Rebecca, "What time?"

"Noon. If it's so important, you can find Tasha there, handing out the candles."

Billie glanced at her watch. To make the vigil, she'd have to wake David, and he'd be pissed. On the other hand, this was work. This was paying the bills.

She had been deliberating so long she hadn't realized Rebecca had hung up. Well, that was rude. Also Rebecca really shouldn't be giving out people's whereabouts to a stranger on the phone. Safety Brigade 101.

"Who was that?" Shari asked.

"Nothing," said Billie absentmindedly. "Work stuff."

"You have a job?"

"Yeah," said Billie. "I'm working for the Russos."

"Like Ken," said her mom.

"Did Ken work for Paul Russo?"

Shari looked confused. "I-I don't know. I'm not sure."

Billie wouldn't push. "I do investigative work, like Gramps used to do."

"Right," Shari said, but she didn't seem convinced.

Just then, Gramps rounded the corner, whistling the opening song to a British crime drama he streamed on his phone. "The detectives don't carry guns over there. Why is that?" he had said on multiple occasions. "Seems stupid."

"Where you coming from in such a good mood?" Billie asked.

"*Nagel's*," he said. "I was drinking coffee with the fellas."

"And Bernice," Billie said with a wag of her brows.

"Would you cut that out?" But Gramps was smiling.

"Can I ask a favor?" she said.

Gramps's eyes darted to Shari. "Let me guess."

She tossed her keys up in the air and caught them. "I'm hitting the pavement," she said. "Like you taught me."

"This case is over. From what I hear, the Russo kid is good for it."

"Oh yeah? Who told you that?"

He coyly glanced around. "People."

"Uh huh. Well, I'm getting double the usual rate to prove he isn't."

Gramps raised a gray, bushy eyebrow.

Mrs Rodriguez passed them on the sidewalk, dressed in a purple sweatsuit. She stopped and goose-stepped in place. Jutting her chin at Shari, she said breathlessly, "How's she doing?" Then louder, "How are you doing, Shari?"

Shari simply blinked wide-eyed at the woman.

"It's me, Lupe Rodriguez," she said even louder.

"She's fine," Billie snapped while Gramps muttered *yenta* under his breath. Then, more kindly, she said, "Seriously, Mrs Rodriguez, you don't have to worry. We have it covered."

Mrs Rodriguez gave them both a doubtful look.

"We'll call you if we need a referral to Happy Sunset," Billie added since her neighbor didn't look as if she was ready to take no for an answer.

"Safe Horizons," corrected Mrs Rodriguez.

"Of course," said Billie.

Mrs Rodriguez didn't seem satisfied, but she left anyway, much to Billie's relief.

Gramps massaged his temple. "Where was I before that yenta showed up? Oh, the Russo case. It can't always be about money."

"Oh no? Our house is falling apart, and we need to hire help. Even someone to clean out the gutters."

"I can clean out gutters," he said defensively.

"You get on a ladder and I'll need cash for your funeral."

He was not amused. "Where you off to anyway?"

"I need to talk to a student at Kentwell. A Safety Brigade officer."

"A what?"

"A Safety Brigade officer. It's a student who escorts other students to class. For safety."

Gramps dismissed this. "You girls are so paranoid."

"You were a cop," Billie pointed out. "You've seen the worst people can do."

He shrugged. "I don't get how talking to a safety escort helps you."

"I'm following leads. Just like you told me to do."

"Rule Number 3," he said. "The quickest way from Point A to Point B is–"

"A straight line. Yeah, yeah. I know. Just hold down the fort. David's sleeping." Billie waved goodbye and jumped into the car.

CHAPTER NINETEEN

The sun hit dead center when the crowd began to form for Jasmine's vigil. Billie was surprised to see that Tommy's roommate, Glenn, had arrived, hands shoved into his pockets, looking perfectly morose.

It couldn't have been easy for him to be there, but it was nice of him to show up for Jasmine.

Billie spotted a few of her old professors and administrative staff in attendance as well.

Voices were muffled but jovial. She wondered who had come to mourn, who had come because of a fear of missing out, and who had come to livestream this for their Instagram account.

Nuri O'Brien stood in the front near a podium, wearing her Safety Brigade officer badge, and passed out small white candles on cardboard circles while the girl next to her – tall with dark skin and hair and wearing a long coat trimmed in fake fur, also with a badge – lit each candle with a silver lighter.

Billie recognized her from Jasmine's Instagram feed. Tasha Nichols.

Excellent.

She approached the pair and nodded in greeting.

Nuri said, "Thanks for coming." She passed Tasha the candle, but the girl eyed Billie suspiciously and didn't even bother to light the wick.

"You're the PI working for the Russos?" Tasha asked, but it didn't sound like a question. More like an accusation.

"I'm really trying to get at the truth," said Billie lamely.

"Uh huh," said Tasha.

"Tasha," Nuri warned. "Take it easy."

"I will not take it easy," Tasha said as she passed a lit candle to a student lined up behind Billie.

"I'm sorry for your loss," said Billie automatically. "I'm trying to help Jasmine. I want to know who killed her."

Tasha scoffed. "And yet you're working on behalf of a very credible suspect."

Billie should've realized that a girl who presided over a club devoted to solving cold cases would easily make assumptions of guilt. Often, the suspect *was* guilty. It was lack of evidence that prevented the police from making an arrest.

Clearly, Tasha assumed Tommy was guilty.

"Money can buy the best defense," Tasha added.

"If that were true, they wouldn't have hired me," Billie joked, but Tasha didn't laugh. Then, more seriously, she said, "Let's give him the benefit of the doubt."

Tasha put her hands on her hips and snorted. "You can do that, but I know a man is responsible."

"Can we talk?" She waved Tasha over to a quiet area by the lamppost.

Tasha gave Nuri what Billie could only interpret as a helpless look. Nuri opened her mouth to say something, but then more students had lined up for candles.

Tasha glanced at the sky as if trying to conjure help from a heavenly being only to give up and join Billie a second later, away from the mourners.

"Listen," said Billie, "I want to ask about a skinhead who might've followed Jasmine around."

Tasha exhaled. "I wouldn't know who he is."

"If I showed you a picture, you might recognize him."

"All skinheads look alike to me."

Billie dug up Damon Shane's photo and showed it to Tasha.

Tasha pointed a polished fingernail at the picture. "I think that's the guy I saw lurking in the shadows, but–"

Billie slipped her phone into her pocket. "But what?"

"He was around, but Jasmine said a guy who had been following her had a tattoo on his eyelid. That was who she was afraid of."

"Ian Dryden," Billie supplied.

"I don't even wanna know his name," said Tasha dismissively. "Anything else?" Girl had a vigil to run.

"Can I see your call logs and volunteer registry?"

Tasha knitted her brows in confusion.

"For the Safety Brigade," Billie explained. "I want to see if Jasmine had requested an escort the morning she was murdered and who might've attended her."

Tasha gave Billie a hard look. "Hit me up later. I have a friend to memorialize, and if I don't get back soon, Nuri is going to say something insulting to someone."

Billie glanced around her and peeked as Nuri greeted mourners. "Does she do that a lot?"

"Girl hasn't met a microaggression she doesn't know," Tasha replied with a snort.

"Why are you friends with her?"

"I wouldn't call us friends exactly. But Jasmine said that Nuri grew up differently and that we needed to be patient with her and educate her, but I find it all so–"

"Exhausting?" said Billie.

"Yeah," she said with a sigh. "Anyway, if there isn't anything else…" Tasha was already heading back.

Billie shook her head and stepped away as Tasha returned to her girl group. They took turns hugging her and reassuring her that Jasmine would've been very touched by the tribute. No one said anything to Nuri, though, even as Nuri broke into sobs.

Billie backed away and let the crowd swallow her up. She felt a tap on her shoulder and turned around to find Nicole, dressed in a wool coat, with her hands shoved into her pockets to keep them warm.

"What are you doing here?" Billie asked.

They eased their way into the back of the group so as not to appear rude to the mourners.

"I issued the permit for this, so I thought I should attend." She examined the crowd. "Truly tragic."

Some students began playing dirges on their phones, macabre and campy, as if providing the soundtrack to a performance rather than a genuine vigil.

Billie leaned into Nicole and whispered, "So, Calvin." Nicole looked expectant. "Please tell me you ran the background check."

"Yes."

"And?" asked Nicole. "Wait, don't tell me. He's got priors. No, wait. He has a restraining order against him."

"Does he give off those kind of vibes?" Billie asked, surprised.

Nicole slumped. "Not really. He seems like a mama's boy, honestly, but you never know."

"Okay, chill. Calvin seems decent, at least on paper. Worst thing I could find was two campus parking tickets and a citation for loud music his freshman year," said Billie, who had conducted the background search rather than sleep last night. "He also got a fine for tossing an apple core years ago at High Point State Park. Deal breaker?"

Nicole pursed her lips, clearly considering it. "Not sure. I mean, who likes a litterbug? Our earth is in crisis."

"It was an apple core. You just want an excuse to say no to him," said Billie.

Nicole sighed. "Probably. I mean, my ex looked decent on paper too. If you hadn't been there that night and hit him with the pepper spray, who knows what he would've done to me."

They were both silent for a moment as they listened to Nuri speak about Jasmine's attributes. Her kindness. Her generosity. Her tenacity.

For a brief moment, Billie felt a sense of gratitude. If she was to succumb to her mother's disease, she had time in her back pocket. Unlike Jasmine.

She turned to Nicole. "I'm sorry that I've been a shitty friend. My life is overwhelming and chaotic, but that's not an excuse."

"No, I should apologize. So you missed my mama's barbecue and my birthday dinner and my master's graduation and my—"

"I think we both get the point," Billie interjected.

Nicole laughed. "That wasn't what I was trying to do. I'm just saying I should've been more supportive and empathetic. I missed you, you know? And I got pissy about it rather than asking how I could help you."

"It's okay," said Billie. "Really."

"Speaking of how I can be more helpful," Nicole began. "My friend in Financial Aid said Jasmine was not on any sort of assistance package."

"No scholarship?" asked Billie.

"No scholarship and no loans that we're aware of."

Billie stared at Nicole. "Girl passed herself off like she was the daughter of migrants, or at least she didn't correct her friends when they made that assumption, but I think she comes from money."

"Her tuition is paid in full every semester," said Nicole. "Wire transaction from a bank in the Caribbean."

It had to be the parents who supported Jasmine.

What if she had been the one with cash and not Tommy? What if she had been his sugar mama?

Nicole jutted her chin toward a cluster of sobbing girls. "This is too depressing. I'm gonna go home and snuggle my cat."

"You should call Calvin," added Billie.

"Maybe," she said. "If you agree to a double date. Safety in numbers."

"Can't I just be a third wheel?"

Nicole raised a brow. "No detective?"

"It's complicated," she replied.

"Seems so high school. I thought we were past that 'let's go as a group' thing, but it feels risky to see a guy alone, even in a restaurant. Like, what if he follows me home? What if he breaks into my house?"

"I get it," Billie said. "I do."

"Aaron would murder any man that threatened you," said Nicole matter-of-factly.

"Didn't we just agree that we don't want violent boyfriends? Gangsters only seem romantic on *The Sopranos*. Most days, you gotta worry if your man is getting picked up in a police cruiser or a hearse."

"I'm going." Nicole hugged Billie. "Glad we talked."

"Me too," said Billie as she watched her friend take off toward the staff parking lot. She kept her eyes on her silhouette until she reached the car.

Billie returned to combing the growing crowd.

She spotted a face she did not expect to see in a group of mourners. He was wearing a black hoodie and trying to blend into a group of guys who had been tossing a ball around. His broad shoulders hunched. His face, all scruff and sharp angles, slacked.

Damon Shane.

He had been on her mind so much she wondered if she had conjured him.

Once the slideshow went up on the projector screen behind the podium, he took that as his cue to split.

Billie followed him. She ducked her chin and tailed him as he rounded the corner by the student center and headed into the parking deck.

All she wanted was a license plate number so she could get an address at which to conduct her own stakeout. Like any normal person.

She had just passed the elevator when her elbow was roughly yanked from behind. Damon pressed her up against the garage wall and growled, "Why are you following me?"

He removed a gun from the waistband of his pants. Billie held up her hands, but there was no place to retreat. She had broken Gramps's Rule 4: Don't take stupid risks.

She stared at the muzzle glinting in the inferior parking garage light. "Don't shoot."

"It's not you that I have this out for," he said.

"Who are *you* scared of?"

Damon's eyes searched the entire parking garage before he stuck the gun under his shirt. "You need to be careful. I wouldn't be protecting a guy like Tommy Russo."

"Why not?"

But Damon wouldn't say.

"What do you want with Tommy?" she asked.

"He owes me money, and he bought a gun off me."

"To protect himself against Ian Dryden, who was following Jasmine around." Billie pointed to her eyelid. "He has a tattoo there, right? Jasmine told her friend about him. Easily recognizable."

"We're all marked. Just in different places. Ian thinks he's the real deal. Not scared of nothing."

"Why was he following her?"

He spat, "To keep Tommy in line. Make sure he held up his end of the bargain."

"Which was?"

He didn't answer. He simply leaned in close, too close. He smelled rank, like weed and sweat. "I'd stop asking questions if I were you." He bared his teeth like a Doberman, and Billie swallowed a hard lump in her throat. "Tommy Russo made enemies of a lot of dangerous men, including your people, the Goffs."

Billie didn't think now was the time to take offense at the "your people" thing.

"Tommy Russo's going to pay for what he did," said Damon. "One way or another. You don't want to get caught up in it."

"Like Jasmine got caught?"

He stiffened. "The one time I–" He stopped himself. The one time he wasn't there to watch her? He walked away.

Billie called to him, "We're not done here."

But apparently, they were. Billie read his license plate number and recited it several times until he had driven away. Then she scribbled the numbers on her palm. For some reason, she wasn't scared of Damon Shane. Maybe because he was low level. Maybe because he didn't have it out for her. Then again, he worked for someone who did.

He seemed – dare she think it – guilty, but not because he had done something wrong.

It didn't make sense.

Billie ran across campus to her own vehicle, which was parked under a tall streetlamp, and hopped inside. She immediately locked all the doors.

Her cell phone vibrated.

Nuri O'Brien had texted Billie a photo of a black car. *My coworker at the* Ugly Mug *took this pic. Look at the driver. Is he familiar?*

She slammed her head against the seat. Sadly, he was.

Billie knew where she was headed next. And this time, she would make sure to bring the pepper spray.

CHAPTER TWENTY

Billie reclined in Matty's chair with her feet up on the desk, twirling a pen and listening to Mama Ree sing her third Lady Gaga rendition of the evening. Then the light switch flicked on.

She didn't glance up, just dropped the pen onto Matty's desk. "You must think I'm an idiot."

"Hardly," said a familiar voice, only it was not Matty's.

Billie's feet dropped to the floor.

Aaron Goff, dressed as if he had just emerged from a *GQ* ad, stood in the doorframe, eyeing her appreciatively. "Lookin' good, Billie."

She wasn't, but she couldn't find her voice to contradict him.

On the other hand, Aaron looked sharp and effortless in a green button-down shirt with just a bit tucked into his jeans. He wore expensive leather shoes and had a Swiss timepiece on his wrist. His hair was recently trimmed. His skin was tanned, no doubt from his stint in Israel.

She noted another change – a scar, a thick pink line that traveled from his earlobe to his collarbone.

He pushed off the molding and entered the cramped office, closing the door with his foot. As he inched toward Billie, she rolled the chair as far back as it would go until she hit the file cabinet.

Suddenly, it felt as if someone had twisted the thermostat all the way up.

Aaron put his arm on the cabinet and leaned over her. His lips were red and full. He smelled like cologne and whiskey. He smelled like a memory.

Billie couldn't find her breath, let alone catch it.

If she wanted to, she could grab the back of his head and kiss him.

She had just attended a vigil for a dead twenty-one year-old girl. With Billie's uncertain future, she should be taking what she wanted – to hell with the consequences. But to do so would muddy her whole life.

The thing about pleasure was that it was fleeting, while pain felt interminable.

"Why are you here?" Aaron asked before straightening up and giving her space.

She wobbled to her feet like a newborn colt. "I'm working a case."

He raised his brow at that. "What are you doing in our office?"

Our? Since when did Aaron take any ownership of the *Malta Club*? She let that comment slide.

"Matty said that he fired a dancer because she stole a few hundred bucks from the bar register, but I discovered that he's been following her best friend. He wouldn't be doing that for petty cash. We're not talking chump change, so what are we talking about?"

Aaron's fingers danced over the objects on his brother's desk. Paperclips. Post-it notes. Then his eyes caught hers. "Where's this girl now?"

"Dead."

"So why tail the bestie?" asked Aaron.

"You tell me."

Aaron casually leaned against the desk and crossed his arms. He knew what he was doing, trying to chisel away at her guardedness. "You're sure that it's my brother who went after this girl? Doesn't sound like him."

Billie swiped through her cell phone until she found the image that Nuri had sent. Billie stepped closer and held it up for his inspection. She willed her hand not to shake.

Aaron smirked. "Could be anyone."

She stared at Aaron's neck, where the whiskers were starting to fill in except over the scar. No hair would grow there. She traced the line with her finger. "How'd this happen?"

His Adam's apple bobbed, and he grabbed her hand. Held it tight. "Not important." His eyelashes fluttered. "My brother has his reasons for doing what he does."

"I know his reasons," Billie said softly. "I just need to know if they ended in murder."

Aaron laughed coldly, dissipating the sexual tension and replacing it with something else – something akin to resentment. "I forgot how you Levines like to look down on us from that moral high ground. How's it up there? Cold? Lonely?"

Billie stepped back, giving him ample space, no longer weak-kneed. "And I forgot how you Goffs see people as expendable, especially if it interferes with your bottom line. We're either with you or against you, right?"

"You know nothing of loyalty," he bit back.

"I don't recall shoving *my* tongue down Jenn Herman's throat."

"Jesus, Billie, that was tenth grade. And she caught me off guard." He wouldn't look at her. "Besides, you know that's not what I mean."

"You were going to Israel," she said, addressing the elephant in the room.

"I asked you to come with me." Now his eyes found hers.

"I didn't want to go," she began.

"Bullshit. You've always wanted to travel."

"Well, I didn't want to be the Bonnie to your Clyde, all right? All I would need is to get caught in some heist in Tel Aviv and have you cut me loose to save your skin."

Aaron blanched. "Is that what you think I would do?"

"You're a criminal," she said coldly.

"Maybe so," he said, pushing off the desk and moving toward her. There wasn't enough room in this tiny office for this level of confrontation. "But I'd never sell you out, and *you* know that."

"You only asked me to come with you because you knew I couldn't leave," she said softly.

"You think I asked you to run away with me to be nice?"

"You were naive."

"I told you I would pay for someone to help–"

"You've got to be kidding me. You know Gramps would've never allowed for your blood money to take care of my mother."

Aaron threw up his hands. "Gramps, of course. God forbid we go against the great William Levine."

"And what about your father? Passing down the long, proud tradition of gangsterdom. Teaching one son to launder money through a strip joint while the other is off – what? What have you been doing these past few years? How did you get hurt?"

"I can tell you what I've *not* been doing. And that's being stuck here, constantly ruminating about the one good thing I had and lost." He pushed her against the closed door and caged her with his arms. "Tell me you let me go because of who I am and not because you're afraid of what you'll be in thirty years."

Aaron was right. She was afraid. If there was anything Billie had learned, it was that they all turned into their parents eventually.

Neil Goff had been married to a woman whom he had cheated on a bazillion times with dancers whose names he couldn't remember. And when his wife had left him, he hadn't noticed she'd split town until the housekeeper complained she hadn't been paid in weeks.

There was no way Aaron would stick by her when she got sick. Billie's dad certainly hadn't. Why should she believe that Aaron would be any better?

Even Matty wasn't able to handle David's bipolar diagnosis. The Goffs were experts at talking a good game, but when shit got hard – *really* hard – they were relieved to find their burdens lightened.

So Levines, in turn, got good at lying. They were well versed in saying what they needed to say in order to protect their already-hardened hearts.

"It's because of who you are," she said.

Aaron uncaged her. "Well, it's good to know where we stand."

One would have thought it would be easy for Aaron to hear that Billie couldn't be with him because of something he could easily change, but being a mobster was in generations of Goff blood. It was as looped into his DNA as Alzheimer's might be in hers.

But Aaron only ever thought in extremes. Black. White. Them. Us.

All or nothing.

Come away with me or lose me forever.

He couldn't see the other side – that her having not gone with him, having broken his heart, was a gesture of love.

Because when you truly loved someone, you gave them what they didn't even know they needed. Even though it hurt like hell to do so.

"I gotta go," she said. "Tell your brother that we're not done here."

"Tell him yourself," Aaron said before slipping out the door, not even looking at her, not even saying goodbye.

CHAPTER TWENTY-ONE

Later that day, after several errands and a meager dinner off Wendy's value menu, Billie had headed home to find David's Cutlass sitting in the driveway behind Gramps's Oldsmobile. So she parked her car in front of Mrs Rodriguez's house and hoofed it up the hill.

A voice hissed at her from the open window of a black Acura that was idling alongside her neighbor's mailbox. "Get in, Billie."

She sighed and pivoted on her heel. She opened up the passenger's-side door and dropped into the seat.

Matty glanced in the rearview mirror. "Aaron said you wanted to talk. So let's talk."

The heat was pumping through the vents, and Billie began to sweat underneath her coat. She unwound her scarf. "You lied to me."

"About what?"

"Don't be coy. You said you fired Jasmine because she lifted petty cash from the bar register, but that's not the truth, is it?"

Matty's eyes darted to the mirror. From there, he had a perfect view of David's bedroom window. Was he thinking about Billie's brother or trying to compose another lie?

"Hello?" she said, annoyed.

Matty reached into the center console, plucked out two pink rubber bands, and dropped them into her lap.

She lifted them to the interior light to examine them, but she already knew what they were. Back in the day, mob-owned clubs had wrapped their cash in distinct colors to identify the money's familial origin. The Bianchi crime family used blue bands with lips on them. The O'Rourkes used green ones with clovers. "Super original," Neil had said once with an eye roll. The Goffs tied their stacks of cash with pink bands, stamped with the Hebrew letter gimel, symbolizing wealth. Fitting if not too on the nose.

Billie stretched the bands as if she intended to slingshot them across the street. One band usually held a stack of ten thousand dollars. If he had two bands, that meant... "Jasmine stole twenty grand?"

"Looks that way," Matty said. "Those bands fell out of her stilettos."

"That doesn't mean *she* stole the money. They could've been planted. Don't you keep your money locked up?"

Matty looked down at his lap and picked at his fingernails. "In a safe."

"So how would she have cracked it?"

"She didn't. After tallying the liquor sales, I put that night's earnings in a black deposit bag on the bar. I was on my way to the bank, and she switched them without me looking."

"How did she do that?"

Matty sighed and glanced out the window. "I was distracted. I left the cash unattended for a few minutes. All the girls had clocked out. I thought the club was empty. I didn't realize she was still there."

Billie sat back in the seat and stared across the street as the neighbor kid dragged his trash cans to the curb. "What were you distracted over?"

Matty cupped his hand and ran it over his chin. "I was busy."

"Doing what?" And then it occurred to her. His pink cheeks. His failure to make eye contact. "Ohhhh, you mean you were *getting* busy?"

But Matty didn't look appreciatively embarrassed. He looked ashamed. Neil Goff had never given a rat's ass about his son's sexuality, which was pretty surprising considering his generation and his deference to machismo bullshit. He didn't care who Matty banged as long as it didn't interfere with the family business. Only this time, apparently, it had.

"Was it worth it?" she asked.

Matty's gaze traveled to the mirror. "No. Just stress relief, that's all."

Billie thought of Detective Morales. "Did it work?"

Matty leaned against the headrest. "What do you think?"

She stared through the windshield at the empty street. She and Matty were similar. Neither of them were good for the people they loved.

"My dad wasn't even mad," said Matty. "I mean, at first, he was. He wanted to murder me. But then he got over it, I guess."

Billie turned in her seat. "Your dad got over losing twenty grand?"

Matty smiled softly. "My fuck-up was the perfect opportunity to get Aaron to come back. Dad doesn't think I can run the *Malta Club*, take it to where he wants it to go. Now Aaron's home. Win-win."

"Where does Neil want the club to go?"

Sighing, Matty said, "Back in time. He wants it to be like the days when he was young. When my grandfather was around. When we still had influence. When the other mobs would bow down to us. But I want to go legit. I don't want to end up in the pen with Ian Dryden as my cellmate."

"That's smart," she said.

"Yeah, but Dad doesn't think so. I'm twenty-eight years old, and I spend most of my days cooking the books so he can clean money. He wants me to be tough, but I'm not, Billie. Did I ever tell you the time my dad instigated a fight between me and Ian?"

Billie shook her head.

"He and Colfer took bets on it like it was a cage match. I threw one punch and missed." Matty laughed sadly. "Ian clocked me and broke my ribs. So Aaron went after him. Took him down in one shot. My dad doesn't care that I'm gay. He just cares that I'm soft."

"So you're not a hardened criminal," said Billie. "That's a good thing."

"Not to him."

Billie exhaled a long breath. "What's this stupid history with the Goffs and Torn Crosses?"

"You mean besides the anti-Semitism and Holocaust denying?" asked Matty.

"Yeah, besides that," said Billie.

"Honestly, all this beef is over a woman. Starla Wells."

"The Dancing Queen," Billie said softly.

"You know of her?"

"Her name came up," she said.

"She was a performer. She used to strip, but it was like an old-timey burlesque number with feathers and masks, and the guys used to eat it up. She was also one of my dad's most trusted friends. He didn't respect a lot of women, but he adored her even though she once worked for Colfer Dryden at his place, the *Lucky Lous*."

"Never heard of it," said Billie.

"It burned down in the eighties," he said. "Anyway, it was rumored that Starla had a diamond worth a lot of money and that my dad had her whacked so he could get his hands on it. My dad swears he didn't touch her. Like I said, he adored Starla. He probably would've married her, but...anyway, he blamed Colfer and still does, because Colfer's reach magically expanded after Starla was murdered. If my dad could've taken out Colfer without starting a world war among the mobs, he would have."

"What was so special about this diamond?" Billie asked.

"It was, like, eight carats or something. Worth a cool half mil."

"Jesus."

"Yeah."

"How did a dancer get a diamond like that?"

"Who knows?" Matty shrugged.

They were both quiet for a moment.

Finally, Billie said, "You realize that this looks bad? I mean, you're claiming Jasmine stole twenty grand from the *Malta*, and now she's dead."

"I get how it looks," he said wearily.

"And you're surveilling her friend. What for?"

"Making sure she's not flaunting cash. You never know, she could've been in on the scam."

Billie raised a brow. "The girl works as a barista. I can assure you, she's poor like the rest of us. Well, poor like me, not you."

"I was trying to be certain."

"Why not Tommy?" she asked. "Why aren't you following him? I mean, it's just as likely he has the money, right?"

Matty cracked his knuckles. "My old man specifically told me to lay off him. Said if Tommy was involved, then Paul Russo would make it right."

"Your dad knows him?"

"Back in the day, the Torn Crosses were known for jumping dock workers and stealing imports, so Paul used to pay my dad's crew to protect his shipments at the seaport." He added, "Paul Russo wasn't always so clean. He used to import diluted olive oil and pass it off as the pure stuff. He needed my dad's connections to move it. They had a mutually beneficial partnership."

Billie massaged her temples. This case was dizzying.

"There was a task force or something that was investigating Russo, but it never came to anything. You can ask your grandfather about it."

If Gramps had known Paul Russo was crooked, Billie would've thought he'd mention it.

"But then Paul went legit and hired an armed guard service," Matty said. "He's switched companies a bunch of times. Probably'll switch again."

"Why?"

"His latest shipment was stolen. Inside job."

"What was taken?"

"Olive oil. Street value, a mil. Usually, you can clear half that."

"There's still a black market for that?" Billie asked.

Matty snorted. "There's a market for everything." He fussed with a loose thread on the leather steering wheel. "Billie, you gotta take the heat off us. A detective's been sniffing around the club. Around me specifically."

"Your dad doesn't have any cops on staff?"

"Not in the BCDB," he said. "Not since some guys retired."

Goff's power truly *was* diminishing. "While I appreciate the influence you think I wield, I'm not sure I have magical abilities to prevent the police from sniffing around a well-known mob joint such as the *Malta Club*. Especially when one of their dancers ended up dead."

"You're banging that detective," he said matter-of-factly.

Billie stared at him, open-mouthed. "That's none of your business. Do I tell David who you're screwing?"

His eyes darted back to our house.

Billie rubbed her throbbing temples. "Maybe your dad wouldn't go after Tommy, but Jasmine was fair game, right? Neil is all about brute strength. Can't look weak. How would it appear to the other girls if he just let something like twenty grand slide?"

"Billie," warned Matty, sensing what she was getting at.

She stared at the line of cars parked along the street. "Killing people and making it look like an accident is your dad's signature move. Follow her to Percy Street. Beat her to her death." She wiped her hands against each other. "Problem solved."

Matty bit the inside of his cheek. He knew she was right. Neil Goff was a scary son-of-a-bitch who dealt in violence and intimidation. No threats from him. Only promises.

Matty leaned across her lap and opened the passenger's-side door. "Time to go."

Billie rewrapped her scarf and slid out of the car. As she watched Matty pull away, she wondered why he had come here tonight. He had told her the truth, but he had also shone a giant spotlight on his family. The Goffs were mobsters, and they handled their affairs like mobsters.

Stealing twenty grand from them was a first-class ticket to a trip off a cliff. Or stuffed into the trunk of a car.

So was, she realized, poking one's nose into their business.

Perhaps he had come here to warn her.

CHAPTER TWENTY-TWO

Billie awoke the following morning to her cell phone blowing up with messages from David. Apparently, he had offered to cover a double shift and was at work, sending her the week's grocery list one text at a time.

After showering and making her mother breakfast, Billie plucked the coupons from the fridge and gathered the canvas bags.

Shari sat at the kitchen table and vacantly stared at television news anchors.

"Where's Gramps?" Billie asked aloud, forgetting that her mother wouldn't be able to answer.

To Billie's surprise, Shari said, "*Nagel's.*"

Not ideal, but it might be good for Shari to get out of the house, although anything that veered from her routine could be problematic.

Not that either of them had a choice. They needed food.

Billie turned off the TV and said to her mom, "Let's get you dressed. We're going shopping."

Thirty minutes later, Billie had both of them in the car and headed for the ShopRite in Englewood.

Grocery shopping for four adults was rife with disordered nitpicking. Everyone required something special. Nondairy creamer for David, but only the one in the blue bottle because it had fifty percent coconut milk as opposed to the brand in the green bottle that contained some chemical that gave David gas. But none of that almond milk shit for

Gramps (his words); he specifically liked the Bailey's Irish whiskey-flavored creamer, which was a surprise to no one. Shari only ate one kind of canned tuna for lunch, and most times, it wasn't on sale. And Billie? She required Vintage seltzer by the truckloads. Plain flavor in the can. No plastic bottles – they never stayed fresh long enough to keep the fizz, and she also felt guilty about them landing in the ocean. If she couldn't drink alcohol, she would, at least, be carbonated.

Billie was opening a freezer door to get her grandpa's favorite ice cream (lime margarita sorbet – again, surprise to no one) when her mom said, "We don't have tomatoes."

"We don't eat tomatoes out of season." That wasn't Billie's rule; it was her mom's.

"I want tomatoes," Shari said, clearly frustrated.

"All right." It wasn't on the list, specifically because they tasted like air outside of the summer months, but Billie wheeled the cart back toward the produce aisle.

Billie asked her mom to pick them out but found her walking toward the bananas.

Billie pointed to the bunch in the cart. "We already got bananas."

Shari glanced at the cart, where a spot of bright yellow peeked out from underneath a mountain of boxes. She dismissed that. "I want more."

"You don't even eat them," Billie sniped.

Shari huffed loudly and threw down the plastic bag. A female shopper gave them both a look.

"Okay," Billie said, placating. "Let's get more bananas."

"No," her mom snapped. "Forget it."

Just then, Billie's phone rang. The shopper gave her another nasty look as she took the call. "Hey, Nic, I'm at ShopRite. Can we chat later?" Billie said.

Shari was walking around the produce section, picking up various fruits and vegetables and slamming them down in anger. A man in a red vest, who was stacking boxes of clementines, watched her suspiciously.

"I'll take care of that," Billie told him.

"We got a problem," Nicole whispered. "Tommy Russo got busted sneaking into Jasmine's dorm room. Campus Police are holding him, but the provost is talking to Chief Mancini, trying to grease the wheels. No doubt Paul Russo just made a sizable donation to Kentwell. Anyway, I think you should get here and find out what he was doing in her room."

"I'll be there as fast as I can," Billie told Nicole. "But my mom is with me, and no one is at home." It was a big ask and one Billie felt guilty mentioning. "Would you be able to look after her? Just for a second?"

"Of course," Nicole said without hesitation.

"Thanks." Billie disconnected the call. She mouthed "Sorry" to the produce worker and then turned to her mother. "We gotta check out."

But when she turned around, her mom was gone.

CHAPTER TWENTY-THREE

After Billie had found her mom wandering the parking lot, looking for the old family Volkswagen, which they no longer owned, Billie belted Shari into the passenger's seat of the Hyundai, something her mother did not appreciate.

Shari slapped Billie's hand away even though Billie was the one who was angry. "You can't leave without saying anything."

"I'm not a child."

No, she wasn't, and that was the problem. At least Billie could reprimand a child. Take away dessert or a favorite toy. Establish consequences. Also, children, in Billie's limited experience, remembered everything. No detail was lost to a five year-old.

Her mom was a grown woman who could no longer care for herself. Billie was old enough and mature enough to comprehend that parents were vulnerable just like anyone else. But she still felt too young for this shit.

"We need to run an errand before we go home," said Billie.

"We can't. The meat will spoil."

"We didn't buy meat. We didn't buy anything because I had to abandon the cart to find you." Billie could send Gramps to the market later with a list.

"Where are we going?" Shari asked as Billie climbed into the driver's seat and jammed her key into the ignition.

"Kentwell College."

"Are we late with the tuition?" her mom asked.

"No. I just need to help a client."

"Who?"

"Tommy Russo."

"The olive oil shyster."

"Not him. His nephew." Billie looked at her mom, stunned. "You know that Paul Russo used to deal in phony olive oil?"

Shari just shrugged. "I guess."

With anyone else, Billie would follow up. Unfortunately, Billie wasn't sure which of Shari's memories were real and which were a trick of light.

Billie started the car and left the ShopRite.

The minute she arrived at the administration building, Nicole took her aside and whispered in her ear. "Paul Russo is with him now. Conference room." Then, to Shari, she said, "Mrs Levine, would you like a cup of tea?"

Shari's eyes bounced frantically from Billie to Nicole to Billie again until Billie said gently, "This is Nic Mercier. My friend. We were college roommates."

Shari visibly relaxed and smiled weakly. She probably didn't recognize Nicole but was willing to trust a kind face.

Nicole gently steered Shari toward the kitchenette. "We go way back, don't we, Mrs Levine?"

Billie exhaled for the first time all morning. She pushed open the conference room door and took a seat across from Tommy. He didn't look well. He definitely didn't look sober. His shirt was wrinkled, and the cuff was torn. His eyes were glazed. Paul Russo didn't look much better. His clothes were impeccable, but he sat hunched as if he could will himself to disappear if he made himself small enough. Something about Tommy drove a man who owned a megacorporation into the saddest version of himself.

Paul ran a hand over his scruff and then reached for the pitcher of water that sat in the center of the table. He poured a glass and slid it over to Tommy, who waved it away. "Tommy got caught breaking into Jasmine's room," explained Paul.

"So I heard," said Billie. "I can't stress this enough. You need to stay at your uncle's place for your own safety. The Torn Crosses are after you. Don't you get that?"

"His debt is paid," said Paul.

"I highly doubt you can wash away Ian Dryden's prison sentence," she replied.

"I'll hire private security for him," Paul said.

"And be a prisoner?" Tommy whined.

"Better than being dead," she snapped back. "What were you looking for?" It was a test, and she already knew the answer.

Outside, a few employees passed the open window. Paul got up and closed the blinds.

Tommy said nothing, so Billie supplied the response. "Twenty grand."

Paul tugged too hard on the pulls, and the blinds crashed together in a metal cacophony, but he couldn't have been too surprised, since he was in on it.

Tommy glared at Billie before he lunged across the table and grabbed her wrist. "I'm not paying you to investigate me."

Billie jerked out of his grip. "You'd be wise not to put your hands on me, especially since I'm trying to help you."

He scoffed.

Paul Russo sank his fingers into Tommy's shoulder and pressed him into the chair. "You're not paying her. I am. And it *is* an investigation into you. We're trying to get you off the hook." Then, more softly, he asked Billie, "What's this about?"

But Billie wasn't in the mood for lies. "Neil Goff doesn't just dismiss stolen gimels, not without something in return. What did you promise him, Mr Russo? To pay him back with interest? Double, triple his loss?"

Paul Russo dropped into the seat. He didn't deny it, which meant Billie was right.

She glanced at Tommy next. "Was it your idea or Jasmine's to swipe the twenty grand from the *Malta*?"

Tommy stared at the closed blinds and scratched his jawline

with dirty nails, perhaps buying time to build a lie. "Mine," he said finally. "And she wouldn't give it to me. She said she would hide it and we'd split it later, but she never did."

"Thomas," Paul warned.

"So that's why you went to her room," Billie supplied.

"Maybe Thomas should stop talking," said Paul as he rocked back in his chair.

"I'm not the cops," she said. "If he killed Jasmine, then I need to go to the police. But right now, you both seem to be involved in a hiccup with a very prominent Jewish mobster."

"Where are you on his alibi?" asked Paul.

"Nowhere," she said, leaving out what Glenn had said. "On Tuesday, he's still unaccounted for."

Paul squinted at Tommy.

"But here's a bright spot," said Billie. "Tommy can't possibly be the bureau's only person of interest. Not with Neil Goff in the picture. I can ask around."

"No," Paul said quickly. "In light of what we know, or don't know, the less we involve the police, the better. They're not on our side."

Why wouldn't they be? Paul Russo was a wealthy, powerful New Jersey businessman. Everyone was automatically on his side.

"All right," Billie said, unconvinced. "There's more. Damon Shane–" Tommy stiffened at the name "–was at Jasmine's vigil last night."

"There was a vigil?" asked Tommy, now sorrowful. That kid could shake off one persona to swap it out for another – going from angry and accused to mournful boyfriend – in a matter of seconds. Billie felt as if she couldn't keep up.

"You bought a gun off him," Billie said.

"Christ! A gun?" Paul got up from the table and ran his hands through his hair. He then pointed a finger at both Tommy and Billie. "That tidbit doesn't leave this room."

"So you went to Jasmine's room hoping to find the cash,

thinking you could what – bribe the Torn Crosses to get off your back?"

Tommy nodded. "I thought if I gave them the money, they would leave me alone."

"You put Ian Dryden away," she said. "Why would you think they'd let that slide?"

"Because I'm a moron," he said sullenly. "And it doesn't matter. The money's gone."

"The cops combed her room," Billie pointed out.

"She used to hide stuff in a hole behind the molding. The police would never think to look there. She probably spent it on one of her stupid clubs. Everyone is always asking her for money."

"Like who?"

"Tasha for one."

"Nuri?"

"Probably."

"Does the name Starla Wells ring a bell?"

"No," he said, confused. "Should it?"

"Shit." Paul jumped to his feet. The glass overturned, and water ran down the table in streams.

Billie continued, "Ian Dryden is not gonna stop until you're dead. I don't think I need to remind you that you're in a world of shit."

Tommy wouldn't meet her gaze.

There was a knock on the door. Nicole opened it up and said softly, "The provost would like to meet with you, Mr Russo."

Tommy rose from the chair.

"Mr *Paul* Russo."

Tommy plopped back down.

Nicole left and returned with paper towels, which Paul grabbed gratefully before leaving the conference room.

Billie turned on Tommy. "Did you kill Jasmine when she tried to get you to go to rehab?"

His eyes grew wet. "No."

"Where were you on Tuesday?" She slammed her hand on the table.

His eyes darted to the closed door, the one Paul Russo had just stepped through. Whatever Tommy had been doing, he didn't want his uncle to know about it.

"I will find out," said Billie as she rose from the chair, hoping that her words would sink in. She leaned over the table. "And then, you're done."

She left the room and joined Nicole, who was sitting with Shari at a small table. Two cups of tea sat in front of them. Her mom's cup was still full.

"I was just telling your mom some college stories," Nicole said.

"Hopefully, you left out that time I got drunk and climbed through Andy Bergen's dorm window by mistake."

"Nope," said Nicole with a playful smile.

The provost's door opened, and Paul Russo left looking worn but with less weight to his shoulders. Bribery had a way of smoothing things over.

Paul approached Billie and gently patted her shoulder. It was a paternal gesture that Billie appreciated. "I know you're trying your best, Belinda," he said. "I'm grateful. Truly."

Shari suddenly brightened. "Is this your professor?"

"Oh, no, Ma. I graduated."

"Oh."

Billie turned to Russo, wondering if she should explain her mother's condition, but she saw the tension return to his face. She didn't have to. He knew.

"I should go," he said to her. "We'll be in touch."

When Paul left, Shari said, "He looks like the olive oil shyster."

Billie smiled with relief. "Yeah, Ma. That's exactly who he is."

CHAPTER TWENTY-FOUR

"Welcome to the Murder Girls podcast. I'm Jasmine Flores."

"And I'm Nuri O'Brien. And this is episode fifteen if anyone is keeping count. We're calling it 'Wells, Wells, Wells.' Punny title. I like it."

"So, what's up, Nuri? Como estás?"

"Well, I'm drowning in schoolwork and coffee. You?"

"Same. Except not the coffee part. But I've been hella busy. Which is why today's topic is based on the most recent paper I wrote for my criminology class."

"No shame in killing two birds. "

"Would that be a murder of crows?"

"Ooh. Jasmine – one; puns – zero. So, which case are you discussing today?"

"Today, I'm going to talk about Starla Wells, the Dancing Queen. She was fierce and fabulous and, sadly, cut down in her prime. Buckle up, Murder Girls. It's going to be a good one."

Billie paused the *Murder Girls* podcast and hunched low in the driver's seat. She was parked at a gas station across from the *Malta Club* with a DSLR on her lap and fussing with the telephoto lens that Gramps had gotten her for Hanukkah. She still suspected it had fallen off a truck.

Billie held up the camera and snapped photos of the back door, which was used by delivery men and dancers and sometimes delivery men *with* dancers. That was typical quid pro quo for the *Malta Club* and another reason it was hard to remain Aaron's girlfriend. Jenn Herman notwithstanding, Billie was pretty certain Aaron had lost his virginity to a stripper before he claimed he had lost it to her.

Billie checked the time. Gramps had assured her that he was home and awake enough to keep an eye on her mother. David was already at work, and it was nearly impossible to surveil the *Malta Club* during the day. Someone would notice Billie's car parked nearby. Although, at some point, she would have to get back inside the club to retrieve an item she had conveniently left behind.

The back door opened, and Matty came outside, clad in a puffy jacket. He removed his cell phone from one pocket and a joint from the other. He lit up, took a drag, and scrolled through his phone. Mama Ree poked her face out and said something to him. He sighed, stubbed out the joint, and went back into the club.

A few minutes later, a dancer emerged wearing a long wool coat. Billie recognized her face – Shonda, Jasmine's nemesis, who had fair criticisms of her podcast topics.

Shonda shoved her hands into her pockets and shifted from one foot to the other. No doubt she was wearing nothing but a G-string under there. She didn't reach for a cigarette or her cell phone, so what was she doing outdoors on a cold evening?

Just then, a man dressed in a thick jacket and a knit cap sauntered over with his chin down and his hands deep in his pockets. Billie's heart stopped. She fumbled for the pepper spray from the center console and was just about to risk exposure to run over there and stop him when Shonda broke into a grin. She opened her arms wide and enveloped him in a hug.

Billie lifted the camera and peered through the lens just as the dude brushed his hand across Shonda's cheek.

What the hell?

Billie snapped several photos of a torn cross above a row of skulls inked into his fist.

Damon Shane slipped his tongue into Shonda's mouth, and her body responded in kind.

Was this a transaction? A hand job, fine. But anything more involved was strictly off limits because Neil Goff did not want the heat. He didn't need his club closed down because of solicitation. Plus it made Matty feel gross.

Damon opened Shonda's coat and pressed her against the brick exterior. Billie had been right; Shonda wasn't wearing anything but a G-string. In this case, it proved efficient. Shonda's eyes rolled back slightly, and she smiled as if in a drunken haze while Damon pulled down her thong. He nuzzled her neck and brought one of her thighs around his waist.

Billie lowered the camera as heat traveled throughout her body. She was immediately reminded of Christmas Day seven years ago. Neil had closed the *Malta Club* so the girls could enjoy their holiday off.

Aaron had invited her and David to the club to hang out. He had ordered Chinese and Indian takeout, and they ate on the stage while David mixed drinks from behind the bar, right before he got high with Matty in the men's bathroom. Not that Billie had known that at the time.

Billie was making out with Aaron in the dancers' empty dressing room when she glimpsed snowflakes through one of the tiny windows. She grabbed Aaron's hand and dragged him outside.

"It's like a Hallmark movie," Billie said as she watched snow coat the dumpster in a fine powder. The highway was eerily still. The door shut behind them, and she asked, "Are we locked out?"

Aaron laughed and shook his head. A key dangled from his pointer finger.

"It's so quiet," she said.

He stared at her for a moment with a goofy grin before he led Billie over to a patch of building where a little portico offered protection from the weather. It also obstructed the view from

Route 17. Aaron kissed her neck and ran his hands up her sweater.

She protested slightly, thinking this was the worst place for a hookup ever. But as the snow fell and they were enveloped in silence, it felt as romantic as if they had been fooling around on a bearskin rug beside a fire.

Aaron and Billie had been stealing kisses since they were fourteen. They'd been sleeping together since they were seventeen. But they'd never really tagged themselves as a couple. Never called each other boyfriend or girlfriend.

Not without Gramps dropping dead from a heart attack. And not without Neil Goff telling Aaron that marrying straitlaced Jewish girls was nothing more than a good front.

And not without every girl in their high school targeting Billie in the hallway.

Billie said to him, "You're my Hanukkah present." Which she had regretted the minute it left her lips.

But instead of laughing, Aaron whispered, "I don't deserve you." He stared into her eyes and brushed the wet hair from her face. Billie was a forest fire, her lust all-consuming and destructive, and Aaron was the accelerant.

He tried to take off her jeans, but she shook her head. Screwing against an alley wall only looked hot in the movies. It was not a realistic spot for sex. "Let's go back." She grabbed his hand and ushered him inside.

As they stumbled through the hallway, Aaron whimpered something about missed opportunities.

Billie laughed but then halted. "Do you hear that?"

A grunting noise came from inside the storage room. Aaron waggled his brows. "Someone is getting it on."

That someone could only mean David and Matty. No one else was supposed to be there.

Aaron put his finger to his lips.

"Don't," Billie whispered. She could only imagine David's mortification, and he'd been constantly on edge, his mood swings a pendulum she couldn't stop.

But Aaron had ignored her. He gently turned the knob and flung open the door. Only it wasn't David and Matty getting busy.

In the corner stood Neil Goff. His muscleman massaged bloody knuckles. A man, shaved head with a torn cross tattoo on his neck, sat tied to a chair in the center of the room. His lip was split open, his eyes bruised and swollen.

Billie's eyes watered.

Neil growled and spat at Aaron. "Get out of here."

"Dad," Aaron began. "You said I could have the place."

"They have to go."

"We've been drinking. No one can drive."

"Then you better flag a taxi."

"Are you kidding me? It's snowing. It's Christmas."

But Neil looked as if he was an eyelash's width from rage.

The man in the chair laughed. He then gurgled, his throat likely coated in blood, and coughed. He spat a red mess at Billie's feet.

Trying not to vomit, she swallowed the phlegm in her throat and whispered to Aaron, "I'll get the boys."

Aaron shook her off and gritted his teeth. "It was time for you to go anyway."

"Not one word to your old man," Neil growled at Billie as she sprinted down the hall and darted into the main area, where she found Matty and David pressed up against each other at the bar. "Neil's here."

David and Billie trudged to the *WaWa*, where they phoned Gramps to come and pick them up.

He was livid that they had been drinking.

He would've been more upset if he had known about the man tied to the chair. Gramps wouldn't have called the police – he wasn't so stupid as to get in the middle of a Neil Goff-and-Torn Cross beef – but he would have never let Billie near Aaron ever again. She would have never risked it.

Now Billie wondered how Neil would feel about Damon Shane, a Torn Cross gang member, lurking outside his club.

Would he go after him? Tie him to a chair? Interrogate him until he disappeared from the face of the earth?

Because that was what had happened to Colfer's brother-in-law.

Billie glanced up at the *Malta Club* to see Damon zipping his fly and Shonda smoothing down her braids.

Wham, bam, thank you, Nazi. It was not as if the girl got unionized breaks.

Billie sighed and was wondering how much longer she should stay there when a rap at the door made the decision for her.

Aaron stared at her from the other side of the glass.

Shit.

Rule Number 5: don't get made.

Billie hastily shoved the camera inside her bag. "I'm leaving."

"Come on, Billie," came Aaron's muffled voice. "Open up. I'm not mad."

Billie scoffed.

"Please," he said.

Her resolve dissipated. She sighed and unlocked the door.

Aaron slid into the seat and blew warm breath into his hands.

"So you're surveilling us now?" he asked, but there was no resentment in his voice.

Billie detected a little teasing. "I don't have to explain my job to you."

His expression said she kind of did. "I don't see how a dead dancer has anything to do with us," he went on.

She stared at him, having forgotten how callous he could be. "You're kidding, right? She worked here." Billie stabbed her finger in the direction of the *Malta Club*. "At your place of business. She stole money from you." Translation: she stole money from Neil Goff.

"Okay, I get that it looks bad."

Billie slammed back into the seat. "How have the police not been on *your* ass?"

"Who's to say they haven't?" He examined the interior of the car, which, admittedly, was a mess of fast food bags and surveillance equipment. "Your friend with benefits, Detective Morales, stopped by to see me."

"How do you–" Billie waved this away. It didn't matter.

He then dropped a pen into her lap. "You left *that* in Matty's office."

She picked up the black ballpoint, which was really a sixteen-hour voice-activated recorder she had purposefully forgotten yesterday.

"I imagine that wasn't cheap," Aaron said.

"No, it wasn't." She couldn't even bother to deny that it was hers.

"I'm not a goddamn chump," he snapped.

"I didn't say that you were."

"You treat me like one."

"No," she said emphatically. "I treat you like a criminal, which you are."

"You're not allowed to record us without our permission. I know the law. Rookie mistake."

"I know the law too." She just didn't take it into consideration when Aaron was involved.

He turned to her and touched her bottom lip with his thumb. "I wish you were more afraid."

"You're not that scary."

"I don't mean of me," he said.

Aaron ran his thumb across her cheekbone, and it took all her willpower not to lean into his touch. Then he skated his hand down her neck, stopping at the collarbone.

Billie didn't flinch, but she thought Aaron had.

"Did you know that one of your dancers is sleeping with a Torn Cross gang member?"

This gave Aaron pause. "Why are Nazis still a thing?" He snatched back his hand and shook his head. "Matty'll handle it."

"Handle it how? Give the girl a psych eval?"

That made him laugh.

Billie said, "He told me that your dad wants you to run the club."

Aaron sighed. "I have bigger things in the works than scrubbing money in a strip joint. He glanced at her. "You want to go to Morocco?"

What an asshole thing to say. Did she want to go to Morocco? Yes. Could she? No.

Billie faced forward, hands on the steering wheel. "Can I drop you off anywhere? I really gotta get going."

Aaron smiled and bit his lip. He looked as if he wanted to say something, but whatever it was, he swallowed it whole. "See you around, Billie." Then he got out of the car.

CHAPTER TWENTY-FIVE

That same night, Nuri had messaged Billie and asked her to stop by Fellman House so they could talk without a pesky coffee shop boss clucking his tongue over shift breaks.

Nuri greeted Billie with a cup of tea, and they settled into overstuffed couches near the window in the student lounge.

"Love your shirt," Nuri said as she sipped from her mug.

Billie glanced down at herself, having forgotten what she was wearing. It was a cropped top with a neon floral print that she'd picked up on eBay for ten bucks plus shipping.

The outfit was quite loud compared to Nuri's, which was black leggings and a cardigan coated in lint. Underneath, her gray T-shirt read "Murder Girls Suspect Everyone" in bold black letters. Seemed like a simple enough design. Billie wondered how much it had set her back to have those made.

"I've been thinking that it has to have been a Goff who was following me," she said as she stared out the window. A fine drizzle coated the glass panes.

"You're warm," Billie said.

"Must've been his son, then, or someone who works for him," said Nuri.

Billie didn't confirm because she didn't have to.

Nuri folded herself into a small package and sipped her tea. "Why would they care about me? Is it because of the podcast?"

Shonda had alluded to this – that the girls' loose lips might have sunk their ships. Billie could've mentioned the stolen twenty grand, but she decided to keep that to herself. She wanted to hear Nuri's theories.

"We did a few episodes where we talked about Neil Goff and his connection to missing people," Nuri added.

"Such as?"

"Colfer Dryden's brother-in-law."

Billie knew firsthand what had happened to him, but she intended to bury that secret in a mile-deep grave, never to see the light of day. "That guy was a Torn Cross lieutenant who set fire to a synagogue in Fort Lee and nearly beat one of the *Malta*'s dancers to death. He wasn't missed. If Neil had taken him out, even the detectives would've shaken Neil's hand."

"*Allegedly* set fire to," Nuri clarified. "I *heard* that Neil Goff set him up and then killed him to cover up the crime."

Billie cocked her brow. "No way. Neil Goff is many bad things, but he's also a good Jewish boy. He would never burn down a temple, not even to take out a Dryden in the process."

"Do you have proof of that?" she asked.

"Did you have proof of all Goff's crimes before you called them out on your podcast?"

Nuri said nothing.

"Call it gut instinct," added Billie.

"My gut says that Neil Goff wants me dead." Nuri blew her bangs off her forehead.

"He's dangerous for sure," said Billie.

"Sneaky too."

"I suppose there's that," said Billie.

"Yeah, he can get away with a lot. Doesn't he have, like, rich people in his pocket? State senators and stuff?"

That was news to Billie, but she wouldn't put it past Neil to buy influence in North Jersey.

Tapping her chipped nails against her mug, Nuri considered something. "How'd he get into a life of crime?"

"Family business," said Billie.

She sipped her tea and shrugged. "He doesn't seem the gangster type at all."

"In what way?" Billie asked cautiously even though she felt as if Nuri was the one skating close to the edge.

"Don't get me wrong," said Nuri. "It's just, if you saw him on the street, you'd think he'd be the defense lawyer for Bernie Madoff." She laughed and then glanced at Billie to make sure she thought it was funny too.

And she might've laughed if Gramps had cracked the joke, but it landed oddly coming from Nuri because there was this whole history of genocide, anti-Semitism, and generational trauma that tied Jews to certain professions, but sure, let's chuckle about how a well-dressed Jewish man had to be a banker or lawyer.

Too tired for a teachable moment, Billie could only think to say, "Bernie Madoff is dead."

"Right, but that wasn't the point I was making," said Nuri.

But Billie got the point. It was Nuri who didn't.

Billie decided to change the subject. "Why did Jasmine strip at the *Malta Club*?"

Nuri blew across her hot tea. "The money, I suppose."

Stripping paid the bills, but Jasmine's bills seemed like they had been paid by her parents. "What do you know about Jasmine's folks?"

"Nothing. She didn't really talk about them. Said they didn't get her and what she was into." She used air quotes around that last part. "I got the impression she was embarrassed by them."

"Is that why you thought they were poor immigrants?" Tommy had made a similar assumption.

Nuri's flush grew. "They weren't?"

"Not that I can see," Billie said.

"Why did she dance there if she didn't have to?" Nuri's eyes widened. "Unless it had to do with the Dancing Queen murder." She gasped, then slapped her forehead, sloshing her tea. "It was too big a coincidence. The one place she chose to work was the same place that dancer got killed."

"Starla Wells?"

Nuri nodded. "The case has become a pet project of the Sleuth Squad. They're obsessed with Starla. So if what you're saying is true, and Jasmine's parents are well off, then Jasmine must've started working there, like, maybe as an undercover thing. To get info." She glanced at Billie. "If she had told me what she was planning, I would've stopped her. It was a crazy idea."

"Did the other Sleuth Squad girls know what she was getting into?"

Nuri shrugged. "Maybe. Tasha is kinda nuts. I could totally see her sanctioning it, which is insane."

"Because it's dangerous," Billie filled in.

"It's one thing to, like, search online or join listservs about a crime, but it's entirely another to fake a persona and work undercover. Like, who does that?" She shook her head, took a sip of tea, and continued. "Jasmine loved doing the podcast, but she was really extra about it. She'd be up all night, researching murders to discuss. Sometimes falling down these wormholes. Then she'd want to do three-part episodes about them, which sounds cool but can bore an audience. It was becoming too much work. I told her we weren't *Serial*, but Jasmine was really into the research."

"If you're not *Serial*, what are you?"

"A brand. You know? Merchandise and live shows, even if they're at the coffee shop where I work. It's fun. At least, for me, it is. But I don't have a boyfriend with a raging drug addiction who hated all the time I spent on a passion project."

The thing about drugs was that they diverted one's attention from anything that wasn't a fix. Billie couldn't imagine that Tommy gave a shit about Jasmine's podcast or the time she spent on it. He didn't even listen to it. He had told her as much.

"Do you make any money off your podcast?" Billie asked.

Nuri seemed taken aback by the question, then her cheeks turned pink. Ah, the hue of shame. Which meant that she probably didn't. When people made money, they bragged about it– ad nauseam.

"We're trying," she said. "We have a few ads. In turn, we get to sample products."

"Like what?"

"A meal-delivery kit. Hair color, which I actually use." She glanced off into the distance. Her fingers drummed against her mug. "A local bakery subscription box. We're supposed to get a kickback, but it's small." She huffed. "If I could make money off the podcast, I wouldn't be slinging coffee. But don't count us out. We're moving the needle slowly."

Billie noticed that Nuri kept saying *we* and *us*, as if Jasmine was still in the picture. Billie didn't know what it took to run a podcast, but it seemed like a lot of work for one person to do, especially a full-time college student and part-time barista.

"Will you consider a new co-host?" Billie asked.

Nuri sipped from her mug again, but by now, the tea would be tepid. Her eyes watered. "One of the girls from Safety Brigade said she was down to do it, but I don't know. I want someone with a similar vision."

"Such as?"

"Someone who sees it like I do."

"Who won't consider going undercover for a story?"

"Yeah," she said, nodding. "That's a bit much." She sipped her tea. "Anyway, I should lie low for a while, so Neil Goff won't find me that interesting."

Billie smiled wanly. "Oh, believe me, he doesn't."

"Did he kill Jasmine, or was it Tommy?"

"Honestly," said Billie as she set down her mug, "who knows?" She opened her messenger bag and dug out a pen. She really needed to see the Safety Brigade logs. Also she was curious as to how crazy these girls got when it came to true crime. "When does the Sleuth Squad meet?"

Nuri slid her phone out of a neat little pocket in her leggings. She swiped through her calendar and said, "Mondays and Thursdays at nine in the morning, upstairs in the student center." She cocked her brow. "Why? You wanna go to a meeting?"

"Might be worth checking out. After all, as a PI, I'm sort of an honorary member."

Nuri scoffed. "Believe me, that is no club you want to be in. It's hard to talk to people about real-world problems when they're constantly dredging up the minutiae of crimes they discovered on the internet."

Billie sucked her lower lip and nodded. "But that was what Jasmine loved. She was a criminology major. She read all those books. She wanted to be Michelle McNamara. Starla Wells was her Golden State Killer story."

"No, you're right. It's what made Jaz cool. It's just–" She shook her head.

"Just what?" Billie asked.

"It's just that's what the Sleuth Squad does. They do a deep dive into these cases." Nuri looked at her. "*Together*. It's not an individualistic society. You know?"

"No stars," Billie supplied as she rose from the sofa. She was tired, but she still had another errand. She gestured to Nuri's wrist. "I have to say your tattoo is really growing on me. Maybe one day I'll get one. A hamsa to ward off evil."

Nuri also got to her feet and took Billie's mug. "I thought Jewish people couldn't be buried in Jewish cemeteries if they had ink," said Nuri.

Billie dismissed that. "Total myth."

"Really?" Nuri said, surprised. "Well, there's a shop in Bergenfield that does good work if you want a referral. I got really crude ink in high school, and this girl totally fixed it." Nuri grinned then checked the time on her cell phone. "You want me to call the Safety Brigade? Have them walk you to your car?"

"That's all right," Billie said with a yawn. "I have pepper spray." Which was good, because tonight, she had a date with a skinhead.

CHAPTER TWENTY-SIX

Billie had run Damon Shane's license plate and discovered that his car was registered to his grandmother, who lived on a quiet street in Bogota. Damon's mother had hightailed it to Vegas while Damon was doing a stint in a juvenile lockup – real maternal affection – so Damon had grown up under the neglectful eye of his widowed grandma.

Damon's house was similar to the Levines' – two-story, cramped colonial with overgrown shrubs flanking the cement stoop and trash cans with misshapen lids sitting by the mailbox. The mums were nothing more than dried stems in pots.

Billie parked her car in shadows and watched the place. A light shone behind flimsy living room curtains, but there was little movement inside.

Damon Shane. What *was* his deal?

He had belonged to the Torn Crosses before he'd had whiskers on his chin. He had a rap sheet as long as a Torah scroll. And through a string of Google searches, Billie had discovered that last month he had participated in a pathetic and poorly attended whites' rights rally in Newark with a bunch of red hats.

What a dummy.

So then why had he been at Jasmine's vigil? And just as confusing, why was he knocking fronts with Shonda from the *Malta Club*?

And did Shonda know who he ran with? She seemed like a smart girl. That tattoo should've been enough of a signal flare for her to realize that this guy was not who she should be sleeping with.

Billie exhaled, leaned over the steering wheel, and rested her head against the worn leather. When she had revamped Levine Investigations, she knew it wasn't going to be easy, but she hadn't expected to be tailing skinheads and confronting her ex-boyfriend. She had naively hoped she would simply be running from cheating spouses. The easy stuff.

She leaned back and grabbed her bag. She shoved her hand deep inside the front pocket for the spy pen, the one Aaron had so graciously returned to her. She jabbed it with a USB cable and uploaded the audio into her phone.

With her eyes focused on Damon's house, she listened to the recording. At first, it was just a bunch of ambient noise. Papers rustling. Matty making a phone call to his chicken wing supplier. One of the dancers whining about the lineup. And then came Aaron's husky voice. Billie sat up straight.

"Billie, Billie, Billie," he cooed almost breathlessly, as if her name was the only sound his mouth could produce. "I know all your tricks. One might say, I taught you them."

His voice filled the car, and she glanced around nervously as if he might be watching her.

"Remember that time, after prom, when we sneaked away and drove to Teterboro? How we watched the planes fly overhead?"

Billie lost her breath.

"I remember your dress. Baby blue. And so many layers." He laughed.

Billie recalled his hand sliding up her thigh, hidden behind the massive crinoline. She pressed a cold hand to her neck. Jesus, what was he trying to do?

"Did you ever find your underwear?" he asked.

"No," she answered.

"I thought about you a lot when I was in Haifa. There was this cafe by the sea. They served a French press coffee that you would've loved." Then, in almost a whisper, he added, "I wish you'd been there."

She stopped the recording.

The front door opened, and Damon Shane scuttled down the steps in the same dark jacket he'd had on when he had been screwing Shonda against a brick wall at the *Malta Club*.

He seemed innocuous as he stood against the mailbox and lit up a cigarette, as if he was waiting for someone. *Yeah*, thought Billie. *Me*.

Only he didn't know it.

She grabbed the pepper spray off the center console and strode out to him.

Was this a stupid idea?

Yes.

Could she get herself hurt?

Probably.

But there was something about Damon Shane that she needed to understand for herself. Besides, she wasn't being impolite. She had shown up to his house with a gift.

With the spray pointed like a pistol, she halted in front of him.

Damon flicked ash into the gutter, apparently finding her as threatening as an alley cat.

"What do you want, Nancy Drew?" he asked in a bored tone. He inhaled cigarette smoke and blew it in her face.

Billie put down the pepper spray and stepped backward. She tossed him the photos she had snapped of his tryst, which he caught with one hand. "Why are you sleeping with Shonda from the *Malta Club*?"

Damon dropped the cigarette and charged toward her. Up went the spray. He backed away but only slightly.

"You following me?" he growled as he slipped the photos into his back pocket, not even bothering to look at them. "Where'd you even have these printed? Walgreens?"

"Yes," she said. "Maybe you shouldn't have boinked her

against a brick wall where anyone in a parked car with a telephoto lens could spot you. Not exactly discreet."

He shook his head as if he found the whole ordeal exasperating. "You wouldn't get it."

"Please explain it to me. Because as it stands now, Mr Shane, you pop up a lot in my investigation. Your ties to Tommy and Jasmine and now Jasmine's co-worker. Plus, you know, the whole raging skinhead thing."

He scratched the side of his nose and glanced around the empty street. It had to be pushing eleven o'clock. "I got jumped into the Torn Crosses when I was a kid, okay? When I had no one and nothing. And once you're in, you're in."

"So you don't espouse their racist beliefs?"

"When it comes to women, I like to taste the rainbow."

"Lovely. Does Shonda know about your ties?"

"She does, but we're working on a plan to get me out."

"You just said that being in the Torn Crosses is for life."

"There are some parts of this country out of Colfer's reach. It's not impossible for me to disappear."

A dog barked from someone's yard, startling them both. Billie thought about Damon at Jasmine's vigil. The white of his eyes bloodshot and damp. The rage he drummed up whenever Tommy was mentioned.

"Did you care about Jasmine?" asked Billie.

Damon ran his hand along his scruff. "I listened to her podcast. I liked what she had to say. She cared about victims."

"It was more than that, wasn't it?"

A sad smile crept along his face. "Something about dancers. Yeah, I thought she was beautiful. Why she was dating that junkie loser was beyond me. Plus she had balls."

"Meaning?"

"Tommy had a price on his head," he said.

"Because he ratted out Ian Dryden to the cops and got him put away."

Damon pointed at her. "You've been doing your homework.

Anyway, Jasmine confronted Colfer and offered to buy Tommy's safety."

"With what money – Oh! Let me guess. She gave Colfer twenty grand for Tommy to be left alone." Maybe it hadn't been Jasmine's intention to steal those gimel stacks from the *Malta*, but she'd sure found a reason to spend them.

Damon flicked his lighter several times and lit another cigarette "Only the twenty grand wasn't enough. His son did five years. It was just a down payment."

"A down payment for what?"

Damon glanced at his phone. "Shit. You gotta get outta here."

"Wait, we're not done. I need answers."

Headlights came around the bend.

"Now!" Damon barked. He dropped his cigarette and grabbed Billie's arm, pushing her into the nearest shrub. "Stay down."

She crouched into the bush and winced as a thorn scraped her cheek. She peeked in between the branches and spotted a black pickup truck sidling up to Damon's garbage cans. He leaned into the open passenger's window and fist bumped the dude who was sitting there.

Shaved head. Pointed chin. Torn Cross tattooed on his eyelid.

Speak of the actual devil.

Ian Dryden.

What *did* one call a group of skinheads? A gaggle? A pod?

"Hey, Ian," Damon said loudly.

Billie crouched lower.

"Did you take care of Tommy?" Ian asked.

Damon twisted his neck slightly as if to try and glance her way. "Not yet."

Ian pointed to the beefy, bearded driver. "Dunphy'll do it."

"It's not safe. Cops are pressing him," said Damon.

"That's why you gotta get it done. Fucker is flapping his mouth. I knew we should've taken care of him years ago. Nice and painful-like." He spat onto the sidewalk, barely missing Damon's boot.

Damon flexed his fingers at his side. He was frightened of Ian Dryden. Any sane person would be, not because Ian was bigger or thicker but because he was unpredictable, skating the edge of sanity. "I'll get him."

"You better." Ian reached out and gripped Damon's shoulder. Damon winced. "Two days, max. Only a matter of time before that Russo kid sings." Ian grinned and roughly pinched Damon's cheek. "What would we do without you, Shane?"

Ian stared at Damon a beat too long before he nodded at Dunphy to drive off.

When the taillights had crested the hill, Damon fished for another cigarette, which he lit with trembling fingers.

Billie scrambled to her feet and brushed off dirt and leaves. She hadn't realized how shaken she was until she teetered uneasily on her feet. "What was that about? What will Tommy sing about? What did he see?"

Damon leaned against the mailbox and tapped the ash against the metal lid. "Better you don't know, Nancy Drew."

"Come on, man," she said exhausted. "Tommy is jerking me around. You're jerking me around. Don't you want justice for Jasmine? If Ian had murdered Jasmine, would you tell me?"

"Depends. Do you have a death wish?" Damon inhaled the nicotine. As he exhaled, he said, "Why don't you ask Tommy about his uncle's olive oil shipment? The one that got hijacked on Tuesday morning."

Olive oil. Street value: a mil.

"The Torn Crosses stole Paul Russo's olive oil." Man, that sounded ridiculous.

"I was not in on it," Damon said as he stared her down. He stubbed out the cigarette on his boot and stepped on the butt. "You got that? I know you're tight with the Spanish detective."

"Colombian," she corrected.

"Whatever."

She exhaled. "You weren't in on it, but Tommy was?" Her brain kept spinning. "So, the twenty grand was a down payment for Tommy's safety. I assume the rest of the deal was contingent on him getting the Torn Crosses the exact information on when and where to hit the containers."

Nicole had mentioned that Tommy had worked in the Russo offices for one week. Perhaps it had been long enough to get what he needed regarding the import schedule and get out. "He was there at the seaport when they hit the containers. That's why he can't offer up an alibi. Because he was there with–" she looked at him "–*your people.*"

Damon pressed one finger to the side of his nose, the other he pointed straight at Billie. "Ding, ding, ding, ding."

"And now the Torn Crosses want him to disappear?" she asked with a raised brow. "Because he served his purpose."

Damon stared at her, challenging. "You gonna warn him?"

"If you're trying to change your life and run off with Shonda, do you really want a murder hanging over your head?"

Damon shrugged. "Like anyone cares about him. And if I don't, then Ian will come after me, and I don't want to die for that piece of garbage."

"Tommy doesn't deserve to die."

"Neither did Jasmine."

"Is that what this is about?" she asked. "You think he's responsible?"

Damon pressed his lips together. In the streetlight, he looked like a sullen man with a broken heart. A broken heart that he attempted to heal with a stripper's tongue.

"Dude," she began. "Don't give me a sob story about how you loved Jasmine when you're with Shonda."

"I *liked* Jasmine," he snapped. "But she hated me for–"

"Stalking her."

"It was a front," he explained. "I told Colfer that I would watch her, scare her a little, but really, I was keeping an eye on her. Ian had been threatening her, a reminder for Tommy to keep quiet."

"But now she's dead. Seems likely that Ian killed her."

The Torn Crosses were tying up loose ends.

Damon didn't refute this.

Billie ran her hands through her hair. This case was so much more complex than she had realized. So many threads. So many players. All she was being paid to do was find evidence of Tommy's innocence, except his actions clearly had put Jasmine in the crosshairs.

Damon relaxed his shoulders, but his eyes remained alert. "Jasmine said if I helped her and protected her, she would pay me enough money to get out of Jersey."

Billie asked, "And how was she going to do that?"

Damon shrugged. "She said she was coming into funds."

"Coming into funds?" she repeated.

"That's right." Damon pushed off the mailbox and smirked. "Girl was full of surprises."

Billie leaned against a tree. Jasmine was a risk-taker. She had stolen money from a mobster and confronted a notoriously dangerous skinhead. She had been incredibly brave and incredibly stupid.

Either she really loved Tommy or he was some kind of means to an end. What had she been getting out of that relationship?

Damon held out his pack of cigarettes to Billie. She shook her head.

"Figured a nice girl like you didn't smoke."

"Now, there's an idea," she said. "Kill myself faster."

Her cell phone buzzed with a text message from Detective Esteban Morales.

Billie smiled to herself.

"Booty call," said Damon. Not even a question.

She walked toward her car.

"Be careful," he called to her.

"Likewise," she said.

CHAPTER TWENTY-SEVEN

Billie slid onto the barstool next to Detective Morales at the *Wagon* and ordered a seltzer and lime.

"You're out pretty late," he noted as he sipped from a pint glass half full of Guinness. His tie hung loose around his neck. His shirt sleeves were rolled up to his forearms.

"Work." Billie squeezed the lime into her drink and dropped it on the cocktail napkin. Then she said, "Speaking of–"

"No. No. You're not going to coerce info out of me that way." He cocked his brow in a seductive manner.

"Oh, yeah," she teased. "In what manner can I coerce information out of you?"

Morales laughed softly and then chugged the remainder of his beer. He signaled for the bartender to settle up his tab just as Malley lumbered out of the men's room.

"What the–?" Malley said with confusion as Morales tugged Billie toward the door. "You're my ride."

"Chen'll drive you home," Morales said as he and Billie disappeared into the night.

Morales pressed her up against his car and kissed her deeply. Billie snatched the keys from him.

"I had one beer," he said.

"You taste like you had more than one," she said before climbing into the driver's seat of his Toyota.

He scoffed but got in, his mouth stretched into a grin.

"I live on Elm," he said.

"I know where you live." She started the car. "Remember, I'm good at what I do."

"I'm banking on it," he said.

By the time they arrived at his house – a two-family bilevel that he shared with his sister and her kids – Morales had stripped off his tie and was unbuttoning his shirt. He nuzzled Billie's neck. "Why aren't we doing this all the time?"

Billie flicked on the light in the living room and shucked off her bag. Morales steered her toward the couch and eased her onto the cushions.

She kicked off her Converse low-tops as she pulled him on top of her. She nibbled his earlobe. He groaned.

"Did you ever get a definitive time of death on Jasmine Flores?" she asked.

He broke away and stared at her. "*En serio?*"

She went back to kissing his neck. "Yes. Time of death?"

He sighed as her hands traveled toward his waist. "Tuesday. Between 7 and 9am."

"Have you found her missing earring?" She undid his belt.

"No."

"Did her phone records show any outgoing text messages to confirm who she was meeting or what she was doing?"

"She sent Tommy a text. Said she was going to pick him up at Percy Street," Morales said as he slipped her shirt over her head. He tugged on her bra straps and pressed his lips to her sternum.

"Night before?" Billie unzipped his pants.

"She called a friend. Tasha Nichols." He kissed her stomach.

"What about her parents?" She gasped. Her underwear band was in his teeth. She stopped him for a second, and he popped his head up.

"They own a bunch of resorts in Central America that are big with Canadian tour companies. They are very wealthy."

"I wonder why she didn't tell Tommy this."

"Some kids are embarrassed about that stuff. They think it

doesn't give them cred." He got to his elbows and licked her bellybutton.

Her head lolled back. "I know Tommy's alibi," she said. "But it doesn't make him look good. He was in a bad spot."

"Can anyone verify that?"

"I don't think the Torn Crosses are going to back him up," she said.

"That doesn't take the suspicion off him," Morales said, his voice husky.

"Colfer and Ian Dryden want to burn loose ends, meaning they're going after Tommy and anyone associated with him. They have motive for Jasmine's murder."

"The Feds have a keen interest in the Torn Crosses, so you should be happy."

"That's good."

"And the *Malta Club*," he said.

That was bad.

Morales pinned Billie's arms behind her head and stared at her lips. "Anything else before we get down to business?"

"I thought we were talking business."

He smirked.

"What do they want with the *Malta Club*?" she asked, her voice having lost a bit of the flirtation.

"Don't know, but they want Aaron Goff in cuffs now that he's stateside."

"What?" She bolted upright and knocked her forehead into Morales's nose.

"Jesus, Levine," Morales grumbled while he rubbed at the soreness.

"Sorry," she said quickly. "Why do they want Aaron? He hasn't done anything." Yet.

"I forgot you guys have history."

"It's in the past," she said. Sorta. "It's Matty that I worry about. He and my brother are really close, and I would hate to see him–"

"Save it. I know who you're concerned over, and it isn't Matthew Goff. Or it isn't *just* Matthew Goff." Morales tucked in his shirt and zipped up his pants. He sighed.

She suddenly felt exposed. She scrambled up, grabbed her shirt, and slipped it over her head. She buttoned her jeans and shoved her feet into her sneakers. She reached for her bag.

"You don't have to go," he said with an exhalation. "I thought that's why we did this. To forget other people."

But that didn't make any sense. No one wanted to be with someone who was thinking about someone else.

Anyway, the mood was ruined. She had ruined it. She shouldn't have reacted so strongly to hearing Aaron's name, but it was a reflex. No different than if the doctor hit her knee with a hammer.

Swinging her bag over her head, Billie went to the door.

"Let me drive you home," he said.

"You're still buzzed. I can smell it through your pores. I'll grab a Lyft." She had her phone out and was scrolling through the app for a ride.

Morales said, "Maybe we need a breather from each other."

She paused in her search, gave him a long look. "Sure."

Morales gave her a curt nod before he headed into the kitchen.

She left him scrounging for a beer in his fridge and went out to wait for the car.

CHAPTER TWENTY-EIGHT

Billie arrived home just as David was pulling his Cutlass into the driveway, the engine popping and sputtering as he cut the ignition. He got out of the car and smiled dreamily. His lips were red and raw.

Maybe Billie hadn't gotten laid, but it sure looked as if David had enjoyed his evening.

Billie strode toward him and said, "Fun night?"

David shrugged, but a grin lit up his face. "What about you? What were you up to? Partaking in a millennial vintage perhaps? A bottle of Esteban Morales?"

"Not quite."

He furrowed his brow. "Everything all right with the handsome policeman?"

She grinned. "We're better off as friends, I think."

They stared at each other for a moment before David gestured dramatically for Billie to lead them up the stoop.

She unlocked the front door and went inside, kicking off her sneakers and tossing them into the foyer closet. David shrugged off his jacket and hung it up. "I'm thirsty," he said. "Restaurant food is so salty."

"You sound like an old man," whispered Billie as she followed him into the kitchen.

David flicked on the light to reveal Gramps slumped over at the kitchen table. Billie darted over to him and shook him. "Gramps?"

David seemed less concerned. He lifted a bottle of scotch

off the table. "Well, I guess he had a good night."

"I'll check on Mom," Billie said. "See if you can rouse him. Get his ass to bed."

"He can't be relied upon to watch her," David said.

Billie huffed out a noise of disgust, but she wasn't so quick to agree. If Gramps couldn't be counted on for some of the caretaking, that meant Billie and David needed to pick up more of the slack, and she just didn't see how they could manage that right now.

She ran upstairs and gently opened the door to her mother's bedroom. Her sleeping form faced the window. Her chest rose and fell. Billie realized, sadly, that it was like checking in on a child. She looked so helpless and so normal. When she was asleep, it was impossible to tell that she often forgot to eat breakfast or brush her teeth.

Billie closed the door just as David was coming up the stairs with a glass of water. "He can sleep it off on the couch." David ran his hands over his chin and leaned against the wall. "We need to think about a place."

"What place?" Billie whispered as she led her brother down the hall and into his room. She shut the door so as not to wake their mother.

"The one Mrs Rodriguez said. We should consider it. Gramps–" he jutted his thumb behind him "–can't be trusted to babysit a puppy, let alone Mom. And you're always working."

"What if she wastes away without us?" said Billie. She noted the pleading in her voice. It sounded like the desperation of a woman thirty years in the future who didn't want the same fate.

"It's not like it used to be. I work in a similar facility. The Girl Scouts organize bingo, for chrissakes. We have therapy dogs and live music. Last week, we had a ska band. Yes, that's weird, but it's far more interesting than her sitting on the couch, watching her soap."

"I know taking care of her is hard, but I'm not ready for her to leave yet. Plus we can't risk sending her to a bad place."

David sighed. There was some truth to what she was saying. Last week, there had been an article in *The Bergen Record* about an adult rehab hospital that got shut down because the staff were starving patients to save money.

"Why don't we try to get Gramps to sober up first?" Billie suggested.

David scoffed. "Mom has a better chance of getting her memory back than *that* ever happening." He rubbed his eyes. "And I don't know if that's really fair to him. He's old and retired. He likes getting sloshed with his buddies. It doesn't seem right to ask him to be a caretaker at his age. Especially since he stuck around when Dad didn't. Don't we owe him something?"

Billie couldn't answer. It wasn't because David was wrong but because he was very right.

David opened his door. "I gotta get to bed. I have work tomorrow." He glanced at the clock. "Correction, I have work today."

Billie nodded. She knew that he took the brunt of Mom's care. He stayed with her during the day and worked the overnight shift. "Sleep as late as you need to," said Billie. "I'll wake up early and pick up more of the slack."

She would try harder. If she didn't want her mom going to a facility, then she needed to show everyone that Shari could be properly cared for at home.

Billie just needed to make more of an effort.

David stared at her.

"What?" she asked.

He sucked on his bottom lip and then sighed. "Are you going to be willing to do this alone?"

"What do you mean?"

"At some point, I want to move out."

"Huh?" she said, surprised.

"I'm pushing thirty," he said as if that mattered. "And I'm feeling healthy–"

"Yeah, but how long will that last?"

He gave her a look.

"Sorry," she said. "It's just you know how you get."

"Yeah, I know." He looked at her hard. "Are you worried about my health or the fact that you lose a babysitter if I move out?"

Billie couldn't answer.

"That's what I thought." He nodded for her to leave and then closed his bedroom door.

CHAPTER TWENTY-NINE

Shari was still sleeping when Billie rolled out of bed at eight o'clock. In her college days, Billie could sleep until lunchtime without waking up to pee, but not anymore. The longer she stayed in bed, the less she got done. Adulthood was a bitch.

Gramps was sitting at the kitchen table in a T-shirt and boxer shorts with the entire coffee carafe at his disposal. His whiskers protruded from a wrinkly chin.

"Rough night," he said even though Billie hadn't asked a question.

"Are you talking to yourself?" Billie plucked a chipped mug out of the dishwasher and went to pour herself a cup of coffee, which was like trying to get oil out of a tapped well. She only managed to procure coffee grounds.

"Sorry," Gramps said with a shrug as if he wasn't capable of making a second pot.

Billie could feel the tension coil its way up her spine. It wasn't the coffee. Part of her wanted her grandpa to be sober enough to help out, but the larger part of her wanted to scream at her father for abandoning them all.

People used to comment on the strength of the Levine genes. How much David took after their father, not just the nose or eyes but the way he stood, the way he talked. "They're so much alike," they'd say. "All a clone of William Levine." And Billie would always disagree because, unlike their dad, Gramps had stuck around. He had come back to Teaneck to help with Shari, to make sure David was taking his meds. But recently, Billie had noticed how apathetic Gramps had been regarding his role in the family. He spent more time at *Nagel's* and the *Clam Bar* than he did at home.

Gramps had really liked retirement in Florida, and he'd had to give it up to come back here.

Shari poked her head into the kitchen, wearing her bathrobe, greasy strands of hair framing her face.

"You want breakfast?" Billie asked her brightly.

She shook her head. "Can you put my story on?"

"Why don't you take a shower and get dressed?"

"I wanna watch my story." She shuffled away without a response from Billie.

Gramps slumped lower into his chair. "Take her to the movies."

Billie sighed. "She can't follow a storyline."

He shook out the newspaper and peered through his reading glasses. "Teaneck Cinemas is playing a special showing of *Driving Miss Daisy*."

"Really?" she said, surprised.

He shrugged. "Some fundraiser they're doing for that Israeli food bank."

"Worthy cause." Billie perked up. Her mother loved that movie, and the plot might be safely tucked away in her long-term memory. It was worth a shot. "That's a good idea."

"Ma! Go get dressed." Then Billie winced, totally forgetting that David was still asleep. She whispered, "We're going to the movies."

When Billie and her mom had left the movie theater, Shari seemed in better spirits. "I remembered some of it," she said brightly. "The movie. The old woman."

"Jessica Tandy," said Billie, who only knew the actress's name because of the credits.

Shari shoved her hands inside her coat pockets, quiet for

a moment as she stared at the row of shops. Then she asked, "You want an ice cream cone at *Bischoff*'s?"

She remembered the parlor's name, too.

Things were looking up.

The sky was the color of dust, and the air had gotten so cold it stung Billie's nostrils with every inhalation. But who was she to say no to coffee cookie crush? "Sure."

They were about to cross the street when Billie clocked Tommy Russo walking briskly toward the jewelry exchange across from the CVS. His hands were shoved deep inside his pockets, and he was walking with the purposefulness of a man with an ill-conceived plan.

What was he doing in Teaneck? In broad daylight? He had a bounty on his head. Every Torn Cross gangster within a hundred miles was hunting him. Was he insane?

No, Billie realized. Just strung out and in need of a fix. She sighed, thinking that rehab couldn't come fast enough. Unfortunately, Tommy didn't seem as if he wanted to be helped.

Billie crossed the street with her mom, and they slid into a booth at the ice cream parlor. Billie imagined Tommy's trajectory as he walked down the block. She sent him a text message.

I saw you. Go back to your uncle's before Ian Dryden finds you.

She pictured him checking his phone and glancing around the busy street, ignoring her warning like a moron.

A waitress came and took their order.

"Coffee cookie crunch," said Billie. "In a bowl with chocolate sprinkles."

"And for you?" The waitress turned to Shari.

Shari hadn't even opened the menu, not that she needed to, as they'd been coming here forever, but she became increasingly flustered as the waitress stood there with an expectant look. "Um…um."

"Vanilla, hot fudge, rainbow sprinkles," Billie answered, looking at her mom. "Right?"

"Yes," Shari said with a weak smile.

The waitress jotted down their orders and left.

Would a nurse at a facility know her mother's favorite ice cream? No.

"We should visit David at work," Shari said.

"He's at home, sleeping," Billie said as she jotted off a text message to Paul Russo.

Spotted Tommy in Teaneck. He has a price on his head. He shouldn't be out.

"Who are you talking to?" Shari asked.

"Olive oil shyster," Billie answered with a grin. "His nephew's in trouble."

"Are you working with Ken?" Shari asked.

"No," said Billie, confused. "Did Ken work private cases?" She shook her head. "Never mind." They were having a nice afternoon, and Billie didn't want to upset the peace by getting her mom frustrated over a memory she couldn't grasp.

Shari said nothing after that, and they ate their ice cream in silence, Billie glancing at the phone screen every minute, waiting for Paul Russo or Tommy to get back to her. No one was taking this seriously, and they needed to.

After the waitress collected their dishes, Billie paid the bill and tip and drove her mother home.

She deposited Shari on the couch in the living room. Gramps noted that Billie was still wearing her coat. "Going back out?"

"I spotted my client in town," she said. "Up to no good."

"The boyfriend?" Gramps said. "He did–"

"It," she finished. "Yes. I know."

Gramps glanced into the living room. Shari had plopped down in front of the television. "I'll take care of things here. Go and come back."

"You sure?" Billie peeked in on her mom, who was sitting contentedly, a faraway look on her face, but that wasn't unusual. "She seems to be having a good day."

"Then it will be fine." Gramps gestured. "Go. Go. I got it."

Billie didn't need to be told twice. She muttered thanks and sprinted toward Cedar Lane in her denim trench and Doc Martens. No sense in searching for a parking spot if she didn't have to.

She weaved in and out of pedestrians and sidled up to the jewelry exchange window where she was sure Tommy had gone.

But he wasn't inside.

Mario was, though, standing by the counter with an eye loupe pressed into his socket. He was a beefy man with a shiny head and thick fingers.

When Billie went inside, a bell jingled at her entrance.

Mario dislodged the loupe and looked up. "Billie Levine, to what do I owe the honor?"

He and Billie hadn't done much business together, but he and Gramps had history as far back as when Mario used to be an errand boy for the Bianchi crime family.

She went right up to the counter and showed him a photo of Tommy on her cell phone. "Did this kid come in?"

"You know you're a kid too?" he said in a thick baritone.

Was she? Most days, she felt like an old lady. "His name is Tommy."

"Yeah, yeah," said Mario, gesturing to a pile of jewelry. Necklaces with amber stones. Rings encrusted in tiny emeralds. A watch with a leather band. "See anything you like?"

She picked up a man's watch. It wasn't a Rolex or anything, but it didn't look cheap. The initials CD were etched into the gold back. Whose stuff was this?

Mario's cheeks were ruddier than usual. He was downright giddy. He examined a gold ring with a dark-blue stone, and his lip twitched. His tell, according to Gramps, who had played quite a few hands of poker with Mario. This wasn't some pile of costume jewelry.

"Good shit," said Mario. "Interested?"

"It's all real?" she asked.

"I paid him fairly," he said with a bemused expression. "Kid's just gonna shoot it up anyway."

She took out her cell phone and waved it at Mario. "Mind if I take a photo? See if my mom likes any of this?"

He gave her a dubious look but said, "Be my guest. I'm legit."

Billie snapped a photo of the watch and ring and sent it off to Paul Russo. *Look familiar?* she texted.

Mario shook his head at himself, as if he knew Billie was trying to set him up. *Just like her grandpa.* "If they want it back, they gotta buy it."

Billie pocketed her phone. "Of course. See ya."

As she walked home, Billie considered the initials CD.

Roxane Russo's maiden name was Donovan.

CHAPTER THIRTY

Billie grabbed a can of seltzer from the fridge and plopped down at the kitchen table. "I think I might need to find work that allows me to be here, like, all the time."

"There's no such job," Gramps said unhelpfully. "Not with your qualifications."

"Thanks," she said dryly.

"You wanted to major in English." He smirked. "What's with the guilt?"

"No guilt." But it was a lie. The whole time she had been sitting with her mother at *Bischoff*'s, all she could think about was Tommy and the Torn Crosses. It wasn't healthy, and it wasn't fair to Shari.

"You want me to put in a call to those insurance companies?" he asked. "Roger from Royal Life owes me a favor."

"Maybe." Billie took out her cell phone and pulled up a job-search engine. "I still gotta be out in the field, right?"

"Yeah, but the hours are steady, and there's health insurance."

She glanced at him. He had shaved since this morning and combed his hair. "What would I be doing?"

"Tailing people, trying to prove fraud cases. During daylight hours. Pay isn't great, but it's steady."

Detective Malley had suggested she work for his friend at her investigative firm, but that would mean Levine Investigations would take a back seat.

She wasn't ready to give up the family business.

Billie blew her bangs off her forehead. "I can't be reliable. What if there's an emergency?"

Her phone dinged with a text message from Paul Russo.

I appreciate your concern regarding Tommy's safety, but I think we can assume he is off the hook with BCDB. I'm ready to end your contract.

Billie held up her phone. "The case is over anyway. I'm being fired." She sat back and exhaled. "Honestly, I'm relieved."

"Tough one, huh?"

She massaged a kink in her neck. "Too many players."

"Do you really think that the boyfriend's *not* good for it?"

"I didn't used to, but now–"

"Now what?"

"He's got a mean streak and shady friends. Like real lowlifes."

"He's your guy."

"But the cops are now turning their energies toward the Goffs."

Gramps snorted and then huffed. "Let the Bergen boys deal with this. I don't want you going to the *Malta Club*."

"I'm not a teenager anymore," she said defensively. "I can handle myself around Aaron."

Gramps opened the fridge and took out a can of beer. He pressed back on the tab and rejoined her at the table. "He's not a kid anymore either. He's just as big a player as his dad, maybe more so. My contacts told me that his stint in Tel Aviv was no small job. He nearly got taken out, and he's lucky to be alive."

That explained the scar and the secrecy.

"Our paths won't cross anymore," she told Gramps as she browsed local job postings. Billie laughed. The first gig to come up was for an exotic dancer at the *Malta Club*.

She then entered *remote* into the search bar, but everything that popped up sounded like a scam.

Make thousands working from home!

Yeah, right.

Pops belched. "I'll leave you to your job search." He headed into the living room.

"Take it easy on the six-pack, will ya?" she yelled at his back.

He belched again.

Billie squinted at the computer screen. There were some legit gigs. Online tutoring, except she needed a degree in education. Audio transcriptionist that paid a whopping $314 a month. Human resources and programming positions, but nothing she was qualified to do.

She could waitress. A cousin of Nicole's needed cocktail servers in a fancy club in Manhattan. Pay was great but not steady, although she might be able to make her own hours. If the money was decent enough, maybe they could hire an overnight caretaker.

Then, without thinking, she googled Safe Sunset Memory Center. *Showing results for Safe Horizons Memory Center*, Google said, as if trying to make a point – you can't even remember the place's stupid name.

The website featured glossy images of a redbrick exterior and a canary-yellow sign out front. Cherry blossoms bloomed in front of the building. There was an Asian woman in pink scrubs standing beside a patient in a wheelchair, and they were underneath the tree, marveling at the floating petals. Props to whoever ran their marketing campaign. This place looked like paradise.

There were several photos of the inside, all staged, of course. The dining room was large and had long tables covered in linens like a fancy restaurant. Another photo showed a magician performing, and another photo showed several golden retrievers. It was just as David said. It looked so lovely, Billie thought she might enjoy living there herself.

In a few decades, I may get the chance.

On the contact page were the name and photo of a blond woman in glasses. *Email or call for a free tour.*

Billie knew that a place like this wasn't cheap. She could set up an appointment to get information only to be disappointed when they couldn't get her in. And a cheap facility was out of the question. In this case, expensive meant better. It just did. The more luxurious the place, the more they paid their staff, the better staff treated patients. Places like Safe Horizons didn't have high staff turnover, which meant patients received consistently good care. Billie couldn't risk anything less than that for her mom.

She closed the laptop and pushed it away. What the hell was she going to do?

Later that afternoon, Billie went for a run in Overpeck Park. She liked to jog the trail alongside the creek, but the water reflected a pewter-gray sky, making it look like a stainless steel slab at the morgue. The marsh was dry and cracked. The willow branches drooped like lifeless puppets.

Every step felt like a struggle. She couldn't summon the energy to maintain her pace, but she needed to keep her heart pumping and the blood flowing. This was good for her, she reminded herself.

She worried about getting complacent. It was so easy to make excuses, to slack off. Could skipping a run really make a difference in whether she lost her memory at fifty-five or fifty-eight years old? If she ran a fourth day, could she stave off the disease until sixty?

The problem was that she didn't know. She could find out if she was a carrier for the early-onset gene, but even then, it couldn't assess her risk with hundred percent certainty. And all the runs in the world wouldn't make a difference.

Billie liked to know things. She hated gaps in information and despised ambiguity. Except her whole future was anyone's guess, and she couldn't stand it.

She kept on running. The tip of her nose was cold, and her hair was wet with a fine mist. At some point, while she was lost in her own thoughts, it had begun to drizzle.

She stopped to use the bathroom in the Ridgefield Park area near the baseball diamond. There was no game today, not on a cold Tuesday morning in November.

In fact, the whole place seemed deserted.

She went into a stall to pee, heard the restroom door open and close. She finished her business and approached the sink to wash her hands.

Glancing up, she spotted a face in the bathroom mirror.

A male face.

She whipped around.

A tattooed eyelid blinked at her.

Ian Dryden.

Billie's stomach dropped, and a cold sweat erupted in her armpits. She eyed the door then opened her mouth to scream.

But Ian wagged a finger at her. "No, no, no. Got my man stationed outside. You're cornered." He smiled with no teeth.

Billie glanced around, wondering what she could use as a weapon, but there were only sinks and soap dispensers.

Her throat felt like sand. "What do you want?" She managed to keep her voice firm, tough, but she couldn't look him in the eye. Not with that swastika inked into his skin.

Ian approached her slowly, as if trying to capture a lost pet, and touched her cheek. His nails were stubby and bitten. "Give Tommy Boy a message," he whispered in her ear. His breath smelled bitter. "I will get him. And if not him then you."

"What do I have to do with anything?"

"You're poking your big nose into business that doesn't concern you."

She swallowed.

A high-pitched whistle came from outside. Ian squared his shoulders, but he looked disappointed.

"See you around."

When he turned, she noticed a sparkle in the florescent bathroom lighting. Whatever he was wearing caught the light just so that it blinded her for a moment.

CHAPTER THIRTY-ONE

On Wednesday morning, Billie drove out to Paul Russo's mansion to collect her fee. Paul had suggested Venmo, but Billie said that she was required to receive the payment in person. It was a dumb provision that Gramps had put in the contract years ago. She guessed that after he had gotten stiffed one too many times by deadbeats who claimed the check was in the mail, he'd amended his contract. She'd have to look into getting that amended again, because modern times called for modern conveniences.

Also the Russo house made her uneasy.

Louise, Roxie's nurse, answered the door in her scrubs. Her dark hair was covered by a brightly patterned scarf. She warmly welcomed Billie inside and then led her to an office space off the kitchen. It was a well-appointed room with a mahogany desk and breezy curtains that faced the covered patio. Billie assumed that this was a managerial space – it seemed too feminine for the likes of Paul Russo. Louise opened up a large checkbook and uncapped a silver pen.

"Not to be rude," said Billie as she handed Louise the invoice, "but I always assumed a guy like Mr Russo would have, like, a butler."

Louise laughed good-naturedly and wrote Billie's name on the check. "He has a cleaning crew, but Mr Russo says that the only person he trusts to manage his household is himself. You know men. They think their way is the best way." She ripped out the check. "Mr Russo told me to triple your rate."

"That's not necessary," Billie began.

But Louise waved that off. She clucked her tongue. "You earned it. Tommy's a handful."

That he is. "Can I ask a question? Why does Mr Russo care so much about Tommy? I mean, from what I've heard, Tommy's parents don't even bother."

Louise nodded thoughtfully. "Mr Russo's just one of those men. Protective." She smiled. That was all the explanation needed. "Anyway, he told me to tell you that he's very indebted to you. You kept his boy outta trouble."

Not quite. Ian Dryden was still looking for him.

"Tell Tommy he's not in the clear yet."

Louise narrowed her gaze at Billie as if she was in on the secret. Then she passed Billie the check. Billie nearly choked on her tongue when she saw the amount.

"Where is Mr Russo? So I can thank him."

"At work."

Billie had been so used to seeing him during daylight hours that she had forgotten he ran a huge international food corporation. She held up the check and waved it like a parade flag. "Well, thank you."

Louise nodded at her hand. "There's plenty more where that came from. Mr Russo is a good reference. He knows plenty of people who need investigative services."

"I don't think I'll be doing this much longer." Billie sighed and rubbed the bridge of her nose.

Louise bit her lip. "You all right, honey?"

Wasn't that the million-dollar question?

"My mom has Alzheimer's disease," Billie explained. "Early-onset."

"Oof," Louise said sympathetically. "That's rough. Miss Roxie has late-onset. Got diagnosed a few years ago. It's tougher when they're younger." She enveloped Billie in a hug. "You should've seen Miss Roxie in her heyday. A stunner. Impeccable taste. And smart. And boy, did she know her–"

Louise's voice was cut by a scream, followed by the sound of shattering glass. A vase? A plate?

Louise's eyes widened, and she darted into the hall. Billie sprinted after her into a bedroom.

Roxie was tossing figurines off the fireplace mantel and throwing them at the floor.

"Miss Roxie!" Louise cried.

"You're stealing!" Roxie said, her arms poised high above her head, her fingers clamped around a statuette.

"Don't be silly, Miss Roxie," Louise said, her voice calm. "I would never do that."

Roxie fumed and raised the statuette even higher. "My watch is gone!"

"Tommy is stealing from you," Billie shot back.

Roxie's eyes were wild, her pupils practically vibrating with rage.

Billie stood in front of her and grabbed the little brass statue, tugging it gently from Roxie's grip. She passed it to Louise. "He sold your belongings." Billie took out her cell phone and flipped through the photos she had snapped at the jewelry exchange until she landed on the picture of–

"My brother's watch," Roxie whispered.

"Her brother's dead," Louise whispered into Billie's ear. "That watch meant a lot to her." Louise clucked her tongue. "I need to speak to Mr Russo about this. He must put everything in the vault."

"No, I like having my things here with me," Roxie said almost in a whine. "Where I can see them. Where I can count them. Some are lost."

"We'll find them," Louise said reassuringly.

Roxie began to cry. "I don't remember where they are."

Louise went over to comfort her, wrapping her in a hug. "It's all right, Miss Roxie. We all forget sometimes."

But it was more than forgetfulness. And it was a lot more than sometimes.

Louise said to Billie, "You should go. I got it from here."

Billie nodded numbly, but inside, she was shaking.

Roxie wailed.

"Shh," Louise cooed.

Billie slid the check into her jacket pocket and showed herself out. She practically threw herself down the front steps, so desperate to get to the Hyundai that she didn't spot the black town car idling outside the curb until the window rolled down.

A man with a flattop rested his hands on the steering wheel. His knuckles were bruised, and his eyes bored into her. "Mr Goff would like to see you."

"Now's not a good time," she said, retreating.

"Get in the car, Ms Levine. It wasn't a request."

"Oprah taught me you should never go to a second location." Then she bolted toward her Hyundai. Billie heard the click of a gun. She stopped and turned around slowly. She had gotten less pushback from the skinheads.

"You wouldn't," she said with way more certainty than she felt.

"I'll shoot you in the leg. Mr Goff said you don't have health insurance."

"Assholes. All of you."

He held out his hand for her car keys. "I'll see that my man drives your vehicle back to the *Malta Club*."

Even the goon had a goon. How many men worked for Neil?

"Does Aaron know about this?" she asked him as she climbed into the backseat of the town car.

He didn't respond as he peeled out of the Russos' nice neighborhood.

CHAPTER THIRTY-TWO

By the time Billie and Neil's henchman arrived at the *Malta Club*, Billie had imagined a dozen or so gruesome ways she would be murdered and dismembered. Aaron didn't know she was here, which meant he wouldn't be around to stop whatever Martin Scorsese shit Neil had planned for her demise.

The henchman ordered her out of the car. Then he grabbed her elbow and shoved her through the back entrance, steering her past Matty's office and toward the dance hall. His gun shifted in his holster.

"Quit manhandling me," she said, to which he responded with a huff.

The club was awfully quiet for an afternoon. "Where is everyone?" An empty club was not a good sign. It was devoid of witnesses.

He led her to the main room, which was pitch black aside from the glow of the exit sign reflected in the polished dance floor. He roughly pushed her into a chair. Without windows and lights, it was like stepping into an endless void. Billie would've given anything to see Mama Ree's false eyelashes blinking at her while she adjusted the mic stand.

This was all shades of wrong.

"Can I get water?" she asked the man.

He grunted. Was that a yes? Probably not, as she still heard him grumbling.

What was Neil Goff's game plan here? To shoot her on the dance floor? Seemed messy.

Suddenly, a bottle was thrust into her face. She snatched the water, amazed her hands weren't tied, and twisted off the cap. She sloppily gulped down the water, the liquid splashing the vintage T-shirt she had bought from a flea market in Englishtown.

Life was short; she should've gotten the acid-washed jeans that went with the top.

Then she wondered, if the henchman had gone off to get her water, who did she hear mumbling in the room?

The lights flicked on, and she had her answer.

His lips were split down the middle, blood oozing onto the collar of his shirt. His left eye was swollen and raw, his right eye tearing. His nose might've been broken. His hair was mottled with blood. Billie wanted to look away, but she couldn't.

Damon Shane.

Someone began a slow clap. Neil Goff emerged, dressed in his finest Brooks Brothers shirt and slacks. The kicker was the loafers with no socks, as if he was headed out to brunch in Boca Raton and not on his way to fit her and Damon for matching pairs of cement shoes.

"So glad you could make it, Billie. I hope you like your gift." Neil gestured to Damon. "Although one wonders if you deserve it. After all, I believe I have you to thank for getting the Bergen boys up my ass once again." He thumbed her chin and forced her to look at him. "You Levines can never mind your own business, can you?"

Billie jerked out of his grasp and then glanced at Damon, whose head lolled to one side. "What's he doing here?"

"Oh, haven't you heard? Nazis are back. Like measles and polio." Neil walked over to Damon and roughly grabbed his bleeding chin, holding up his head for Billie's inspection. "Anti-Semitism is on the rise. My neighbor is afraid to stick her electric menorah in the window. In this day and age?"

"Neil–"

"You got the detectives bureau all up in my business, Billie. Not just mine but my son's. You know how I hate that."

That seemed like a stretch. The BCDB were connecting dots. Jasmine had worked at the *Malta Club*. There was no way the Goffs would avoid questioning, Billie or no Billie. But it was Neil they should zero in on, not Aaron and not Matty. "So you've beaten up Damon to punish me?"

Neil gripped Damon's chin again, squeezing harder, and Damon winced. "No, I've smashed his face in because he's going to confess to the dead girl's murder."

Damon jerked his head out of Neil's grasp before he spat blood on the floor. Neil raised his fist as if to backhand Damon but then glanced down at his shoes and must've thought better of it.

Neil waved Billie over, grinning and gesturing hurriedly. He bent down and put his hands on his knees. He glanced from her to Damon.

Billie exhaled and got up from the chair. She walked over and crouched next to Damon. "Did you kill Jasmine?"

He could barely open his mouth. "No."

Neil slapped Damon's cheek. "That's not what you'll tell the nice detectives if you want to see your girlfriend alive."

"Shonda?" asked Billie.

Neil retreated into the darkness and returned, dragging a tear-stained Shonda behind him.

"No, no, no," Shonda said through hiccups. Her eyes darted to Damon, and her lips trembled. She glanced at Billie, her chest heaving with panic. "He had nothing to do with Jasmine's death. He doesn't even want to be a Torn Cross member anymore."

Neil considered that. "Aw, but like Judaism, you're in it for life, kid. Also, I don't care." He took his gun out of his waistband, clicked off the safety, and pressed the muzzle to Shonda's temple.

Billie turned to Neil in a frenzy. "You think killing an innocent girl is going to get you off the hook with the BCDB? That's insane."

Neil looked at her with steely eyes. "I kill her. Maybe I dispose of him too. And then I dump their bodies in Colfer's trailer park backyard. Cops nab Colfer." His eyes brightened. "I'm killing a bunch of skinheads with one stone." He grinned and rubbed his chin stubble. "Damn, that's a good idea. I should just do that anyway."

"Shonda is not a skinhead, Neil. She's your employee. And killing her won't get the cops off your back for Jasmine Flores."

Shonda looked at Billie then Damon then Billie. Then Neil's gun. Billie saw that Shonda was desperate to make a choice. "I'll confess to her murder."

"No," said Damon weakly. "You didn't do anything. I'll do it."

"Again," said Neil, "I'm starting to think I overplanned this. I could kill two people and get rid of all my problems." He took aim with the gun then lowered it. "Or I could toss her to Colfer."

"No!" Damon cried. "Not that!" He squirmed against his bonds.

"Neil," said Billie. She took a step toward him, but his bodyguard grabbed her shoulder and hauled her back. "Please."

Shonda licked her lips and shifted nervously. Billie watched the girl's eyes dart from Damon to Neil as if she was trying to weigh her options. Finally, she cried, "Starla Wells's diamond!"

Neil stared at her then. "What did you say?"

"Starla Wells's diamond," she repeated. "Does that interest you?"

"Shonda," Damon warned.

"What do you know of it?" asked Billie.

Shonda eyed Neil's gun. "Jasmine knew about the diamond, and she knew who had it."

"How?" said Billie.

"I never asked her," Shonda snapped as if Billie's question was going to upend this whole ordeal.

Neil lowered the gun and stared at Shonda. "Are you lying?"

"No! I overheard her on the phone with someone, whispering about Starla's diamond. She said she knew how to get it, but it would be dangerous. Said it would prove everything."

Damon eyed Shonda warily before giving an almost imperceptible nod of his head. But Billie caught it. So did Neil.

"What else?"

"No," warned Damon.

Shonda bit her lip as Neil raised the gun. "She mentioned Colfer," she said rapidly. "Colfer must have it. He never sold it like everyone thought."

"Fucker," Neil growled as he flexed his fingers. "I knew that son-of-a-bitch killed her for it." Neil gestured with his gun and turned to Billie. "That girl found out what Colfer did, and *he* stuffed her in a trunk."

Billie glanced at Damon to see if there was a flicker of truth to this, but Damon gave nothing away.

"I got an idea, Nancy Drew," Neil said to Billie. "You prove that Colfer murdered Starla Wells, and I'll let Damon and his girlfriend go. Hell, I'll even give them a few grand to start a new life together. But I want Colfer Dryden brought down for this."

Billie staggered backward. "Neil, I don't think I can–"

"Don't do it," said Damon. "If Colfer gets his hands on you, you'll wish to die."

Billie thought of Ian in the ladies' room at Overpeck Park. How close had she come to a slow, painful death? Her pulse popped, and she began to pant. She had just decided that she needed to get out of the PI business. She had a sick mom at home, an old grandpa, and an overworked brother. Everyone needed her. And now she had to put herself out on a limb to protect a skinhead and his girlfriend so a mobster could enact his petty revenge?

"Neil–" Billie began.

But her excuses were cut off by Shonda's sobs. "Please," said Shonda.

"Deliver Colfer Dryden to the cops," said Neil as he handed his gun to his bodyguard. "Or else the next time your brother sneaks out of my son's office, I'll make him disappear."

She gritted her teeth. "You lay a hand on David, and I'll destroy you."

"Well, now it sounds like a fun competition."

They stared at each other in a standoff.

Finally, Billie said, "What assurances do I have?"

Neil grinned. He knew he had her.

"If you want assurances, you won't get them from him," came a voice.

Aaron sauntered in, dressed in his bomber jacket, hands thrust into his jean pockets. He glared at his father. "The fuck you doing, Dad?"

"Business," said Neil.

Aaron shot Billie a look, but his eyes didn't linger on her. "I'll make sure everyone stays in their respective corners while you look into–" he waved his hands around "–whatever bullshit this is."

Billie shifted nervously, but Shonda seemed visibly relieved. Only this further complicated matters for Billie.

"If Olivia Benson over here does what I ask, no one has to worry," said Neil. "So get your BCDB pals off our asses."

"Don't touch my brother," she growled.

Neil held up his hands in surrender, but that wasn't a guarantee.

Billie wasn't equipped to handle this kind of investigation, but did she have a choice? She either dug up Starla Wells herself or was responsible for Neil plugging holes in Damon and Shonda's bodies.

"I'll help you keep them safe," Aaron whispered to her, his fingers sitting gently on her shoulder. "We won't let Neil win."

She gently shrugged him off. Gramps was right. She should've never gotten involved with the Goffs. Aaron complicated everything, and his father was a total psychotic prick.

"Get me employee records," she told Aaron. "Anything with Starla's name on it – an application, a receipt – I want it."

He nodded. "I'll see what I can do."

She turned to Neil, emotionless. "Is my car outside?"

Neil nodded with a grin as wide as the sea. "Out front."

She leaned down and whispered in Damon's ear, "Nancy Drew always wins in the end."

Damon blinked several times but said nothing. She guessed he wasn't holding out hope.

"All right, get them out of here," Neil said to his bodyguard. "I gotta open the club."

Billie stumbled down the back hallway, her hand sliding against the walls for support, and out the door. She emerged into drabness and sucked in the frigid air.

Aaron appeared a moment later and called out to her, "I'm sorry. I had no idea he would do this."

But Aaron could no more apologize for his father than she could for hers.

She waved to him and got into her car.

CHAPTER THIRTY-THREE

Billie stood in the shower with her eyes closed. She rested her forearm on the cold tile while water ran down her back in rivulets. She had already scrubbed her body raw, desperate to wash the invisible film of the *Malta Club* off her skin. But it was no use. She felt dirty and used.

Aaron had texted her earlier. He promised to place Damon and Shonda in a motel where only he would have access while Billie untangled this mess.

And what a mess it was.

She turned off the water and stepped onto the bathmat. She wrapped herself in a towel, soft and worn from years of use, and rummaged through the vanity drawer for a comb.

When Billie had suggested she become an investigator, Gramps had warned her about the repercussions.

"Once you sign that contract, you're in it," he said. "Whatever it is. And it can get lonely."

And like a dopey twenty-something-year-old kid, she had brushed him off. "I can handle being alone." But she realized now that wasn't quite what he had meant.

She had taken Tommy's case, thinking all she had to do was unearth a college kid who had ghosted her boyfriend, only to have fallen into a black pit of murder, kidnapping, and a decades-old gangster feud involving a dead dancer. Not to mention the unintended consequences for her mother and her own hazy future.

And somehow, she had put David in danger.

Other women Billie's age were simply trying to navigate new careers and online dating. She wished a Tinder profile was the most stressful part of her life right now.

She parted her hair down the center and mindlessly dragged the comb through her short strands.

And what about poor Jasmine Flores?

She had been a criminology student from a wealthy family who took a job at the *Malta Club* in hopes of finding out what had happened to Starla Wells. What kind of girl did something like that?

Maybe the same type of girl who dated a mobster's son because she thought it was sexy and romantic. Because she thought she could save him. Because she thought he might save her.

Jasmine had tried to rescue Tommy, and look where it had gotten her – mixed up with dangerous skinheads, bargaining for a life with a diamond.

If Jasmine had really known the location of Starla Wells's diamond, then she'd been sitting on a tinderbox of information. That jewel could provide enough money to restore Neil's prominence.

Billie's brain burned just thinking about it.

And what choice did Billie have in all this? Did she want to be personally responsible for the deaths of two people – Damon and Shonda? Not when she could stop it.

And David? She would do anything to protect him.

She sighed and leaned against the sink. She needed to reconsider everything she already knew.

A knock on the door interrupted her pity party. "It's unlocked," she said, exhausted.

David poked his head in and fanned the humid air with his hand. He held out her cell phone. "It's been blowing up on the kitchen table for an hour. Thought you might want it."

She cinched her towel tighter and exited the bathroom. A

chill traveled through her body, but she wasn't sure if it was the cool, dry air or the text message snippet she glimpsed on the home screen.

It was from Morales.

Tommy's dead. Overdose. Body found in Percy Street Garage.

How convenient for Ian Dryden.

She fell back against the wall. "Shit," she said, the word coming out like a breath.

"What?" said David.

"My client's dead."

"The Russo Foods guy? Wouldn't that be, like, big news?"

Billie shook her head. "No. His nephew. Heroin addict."

That gave David pause. He was probably thinking about his own close call, back before he had been diagnosed and put on a decent med regimen. "So now what?"

Billie shook her head. "I don't know." She looked at her brother. He was dressed in pressed slacks and a button-down shirt that brought out the gold in his eyes. Not a wrinkle to be seen. "Where are you going?"

"I have a date," he said simply.

"You need to be careful," she said.

"With my date?" He sounded amused.

"With Matty," she said.

"If you're worried about my feelings–"

"Not your feelings. Your life."

He laughed outright.

"I'm serious," she said. "Neil is dangerous, and he might try to hurt you to get to me."

He laughed again and then stopped. "For real?"

"It's this case–"

"I thought this client wasn't a client any longer," said David.

"He's not."

"Then why are you still involved?"

Because she had no choice. Because Tommy had signed a contract. And now because Neil Goff was holding two people hostage until she came through on a promise she should never have made.

"Stay away from the *Malta Club*," she told him.

"Now you sound like Gramps."

"Yeah, well, he's right on this."

"Are you going to stay away from Aaron?" he asked, challenging.

She sighed but didn't say no.

"Maybe this is not the right career for you."

She glanced at her phone. "Did you always know you wanted to be a nurse?"

"When I was four, I wanted to be a firefighter." He laughed. Then, more seriously, he went on, "I did know that I wanted to help people. It makes me feel good to care about others. It takes my mind off – well, my own mind."

"I like helping people, too," she said.

"But at whose expense?" David tapped his temple. "I know you're worried about what will happen when you're older, but you can't predict the future. I don't know when I'm going to have a manic period or depressive episode. I don't know if my current diet of meds will stop working one day. I don't know if Neil Goff will jump out of the bushes and shoot me."

"David, that's not–"

"But I'm not going to live my life in fear." He checked his phone before slipping it into his pocket. "I refuse to let circumstances out of my control dictate how I live my life. Don't feel sorry for yourself."

"I'm not feeling sorry for myself," Billie said defensively.

"You kinda are."

"I'm not–"

"You *are*. I know you. You're pissed about how life has doled out unfair shit for us. My bipolar disorder. Mom's Alzheimer's. Dad leaving. And you – you're definitely not doing the things you'd thought you'd be doing. Going to Europe. Learning a new language. Being snooty."

"David–" But she was smiling. He had a way of making everything feel less dire than it did in her mind.

"You're real smart, Billie. Smarter than anyone else I know. And you're a good person with bad taste in men. Family trait. But ask yourself: do you like this job? Or are you just doing it because you think it makes it easier on the family? Which, by the way, it doesn't."

She sighed. "I do like it, but it's also so tough."

He stared at her for a beat. "Most things that are worth it are." He shoved his hands into his pockets. "I can take care of myself. Worry about you." He pressed his mouth into a tight line and went downstairs.

CHAPTER THIRTY-FOUR

Billie sat on her bed with her legs crossed. She was dressed in sweats, her damp hair having left a wet splotch on the back of her collar. Her attic room was warm and cozy.

She glimpsed snow flurries outside her window, which reminded her that winter was en route. She and the cold never fully jived. If it was up to Billie, she might be living her salt life on a beach somewhere in the Caribbean. Maybe learn to scuba dive. After she learned Spanish, of course.

She sighed and opened up Starla Wells's old employee record that Aaron had dug out of Matty's file cabinet. It had been delivered to Billie's front door by Neil's henchman.

She would not bother to learn his name.

There was only one document inside – a job application with Starla's name, address, and phone number. No Social Security number.

It turned out that Starla Wells had been her real name, or at least that was what she wrote down. And that she had once lived in an apartment complex in Paramus that had been razed a few years ago to make room for an assisted-living facility.

Her birthdate was listed as March 3, 1959. That put her at age 32 when she died. So not young. Not old either. Just in her prime.

The birthdate proved helpful. Maybe Billie could find something online. Only when she conducted a preliminary search, she was hit with very few newspaper articles – the ones without a paywall – that regurgitated what she already knew: a youngish, hot stripper was stabbed to death outside the *Malta Club* in June of 1991. There were no leads, but the cops thought it was a mugging gone wrong. The BCDB didn't have enough to pin the crime on Neil Goff, and Billie would have bet her bat mitzvah money that they had wanted to.

She closed her laptop and stood up to stretch. There was only one other person who could help her with this, and he was downstairs sleeping off whiskey sours.

Perfect timing.

Billie went into the kitchen to find Gramps slumped over the table. She tapped his shoulder. He didn't wake. She shook his shoulder. He stirred. She took a drinking glass from the cupboard, filled it with tap water, and spilled it over his head.

Gramps jerked awake. He sputtered and whipped his head around. Water droplets flew off his forehead and onto Billie's shirt.

He groaned and then reached across the table for a napkin. "Whatcha do that for?" he grumbled. He blotted his pale skin while she went into the refrigerator for a can of seltzer. She pulled back the tab and plunked the can on the table. Bubbles popped inside.

He grumbled something about being *totally sober*, but he slurred his speech. Billie's patience was as thin as her grandpa's hair.

"Sorry, but I require supervisory help," she said, leaning against the sink and crossing her arms. She watched him drink his seltzer for a moment. "Can I have access to your old case files?"

Gramps ran his hand over his face and belched. "Huh?"

"Your case files," she repeated. "Everything you got on the Dancing Queen murder. Starla Wells?"

"I know what you mean, and you can't have them." He burped again.

That got her attention. She straightened. "What do you mean I can't have 'em?"

"I mean they were destroyed in a flood."

"A flood?"

"Hurricane Floyd."

"Hurricane Floyd?"

"You were a toddler when it hit. Anyway, the storage facility got a deluge."

"A deluge?"

"Would you stop repeating everything I say as a question," he barked. "It got a deluge of rain, and my case files were destroyed."

"Wow," she said with a hint of dramatic flair. "I'd imagine that such devastation would've put Paretsky's out of business."

Gramps shrugged. They were both quiet for a moment. Then he said, "I don't want you following up on this case."

"Yeah, I got your intention."

"I'm serious, Belinda. This isn't something to monkey around with. You got a lot of big-time players. The Torn Crosses. Neil Goff. Not to mention there were some shady policemen who had a hand in a cover-up."

"Shady cops? Who?"

"Doesn't matter," he said, dismissing the question. "I couldn't solve the case. You won't be able to either."

"Thanks for the vote of confidence."

"It's not that I don't think you're capable, but it's dangerous. Colfer Dryden and his dummy kid are no one you want to be snooping around."

She knew that firsthand. She decided to change tactics. "Was it a random mugging?"

"Could've been. She wore that diamond around her neck. Someone was bound to pluck it off her body at some point."

"Why so callous?"

He sighed. "I don't know. This case always bugged me. She was always surrounded by ruthless criminals, but maybe it was a random hit."

"My money is on Colfer," she said.

"Let this case go," he said. "I thought you were done with this anyway. You're gonna find an office job."

"Maybe I'm not meant for an office," she said. "Like you."

Gramps harrumphed.

"Jasmine claimed that she knew where to find Starla's diamond," said Billie thoughtfully. "Maybe someone at the *Malta Club* knew something that they shared with her. Someone like Mama Ree."

Gramps turned in his chair and pointed an arthritic finger at her. "Don't go near the club."

Billie sighed. It was no use arguing with the old man. He still thought of her as a naive fifteen year-old kid. He forgot that he had gifted her his business and that she was old enough to handle cases, whatever they were.

She slid her car keys off the kitchen countertop.

"Where ya going?" asked Gramps, his eyes narrowed into slits.

"Nowhere you gotta worry about," she said.

"Billie," he called after her, but it was too late. She was already out the door and shrugging on her coat.

CHAPTER THIRTY-FIVE

Paretsky's storage facility was in a rundown, converted parking garage in Rochelle Park, tucked behind a 7-Eleven and nearly invisible from the highway. It was the kind of place that didn't see the business of a Public Storage and for good reason. The rates were cheap, but so was the security. No gates. No working cameras. It was patronized by criminals and poor PIs alike.

Brian Paretsky had been in David's graduating class. Her brother used to joke that Brian once had the hots for Billie, which she was hoping to exploit.

She went into the small manager's office and tapped a silver bell that sat on the counter. The space smelled like a combination of weed and Pine-Sol. She heard a toilet flush and the rustlings of a man attending to his own needs. Brian hustled out from the back. Billie hoped he had made time to wash his hands.

He was burly and had light-brown hair and a wide nose. His polo shirt was too tight, and his pants were too loose.

He halted at the sight of her. "Billie?"

"How's it going?" she said lightly. She tucked a strand of hair behind her ear in an attempt to look demure. It must've worked, because Brian broke into a grin.

"I haven't seen you since high school," he said.

"Oh, you know. Same old. Same old." She realized she was answering a question he hadn't asked. She leaned across the counter and batted her eyelashes. She felt ridiculous.

She probably looked ridiculous. "Actually, I took over my grandfather's private investigative business."

"That's cool. I think I heard about that."

"Yes. Totally cool." She smiled again. "So my gramps rents a storage unit here with all his old case files. And I was wondering if you could let me in."

"Did he give you a key?"

She leaned over further and whispered, "He's getting on in years and forgot where he put it."

Brian ran a hand over the back of his neck. "Sorry to hear that. I mean, your grandfather and your mom, both with Alzheimer's. That's gotta be tough."

Billie dropped her smile. "Yeah," she said curtly. "So anyway, can you let me into his unit? It's just old case files in there. Nothing of value to anyone."

Brian glanced behind him as if checking for eavesdroppers, but no one else seemed to be there. Not to mention that his pops owned the facility. "Yeah, sure, Billie. I'll let you in."

He opened a desk drawer and pulled out a key. "Master," he said by way of explanation. "But I gotta open it for ya."

She nodded and allowed him to lead the way down the hall and past the elevators. "You should join our local small-business association. It can help you network and get discounts."

"Sounds good," she said absently.

They rounded the corner and stopped in front of a small orange door with #1120 on it in peeling vinyl.

"Your grandfather insisted on a first-floor unit," said Brian.

Of course he did. God forbid he get a little exercise going up stairs.

Brian pushed his key into the lock and toggled the switch. Then he bent down and hefted up the garage door.

"Let me know when you're done, and I'll lock up," he told her.

"Thanks," she said.

Brian gave her a long look as if he was trying to work up the nerve to say something – maybe he wanted to ask her out on a date – but he must've thought better of it. He smiled sadly to himself and returned to the office.

For a second, Billie wondered if he had lost his nerve or if it was something else that prevented him from coming on to her.

Eh, it didn't matter.

She flicked on the light and examined the space. *Flood, my ass.* Boxes were piled high. A club chair and a floor lamp sat in the corner. Billie closed the door to salvage some of the heat and turned on the light. She ran her fingers over the boxes, trying to make out the faded marker, to read her grandfather's indecipherable handwriting. Some boxes were labeled by year, others by case.

She restacked a few boxes to one side before she found one that was simply labeled, *Malta Club*.

She took it out and brought it over to the club chair. She sat down and flung off the lid. It was packed with file folders that had names scrawled on the tabs. *Neil Goff. Matthew Goff. Aaron Goff.*

Glad to know Gramps had been keeping dossiers on his grandkids' ex-lovers.

She finally found a stack of folders bound together with a rubber band. *Starla Wells* was written on the cover.

She undid the bundle and skimmed through the contents. She first found photographs, likely taken with Gramps's old single-lens camera. There were close-up shots of Starla outside the *Malta Club*. In one photo, she was wearing a tight miniskirt and heels and sharing a cigarette with Neil Goff. In another, she was kissing Colfer Dryden in the front seat of an old Buick. Blech. Another photo simply showed her neck and the megadiamond near her clavicle.

And then there was one photo that made Billie a little awestruck. Starla was sitting in a booth at *Nagel*'s. Billie spied Bernice, thirty years younger, slightly out of focus, in the background. Starla sat across from an identifiable man. Her head was tossed back, her red mouth open and wide, and her hair fell around her shoulders like a mermaid's. The man must've said something outrageous to elicit that kind of laugh. Billie wondered how many men had strived to make her that joyful. There must have been a lengthy line to her dressing room door.

All that didn't explain why Gramps had been tailing Starla long before she was murdered.

There was a note written in his cursive.

ME: Stabbed fifteen times.

ME? Medical examiner. Where was the report though? Also fifteen times seemed…excessive.

Billie shook the box and glanced inside to find little cassette tapes in the bottom. She knocked the tops off more boxes until she found an old-school handheld tape recorder. She popped the cassette inside and pressed Play.

Immediately, she heard the roar of a crowd – mostly men – and then cheering. Some whistled. Some whooped. Then a voice. Mama Ree. Billie recognized it right away.

"Welcome, Maltesers," she said. "It is my privilege to announce tonight's performance. Give it up for your favorite girl and mine, Ms Starla Wells."

There was more applauding. More screams and catcalls. Some dude yelled, "We love you, Starla!" Another cried less eloquently, "Take it all off!"

The introduction to "Dancing Queen" by ABBA played. Then a voice, husky and sultry, huffed into the mic. "Hello to all you beautiful, sexy people in the audience. Are you ready to blow off some steam?" More cheering. "I'm ready to blow, too." More whistling. "I'm so honored to dance for you all tonight. I promise to make it worth your while."

Billie imagined her grandfather sitting in a strip club while Starla Wells gave the audience what Billie could only equate to verbal foreplay. Talk about the sleazy parts to the job. Except Starla didn't sound sleazy. She sounded sincerely honored, almost. Billie sensed that Starla loved being the center of attention, and she now thought she understood the Sleuth Squad's obsession with this case. Starla was magnetic, even in death.

The music changed from the disco-style tune to a jazzy number. The crowd settled a bit, but even Billie could sense an undercurrent of sexual tension. They were all waiting, entranced. Starla was no run-of-the-mill stripper. She was a performer. She was as her name suggested.

The music picked up. There was a drumbeat. Then the crashing of cymbals. The crowd roared. "Naughty thoughts," Starla cooed. "Wanna see what's under these fans?"

Billie began to sweat and squirmed in the club chair. This was like watching Shonda and Damon have sex outside the *Malta Club*.

Starla Wells's sexuality oozed from the recording. She was the kind of woman who could make you feel things. Dirty things.

Dangerous things.

She brought out impulses.

Maybe a customer got handsy. Went out with her in the back alley, tried to lift her skirt and stabbed her instead.

But she had been stabbed fifteen times.

Would a mugger do that?

And what was Jasmine's connection to all this? It had to start somewhere.

Something had happened at the *Malta Club*, and Jasmine must've found out about it. That Billie was sure of.

The Torn Crosses were skilled in tying up loose ends.

Maybe they'd tied these ends together.

CHAPTER THIRTY-SIX

Billie snagged her usual spot at *Nagel*'s and pushed a box of her grandpa's old case files into the corner booth before sliding in after it.

The deli was quiet. The old folks, like Gramps and his groupies, were part of the morning crowd, preferring coffee and bagels to cream soda and pastrami. All that was left were the young couples, clustered around tables, heads bent over a vinegar-based coleslaw, gabbing about politics and podcasts. They had probably just come from a concert or late movie.

Billie thought she should try that sometime.

Bernice sauntered over, her apron impossibly pristine, her hair so stiffly coiffed that not even tornado winds could upset a strand. She set a mug in front of Billie and filled it with dark coffee. Then she nudged the bowl of creamer toward her.

"Working hard?" asked Bernice in her thick Jersey City accent. She pushed down her reading glasses and peered over Billie's shoulder. "Starla Wells? I haven't heard that name in years." Except it came out sounding like *yeeahs*.

Billie took a sip of coffee and reclined against the vinyl cushion. "What do you know about her?"

Bernice shrugged before she leaned down and whispered, "She and Malley had an arrangement."

"An arrangement?" said Billie, realization dawning on her. The photo. The man cracking a joke with Starla. "With Detective Doug Malley?"

"Yeah, that's right. He would sit on the barstool, order her usual – turkey on rye, sometimes a black and white, but always the turkey – and wait for her to pick it up. She'd leave. Then he'd leave. One night, they ate together."

"Did they ever *leave* together?"

"No, they weren't a couple. Like I said, it was an arrangement."

Well, that *was* an unexpected tidbit. Gramps had said something about shady cops, but Malley never came across as corrupt. No way would Morales the Boy Scout partner with Malley if he wasn't on the up-and-up. Then again, how would Morales know about the kind of cop Malley had been thirty years ago?

"You sure Starla and Detective Malley didn't have a fling?" asked Billie. In his heyday, Malley had left a lot of women in his wake.

"You could ask him. He loves to kiss and tell," Bernice said with a wink before walking away to refill another customer's coffee mug.

Malley had said he had worked Starla's case, but he had never made decent headway. Billie would have to chat him up. She would need to chat up a lot of people.

Opening her leather bag, she removed a pen and notebook and started to make a list of potential interviews. The first names she wrote down were Malley's and Mama Ree's. Both had known Starla back in the day.

She sipped more coffee and rummaged through the box. She flipped through a manila folder and skimmed various documents including Starla's rental agreement. Starla had listed Neil Goff as her one and only reference.

She also found sketches done in soft colored pencil of a nondescript building with glowing marquee lettering that read, "Diamond Girls."

There was also an old yet still glossy magazine article out of some publication called *Dance Hall Monthly*. Was that, like, a strip club trade journal? Billie laughed, imagining Neil "the Goffather" Goff signing up for a subscription.

Her eyes scanned a headline for a short article in its Club News section.

STARLA WELLS BRINGS HER STRIP TEASE TO THE MALTA CLUB

The Malta Club *just announced its latest addition to its sultry lineup. The veritable Starla Wells, a popular cabaret dancer, is joining Neil Goff's band of bawdy babes* (oy vey, who wrote this?). *Goff enticed her away from the* Lucky Lous. *Lucky Neil, indeed.*

She took out several more folders and combed through them. Gramps had collected any and all news clippings that referenced Starla. Then she found this one:

LOCAL STRIP CLUB DESTROYED IN ARSON FIRE

The Lucky Lous, a gentleman's club in Hackensack, was destroyed in a fire that arson investigators have labeled as suspicious. The club, owned by Colfer Dryden, who has been arrested numerous times for assault, armed robbery, and hate crimes, told investigators that he believed Neil Goff was responsible for the fire.
Investigators have yet to comment. One firefighter was hurt in the blaze.

Billie rested her head against the vinyl booth. So Starla Wells used to dance at Colfer's club. Then Neil Goff poached her. That must have made Colfer really mad. One might even say vengeful.

Speaking of mad, Gramps was heading straight toward her, his face red and his nostrils flaring like a bull in a Spanish arena. Billie sat up straight as her grandpa took the seat across from her.

"What are you doing here?" she asked. "Who's with Mom?"

"The yenta." Then, more specifically, he added, "The neighbor." He gestured for Bernice.

She scuttled over with a mug of coffee and a flirty smile. "Hiya, Bill," said Bernice with her hip jutted out. "Can I get you anything to nosh on?"

"I'd love some of those half sours if you got 'em," he said with a grin. "A cup of matzoh ball soup, too."

"Coming right up." She winked at him.

Billie leaned over. "You left Mom with Mrs Rodriguez?"

"It was an emergency. It appears someone, *you*, broke into my storage locker. Paretsky Senior called me about it."

"Snitch," Billie grumbled.

Gramps smacked a Sweet 'N Low packet against his palm then tore off the top. He tapped it into his coffee. "I told you to stay outta there."

"You also told me your records were destroyed by a flood, so excuse me for not feeling appropriately guilty."

Gramps took a sip of coffee just as Bernice returned with his soup. She bent over suggestively and set down a packet of saltines next to the bowl. Billie caught a panoramic view of her cleavage.

"Thanks, doll," he said.

"Doll?" said Billie once Bernice had sauntered away.

"It makes her feel sexy," he said.

"Gross."

"Anyway, I see you stole my boxes. So what have you got?"

"You don't know what's in here?" asked Billie.

Gramps sliced the matzoh balls with a spoon. "I mean, what's your interpretation?"

"Oh." She gestured to the newspaper articles. "It now seems obvious that Colfer killed Starla as revenge against Neil for the fire that destroyed his club. And he stole her diamond."

"You don't say." Gramps shoved a matzoh ball into his mouth and stared at her.

"I take it you don't agree."

He swallowed and sipped his coffee. "I shook down Colfer."

"Don't tell me. He had an alibi." Billie plucked a half sour from a dish and chomped down on it. The brininess clashed with the coffee taste in her mouth, but it was satisfying nonetheless.

"He was shacking up with one of his girls in a sleazy motel down the shore. FBI's tail confirmed it."

"The FBI were watching him?"

"Like a hawk."

"Who was the chick?"

"Some side piece. Crystal Dean. Barely legal."

"If his alibi so easily checked out, then why did Neil think Colfer killed Starla?"

Gramps considered that. "Colfer suddenly went from small-time racketeering to a full-blown drug trafficking network. Neil was convinced that Colfer could have only done that if he had a half-million-dollar investment."

"Jasmine told someone she knew where the diamond was. If Colfer had sold it, how would Jasmine know about it?"

"Excellent question," Gramps said. "I'm curious as to how you acquired your intel."

Billie ignored that. After all, the PI asked the questions. "Was Colfer ever in love with Starla? Is that why he was so upset that she went to the *Malta Club*?"

Gramps looked thoughtful for a second. He scooped up another matzoh ball. "Everyone was in love with her. She had that effect on people."

"Even you?"

"I only had eyes for your grandmother – best tuches this side of the GWB. But in another life, sure, I might've ended up with a girl like Starla. She was funny and sexy and strong. She didn't talk much about her personal life, but she had mentioned that she had struggled in her youth. Anyway, Colfer probably did love her, but you can be in love with a person and still hurt them. Colfer loved by squeezing the life out of something like a toddler with a puppy."

"Some metaphor." Billie thought of Aaron. They had hurt each other frequently. Not in the same vein as Colfer and Starla, but painful nonetheless.

Gramps continued, "I think Colfer thought that Starla was going to stick by him, be the main attraction of his club, get him on the map. But she saw the white supremacist writing on the wall and got out of there." He pushed around the sketches. "She had dreams to open her own Las Vegas-style shows with girls like herself."

"That couldn't be cheap," Billie pointed out.

"Guess that was what the diamond was for," said Gramps.

Billie imagined Starla sitting down to sketch her club's design. The light in her eye as she created the business of her dreams. Poor girl. To have died with it nearly within reach. "Do you think Colfer sent one of his goons after her? His brother-in-law was pretty ruthless, even by Colfer's standards."

Gramps slurped some broth and then set down his spoon. He looked at Billie squarely and said, "Possibly, but he's been missing for seven years. We can't exactly ask him." His brow went up.

"I don't get why Starla flaunted that big stone around anyway," said Billie. "Seemed risky. It was not like she was wearing it to High Holidays services. She was wearing it around gangsters."

"If there is one thing you should know about Starla, it's that she lived her life on her terms, and people respected that. Everyone loved her."

"Someone didn't," Billie said, reaching for another pickle. "She *was* murdered. So if not Colfer, who?"

"I didn't say Colfer was innocent. Apparently, Starla had given Neil information that Colfer had supposedly passed along to her in confidence."

"What kind of info?"

"Shipments from overseas that the Goff boys managed to snag before the Torn Crosses even have a chance to blink."

"The olive oil?"

Gramps clicked his tongue. "One thing you gotta realize is that all these mobsters want a piece of the same pie."

"Who knew that Jews and white supremacists would have the same goals?"

"Relevance and influence," Gramps said, gesturing with his coffee mug. "Everyone wants that."

CHAPTER THIRTY-SEVEN

When Morales texted Billie and asked her to meet him at the *Wagon*, Billie left Gramps to his matzoh ball soup and traded her deli booth for a barstool.

Billie expected that things with the handsome detective would be a little awkward in the wake of their ill-fated hookup at his place. Her mind had been too cluttered with the case and with Aaron, and Morales had made it clear that he was sick of her baggage and hang-ups as well.

She spotted him at the end of the bar, still clad in his suit and tie and nursing a whiskey. He must have sensed her watching him, because he turned around. He didn't greet her with a smile, but his eyes scrunched up at the corners, which made Billie think he was trying to suppress a grin. He had probably forgiven her by now.

She plopped into the seat next to him and ordered a seltzer with grapefruit juice.

"Fancy," Morales remarked. He'd asked her once why she didn't drink, and she just told him that she didn't like the taste. But he had probably guessed. He'd met her mom, and he was a good detective.

The whiskey glass hovered around his lips. "So I take it you got my text? You didn't respond."

Billie dropped a few dollars on the bar, but Morales waved it away. "It's a soda."

She tugged the cocktail napkin closer to her and picked up the glass, slick with condensation.

"You said you wanted a breather from me."

"This is business," he said, not unkindly. Just matter-of-fact.

"You still think Tommy is good for Jasmine's murder?" Billie asked.

"Doesn't matter what I think. Not my case. Anyway, Richards knows what he's after."

Billie nearly choked on the carbonation. "You mean the Goffs. Why? When the Torn Crosses are involved."

"Billie," Morales said with what sounded like pity. "Jasmine Flores stole two gimels from the *Malta*. They're gonna lean into them hard."

"Colfer Dryden is involved in her death," she said with conviction. "I know it. And Matthew Goff has no history of violence."

Morales snorted. "He has a rap sheet."

"From adolescence."

"He's into racketeering and money laundering."

"You don't know that."

He stared at her. "Your friendship with the Goffs is clouding your judgment."

He wasn't wrong there.

"*How* do you know that Jasmine and Colfer Dryden crossed paths? Tommy used to buy off the Torn Crosses, but that's it."

"That's enough." Billie wasn't quite ready to reveal her hand. She didn't want Morales to draw a connection between Starla's coveted diamond and the Goffs since Detective Richards was so antsy to get Matty into an interrogation room. Also it would put her whole mission at risk, not to mention Damon and Shonda. Aaron squirreling the two of them away in a hotel room for their own safety – because they were essentially being held hostage by his father – wouldn't change Morales's mind about who the bad guys were.

Also she wouldn't put David's life in jeopardy. Not for Morales or any man.

Morales said, "Maybe the Russo kid overdosed on purpose because he killed Jasmine."

"If that's the case," she said, "then why look at Matty, err, Matthew Goff?"

"Because she worked at the *Malta Club*, and he has motive."

"But the Torn Cross—"

Morales cut her off. "Richards talked to his buddies in domestic terrorism, but even they couldn't see how Jasmine had any involvement with them. She would've never gotten an audience with Colfer. It just wouldn't happen."

An audience. As if Colfer was a king. Yeah. King of meth and swastikas.

And the only one who could corroborate that would be Damon, who was not readily available to comment anyway.

"Besides," he continued, "they're trying to tie Colfer to a smuggling group that's arming supremacists in the Southwest. They're not gonna jeopardize that for some stripper."

"Some stripper? Seriously, Morales?"

"Not my words." He sipped his whiskey slowly, his eyes flitting from her to the television screen showing a soccer match in Manchester.

They said nothing for a moment. Billie gulped down her soda, burped quietly to herself, and looped her bag strap around her shoulders.

That got Morales's attention. "You going?"

"It's late. I'm exhausted, and tomorrow, I got a lot of shit to do."

"This case is over, Billie. What else do you have to do?"

She answered that question by leaving.

Outside, the air had gotten so cold she could see her breath. A group of smokers huddled under their coats, inhaling nicotine as fast as their lungs could expand. Doug Malley stood in the center, shifting in his loafers, his wool coat open to reveal a protruding gut. A lit cigarette dangled from his fingertips.

Wasn't this serendipitous?

"Malley," she called over to him.

"Levine, is that you?" He took one last drag and flicked the butt into the street like a common litterbug. He lumbered over to her then whispered, "You heading home with Morales?"

She reared back. As if it was any of his business. "No," she said flatly. Then she doled out a lie. "He left."

Malley leaned past her as if to get a better view of the bar. "You're kidding, right? He's my ride."

"Left in a hurry. Said something about his sister's kid."

"Son of a bitch," Malley said.

"Chen can drive you home."

"Chen's gone."

"I'll take you," Billie said lightly. As if it was no big deal. As if she wasn't internally pleading for him to agree.

Malley scrunched his forehead then glanced again at the bar's entrance. "You sure? I'm in Ridgewood."

She moved her frame into his line of sight. "Absolutely. I don't mind."

Malley scratched his cheek with a bitten fingernail. "All right." Then he followed her to the car.

Billie unlocked her Hyundai, which was parked at the meter across from the bank, and watched as Malley stuffed his oversized body into the squat sedan.

He glanced around the car's interior, his gaze meeting fast-food wrappers and empty cans of seltzer, and huffed. "Reminds me of my early stakeout days." He patted his stomach. "That's why I got so fat."

Billie turned the key in the ignition, pulled the car onto a deserted Cedar Lane and headed toward Route 4. "Yeah, well, lucky for me, I got a fast metabolism."

"Yeah, they all say that until..." He glanced down again, gesturing to his belly.

"You've been a detective a long time," Billie began.

"That I have."

She kept her eyes on the taillights in front of her. "What was the *Malta Club* like in its heyday?"

"In its prime?" Malley shook his head. "I was a kid back then. When Neil's father was in charge, there wasn't a beat cop in Bergen County that didn't spend half their paycheck on the girls. You gotta remember, it was like the Playboy mansion over there. Ladies just as beautiful as Hef's bunnies. My old man would talk about them like they were movie stars. Not to my mother or anything, but to his cop friends. I'd overhear them bullshitting. Then Neil took over. And it was coke. The girls got strung out. The nineties were no better. Heroin chic." He scoffed. "It's just not the same anymore."

"What do you mean?" asked Billie.

"The glamour's gone. Now you got the Eastern Europeans. Half the time, you can't be sure they're not being trafficked."

"Not at the *Malta*," said Billie. Matty would never let that happen.

"At the *Malta*, it's college girls trying to pay the bills. Nothing kills sex like seeing a girl on stage young enough to be your daughter. Mama Ree's great, but I wish they would expand the cabaret."

"You mean like Starla Wells?" she asked as she carefully took the Saddle River exit.

"Yeah," Malley said wistfully. "She was something."

They were both quiet for a moment. Then, "Were you in love with her?"

That perked him up. "Who told you that?"

"It was said that you had an arrangement. You treated her to turkey on rye and black and whites."

Malley shook his head to himself and whispered, "Bernice. Unbelievable. Thirty years and she tells *you*."

"So did you date her?"

Malley sighed and gestured for her to make a turn at the light. "No, we didn't date."

"Then what was she to you?"

Malley ran his hands down the scruff on his neck. His eyes widened, and he shook his head sadly. "I'm such a stupid detective. Did Morales even bail?"

"No," she said.

Again, he shook his head, chastising himself for his idiocy. "They should take my badge for getting into your car. It's that baby face of yours. That's why I didn't see this coming."

"Come on, Malley. Starla's dead. What does it matter now?"

He sighed, glanced around the street as if someone could eavesdrop, and grumbled, "She was my CI."

Oh. Confidential informant. "Shit," Billie said. That complicated things. "How did that even happen?"

Malley pointed to a street sign with a thick finger. "Over there. Turn left."

Billie palmed the steering wheel.

"You can stop here."

She parked in front of a tired-looking split-level house with a brick exterior and a postage-stamp-sized front yard.

Malley exhaled and got out of the car. Billie followed.

He sighed again, wearing his exasperation like a cheap suit. "Whattaya doin'?"

"We're not done talking," she said, climbing his stoop.

He gestured around. "The neighbors are gonna think you're my girlfriend."

Billie snorted. "No one's gonna think that." She waited while he fished out his keys.

Malley pursed his lips, probably agreeing that she was right, and unlocked the front door. He pushed it wide open and gestured hurriedly for Billie to enter. He flicked on the light, illuminating a living room with worn carpeting and a leather sofa that had been scratched to death by an unseen pet. He tossed his keys into a catch-all bowl on the coffee table, shrugged off his wool coat, and draped it over a dining room chair. He went into the kitchen. "Can I get you a water?"

She stood awkwardly in his living room. "Do you have any info here on Starla's murder?"

"Does this look like an evidence lockup?" Malley slammed the fridge door and leaned against the doorframe that separated the kitchen from the living room.

"Come on," she said. "I need newspaper clippings, stuff that hasn't been digitized."

He twisted the plastic cap off the water bottle. "You gonna tell me what this is really about?"

Billie shrugged. "You gonna tell me how Starla became an informant?"

Malley chugged the water and glanced up at his popcorn ceiling. "She was responsible for the arson fire at the *Lucky Lous.*"

"Why?"

"She said she was trying to get away from Colfer."

Billie dropped onto the sofa. "For real?"

Malley nodded. "For real." He set the plastic bottle on the coffee table and opened the door to a coat closet. He hefted a black binder from a shelf and set it down in front of Billie. "A firefighter was hurt in the blaze. She could've done serious time." He opened it up to reveal yellowing articles in plastic sleeves. "There. All yours."

"What were you hoping to get out of her? Stuff about the Torn Crosses? The Goffs?"

"Among others," he said vaguely. "She had intel on several ongoing cases."

"If Colfer Dryden had found out what she had been doing, he would've killed her. Slowly."

"No one knew what Starla was doing," Malley said. "Only me. If she had something to share, she would go to *Nagel*'s, put in an order. Bernice would call me. I'd come. Pay for the food. And we'd leave separately. Then I'd follow her out to the parking lot, and we'd talk."

"That's not a foolproof plan. You sometimes ate together. A

Torn Cross member could've easily been tailing Starla," Billie pointed out as she flipped through the binder.

"Colfer's people wouldn't be caught dead near *Nagel*'s," he said.

Billie blinked up at him. "But Neil's guys went there." She found Malley's chicken scratch on notebook paper. He had written down dates and events just like Jasmine had done on the notecards.

May 1990. Starla Wells gets booted from Pembroke Hotel after a drunken altercation.

She pointed to his crossed-out notes. "Nothing here?"

"False lead. She was having a drink at the bar when she was told to leave."

"Why?"

"Someone recognized her from *Malta* and wanted her gone. Complained that she made the place trashy."

"That's obnoxious," said Billie. "What about the 9-1-1 call from Jasmine's cards? I think it was December. You don't have it here."

His eyes narrowed, creating a little ridge. "Must've not been important. And I'm not continuing down some rabbit hole a college student drummed up. It brings up bad feelings."

"Because you think you failed her? Starla could've been killed because they knew–"

"Don't you think I know that?" he barked. "You know what? Take the binder. There's nothing in there that I haven't looked at a million times. Just go home."

Billie rose from the couch. "Thanks." She grabbed the binder while Malley held open his front door.

"Morales was right," he said as she maneuvered down the front steps. "You are more trouble than you're worth."

"Wait." Billie turned around. "Morales said that?"

But it was too late. Malley had already shut the door on her.

CHAPTER THIRTY-EIGHT

Billie sat cross-legged on her bedroom floor. She'd kicked off her Converse low-tops and traded her sweatshirt for a pajama shirt. A cup of coffee sat beside her, nestled in a floral-rimmed china saucer. The binder that Malley had given her was open wide like the wings of a giant crow.

Malley was correct in that there wasn't anything in here that proved revealing, just newspaper clippings on Starla's disappearance. A few enlightened reporters expanded upon the dancer's origin story but not by much – she had been a party girl who frequented Manhattan's club scene until she got embroiled in organized crime, but it was all fairly vague.

As time elapsed, the articles became shorter and shorter, getting relegated from the front page to a two-inch box sandwiched between local events and the daily comics. And then finally they disappeared altogether, just like Starla.

Even the detective's notes went from careful, tidy handwriting to frenetic, frustrated scribblings.

Sighing, Billie opened her computer and shifted it onto her lap. The processor whirled and churned as it woke up, hesitant to do business at this late – or early – hour, depending on how she looked at it. Before all this, Billie had been so focused on Jasmine's connection to Colfer Dryden that she hadn't thought to connect synapses between the girl and Starla Wells, but she would now.

The crimes were so similar. Pretty girl dies, and her jewelry goes missing.

Billie opened Reddit and entered Starla Wells into the search bar. Plenty of cold cases had subreddits devoted to them, and Billie figured that this one would be no different.

She didn't find a Starla Wells exclusive subreddit, but she did find one for the Sleuth Squad with over a thousand members and two moderators: **u/TashaNickels** and **u/JasmineFlowers12**.

Billie settled in against the foot of her bed and yawned. She skipped the top thread, which was a post memorializing Jasmine, and scrolled down. She saw a bunch of posts with links to the *Murder Girls* podcast and a top post from **u/TashaNickels** banning self-promotion.

Billie wondered if that was a dig at Jasmine and Nuri.

Blinking away the exhaustion, she scrolled down further until she ended up at a thread titled Starla in Italy.

Interested, Billie clicked on it and read.

r/StarlaWells
u/Starlalightbright • 10 days ago

Starla in Italy

My grandma was a cabaret singer in her day and she said that Starla stole a bunch of money from Neil Goff and fled to Italy where she's been living under a fake name. Barletta. Anyone check into it?

u/Teadrinker2345:
No, but I heard she was murdered and buried in a vineyard in Long Island.

u/Taptap:
Witness protection makes the most sense. Or dumped in the Pine Barrens.

Finally, Tasha jumped in and wrote:

u/TashaNickels:

Moderators will start kicking people out of this sub for this kinda stuff. Only real working theories can be posted for discussion.

Billie had to laugh. *Real working theories.* Who determined what was real and what was far-fetched when a dancer with mobster ties went missing? In her estimation, everything was fair game.

Billie glanced at the clock and then closed her eyes. She was exhausted, and even another cup of coffee wouldn't help her now.

Somewhere, she heard her phone buzz. She patted the rug for the rectangular shape and scooped up her cell.

A text from a familiar number lit up the screen.

Aaron.

How are things? Papa Dukes is antsy.

The police must have been making a real nuisance of themselves.

Billie wrote back simply, *Working as fast as I can.*

He wrote back, *I know. Sorry. Night.*

Night, she replied.

She rubbed vigorously at her eyes, sipped her coffee, and went back to the subreddit. After an hour of combing through every wonky conspiracy from Starla being a Disney heir hiding out in the Caymans to her becoming an Instagram influencer, Billie decided to call it quits. She closed the laptop and the binder and shoved them both under the bed.

Malley's newspaper clippings. The subreddit's conspiracies. There was only one girl group that could help her sort through everything.

The Sleuth Squad.

Good thing they had a meeting tomorrow.

CHAPTER THIRTY-NINE

The next morning, Billie popped the last bite of a breakfast muffin into her mouth and wiped the crumbs from her palms. She sipped from an extra-large double-shot latte that she'd bought downstairs in the student center and dragged herself down a long, mauve-carpeted corridor toward a meeting room nestled between the janitorial closet and Kentwell's Greek Life offices.

Her eyelids felt as if they were weighed down by anvils.

She pushed open the door and collided hip first with an oblong conference table. On the far end was a portable chalkboard covered in names and lines that zigzagged across it like a spiderweb.

Billie dropped her bag into a cushioned chair, the upholstery embedded with brown stains, which certainly explained the aroma of stale coffee that permeated the air. She glanced down at the cushion. At least she hoped it was coffee.

She yawned and approached the board with her hands behind her back. She followed the chalk lines as they snaked from one name to the other. She recognized many of them: Neil Goff, Colfer Dryden, Mama Ree, and Detective Malley.

The players. A game of Clue.

Colfer Dryden in the strip club with a knife.

And yet there was one name she didn't know.

A voice snapped, "I hope you didn't touch anything."

Billie whirled around.

Tasha Nichols blew into the room like a storm. She held her

cell phone in one hand and an *Ugly Mug* to-go cup in another. Her messenger bag dropped from her shoulder to the tabletop.

Billie raised chalk-free palms. "Not a thing." But then, just to be a shit, she tapped her finger to the board, smudging a line of white dust as she cleaved the name in half. "Who's Ms X?"

Tasha glanced over at the board, spotted Billie's handiwork, and swiped the chalk from the wooden frame to fill in the letter that Billie had accidentally erased.

"We don't know," said Tasha, not even trying to hide her annoyance. She was the kind of girl who was perpetually irked with the world because it couldn't keep pace with her. "It's a placeholder for a woman who came into the club and threatened Starla."

Billie thought back to the subreddit and the nutjobs popping in with half-assed theories of Starla Wells living her best life in Costa Rica or being buried under the Statue of Liberty. "Have you verified this information?"

Tasha frowned. She was also clearly someone who didn't appreciate being questioned. Billie wondered how well that went over with other Sleuth Squad members.

"We verify everything we can," she said.

Billie pointed to the board. "How? How did you verify it?"

Tasha glanced at Billie and then at the board and then back at Billie. She sighed. "Jasmine had checked into it."

"You must have asked her where she got the information." Billie stared at Tasha.

Again, Tasha sighed. She was clearly put out by all the questions. Alpha types didn't like having to prove their authority, and yet Billie simply wished that people would tell her what she needed to know the first time she asked.

"The drag queen told her," said Tasha, nodding at the board.

Mama Ree. Why would Mama Ree share that kind of information with Jasmine? "What else?"

Tasha stepped up to the chalkboard, her broad shoulders nudging Billie out of the way. She picked up a piece of blue chalk and retraced one of the many lines that connected Mama Ree's name to Starla's. Then she stared at it, quiet, contemplating.

"Tasha?" Billie asked.

The girl shook her head. "Jasmine said she had learned details about the case that would blow everything wide open."

"Like what?"

Tasha turned to Billie, hands on hips, lip jutted out. Defiant and defensive. "She didn't say. She died before she could."

"Is that what she called you about?" asked Billie. "The night before she died, she left you a message."

"How do you know that?"

"I have my sources too. That I verify," Billie added. She spread her arms wide. "This is your club. Your big cold case. If Jasmine knew something, why wouldn't she share it with everyone right away?"

"I'm sure she had her reasons," said Tasha with a hint of bitterness. A flicker in her gaze made Billie think that this was a front. Tasha had no idea what Jasmine had planned to do, and she was not happy about it.

"It isn't my big case," Tasha added. "I mean, not initially."

Billie said. "Not to sound cold-hearted, but on the outside, the Starla Wells murder sounded like a simple mugging. What was the attraction?"

Tasha cocked a brow. "A simple mugging? With Torn Crosses and Neil Goff?"

"Yeah, but you only know that *now*. How did Jasmine learn about this?"

Tasha shrugged. "Jasmine has always been into true crime. She had a blog when she was in high school, and she would discuss all these old cases."

"Like Michelle McNamara," Billie said. "She wrote a popular blog before her book."

Tasha's eyes lit up. "Yeah. Like that. Jasmine always cited her as an inspiration."

Except the Starla Wells case was small potatoes compared to the Golden State Killer. Billie had had so much trouble finding stuff online that she'd had to pester Malley into turning over his binder of newspaper clippings. It didn't explain how it had blipped onto Jasmine's radar.

"So Jasmine turned you on to Starla Wells," asked Billie.

Tasha nodded. "It's what got the Sleuth Squad growing. We're amassing a large following."

"Jasmine was really into that sorta thing, right? Her podcast? She wanted a fan base?"

Tasha waved that idea away like swatting a bug. "She didn't want fans. She wanted to start a movement." She gestured at the chalkboard. "I know when you look at this, all you see are tinfoil hats, but our investigative work might actually solve cases the police can't. The more people who are involved, the more heads working together, the better the outcomes."

"Too many chefs spoil the soup," said Billie.

Tasha gave her a look.

"I went on your subreddit last night. There's a ton of garbage to sift through. Starla's on a cruise boat in the Mediterranean," Billie scoffed. "Stuff like that muddies the work; it doesn't enhance it."

"You're only saying that because you're being paid by the Russos," said Tasha with derision.

Was being paid.

"Jasmine was going to break up with him, you know?" said Tasha.

"I wouldn't have blamed her," Billie said. "He was a mess, but I thought she loved him."

That caused Tasha to cackle. "Jasmine loved our *cause* – Sleuth Squad. But Tommy – he was no good to her."

"Did he hurt her?"

She shrugged. "I don't know, but she got what she needed from him and–" She wiped her palms against each other.

He was no good to her. Maybe it wasn't that he treated Jasmine badly but that he had served his purpose.

"Did you like the Murder Girls podcast?" asked Billie.

"It's all right, I guess. It just skimmed the surface."

"And Jasmine wanted to dig deeper?"

"Definitely."

"It didn't bother you that Jasmine was hiding stuff from you? That she might've solved Starla Wells's murder and didn't tell you?"

"I'm sure she was going to," Tasha said insistently. "But then she died."

"Interesting choice of words. You said *died,* not *was murdered.*"

"That's what I meant." Tasha checked her phone screen and then flicked her gaze to the door. Girl didn't major in subtlety. "Meeting is starting soon. It's only for current Kentwell students."

"I still need to see your Safety Brigade log. I want to know if Jasmine called for an escort and who responded."

"Yeah, sure," she said absentmindedly. "Later."

Billie slid her bag strap over her head and adjusted it on her hip. One thing was for sure – Jasmine hadn't been sharing everything with her Sleuth Squad members. Maybe Tasha was downplaying how that really went over. "I'll go now."

"Great," said Tasha brightly, straightening up. Her cell phone vibrated on the table, but she grabbed it before Billie could see the screen.

"One more question," said Billie. "Will there be a vigil for Tommy Russo?"

"Huh?" Tasha was scrolling through her phone.

"A vigil? Like the one you organized for Jasmine?"

Tasha shrugged. "*His* friends should plan one."

But Tommy didn't have friends, and Tasha knew that.

Billie closed the door on her way out.

CHAPTER FORTY

Shortly afterward, Billie drove her car into the guest parking lot of a luxury building in Hackensack that boasted a gym, lounge, and twenty-four-hour security. Rent was steep, but the amenities were plentiful. Also nothing was too good for Mama Ree.

Billie stepped out of the Hyundai and into the increasingly frigid temps. Her checkered Vans sneakers padded along the asphalt before sinking into the plush carpet that snaked into a gleaming lobby.

She pushed her sunglasses to the top of her head, allowed her eyes to adjust to lemony sunlight that streamed through Windex-streaked glass, and gave her name to a Black man standing behind a marble counter. She felt as if she was checking into a ritzy hotel. *If only.*

"I'm here to see Mama Ree," she said. "She's expecting me."

The guard quirked an eyebrow.

Right. Mama Ree *inside* the *Malta Club* only. "Mr Reece Johnson," she clarified, the name sounding foreign to her tongue.

"ID, please," the guard said in a deep baritone.

Billie complied and slid it across the glossy countertop. He glanced at the photo – her bangs had air-dried wonky that day – and returned her driver's license. Then he unearthed a tablet from behind the counter and swiped a thick finger across the screen, nodding when he must have spotted her name on an approved list of visitors. He provided Billie with a stylus and pointed to an empty box on the screen. She signed her name with a flourish.

"Apartment 4F," he said.

Billie smiled in response, hiked her bag onto her shoulder, and opened the heavy door to the stairwell. For exercise, she hustled up the four flights and found Mama Ree's door, third on the left. She gently rapped on the dove-gray wood.

Billie had seen Mama Ree without stage makeup several times, but she was still taken aback when the door opened to reveal a lithe Black man in a sweater vest and pressed slacks. For the briefest of seconds, Billie thought she had appeared in front of the wrong apartment until Mama Ree grinned and gestured for her to enter. "Come in, come in. Make yourself comfortable on the sofa. I brewed tea."

"Uh, thanks," said Billie, feeling a weirdness settle over her as she made her way toward a small living room that sat opposite an equally small but modern kitchen. "I really appreciate you seeing me on your day off."

Billie plunked into a soft floral couch and set her bag on a red-tasseled rug. The windows were flanked by heavy draperies, and the television was sandwiched between mahogany bookcases that were cluttered with thick hardcovers and tchotchkes.

"Mama," Billie began but then stopped herself. "Reece?" She squirmed in the cushion, said, "Sorry," and shook her head. She wasn't used to addressing Mama Ree as anything but her stage name. She wasn't used to seeing Mama Ree as anything but a glamorous woman with bouffant hair and eyelashes as long as fingers.

"Don't be sorry, Belinda. At the *Malta*, I am Mama Ree, but here–" he gestured, his arms wide "– I am simply Reece. It's what my daddy named me." He settled into the tweed-upholstered chair opposite her and leaned over the table. Picking up a ceramic teapot and pouring hot liquid into delicate china cups, he glanced up at her. "Sugar cube?"

"Please," said Billie.

Reece dropped a white square into her tea. He held out a saucer of butter cookies. "I baked them this morning."

Billie plucked one off the plate and nestled into the overstuffed cushions. Her eyes bounced off paintings in gilded frames and potted plants with long green fronds. A striped cat with a lion's mane slid its body against Reece's pant legs. He scooped up the cat and kissed its head before dropping it back down to the rug.

Billie swallowed the cookie in a bite and sipped her tea. "Not gonna lie, this isn't how I thought your place would look."

Reece raised his brow. "You expected gaudy mirrors and a life-sized canvas of Beyoncé on the wall?"

Yes. "No," said Billie, her cheeks suddenly warm. She certainly hadn't anticipated this apartment, which seemed one cucumber sandwich away from the receiving parlor at Buckingham Palace. The Mama Ree that Billie knew spent her nights reapplying makeup next to a topless dancer who was powdering her ass cheeks after a private lap dance. Billie simply didn't know how to reconcile these two halves of one person. Finally, she said, "It's just hard for me to separate you from the club atmosphere."

"That's fair, honey." Reece sipped his tea and set the cup on a saucer. "Mama Ree is an act that I perform. But if all you ever see is the act, then you'll never recognize the real person underneath."

Clearly, Reece was letting Billie's ignorance off the hook, but his words buzzed around her head. *An act. A performance.*

"You mean like Starla," she said.

Reece smiled, all lips and no teeth.

"She was a performer, like you," Billie continued.

"That she was," he said, flicking the bitterness from his tongue.

She shifted and then fished out a pen and notebook from her bag, heightening the formality of the interview and making her feel even more uncomfortable. She felt as if she was sitting down with a stranger.

She clicked her pen. "Did you two get along?"

"We were friends-ish," Reece said before clearing his throat. "I thought Starla took too many risks. She flaunted–"

"The diamond," said Billie, realizing too late that she had interrupted. "Sorry."

"That and other things," he said dryly.

"Like what?"

"Let's say she hung out with the wrong people," said Reece.

"Like Colfer Dryden," said Billie.

"Starla tried to avoid that man at all costs."

She snatched another cookie and spoke around it. "Did you know that Starla burned down the *Lucky Lous*?"

Reece nodded.

"Did she tell you why she did it? I mean, that's insane. If he had known–"

Reece pursed his lips. "I see what you're getting at."

"Did she tell you why she did it?" Billie asked.

Reece shrugged. "She mentioned something about a transaction. She spoke in riddles like that."

"Transaction implies someone asked her to start the fire. Malley made it seem like it was an act of desperation. Something she did to get away from Colfer."

"Why not both?"

That gave Billie pause. "Do you think Neil made her do it?"

Reece slid a butter cookie off the plate. Before taking a bite, he said, "Don't you think Neil Goff would've relished setting fire to Colfer Dryden's place himself?" He popped the cookie into his mouth.

Billie gave that some thought. He would. She scribbled down a few notes. "If Colfer knew what she had done…" She let the implication dissipate around her. A beautiful woman. A vengeful Colfer Dryden. Billie shuddered at what she imagined. Unlike Neil Goff, Colfer did his own dirty work; he relished it.

"I normally wouldn't disagree with you," said Reece. "But Malley felt awful about Starla. If he could've nailed Colfer for this, he would have. Believe me."

"Doesn't mean Colfer didn't have one of his crew members pick her up."

"I suppose it doesn't," said Reece, offering Billie a slight concession. "But Malley assured me that he couldn't find a link."

"What about Neil?" asked Billie. "What would he do if he had found out about Starla and her arrangement with Malley?"

"He would've killed her," said Reece matter-of-factly.

"Well, there ya have—"

"But he already knew about it." He sipped his tea behind a conspiratorial smile. "It was a bargain they drummed up. He knew that she'd been nabbed by BCDB. He also knew she wouldn't disclose anything." He gave her a pointed look. "You might want to ask yourself what Detective Malley might have done if he had been aware of *that*."

Rule Number 2: I ask the questions.

Billie decided to move on. "What was Starla's personal life like?" She tapped her pen against a photo of Starla that she had found in Malley's binder. "What can you tell me about this diamond she wore? Was that a gift from a suitor?"

"Suitor," Reece said with a chuckle. "How quaint."

"A boyfriend, then?" Billie clarified. "A girlfriend?"

Reece shrugged. "Perhaps."

Billie stared, hoping to tease out a response with silence.

Reece sighed then elaborated, "If she was wearing an expensive new skirt, she would say that it was a gift from her man. Her rent mysteriously paid? A gift from her man. I assumed the diamond came from the same source. At first, I didn't think it was real. I mean, who wore a stone like that around our clientele? But I told you, she was a risk-taker. An unnecessary risk-taker." Reece shook his head as if he was reliving a conversation he had had with Starla many times.

It seemed to Billie that everyone looking out for Starla had inadvertently made her reckless.

Billie suddenly became interested in *a gift from her man*. She glanced up, a thought circling like a buzzard. "Was Neil her sugar daddy?" Starla had been a hot commodity, and Neil always took a piece of the action.

Reece must not have agreed, because that question elicited a snort from him. "A diamond worth half a mil? Neil was in no position to do that. And if he had gotten one off a truck, he would have kept it for himself. He had plans, and that money would've helped him out."

Billie ticked off her questions. "You told Jasmine that Starla had a run-in with a mysterious woman at the club. Could that have been Neil's wife?"

"I doubt it. They weren't even dating yet."

"A girlfriend?"

Reece shook his head. "Starla would've said."

"Well then, how did you know about this woman?"

Reece sighed. "I came in for rehearsal, and I saw Starla blotting her cheeks with a tissue. Someone had scratched her face. I asked 'Who?' and she said–" he raised his chin "–'some alley cat who thinks I'm moving in on her man.'"

"That's it?"

"That's it," he said.

"May I ask why you confided in Jasmine? Wasn't it clear she was fishing for info on Starla?"

"Listen, Belinda, I'm no dummy, but it had been thirty years, and here comes this girl, and she has this desire to solve Starla's murder." He sighed. "After all this time, the cops had given up. The leads were cold, and here she comes, and she *cares*."

Billie thought about how the articles had gone from front page to the back of the newspaper within weeks.

"But what if Jasmine had set her sights on Neil as Starla's killer?"

"I don't think she did."

"Why?"

"Neil and Starla were friends. She was a trusted confidant."

"I find that incredibly surprising. Neil isn't friends with any of his dancers except you. Maybe–"

"Honey, please. You need to move off this," Reece cut in. "Neil did *not* date Starla Wells."

"Why not?"

"She wasn't his type."

"Type? I thought Neil's type was tits and ass, and that's it."

"It wasn't quite that simple. Not back then."

Billie dropped her pen, her patience oozing through her fingers. Maybe Starla Wells wasn't the only one who spoke in riddles. "What am I missing? Neil Goff has always slept with his dancers. He points–" Billie snapped her fingers for effect "–plucks the girl from the dressing room, and takes her to his office…" Her voice trailed off, and she cringed, disgusted that Aaron came from this man. "Well, you know."

Reece looked at her with a bemused expression on his face. "Your grandfather didn't tell you everything he had on Starla."

Billie jutted her chin like a petulant child, suddenly defensive. "I have his files. I've read them."

"What I'm about to say probably isn't in those files." Reece took a delicate bite of the cookie. "Some stuff didn't make the newspapers."

Billie dropped her pen and exhaled dramatically. "Like what?"

Reece sipped his tea as if he had all the time in the world, but Billie didn't.

"Tell me," she urged. "I don't have a lot of–"

"Starla was transgender," he said simply.

"Oh." Billie swallowed, her throat suddenly dry from the cookies, her tongue feeling fuzzy from the tea. "*Oh*."

"Yes, it certainly complicated things for Starla." Reece sat back in the chair and folded his hands in his lap. He examined

Billie as she stared blankly ahead, her brain whirling and churning so heavily she was sure he could hear it.

"Who knew?" Billie asked.

"Who knew about her being born a man?" Reece asked.

Billie nodded.

"Well, I did, and so did Neil."

That surprised her. Neil Goff was a chauvinist.

"Did Colfer know?"

"No. That would've been a death sentence."

"Why wasn't this in the newspapers?"

Reece sighed. "The medical examiner was a friend of Malley's. He might have left it out to protect–"

"The cops who dated her?" Billie finished.

Reece pursed his lips. "I was going to say her legacy. Starla was a woman, no matter how she came out of her mother's womb. Malley and even Neil respected that."

"But this changes everything," said Billie. "Her murder could have been a hate crime."

"Yes," said Reece simply. "It's no safer to be trans now than it was thirty years ago. I do wonder, though, why your grandfather doesn't want you sniffing around this case."

"I never said that."

"It was implied. William Levine is holding out on you."

Billie pinched the bridge of her nose. A headache was blooming. She shook it off. She then wondered if the Sleuth Squad knew about this. "Did you tell Jasmine that Starla was transgender?"

"She already knew," he said nonchalantly.

It hadn't been on the chalkboard, so Tasha Nichols didn't know.

Reece watched her for a second as if examining her. "You and your grandfather are a lot alike. He couldn't see past Colfer and Neil either, which is why he could never get anywhere."

Billie snapped her head up. "What do you mean? I can see past them."

"Neil this and Colfer that."

"They're notorious criminals," said Billie.

Reece pursed his lips and set down his teacup. "I wasn't completely honest when I answered your question about Starla's personal life. She was getting close to someone."

"Who?"

Reece blinked at her and said, "A cop."

"Malley."

"No. Not Malley. Someone your grandfather was friends with. Someone he trusted. Someone he would never pursue."

A cop? That Gramps knew? That could be the entire booth of men who hung out at *Nagel's Deli*. A dozen.

No, not a dozen.

Just one.

"Ken Greenberg," she whispered.

Reece nodded and then tilted up the plate of cookies. "You want some for the road?"

Billie snatched the plate and tipped it into her bag. She dropped her pen and notebook in after them and gathered her belongings. "I gotta go."

Reece walked Billie to the door. "Please send Mr Greenberg my regards. Lord knows your grandfather didn't."

Billie decided to ignore that dig at Gramps. She thanked Reece and scuttled down the stairwell. She pushed open the door and dashed into the lobby, calling to the guard, "Sign me out!" She ran to her car, squinting against the sunshine before skidding to a halt.

The Hyundai sat at a funny angle. The back bummer dipped low, and a gash had been cut into the rear driver's-side tire.

She crouched and ran a finger over the jagged edges. *Shit.*

Had she run over something on her way here?

Except glass and highway debris couldn't have sawed into the rubber like that. A person had done this. Someone had followed her here, and then what? Slashed her tire to scare her? If Ian Colfer had done this, it seemed amateurish. Quite beneath him, really.

She hopped to her feet. A slashed tire could be a distraction. Or worse, a lure.

She spun in a circle to see if anyone was watching her, but she saw no one. Her heel twisted further into a mud puddle, making a soft squelching sound.

Mud puddle? But there had been days of crystal-clear skies, and what rain had showed up had been light at best. The parking lot was bone dry.

Billie swallowed hard and glanced down at her sneakers, which now sat in a viscous berry-red circle. She yelped and stumbled backward, slamming herself into the SUV parked beside her.

Her heart vibrated like a motor.

Her eyes traced a line from the red puddle to her trunk. Tipping her head to the side, she watched as red droplets fell from the undercarriage to the white paint line below.

Something – or someone – sat rotting in her car.

She stepped cautiously toward the trunk and thrust the key into the lock and twisted. The trunk popped. She raised the lid just a few inches and peered inside. Then she slammed it closed.

CHAPTER FORTY-ONE

"I'm glad you called." Aaron unlocked the trunk of his Acura and hefted out a brand-new tire. He rolled it toward Billie's Hyundai, careful to avoid the blood pooling on the asphalt.

"There really was no one else," she said matter-of-factly because there wasn't.

Aaron grinned.

It wasn't a compliment. There simply wasn't anyone else who would be able to deal with the massive amounts of blood in her trunk. Gramps would've made her call the police, and David, despite his nursing background, couldn't stomach cutting into a rare steak, let alone the bloodbath inside her vehicle at the moment. Blood but, thankfully, no body.

If this was some sick and twisted game Colfer was playing, he was winning.

"You don't want to call your detective boyfriend?" Aaron asked with a smirk.

"One, he's not my boyfriend, and two, the BCDB would impound the car. I can't afford to be without wheels right now."

Aaron stared at her for a beat more than was comfortable.

She squirmed beneath her coat. "What?"

He shrugged. "Nothing. You just surprise me sometimes."

She leaned against another parked car with her arms crossed and watched as Aaron jacked up the Hyundai to remove the damaged tire. He'd taken off his coat and rolled up his sleeves to reveal tanned forearms and a tattoo of a hamsa on his left wrist that he had never had when they were together. He had unbuttoned his collar, and Billie caught that scar again.

His souvenir from Israel. What *had* happened over there?

Biting his lip, Aaron tugged off the slashed tire and dropped it to the ground, carefully avoiding the blood that was congealing nearby.

"We gotta hurry," he said just as a gray Honda CRV with a security logo on the driver's-side door rounded the corner and stopped in front of Billie's car.

The guard from the lobby got out.

Billie positioned herself in front of the trunk, doing her best to hide the bloodstains.

The guard adjusted his cap and then took note of Aaron's dress shirt and expensive loafers. "Want me to call a tow?"

"We're good," she said brightly.

"I got it," Aaron called as he tightened the lug nuts. "Nothing I can't handle."

"If you're sure," the guard said, sounding very unsure.

"He's almost done," Billie said with a smile, trying to draw the guard's attention to her face. "He's more rugged than he looks."

That shamed the guard. He lifted his cap to scratch his forehead. "I didn't mean to imply anything. It's just that usually, folks have Triple A."

"Not me," she said. "It requires a membership fee."

Aaron got to his feet and brushed stones and silt from his pants. "I'll get you one."

"I don't need you to pay for an automobile club," she said through gritted teeth.

"Don't be ridiculous," said Aaron. "It's for your safety."

"Then I'll pay for it myself." Billie's voice rose.

"But you can't afford it. You're broke." Aaron pursed his lips. "And I can."

Billie flushed.

The guard's eyes flitted back and forth between them, and

then he backed away. "I'll let you two be on your way, as long as everything is all right."

"Everything is fine," Billie said, staring at Aaron, her nostrils flaring, her fists balling at her sides.

The guard hurried into his SUV and drove off.

Aaron exhaled, his eyes never leaving Billie's face. "Get the bleach."

"The hell you talking about paying for Triple A?" she said.

"I was just trying to get him to go. I figured getting you pissed off would do the trick." He gestured toward the empty aisle. "See? It worked. Get the bleach and paper towels. We need to clean up."

Billie shook off the tension and grabbed the cleaning supplies and a plastic bag from Aaron's backseat. She unraveled the paper towels. "I don't even want to know why you're so good in this kind of crisis."

"I'd prefer you didn't ask," he said as he dropped the tire into his trunk.

She bent down and tried to scoop the blood off the asphalt, collecting bits of rock in the process. Maybe even bits of a person.

She threw the mess into the bag and got to her feet. Aaron gently ushered her aside and poured bleach over the spot.

She sighed. "I'll deal with the rest when I get home."

Aaron scoffed. "And let William Levine catch you? Hell, no. We're going to a place in Paterson. I know a guy who can help."

Billie opened her mouth to protest but snapped it shut. This really wasn't the time to argue. "I'll let you drive."

CHAPTER FORTY-TWO

Billie watched as Aaron's *guy* drove her car into the garage bay. Aaron had said his name was Lenny and to leave it at that. Lenny had a neck as thick as an elephant leg and eyes like two black pits.

She would definitely be leaving it at that.

Smells from the nearby dumpster crashed over them like ocean waves. A seagull pecked at trash scattered in a patch of weeds.

Billie heard the distant hum of cars speeding along Route 80. People on their way to someplace that wasn't a shady chop shop in Passaic County. Billie wished she could trade places with one of the drivers. Any driver would do.

Lenny hadn't even balked when Aaron said the trunk needed to be stripped and wiped down. Of course, Aaron had concluded the conversation by handing over a wad of cash. Billie supposed she should've been appalled by the exchange, but she'd had too much practice observing criminality to be fazed by anything Aaron did anymore. Probably for the best now that she was the one in need of his underworld connections and money. Billie wasn't flush enough to pay anyone off, even disreputable mechanics.

Billie texted her brother to keep him apprised of her whereabouts.

Car trouble. At mechanic, she wrote.

She could picture David sighing dramatically.

He wrote back, *Need me to pick you up?*

She sneaked a glance at Aaron, who was leaning against an old Ford Explorer that had been sitting in the lot so long crabgrass had sprouted from its tires. His sunglasses hid his eyes from the afternoon sun.

No. How's Mom?

Watching TV.

Shouldn't take long. Cya later.

She put her phone away, dissatisfied. She wasn't sure what she expected David to say. *Oh, Mom's gardening in the backyard. She took up cross-stitch. She's making sourdough.*

Billie kicked a rock and shoved her hands inside her pockets to keep them warm.

She and Aaron said nothing for a while, their silence broken by the buzzing of a drill – the kind used to dismantle a car.

"It's a warning, Billie," he said finally, sounding exhausted. "Next time, it will be a body for you to find. Like that girl."

She had already considered that. "I doubt Ian can be bothered to do it twice."

"Billie, this is *serious*." He sounded serious, which sounded bad. Aaron had always treated most things with the gravitas of a circus clown. She could have used that levity now.

"Wait, you mentioned Ian," Aaron noted.

"Did I?" she said with a nervous laugh.

That elicited a look.

"So how are Damon and Shonda holding up?" she asked lightly.

"Dammit," he said. "What happened with Ian Dryden?"

"Nothing." If Billie mentioned that he had followed her into the ladies' room at Overpeck Park, Aaron would volunteer to be her round-the-clock bodyguard. And that was the last thing she needed.

"You're lying."

"Everything's fine." She kicked another rock and watched as it skittered across the cracked pavement, stopping only when it smashed into a rusty hubcap.

"Billie." He practically growled her name.

"You don't get to lecture me on safety."

"What does that mean?"

She traced an invisible line down her neck and raised her brows. It was a shitty thing to do, but he had it coming. Something had gone down in Israel, something that almost got him killed. He wasn't being truthful with her, so why should she be truthful with him?

Aaron pushed off the SUV and dug his shoe into the dirt. "Nice, Billie."

"You gonna tell me what happened over there?"

"No," he said definitively.

"Well, then..." She crossed her arms over her coat and caught her reflection in Aaron's aviator sunglasses. She saw her petulant stance and frown. It was not a good look.

But she wanted Aaron to understand that the truth worked both ways.

He took a step toward her. His shoulders softened. His lips were glossy.

She stepped back, forcing distance. "You wanna grab a bite?" Billie was in no mood to eat, not with the blood and Aaron standing so close to her, but it seemed like a good way to pass the time.

"Diner?" he asked.

She nodded.

"Let me borrow some wheels."

He jogged into the garage, giving Billie just enough space to reclaim her composure, and returned a moment later with a set of keys. He aimed the remote start button toward a car to unlock the doors.

Billie settled into the passenger's-side and took note of the pristine interior. If one good thing came out of this, it was that her Hyundai would get a decent detailing for the first time in its existence.

Aaron drove her to a quaint diner on Railway Ave that

looked like it had been transported from the 1950s. The sign out front boasted that it had "the best coffee in town."

My kind of place, thought Billie.

They grabbed a booth by the window, where Billie had a view of utility trucks. Aaron ordered an omelet. Billie asked the perky waitress for a recommendation but was met with cold indifference as the girl stared, bewitched by Aaron.

"Can't go wrong with French toast," said Aaron, so Billie ordered that.

Why had she thought this was a good idea? She was better off outside the chop shop where she could pace or walk laps, anything to avoid awkward conversation.

She hadn't even realized her knee was bobbing up and down until the coffee cup rattled against the spoon, and Aaron had to place a hand on her leg to stop it from shaking.

"Sorry," she said. The heat from his hand only made her insides rumble even more.

Why was she so nervous? It was just Aaron. Sure, he looked sexy in a wrinkled button-down shirt, tire grease smudged on his neck, and he still smelled like whatever expensive cologne he wore, but it wasn't as if he was a stranger. Billie knew Aaron intimately. There were no surprises left.

Also, she reminded herself, he had left her for some big score in another country.

He had left her.

"What are you sorry about?" he asked.

"I'm sure you had other things to do today," she said. "Not bail me out."

"The only thing I had to do today was babysit Damon and Shonda, who argue like my parents before the divorce."

Billie laughed. Then, more thoughtfully, she added, "You could've just let them go."

"Believe it not, I offered, but Damon was worried that my dad would go after you once he lost his leverage. I assured him that I would not let *that* happen, but the weird Neo-Nazi has faith in you. Said he'll leave when you say it's okay."

"I can't even pretend to understand Damon Shane," she said. "One part skinhead, one part cinnamon roll."

"He got stuck in a life of crime," said Aaron. "I find that oddly relatable."

The waitress returned with a plate of eggs and a smile. She set the food down in front of Aaron, the zipper of her top remarkably lower since she had taken their order. This girl must've been getting occupational lessons at the Bernice Waitressing School of Hard Flirts.

Turning to Billie, the girl said coolly, "Your food'll be up in a sec."

Billie nodded, appreciating the familiarity. "Just like old times," she said with a shake of her head.

Aaron cut up his omelet with a fork. "What?"

Billie blinked at him.

Aaron glanced up, his brows knit together.

"People were always coming on to you when we were together."

"Not true." He took a sip of coffee.

"Very true." Men. Women. Grandmas. Everyone wanted a piece of Aaron Goff, and they hadn't cared that Billie was beside him, sharing a plate of fries or holding his hand in a movie theater. He was a steak, and they were starving.

Billie was hungry now. Where was her food?

"It's always been that way," she said. "You ooze sex."

His mouth quirked into a smile. "I ooze sex?"

Dammit. Now she sounded as if she was flirting.

The waitress returned. She set the plate of French toast in front of Billie, her chest turned toward Aaron so he could peek at her lacey, sheer bra.

When the waitress had sauntered away, Billie pointed at him with her fork. "You can't tell me you've never noticed."

He stabbed his omelet and said, "I don't pay attention to other people when I'm with you."

She laughed nervously and then shoved a bite into her mouth so she wouldn't say something stupid. He might misconstrue it as foreplay.

Aaron leaned across the table and grabbed her hand. "I mean it." He stared at her. Then, more softly, almost sadly, he said, "I love you. I've always loved you. You know that."

Did she? If he had loved her, then why had he left?

"Billie," he began.

But the waitress returned, hefting a coffee carafe. "Fill me up," she said seductively.

Billie glared at the waitress. "Excuse you."

The waitress blushed. "I mean, refill?"

Aaron flushed. He cleared his throat, which meant he was about to lie. "I'm good."

Billie pretended that her toast was the waitress as she sawed into it repeatedly with her butter knife.

"I came back because of you," he said finally.

She shook her head. No, he had come back because he'd had his throat slit. "Then why were you hiding from me?"

He blanched.

"If I hadn't been sitting in Matty's office chair, would you have come to see me?"

"I wasn't sure if you wanted me to." He looked at her for a long time, waiting for her to contradict him, but she couldn't.

Of course she had wanted to see him. She had never wanted him to leave her in the first place.

She pushed away her plate. "We should get going," she said.

Aaron graciously paid the bill and drove her back to the chop shop, where they found the Hyundai sitting in the lot.

He asked her to wait a moment and ran inside the garage bay. Billie watched as he whispered into Lenny's ear. Lenny whispered something in response. They shook hands, and Aaron jogged back to where Billie was standing. He handed her the keys.

"So what was that about?" she asked.

"Nothing," Aaron said, clearing his throat. "Absolutely nothing." A long pause. "So what are your plans for the rest of the day?" He didn't look at her as he asked.

"I have to follow up on a lead," she said almost regretfully. "You need me to drive you back to Hackensack?"

"No," he said. "I can borrow wheels, and one of my dad's guys will return them. You'll be careful?"

"Of course." She pulled him toward her by the zipper on his coat and kissed his cheek. "Thanks for the grub and the bailout." With those aviators on, Billie couldn't see his eyes, but she caught her own reflection – pink cheeks, blown pupils. Her breath came in short bursts as if she'd just completed a sprint in Overpeck.

Aaron licked his lips. "Let me back into your life. Please."

Billie shivered. "It's cold. I should go home." She gave him a slight wave and got into her car. As she drove away, she stared at him through the rearview mirror.

CHAPTER FORTY-THREE

Later that night, Billie sat outside Ken Greenberg's house, which was a rundown two-story Cape Cod only a few blocks away from the Levine home. She inhaled the soft pine air freshener that Lenny had graciously hung from her mirror. For a man who dealt in stolen car parts, he was sure thoughtful about the details.

Billie stared at Ken's darkened living room and wondered when he would return. She had called Bernice at *Nagel*'s to see if he was there, but she hadn't seen him in days. Nor was he at the *Clam Bar*. Billie texted the bartender, who was in her contacts list, to send her a message if he showed up.

All she could do was wait in front of his house.

She sighed and opened the Safety Brigade app. It was still relatively new, and not all the students used it. Basically, it was like Lyft except rather than a car coming to pick you up, the nearest student did. Often, girls didn't call for an escort until it got dark, but Jasmine had been threatened. She might've used it more frequently.

Billie's phone buzzed with a text from the bartender at the *Clam Bar*.

Ken just walked in.

He'd be there awhile. So much for a stakeout.

Billie dropped her cell phone onto the passenger's seat in frustration. She glanced at his house. Shadows crept over the empty place.

He'd be gone for hours. What should she do now?

She peered at his front lawn. A small security sign poked out of a hedge to suggest the house was alarmed. No way did Ken pay a hundred bucks a month to keep his house monitored. He just wanted people to think that he did.

Old cop trick.

Billie pocketed her keys and swiped her cell phone off the seat. She tossed both into her bag and got out of the car. Checking the neighboring houses to see if anyone was outside, she crept up his front steps. She snapped on her latex gloves and tested the door handle to see if it was unlocked. Unlikely but not improbable.

It wasn't, but this wasn't the best spot to break in. Too easy to be seen.

She went around the rear, pushing open a crooked gate, and hustled up the back steps. She tried the door, and the knob twisted easily in her hand. She was a little disappointed; she would have to save her party trick for another night.

She understood that what she was about to do was illegal and that if caught, she could kiss her future PI license goodbye. But she also knew she was running out of time.

She opened the door and entered the dark kitchen. The smells of cooked chicken and stale booze permeated the air. Ken wasn't one to crack a window every once in a while.

She left the lights off and slid her penlight out of her coat pocket then thought better of it. A moving light in a darkened room was far more suspicious to outsiders than a glowing lamp. The neighbors would think that Ken was home. She flicked on the kitchen light.

Ken really did live like a frat boy. The sink was full of dirty dishes. Empty liquor bottles lined the window sill. She sniffed. And was that weed?

This was a terrible idea. Ken didn't live like a man who had murdered Starla and stolen her eight-carat diamond.

She opened the door off the kitchen to reveal an office the size of a bathtub. Like the rest of the house, it was a disaster. A mammoth desktop computer perched precariously on a table. Dust coated the desk chair. Framed certificates with glossy raised seals whose dates ended in the late eighties – commendations from the Bergen County Detectives Bureau – adorned the walls.

Billie went upstairs to be confronted by two closed doors. She opened the door on her right. It was the master bedroom. The queen-size bed was unmade. A joint was stubbed out in an ashtray on the nightstand. She opened the closet and glanced around. Ken's gun safe sat on the floor. If he had taken Starla's diamond, it would be in that safe. Only logical place.

She crouched and stared at the keypad. She clicked on her penlight and shone it toward the numbers. In the glow, she could see which numbers were coated in Ken's grimy fingerprints.

She took out her cell phone and typed the name of the safe into Google. It brought her to a listing on Harbor Freight. She read the specs. Heavy-gauge steel construction and an eight-digit code capacity.

Eight numbers were a lot to remember for a guy like Ken. They were a lot for Billie.

She grabbed a marker from her bag and wrote the worn numbers on the keypad on her hand.

2-6-7-5-1

There was no way to know which numbers were repeated. She couldn't tell if the five was more worn than others.

Ken was roughly her grandpa's age, but she didn't know his birth year. Was he born in 1951? She typed in 7-2-6-5-1. July 26, 1951.

It flashed red.

She reread the specs on the website. This gave her two tries before it locked her out for good.

Shit.

She stood up and stretched her back. She glimpsed a portrait of Ken in his cop uniform framed above the bed. What a weird place to hang a framed photo of oneself.

Unless...she shone the penlight on his uniform. There it was. His badge and the number: 25176.

Her fingers danced over the keypad. The safe flashed green, and a mechanism popped. She pressed down the lever, and the safe opened.

Voila.

She really would need to brag about this to someone later. Maybe Aaron. He would appreciate a good safe cracking, and it was like extending an olive branch.

She opened the door wider and shone her light inside. The first thing she noted was a pile of cash dressed in pink rubber bands with a Hebrew letter stamped on them.

Gimels from the *Malta Club*.

"Kenny, what are you up to?" Billie whispered.

His Glock was sandwiched between a box of ammo and some documents. She unfolded one, a life insurance policy that had lapsed. She then glimpsed stationery with BCDB letterhead.

She opened the letter. It was dated June 1, 1991, five days before Starla Wells had disappeared. It was a disciplinary letter. Ken was being asked to come in for an interview with a department-appointed lawyer to discuss his handling of the Russo Foods investigation.

Billie sat back on her heels. Well, this was something she hadn't expected to find.

Ken Greenberg had mucked up something involving Russo Foods. She wondered if Malley could shed light on it.

She picked through the other objects but didn't see a diamond or jewelry of any kind. She put everything back as she found it and got to her feet. She halted at the sight of the silhouette in the doorframe.

"What are you doing here?" Ken stumbled into his bedroom and fumbled toward her.

Billie smelled the whiskey rolling off him in waves. She thought if she didn't move, he would think she was a drunken nightmare.

"What are you doing in my house, Billie?" he asked again, his grandfatherly tone replaced by a vileness she'd never heard from him before.

"Looking for Gramps," she said, her voice barely registering even in the quiet bedroom.

"No, you're not. You're trying to get me, aren't you? I heard you've been to see Mama Ree." His voice sounded thick and throaty. Menacing.

Billie retreated a step and bumped into the bed. Ken moved toward her. She scrambled to her feet. "Don't do this. Think of Gramps."

"Always with the snooping, you Levines."

He dove for her, and she bolted out of the way.

The safe door was still wide open. Ken's Glock sat there, mocking her. He smiled eerily and snatched it, waving it around carelessly. Or maybe not. Maybe he had every intention of–

"Is that loaded?" she asked nervously.

"What do you think?"

"I think you're drunk, and you should be smart. You don't want to accidentally shoot your best friend's grandkid."

Ken laughed and gestured with the gun. "I told him you'd be a problem."

That stopped her cold. "You told my grandfather?"

Ken laughed and pointed the gun at her.

"Ken!"

A shot went off.

Her ears rang. She cowered. Then patted herself down. The bullet had lodged itself in the wallpaper.

Get out, Levine! Get out!

Billie shoved Ken into the dresser and ran out the door and down the steps. She went out through the kitchen and jumped off the back porch, landing softly in the grass. She got to her feet and sprinted to her car.

Shoving the key into the ignition, she glanced back at Ken's upstairs window just as his figure glided across the glass pane.

She couldn't see his face but knew he was staring at her. Then he brought his hand, the one still holding the gun, to his temple.

"No!" Billie cried, her screams overtaken by a flash of light and the pop of another gunshot.

Ken dropped from view.

Lights were thrown on in neighboring houses. A dog barked. Screen doors opened, squealing on rusty hinges.

With shaking hands, Billie turned the key, started the engine, and sped off into the night.

CHAPTER FORTY-FOUR

Billie bounded up the cement stairwell that led to Nicole's second-floor apartment. The interior hallways were lit in the dim glow of security lights that had been installed after several residents complained about safety, since a woman had been attacked by a man hiding in the shadows. That woman being Nicole and that man being her psycho ex-boyfriend.

Now it was Billie who dragged herself up the stairs, through the canary-yellow light, to seek refuge with a friend. She couldn't imagine going home now, avoiding Gramps's gaze and lying about where she had been. What she had been doing.

Because she would have to lie or risk him never looking at her the same way again.

She had her phone out and dictated a text to her brother.

"I'm staying at Nic's tonight," she said into her cell. "Everything's fine. I just needed a change of scenery." She hit Send.

David wrote back, *I'm worried about you.*

She sent him back a smiley face emoji.

She had briefly considered going to Matty's place, but there was a rumor that Aaron was crashing on his couch. If anyone could understand where her head was at right now, it would be him. But she was low enough and weak enough to know that she wouldn't be able to stop herself from slipping into Aaron's arms.

And then what?

Aaron wanted to be back in her life, but for how long? How long until he left the country again? If they fell back into bed together and things went south, Aaron could escape to Morocco or Tunisia, and she'd only be left with the reminders.

A television, loud and abrasive, blared from one of the adjoining apartments. Someone was listening to a cable news channel at the highest possible volume.

Billie pounded gruffly on Nicole's front door, her knuckles keeping pace with her nerves.

"Nic! It's me!" Billie cried.

Just then, the door across the hall opened. An elderly man peeked his head out, peering at Billie from beneath furry eyebrows.

"Hold your horses. I'm coming," Nicole replied, her voice muffled.

Billie heard the sound of metal sliding against metal and a chain rattling. Then the door opened to reveal Nicole dressed in a floral robe with her hair wrapped in a silk kerchief. A glass of merlot sloshed in her hand.

"Girl, what are you doing here?" said Nicole as she glanced past Billie to the old man across the hall. "It's all right, Mr Zerkofsky. She's a friend."

"Tell her to be more quiet," he said in a phlegmy voice. "It's late."

Nicole gestured for Billie to come inside and shut the door. "Don't mind him. He's the neighborhood watch."

Billie nodded several times, her chin bobbing up and down in a skittish rhythm.

"What's wrong with you?" Nicole sipped her wine carelessly, but her eyes had narrowed into examining lines. "You're making me nervous." She waved Billie further into the apartment, toward the kitchen and out of the cramped vestibule area. She went over to a slip of Formica counter between the fridge and stove to retrieve a bottle of red wine, already half empty, and refilled her glass.

Billie eyed the liquid. Viscous. Warm. A little bite. "Pour me one too."

"You don't drink," said Nicole as she made no attempt, no gesture, to find another piece of stemware.

Billie rummaged through a cabinet until she unearthed an orange plastic cup, a souvenir from a Mets game they had attended together two seasons ago, when Billie still did fun stuff, and held it out. "Pour."

"Jesus. All right." Nicole brushed Billie aside and plucked a clean goblet from inside the dishwasher. She poured a glass and handed it to her.

Billie graciously took it and drank. She hadn't even taken off her coat yet.

"Are you going to tell me what's going on?" Nicole asked as she leaned against the countertop.

Billie felt the wine travel down her throat and hit her belly, coating her entire body in a welcome warmth. She exhaled long and slowly and then pressed the glass to her chest like a shield.

Nicole softened. "You're freaking me out, you know."

"Sorry," said Billie. She took another sip. Then another, waiting for the wine to reach her head, to still her thoughts.

"Careful," said Nicole, "or you'll turn into your old, old man."

"I watched Gramps's best friend shoot himself in the head tonight," said Billie, her voice faltering slightly.

"Christ." Nicole refilled Billie's glass.

"I couldn't stop him," said Billie.

"Did you call the police?"

Billie shook her head. She whispered, "I don't think it would've made any difference. Also I had broken into his house. I'd have to explain that."

"Girl, you need to be smarter about this gig if this is what you want to do," said Nicole softly.

"I don't know what I want to do." Her eyes blurred with tears. "Gramps–"

"Is a tough old dude who has survived a lot. He will survive this."

Gramps survived things by mixing them into a highball and tossing it back. And as she gulped the wine and refilled the glass, she thought she understood why. "I'm responsible for whatever happens—"

Nicole took the bottle from her hand. "No, you're not. You didn't shoot him."

"I was in his house, searching, snooping." She said the last word with a sneer because it was all so ridiculous. She wasn't a private eye. She wasn't a badass mobster's kid. She had grown up watching Aaron and Matty skirt the law so much that she'd thought she could straddle both worlds and still be on the side of good. But she was nothing more than a busybody. A yenta. A twenty-four year-old Nancy Drew.

She wasn't even licensed.

Billie began to cry. Nicole's arms encircled her. She shushed Billie with that kind of soft whispering a mom uttered to soothe an upset child, and Billie relished it. She missed being cared for; she missed maternal affection. She missed being a kid.

She was Atlas, carrying the weight of the world on her shoulders, and man, was she tired.

Nicole rested her chin on top of Billie's head. "I'll make up the couch for you. Sleep here, and you can deal with this in the morning."

Billie sniffled. "What do I do about Ken Greenberg? How do I fix this?"

"Ah, honey, you can't. Whatever decisions he made are his to deal with in this life or the next. My mama always said that those are the rules we all agree to when we come into this world." She unwound her arms from Billie and headed down the hall.

Billie heard the linen closet door open and shut. She grabbed the wine bottle by the neck and carried it with her to the couch. By the time she had passed out, she was still wearing her shoes. But she remembered feeling lighter.

CHAPTER FORTY-FIVE

Billie awoke at dawn to a headache and a fuzzy tongue. Her stomach rolled like a boat in a storm. She spent the majority of the morning sitting on the toilet in Nicole's hall bathroom, her body desperate to rid itself of toxins.

By the time she emerged from the bathroom, drained and weary, her dignity in short supply, Nicole was standing at the kitchen counter in her bathrobe, brewing a pot of strong coffee.

"I am *never* doing that again," said Billie, massaging her temples.

Nicole snorted as she passed Billie a mug. "We all say that, and we all do it again. You want breakfast?"

Billie vehemently shook her head. "I gotta get going." She closed her eyes and sank into herself. Her shoulders hunched to her ears with the realization of the consequences she was going to have to face.

Nicole took the mug and poured the coffee into a travel tumbler. She added skim milk and snapped the lid on top. "You'll need this for the road."

Billie gathered her things, looping her arm through her wool coat as Nicole escorted her to the door. Billie wrapped her arms around Nicole's shoulders and squeezed as if she was clutching a life preserver. "Thank you. Truly."

Nicole patted her back, but before passing her the to-go cup, she asked, "Why won't you date Morales? He'd be good for you, y'know?" Billie opened her mouth to offer up an excuse or a vague response, but Nicole tugged back on that to-go coffee. "Don't you lie to me."

Billie sighed. "I like him, but I'm not sure if I like him enough to fully invite him into my life."

"Because you think he can't handle it?"

"Oh, I know he can't handle it," she said, snatching the tumbler, desperate for coffee. "It's just easier, y'know? Also there's–"

"Aaron."

"Yeah. Aaron."

"Ah," said Nicole with a smirk. "We finally get to the truth."

"Yeah, fine," said Billie, giving up. She sipped the coffee. "What about Calvin? You going out with him?"

Nicole gestured dismissively. "I waited too long to respond, so he's not interested anymore."

"Why don't you just tell him about your ex?" Billie asked. "Explain what happened."

"Pff," said Nicole. "No man wants to hear how an ex fucked you up royally. He'll see me as damaged goods."

Billie pointed at her with the tumbler. "You're not damaged goods. And weren't we just talking about honesty?"

"I want honesty from *you*," she replied. "I don't need to be TMI with some guy around the office who finds me cute."

"You're hot, not cute," said Billie, suddenly feeling as if she would sacrifice all future paychecks if she could stay in this apartment and avoid her life. But alas, she had to go. "I better head out."

Nicole hugged her again and then watched as Billie made her way down a stairwell now lit with buttery sunshine.

The drive home was a blur of ruminating thoughts. Of flashing lights and the popping sounds of gunfire. A car horn blared, and she yelped, feeling unhinged.

The caffeine was probably not helping.

She caught a glimpse of herself in the rearview mirror – eyes dull from lack of sleep, skin blue as a bruise, hair wild and knotted. Her mascara had crusted so that black flakes fell from her lashes, landing on the dark hollows below.

By the time she pulled the Hyundai into her driveway, she wanted to fall into her bed and disappear. But she knew she couldn't do that, not without first settling her debt.

She opened the front door. Voices murmured from the kitchen. Low voices. Hushed and mournful tones. The news about Ken had already traveled to the Levine house.

She swallowed hard, panic flooding her because she knew her grandfather would take one look at her, and he would know. He'd been a good PI for a reason.

She entered the kitchen just as David slammed the fridge door. "No eggs," he said with annoyance.

Except he wasn't addressing Gramps. Gramps wasn't even in the room. Neither was their mother. David was talking to Matty Goff, who sat at the Levines' kitchen table as if he lived there. He was dressed in a black sweater and rumpled jeans. His hair was mussed.

David whirled on her. "Good. You're home." Then, more critically, he added, "You look like shit. I've been calling you."

Billie slid her cell out of her bag and glimpsed all the notifications she had somehow missed. She flicked up the screen and said, "I had it on *do not disturb* by accident."

"What if there had been an emergency?" David asked, his voice rising.

"I just needed the night."

"What's going on with you?" he asked.

Matty's eyes bounced from one Levine to another. He began to rise out of his chair as if preparing to bolt. Which made sense. Running at the first sign of discomfort was Matty's default mechanism. David shot him a look, and Matty sat back down.

David set his sights on Billie. "When you didn't come home, I had to call out sick."

"I'm sorry," she began, setting Nicole's travel mug on the countertop. Then she asked, "Wait – where was Gramps?"

David threw up his hands. "How the hell should I know? He

didn't come home either. The two of you are out partying, and I'm doing all the work."

"David," said Billie, her voice steady despite her blood simmering beneath her skin. "I'm not having fun. I'm working. This is what we agreed to–"

"I didn't agree to this," he snapped. "I work all night. I barely sleep. I have no life. I want–"

My own place, he was going to say.

Billie's eyes flicked to Matty, who was sinking lower and lower into the kitchen chair as if willing himself to disappear. Now she understood why he was in such a rush to move out.

Were they officially back together?

"Maybe we should talk about this upstairs," she started.

"Were you with Aaron?"

That took her aback. "Excuse me?"

David jutted his finger toward the table. "Matty said you were with Aaron."

"I–" Matty began.

Billie cut him off with a look that could have sliced granite. She turned to her brother. "Aaron helped me out of a jam. That's it." She felt salty. How dare he accuse her of romance and trifles when she was clearly trying to save the lives of two people and solve the murders of two others? Not to mention bail her family out of financial hardship. All while trying to behave like a normal twenty-something year-old woman. Her life was nothing but death and near-deaths, and he had the nerve to accuse her of partying like some Jersey Shore reality star. She stepped toward David, her fury on full display. "Don't lecture me about sex when you have Matty here."

Matty colored. "I really should go–"

"No," said David. His eyes cemented on Billie. "He came here to keep me company and to help with Mom since you and Gramps couldn't even be bothered to come home!"

"I texted you. Told you where I was."

"But you didn't ask me if it was all right."

"I didn't realize I had to."

"I can't do this by myself. We need to put her in a home. She wouldn't want us constantly sacrificing our lives for her."

"We don't know what she wants," said Billie. "She can't really tell us."

"Well, I know what I want." David glanced at Matty and tilted his chin, a signal that it was time to go. "We're headed out to breakfast. I haven't had a Belgian waffle in ages. You're on duty."

Billie exhaled. The fight in her was gone, replaced with resignation and hurt. And shame. David was right. Billie relied on him too much to take care of their mother. She needed to pull her weight. "Where is Mom?"

"In the living room, watching her soap," he retorted. "Where do you think?"

But when they went to check on her, Shari Levine was gone.

CHAPTER FORTY-SIX

"I can't believe you lost her," Billie snapped at her brother.

"Me? Maybe if you'd been home, we'd have enough eyes on her." David's breath came out in huffs as they all filed out of the house, sneakers on, laces undone, coats with one arm through the sleeve. A Teaneck police cruiser drove past, and Billie held her breath. But the patrol didn't stop, didn't even slow down.

She exhaled. Maybe that was a good thing.

"Guys," said Matty. "Stop arguing. All right?"

Billie put her hands on her hips and squinted into the sunlight, craning her neck to see down the hill. She wanted to refute Matty – remind him that their mother was *their* problem, hers and David's, and that there was no Goff in this equation. But she kept her mouth shut. In this case, the more hands on deck, the better.

David opened up the garage door and unearthed his old ten-speed bicycle. He wheeled it down the driveway. "I'll head toward Cedar Lane. She couldn't have gone far. Maybe she was nostalgic for a bagel run."

"Why the bike?" Billie asked.

"It's faster, believe it or not. I can sidestep traffic laws."

Matty palmed his car keys. "I'll drive around the neighborhood."

Billie felt flustered, unsteady, not sure where she should go. "I'll–"

"You'll wait here," David ordered as he straddled the bike seat. "In case the police bring her home."

That wasn't what Billie wanted to do. She wanted to get in the car and circle the block or run down the street, screaming her mom's name. Something, anything to burn the anxious energy coursing through her. Standing still was too hard a job, but she didn't want to get into another fight. "Fine," she said. "Fine. Fine."

He quirked his brow at her. "*Are* you all right?"

"Please stop asking me that." She waved him off. "Just go."

A neighbor was dragging a trash can to the edge of the driveway. The plastic scraped along the asphalt, shredding Billie's nerves.

David took off on his bike, but Matty hung back, his mouth opening and closing like a garage door. "This isn't the time," she said, cutting off words he hadn't uttered.

"I didn't mean to tell him about you and Aaron, but it seemed so cute. Like old times. You guys hanging out."

Billie guessed that Aaron hadn't exactly mentioned the blood in her trunk, or Matty wouldn't have used the word *cute* to describe their afternoon together. She swallowed hard. "Do you even know what you're doing with him?" She pointed at the retreating figure of David as he pedaled out of sight, his back blurry and soft in the morning rays.

"I'm not going to hurt him if that's what you mean," Matty said. "He left me, remember?"

"Because you couldn't handle being around him," she said coldly. "His bipolar disorder is not going to evaporate because you sleep over. It's always going to be there."

"I know that," he said almost defiantly.

She scoffed. "We'll see."

Matty unlocked the driver's-side door of his Acura. He stared at her a beat. "You underestimate us, Billie. You think–" he glanced around for witnesses "–because we play fast and loose with the law that we do the same with the people we love."

"He left," she said.

It took a second for Matty to realize who she meant, but

when he did, his shoulders slumped. "He really didn't have a choice."

"Everyone has a choice," she replied, but the minute she said it, she knew it wasn't true. Sure, she could *choose* to dump her mom in some facility. She could *choose* to leave Teaneck and run off to Europe. But really, were those choices? Or just shitty decisions?

"We're Neil Goff's sons," said Matty. "Some decisions are made for us."

Billie had no comeback to that. It was far easier to hate Aaron if he had willingly given her up than if his mobster, murderer father made him leave. "Call me the minute you spot her," she said before traipsing up the stairs and into the house.

Aside from the ticking of an antique clock, the home felt eerily quiet. The air was so still that Billie heard her own labored breathing. She pressed her fingertips to her hairline, and they came away damp with sweat.

Was this the beginning of a panic attack? She dropped into the living room recliner and took deep inhalations. She leaned forward and shoved her head between her knees like she'd seen people do on television. She had no idea if it would work.

When she popped back up, the room teetered in her vision.

She smacked her cheek a few times, lightly at first then harder, trying to coax herself out of whatever mental break was about to happen.

She should call Gramps. He'd want to know about this.

But she did not want to call him lest the conversation turn to *other* topics. Like Ken.

The phone rang.

Not her cell phone but the house line. She scrambled to her feet and raced from the living room to the kitchen, snatching the cordless phone from the countertop. She pressed TALK. "Hello? Hello?"

A voice huffed into the line. "This is Lupe Rodriguez. Can

I speak to David or Belinda?" Then her voice quieted as if she was turning to someone else. "I'm calling your children."

"It's Billie. Is my mom with you?"

"Oh, good. Yes. She's here at my home."

"I'll be right there." Billie disconnected the call. She pocketed her house keys, locked the front door, and took off down the street at a clip, sprinting the one block over. She arrived at the blue colonial sweaty and panting.

Billie hauled herself up the front stoop and knocked rapidly on the storm door, sounding like a deranged lunatic.

Mrs Rodriquez opened up, tossed a dishrag over her shoulder, and took in Billie's schlubby exterior. "You didn't have to kill yourself getting here. She's fine." She opened the door to allow Billie to enter.

"I know, but I didn't want to put you out further."

Mrs Rodriguez raised her brows but said nothing.

Billie stepped into the foyer and noted a pile of shoes next to the staircase landing. She slipped out of her Vans to be polite and set them next to a pair of kids' Crocs. She noticed that her mother's shoes were not there. She followed Mrs Rodriguez into the kitchen, where a red pot bubbled on the stove. The house smelled garlicky and spicy.

Shari Levine sat at the kitchen table. A cup of coffee was set in front of her, but her eyes were glued to a tablet screen. Billie heard cartoon voices coming from the living room, where she guessed Mrs Rodriguez's granddaughter was camped out on the couch.

"She's watching one of my telenovelas," said Mrs Rodriguez, her back turned to Billie as she stirred a pot of sauce.

Billie texted David and Matty, *Found her. At the yenta's.* Matty wouldn't know what she meant, but David would.

Then she went over to her mother and kneeled, the way an adult would address a child, and said, "You can't leave like that. We were so worried about you." She gently tucked a strand of her mom's hair behind her ear. Then she peeked underneath the table. Her mother's feet were clad in dirty white socks.

"I didn't see her shoes," Billie said to Mrs Rodriguez.

"She wasn't wearing any."

"Oh my God," said Billie, her voice choking. Then to her mom, "You left without shoes." She stood, but the stress was a boulder, and she fell into the empty chair.

"I'm sorry," said Shari. "I forgot I needed them."

And that set Billie off. She broke into sobs.

It was such a simple thing. Everyone – even children – remembered to put shoes on before they left the house, but her mother had forgotten. Shari had forgotten to turn off the stove until the entire house smelled acrid with gas. She'd forgotten to twist off the faucet, and the tub overflowed, causing water damage in the downstairs hall closet. She'd forgotten to eat, to drink, to bathe. She'd forgotten the days of the week, birthdays, holidays.

She'd forgotten how to be herself.

Billie had thought she could do this, but most days, she felt as if she was drowning. And perhaps she could muster through it if she didn't also feel like she was confronting her future self at every moment. Staring at a mirror thirty years from now.

Shari stared blankly at Billie. "Why are you crying?"

But Billie couldn't answer. How could she explain to her own mother that she was destroying her slowly?

Mrs Rodriguez placed a gentle hand on Billie's shoulder. "It will be all right, *querida*."

"It won't," said Billie, drying her eyes with a napkin.

"There's no shame in getting help." Mrs Rodriguez placed a brochure for Safe Horizons on the table. Next to that, she set a plate of warm rice and beans. "Eat up. Then you can call them and say that Lupe sent you. My aunt gets a credit."

Billie stared at the food, hesitant to encroach further on Mrs Rodriguez's hospitality. She'd already done so much.

Shari's eyes were still glued to the tablet. She couldn't

possibly understand anything being said on that telenovela, and yet she was occupied. Almost serene.

Billie unfurled the napkin and set it on her lap. Then she picked up the fork and dug in. She hadn't realized that she was starving.

Mrs Rodriguez beamed.

Billie finished her meal and was tempted to ask for seconds but decided she'd imposed long enough. Mrs Rodriguez had been so generous, and Billie wondered how she would repay her. She should get her a Christmas gift this year.

Since Shari didn't have any shoes, Billie texted Matty and asked him to swing by so he could drive them home. When they pulled into their own driveway, David was already there, wheeling his old bike into the garage to be neglected for another decade or so.

David opened the Acura's back passenger's-side door and eased their mother out of the car. The fabric of his T-shirt was darkened with sweat. Matty got out too, stepping awkwardly around the car in case David needed another set of hands. He didn't, but it was a nice gesture.

They were a sight, the lot of them: Shari, her hair mussed and her shoes missing; Billie, wearing rumpled clothing; David, skin glistening from an autumn bike ride; and, of course, Matty, dressed in a gray sweater and dark jeans, his shoes as black as crow feathers.

David patted his sweatpants pocket and took out his cell phone, which buzzed in his hand. He swiped across the screen. "We found her." He silently mouthed "Gramps" to Billie and Matty. Then, "Uh huh. Oh, shit. God. Really? Not me? I'm the nurse."

Billie retreated a step and eyed her Hyundai, parked under a maple tree across the street. She wondered if she could make it to her car before David called her name, but it was too late. He pulled his phone away from his ear. "Gramps is at Hackensack Medical. Ken Greenberg shot himself. He wants you to meet him there."

"Why Billie?" Matty asked.

David stared at her intensely. "He said it had to do with Levine Investigations."

Hands shaking and heart spitting, she took out her car keys and headed straight for the Hyundai. Gramps knew she had been at Ken's place. Somehow, he just knew.

CHAPTER FORTY-SEVEN

The man at the information desk handed Billie a pass and said, "This must be visible at all times while you're in the hospital."

She nodded.

"No live flowers, plants, or fruit baskets allowed," he continued.

Billie glanced around to check that she hadn't actually brought anything like that with her. She hadn't.

"Balloons, silk arrangements, and greeting cards are okay."

She hadn't brought those either and felt ashamed. Ken was in a coma.

The man pointed to the elevators and directed her toward his room.

Billie hated hospitals. The emergency room was one thing – a place you went for a broken bone or stitches. But the upper floors, everything other than labor and delivery, signaled death. She knew she was being irrational, that of course, hospitals treated people and sent them home. But she didn't want to end up here. The numbers weren't in anyone's favor.

She thought of her grandma's last days, confined to a bed, tubes in her nose, needles in her veins, her skin as translucent as tissue paper. A machine had chirped so constantly Billie had wanted to toss it out the window to shut it up.

The elevator doors opened, and she was immediately assaulted by that smell – disinfectant and stale coffee. She passed an empty gurney and the nurses' station. A cookie platter, still wrapped in cellophane, sat on top of the counter, a card taped to the top, unread.

She didn't pause to check in. She knew where she was going.

She found Gramps sitting in a stiff chair next to Ken's bed. His bony knuckles propped up his chin. His eyes were closed.

Billie cleared her throat. Gramps's eyes flew open. "I came as soon as you called," she said, sounding like an actress in a drama.

Gramps shifted in his chair. He rubbed his bushy eyebrows and pushed himself up straighter. One machine beeped. Another kept pace with Ken's breath.

Billie didn't know the names of any of these contraptions. There was a reason David was the nurse and not her. He was a whiz with drugs and anatomy, but it all made her discomfited. She used to say it was because blood and guts grossed her out, but really, she was unsettled by how vulnerable the human body was. A car accident. A bullet to the temple. A brain disease.

Old age really was a privilege.

"What do the doctors say?" Billie asked.

Gramps shrugged. He wouldn't meet her gaze.

Billie spotted another chair by the window but chose to lean against the table, her arms crossed, her posture stiff. There weren't any fake flowers in the room, no cards or balloons. For Gramps to have been Ken's emergency contact meant that Ken had been a bachelor a long time.

Sure, Gramps was a widower, but he had a son – even if he was a good-for-nothing louse – and a daughter-in-law – even if she was ill – and two grandkids – even if they did have their own problems. Gramps had people. People who loved him, and who would mourn him if he had died.

Ken only had Gramps.

Billie felt horrible that she had sped off – that she hadn't bothered to call 9-1-1.

Gramps shifted again in the chair, pushing himself up a bit with his hands. He glanced at the open door as if waiting for someone to show up. When no one did, he said, "I know you were there."

Billie wouldn't insult either of them by denying it. So instead, she said, "How?"

He ran a hand over his scruff. He still couldn't look at her. And that was when she knew – he wasn't avoiding eye contact because he was upset with her or because of *her* guilt. He couldn't look at her because of *his*.

"You've been following me?" she said, pushing herself off the table and taking two steps toward him. She was closer to the bed now, closer to Ken's body – no longer big and lumbering but frail. Brittle. She could hardly imagine he had tried to kill her.

"Why?" she asked, her voice surprisingly steady, considering.

"I was worried about you," he said, almost imploringly. "All this nonsense with Neil Goff and his sons. The Starla Wells case. It got dangerous back then. I didn't want you getting hurt."

"But Neil didn't shoot me. Ken did. He just missed."

He got up from the chair and closed the door.

"Tell me the truth," she said. "Were you really worried about my safety, or were you more concerned that I'd find out that Ken had killed Starla?"

Gramps stared at her then, finally, but it unnerved her. "Do you think I would be friends with someone who had willfully murdered a person?"

"Not intentionally, no. But maybe you disregarded evidence so that you wouldn't have to confront the fact that he killed Starla Wells."

He waved that away. "You talked to Mama Ree."

"She said you ignored Ken's involvement with Starla," said Billie. "They had a relationship in the nineties, when things weren't exactly great for the queer community. Hell, even now, transgender women are still murdered at significantly higher rates than the general population. And don't think I don't hear the 'jokes' you tell when David isn't in the room. You really think Ken, who still uses a very awful Yiddish word to describe gay people, didn't freak out and kill Starla when he found out that she was trans?"

"Okay! Yes, Ken was horrified–" he bit back the word "–*upset* when he learned that Starla hadn't been born a woman, but I know Ken didn't kill her."

"Don't tell me it's because he didn't have it in him, because he shot at me," she spat back.

"He wasn't a saint," said Gramps, which elicited a scoff from Billie. "*But* he wasn't a monster."

"How do you know?" Billie hissed. "And if you are still so certain, why wasn't his alibi in your notes?"

Just then, a nurse entered the room. She unwound a stethoscope from her neck and cast them both annoyed looks. "I can hear your raised voices from outside," she said in a Jamaican accent.

"Sorry," Gramps and Billie mumbled in unison.

"Uh huh," she said, clearly not convinced. "Ten more minutes." Then she left.

Billie exhaled. "You purposefully left stuff out of your files. Why?"

Gramps stared at Ken, looking helpless and old. "Ken was working alongside the organized-crime task force. They were investigating Russo Foods and black-market olive oil. Ken mishandled evidence. It was sloppy police work that unraveled the whole case."

"Did he take a bribe from Paul Russo?" asked Billie.

"They had some type of financial arrangement," Gramps muttered.

"And you know that because you were tailing him? The night of Starla's disappearance?"

"I watched the whole thing go down," Gramps said with a sigh. "June 6, 1991." He turned to Billie. "I didn't put it in my notes because I didn't want it to get out. I didn't tell Mama Ree because

I couldn't trust that she wouldn't report it to Detective Malley."

"Gramps," Billie began.

"You gotta understand, Ken and I go way back. We grew up together. He's a brother. Yes, he's flawed, but he's still family." His voice choked. "I followed you to his house, and I watched you surveil his place. I even told him I would meet him at the *Clam Bar* so he wouldn't return home, but then you went inside. You *broke* in. You know you can't do that. It's against the law. It's against the rules."

"*Your* rules," she said. "That you've broken."

He sat back in the chair and glanced at Ken. "He was so drunk. He didn't know what he was doing. He's never really been a strong man."

Billie's eyes were wet, and her throat was thick with phlegm. "You think that if I hadn't been there, he would be okay?"

He waved that off. "It's because you're getting close."

"Close to what?"

"I'm not quite sure." He looked at her with red-rimmed eyes. "You know what's the worst part? If I hadn't been tailing him that night, the night Starla had been murdered, I would've suspected him of killing her too."

Just then, the nurse returned and unceremoniously announced, "Time to go."

Gramps pushed himself to a standing position. "Come on, kiddo. Let's go home." He turned to Ken and patted his knee. He said sadly, "See you tomorrow, champ."

CHAPTER FORTY-EIGHT

After the ICU, she and Gramps had stopped by *Nagel*'s for soup and a cold pastrami sandwich. He slurped the matzo ball broth and said, "So what are you going to do now?"

Billie moved a bit of coleslaw around her plate and shrugged. "I don't know. Got any ideas?"

"If I had any ideas, I would've employed them thirty years ago." He flagged Bernice over for a coffee refill, and she happily obliged. It reminded Billie of Aaron's interaction with the waitress the afternoon they'd had lunch together.

"Ken said something to me," she said hesitantly,

Gramps looked at her. "What?"

"He said, 'I told him you'd be a problem.' At first, I thought he meant you. He told *you* that I'd be a problem, but that doesn't seem likely now."

"You're a pain in the tuches, but I would never call you a problem," he joked.

"You mentioned that Ken had a disciplinary hearing at work because he got sloppy with the investigation into Russo Foods. He was likely taking a bribe–"

"I never got proof of that," Gramps cut in.

"He had cash in his gun locker," she said softly. "Wrapped in gimels."

Gramps sipped his coffee and slurped his soup, but he didn't add anything other than, "Gimels are Goff currency. What's that have to do with Russo?"

"Maybe nothing, but if he was willing to take bribes from

Neil, then he would've taken them from Paul."

"When that son-of-a-bitch wakes up from his coma, I'm going to kill him," said Gramps without a hint of humor. Then, in a more disgusted tone, he mused, "I can shake down Neil."

"I don't know if it matters anyway," she said, her thoughts whirling. "We keep focusing on the diamond as a motive, but what if this was purely a hate crime?"

"Could be both," said Gramps.

Leaning back in the booth, Billie ruminated on an idea. "Had Starla completely transitioned? You made it seem like no one had suspected that she was trans."

"Malley had told me that she had breast implants and genital reconstruction. So to answer your question, yeah, she had gone through with the surgery." Gramps sighed with exhaustion. "After she was killed, I went to her apartment. Someone had tossed her place. I mean, it wasn't trashed, but desk drawers had been left opened as if someone was looking for papers – documents."

"Hints of her old life," Billie filled in.

Gramps nodded. "I had found a Xerox of a money order under her dresser. Lot of zeroes. Dated years before she died. Thief must've dropped it when he was grabbing her stuff."

"I didn't see that in your files either," she said.

Gramps shook his head. "I left it for BCDB to put into their evidence, but Malley wasn't able to tie it to anything. The account was connected to an overseas shell corporation. Impossible to track down."

"Whoever gave her that money didn't want anyone to know about it," said Billie thoughtfully. "It had to be for gender-affirmation surgery."

"Possibly," said Gramps. "Careful working on assumptions."

"How else would she have paid for it? She couldn't have had health insurance. Did insurance even cover the cost in the early nineties?"

"How would I know?" said Gramps, shrugging.

"You said she spoke of struggles in her youth," Billie began. "What if she was alluding to struggles with her gender identity and not financial problems?"

"Everyone loved her, but no one knew her," said Gramps.

"Someone did." Billie texted Malley under the table. *Need to run something by you. Call me later.* Then she texted Aaron. She'd been wanting to check in on Shonda ever since their ill-fated meeting with Neil.

Need to see D&S now.

Why?

Need clarification on something.

Can't now. At club.

"I'm gonna drop you off, all right?" she said to Gramps as he thumbed through his wallet for cash to pay the bill. Probably another reason Bernice was so smitten with Gramps was that he'd always been a generous tipper.

"Hot date?" he joked, his brow raised in an arc.

If only her life was that easy.

"No," she said flatly. "Business."

"I miss this," he said. "The investigation work. It's almost fun with you in the picture."

"Almost?" Billie smiled. "Thanks."

By the time she had dropped Gramps off at the house, the sky had turned orange. Billie forgot that it got dark so early. The day felt dizzying.

Matty's Acura no longer sat in their driveway. She supposed it was too much to ask that a boyfriend hang around all day, waiting for the swing shift to take over. It was nice that he had stayed for a little while anyway.

She didn't bother to go inside, fearful that David would chide her for going back out. Gramps would make her excuses.

When she arrived at the *Malta Club*, the sun's rays tossed everything in a lascivious shade of blush. She pulled open the heavy wooden door and was immediately assaulted by dance music that popped in rhythm to bright, flashing lights.

Mama Ree, bedazzled in drag makeup, leaned over the bar as she directed a girl in a bikini top and bowtie on how to prepare the signature cocktail. Billie could hear her voice from the entrance. "Tanqueray, my dear."

The hostess, wearing a black miniskirt and sparkly bra top, smiled at Billie. "One?"

"No, I'm not here for a lap–" she stopped, wondering how best to phrase herself so that she didn't come across as a sanctimonious prude "–to see the show. I need to speak with Aaron."

The hostess's smile faltered slightly. "Is he expecting you?" she asked, her voice tight and controlled.

"No, but you can tell him that his ex is here," said Billie with as much salt as she could muster. Which was probably not the best response.

The hostess gestured that Billie should wait a minute before she made a beeline from the stand to Mama Ree at the bar. When her back was turned, Billie darted for the curtain partition and went into the backrooms.

She heard Aaron's voice before she spotted his face. "The books are pristine," he said.

"I know how to keep books," Matty bit back.

"Then why are you spending all this money at Prime Meats when Auggie's will adjust the numbers?"

"Because Prime has decent product and Auggie's shit looks just like that – shit."

"You're losing money that way."

"You mean Dad is losing money?"

"Same thing."

Then the sound of ruffling papers. Drawers opening and closing.

Billie chose that moment to pop her head in with a bright and elastic smile. She pointed a finger gun at Aaron and clicked her tongue twice. "Hey there, Bugsy Siegel." Then, more seriously, she said, "We gotta talk."

Aaron cast her a glance and puffed out his cheeks with air. He squeezed Matty's shoulder, a brotherly gesture that also suggested Matty was not free to go. "We're not done."

Matty leaned back in his desk chair, stretching his arms above his head. "Nothing I enjoy more than a 'cooking the books' lesson from the Bobby Flay of crime."

"Thanks, bro," Aaron called back before motioning for Billie to follow him outside.

He pushed open the door, and they entered the alley, where the dumpsters sat like green leviathans.

She whirled on him. "Hey, Ken Greenberg had stacks of *Malta* cash in his gun safe. Know anything about it?"

Aaron looked taken aback. "No 'hello, how are you?' first?"

"I said, hey." Then, fingers snapping, "Stacks. Gimels. Ken."

"I don't know anything about it," he said, rubbing his shirtsleeves, trying to conjure warmth. It was freezing outside. "He was on the payroll a long time ago. He might just be saving it for a rainy day. Maybe a retirement in Hawaii."

That actually made sense. Ken didn't live like someone who had been taking bribes. If he had never spent the money, then maybe he *was* saving it for something.

"I was also hoping I could talk to Shonda," she said.

Aaron sighed and shook his head.

"Just give me the name of the hotel," she said, attempting to keep her voice self-assured. "I got a few more follow-up questions."

"About Colfer Dryden?" He looked at her then, his hazel eyes nearly black in the shadows.

"No," she lied. "Other stuff."

"Yeah, right." He laughed as if this was all a joke. "No."

"The Drydens put blood in my trunk. They're threatened. Don't you want to know why?" she asked.

Aaron looked past her, toward the roar of traffic off Route 17. Police sirens wailed in the distance. He focused his attention back on her. "They're sadistic, racist pricks. They don't need a reason to screw with you."

"So you're not going to tell me which shady motel off Route 4 they're in?"

"No," he said flatly.

She smiled at him. "But I know it's on Route 4."

The ends of his mouth quirked up slightly. "Listen," he said, his voice soft, almost sultry.

He encroached on her space, forcing her to back up against the brick wall. She was suddenly reminded of Christmas seven years ago and of Damon and Shonda that night she was surveilling the club.

The wall felt cold even beneath her coat. "I should go," she said lightly. "If I'm to narrow down the motel on my own."

He looked serious for a moment. "Colfer is insane. He'll kill you."

"I know," she said, just as serious. The sirens grew louder.

"He won't think you're cute playing at being a PI."

"I'm not playing," she said, pushing off the wall and moving toward him, forcing him to step back. "I'm actually good at this, despite what you think."

He sighed. "I didn't say you–"

"You didn't have to," she shot back. "It's your *tone*."

"My tone?"

The sirens wailed again, sounding close, as if they were parked out front. Lights flashed across Aaron's face.

They *were* out front.

"Fuck," Aaron muttered. He opened the back door and darted inside. Billie followed him. They sprinted down the hallway and through the black curtain that opened up onto the dance floor.

The *Malta Club* was brimming with men now, both customers and cops. The dancers huddled together, watching and whispering as a tall, middle-aged man with a mustache accosted Matty for questioning.

Detective Richards.

Matty shrugged him off hard, even went so far as to raise his fist.

Richards twisted Matty's arms behind his back. Billie caught the glint of handcuffs and heard the detective grumble, "Assaulting an officer."

Matty had played right into their hands.

Aaron shoved aside a customer and charged toward the cadre of policemen but was thrust back by Neil Goff's iron grip. His father hissed something into Aaron's ear, too low for Billie to hear, but she caught the drift in Aaron's defeated gaze.

There was nothing he could do.

Billie, too, watched helplessly as they escorted Matty out of the *Malta Club*.

CHAPTER FORTY-NINE

Aaron stood with his hands in his jacket pockets and watched as the police cruiser drove off with Matty inside. His breath came out in white puffs.

"We should head in," Billie said.

"The club is swarming with cops," he replied curtly. "Your boyfriend's in there."

Morales. "Would you stop calling him that?"

"What? Your boyfriend?" He stared at her. "Isn't he?"

"No," she said adamantly.

"Am I?" he asked softly.

When she didn't respond right away, he swatted the air. "Forget it."

Moths flitted around the neon martini glass, throwing themselves into the light. The parking lot smelled like gasoline from the idling police cars.

"Listen," Billie began, feeling this dreadful need to insert some optimism into this conversation. "Matty'll be all right. Your dad's lawyers–"

But Aaron was in no mood for her reassurances. "I got soft. *You* made me soft. Israel. This dead dancer…this is your fault."

She hadn't been expecting that, and she felt herself grow hot. "I didn't employ a crime junkie to dance in my club without vetting her. I didn't conduct shady dealings with Paul Russo to get his nephew off the hook and hang a girl out to dry."

"No, but because of my *feelings for you*, –" he spat that out as if he was disgusted by it "–I stuck my neck out to protect a skinhead and his girlfriend when I should have let my father handle it like he wanted to. I should've made Damon Shane take the fall."

"But he didn't do it."

"Neither did my brother!"

"Then he'll get off. They don't have anything. That's why they baited him. They wanted him to throw a punch so they could bring him in. God, didn't you learn this lesson in the womb?"

That stopped him. The glare he gave her was hard and bitter. "That's us, right? Criminals from birth."

That shamed her. "Aaron–"

"You don't get to have me both ways." The lights from the remaining police cars flashed across his face. "You've always been attracted to me because I was Neil Goff's kid. I'm dangerous. I ooze sex." He tossed her words back at her. "Good in bed, but that's it, right?"

"Aaron–"

He cut her off again, "Why were you with me all those years? You could've just stayed away. Saved us both a lot of heartache. Because I am never going to change." He held his arms up and gestured around at the club and at himself. "This is what I am. A Goff."

"You're not a murderer," she said.

"I'm whatever my father needs me to be," he said coldly. "After this, I'm going to take care of the problem, and Matty will be home in a few hours."

"Give me more time," she implored.

"You can't stop this. This is bigger than you and your lock-pick kit and your spy pen. You're not a cop, Billie. You have no real power here."

Just then, Detective Morales came outside. He glanced between Billie and Aaron, sensing the tension, and said, "Everything all right?"

Billie glanced at the detective. "Yeah." She stared at Aaron.

"Just getting a lesson on the real world from the expert here."

Aaron shook his head as if trying to rid himself of Billie's naïveté. He stared at the ground but addressed Morales. "You done tearing up my club?"

Morales looked at Billie. "You should head out."

"Don't tell her what to do," Aaron barked at him.

She glared at Aaron. There was so much she wanted to say, to refute, but not here. Not in front of Morales. Her anger was the climbing mercury in a thermometer. "I plan to leave."

But she wasn't going home, and Aaron knew it. He gave Billie a withering look.

But she wasn't pretending. She was a decent private investigator, and Aaron wasn't the only one who was resourceful and sly.

"I'm leaving too," Aaron said.

But Morales simply smiled like the devil. "Not so fast. Detective Richards would like a few words with you and your old man. We're just waiting on your lawyer."

"How long will that take?" Aaron asked Morales, but he was staring at Billie.

Morales shrugged. "Why? You got a date?"

Aaron cursed under his breath. He was stuck, and he knew it.

But that only gave Billie a slight head start. And she was going to need it.

Billie pulled her car into the QuickChek's parking lot and killed the engine next to the air compressors. To find out where Aaron had stashed Damon and Shonda, she needed to think fast.

It would have to be a place where Aaron had connections but Neil didn't. It would also have to be a person who would turn a blind eye to Aaron's dealings and wouldn't call the cops the moment they spotted a Torn Cross tattoo. It would have to be owned, or at least managed, by one of Aaron's friends.

Probably someone from high school, someone he had known a long time, someone he trusted.

Think, Levine. Think.

She dialed Paretsky's Storage Center. A languid voice answered, "Run out of room? We're here to help."

"Brian!" She practically screamed his name into the phone.

"Yeah?" He sounded cautious. Maybe he didn't recognize her voice.

"It's Billie."

That elicited a grumble. "You know, you got me in real hot water with my dad."

"Look, I'm sorry about that." She tried to make her voice sound sorry.

"He said that I should know better than to let a Levine get one over on me."

"Brian, this is important. Life-or-death important."

He huffed, still not convinced.

She added, "You could help me close a big case and save two lives."

"Really?" Stroke a man's ego – that was all it ever took.

"You told me about the local business group. Remember? Said maybe Levine Investigations should be a member."

"Yeah," he said, perking up. "Yeah, I remember."

"So, then you know a bunch of the businesses in it, right? You're like an expert in Bergen County small businesses?"

"I wouldn't say an expert." He sounded sheepish.

Perfect.

"Of course you are. I bet you know everyone."

"Not quite, but almost."

"For instance, who runs or manages a hotel on Route 4? Someone young? Maybe our age?"

He was quiet. So quiet that Billie thought the call had been dropped. "Brian?"

"Yeah, I'm thinking. I don't know. I mean, there are always a

bunch of old-timers who show up to those meetings, except–"
He stopped.

"Except who?"

"Rami Khan. Remember, he was in our school. He's not in the organization, though."

"Rami Khan," she whispered. A smile lit up her face. "Yes! Which place does he own?"

"The Bridgeview Lodge in Fort Lee."

"Thanks, Brian. You are the absolute best person on the whole planet. Don't let anyone tell you different."

"Is this gonna come back and bite me–"

She disconnected the call and started the engine. At this time of night, she could get there in ten minutes. But first, she had to stop at the bank.

CHAPTER FIFTY

The Bridgeview Lodge was a one-story string of rooms that opened onto a dimly lit parking lot. It was rundown and likely to stay that way – the weekly rates were paid by Social Security checks and cash assistance. Anyone else who found this place did so by accident.

Next to heavily draped windows, lightbulbs sputtered, casting a pale glow on the room numbers that clung to the doors with rusty screws. Below were various objects – plastic toys, a wheelchair, plants in cracked pots, even a pink flamingo stuck in a patch of weeds – that sat near the curb. Some people had lived here for years.

Whatever room Damon and Shonda were in was likely to have a bare front. The previous occupants were probably either dead or homeless, their stuff tossed into the dumpster next to where Billie was parked.

Her eyes scanned the row of suites until she found one all the way at the end, plain and missing the doodads in front.

She left her car under a streetlamp, softly closing the door so as not to draw attention to herself. Then, thinking better of it, she went to retrieve the pepper spray from the center console, just in case Aaron got here in time to stop her. She'd never do anything to physically wound him, not permanently anyway. Only she discovered the pepper spray nestled against a gun.

Billie huffed.

The money. The whispering. Lenny from the chop shop in Paterson.

Aaron must've paid extra for that. Waste of money.

She grabbed the pepper spray and left the gun.

Flattening her body against the rough block exterior, she attempted to peer into the window through the gap in the curtains. She caught a glimpse of the television show they were watching – the *Real Housewives of Something or Other* – through the mirror's reflection. Then she spotted a forearm, scarred with ropey lines, leading to a tattoo of a torn cross above a row of skulls.

For a moment, Billie allowed herself a satisfied smile. *Excellent detective work, Levine. Excellent* professional *work.*

She checked over her shoulder before knocking on the door.

The television went quiet. The drapes moved gently as if pushed by a ghostly hand. She heard the rattling of a chain and then the twist of the deadbolt.

The door opened to reveal Shonda in sweats and a Rutgers T-shirt.

"What do you want?" she asked with the jut of her hip.

"We gotta get you out of here," said Billie.

Shonda's eyes flitted around the parking lot. Then she gestured hurriedly for Billie to enter.

Damon, wasting no time, began plucking various items off the bedspread and hastily shoving them into a duffel bag. He barked at Shonda, "Get your stuff."

But Shonda didn't seem ready to bolt simply because Billie had told her she should. "Wait a second. Where's the fire?"

"Colfer found us," Damon said as he tossed a toothbrush and cigarettes into a side pocket on the bag.

"The fire," Billie said with as much authority as she could muster, "is that Matty Goff got taken in for questioning for Jasmine's murder today. Aaron is going to deliver you on a silver platter to Neil if you don't get out of here."

"Colfer must be loving that," said Damon before he flung a skirt at Shonda. "Let's hurry."

"We have no money," Shonda said. "Not even a car."

"I can lend you some cash," said Billie. She wasn't thrilled about it, but she decided she could spare some of Paul Russo's payment for Damon and Shonda's getaway.

"We'll take a bus," Damon said.

"A bus!" Shonda wailed.

Billie cut her off. "You want to take a chance with Neil Goff? Go ahead. But know your mother won't have a body to bury."

Shonda began to pack.

"I'll drop you off at the Greyhound stop in Ridgewood," Billie said. "You're gonna have to figure out where to go and how to get new identification."

"Hurry!" Damon barked again, startling Shonda, who still had that look on her face. The look that said she'd never thought she would have to run.

Billie pointed to the door. "I'll bring the car around."

She let herself out, shoved her hands into her pockets, and trudged toward the Hyundai. She got into the driver's seat and exhaled, grateful that the BCDB's judicious questioning of Aaron was buying her time.

She started the engine and pulled into the spot directly in front of their room. She lifted the lid of the center console and stared inside. No way was that thing registered. What the hell was she going to do with it?

Well, she had one idea.

She got out of the car and turned the knob to let herself back into their motel room. Then she stopped.

Ian Colfer grinned at her with his back to the sink and his hands on the counter. His face was lit by weak light, making his pockmarked skin appear even more pitted than it had the night outside Damon's house. Like Damon, Ian had scars crisscrossing his cheekbones. All the Torn Crosses did – leftovers from whatever rituals they had to perform to get jumped into the gang. It made them look all the more alike – all the more menacing and all the more monstrous.

The only thing that brightened his face was Jasmine Flores's diamond solitaire glinting in his earlobe.

She'd thought she had spotted it in the Overpeck Park restrooms.

"Close the door, Belinda Levine," Ian said with a twisted smile as he flashed his gun. He was taking care of problems.

Jasmine. Tommy Russo. Now Damon and Shonda, and lastly, her.

Removing roadblocks, one by one.

She glanced at Damon and Shonda, who were huddled together at the edge of the bed. Damon gave a subtle nod.

She kicked the door closed with her sneaker and shoved aside a brief moment of panic to make room for a plan. "Aaron's coming," she lied.

Ian laughed. "Doesn't that motherfucker have a Ponzi scheme to run?" He shook his head as if he found the entire notion of Aaron Goff a joke. "Anyway, I can take him."

"He's kicked your ass before," said Billie, recalling what Matty had told her in the car that night.

"Cheap shot," Ian said, no longer smiling. "Sneaky bastard, just like his father."

Billie tried another avenue. "You're never going to get out of this. You think five years was tough? Imagine several life sentences without the possibility of parole." She ticked off names. "Jasmine. Tommy."

"Tommy?" Ian's brows knitted slightly as if he was using all the brain power to get her meaning. Then he grinned. "Nature took care of that on its own, but we supplied the means. We had the drugs delivered to his door. The rest..." His fingers danced in the air as if Tommy's death had been conjured from fairy dust.

"Guess what?" she said. "Still murder."

Ian's face fell. He aimed the gun at her.

Billie's hands immediately went up. "What's your plan here, Ian? You gonna shoot all three of us?"

"How could you suggest that?" he said, pretending to look hurt. He ran his dirty thumbnail down Shonda's cheek. She whimpered, and Damon flinched but held back. Billie stood her ground.

"Maybe I kill Damon and take you and Shonda with me."

She'd like to see him try. "Where's your backup, Ian?"

He glanced up at her. "Huh?"

"Your brothers. Your guard at the door. You didn't come alone, did you?"

"No," he said, but there was a split-second change in his face that told her he had done exactly that. He had come alone. Billie noticed that Damon noticed it too.

Whatever he had come here to do, he didn't want anyone to know. More importantly, Billie guessed, he didn't want his father to know.

Ian stabbed the air with his gun. "I want that diamond. The big one worth all the money. The one the dead stripper had."

"Starla Wells?" asked Billie.

"No, the other one," Ian spat before he turned his head. "The Spanish girl. I know she hid it."

"Your dad tell you that?" Billie asked.

"What?" Ian grew flustered. "Just tell me where it is, and you won't suffer. Much."

"How'd you get Jasmine's earring?" Billie asked, stalling. "Did you take it off her body after bashing her head in? You'll die in prison."

"Only if the police nail me," he said. "I want the diamond. The one you and my dad and everyone is after."

If Ian Dryden didn't know where it was, then Colfer didn't either. Which meant Colfer didn't have it. He'd never had it.

And if he'd never had it, he likely hadn't murdered Starla for it.

So why had Shonda lied to Neil?

"I don't know where it is," Billie said simply.

Ian scoffed. "Fine. Then I'll just take my own diamond."

Billie had no idea what he meant until he grabbed Shonda roughly by the elbow and hauled her to her feet. She cried out, and Damon lurched to reach her until Ian brandished his gun and held it to her temple. "Uh uh," he said in a singsong voice. "I'm the one with the gun."

"Well, that's embarrassing, because I've brought one too." Billie lifted the gun from her coat pocket. She had meant to give it to Damon to take with him for safety, but this seemed as good a time as any to show it off. "It's like we arrived to the party in the same outfit."

She wasn't quite sure how to hold the weapon. It felt awkward in her hand, and Ian knew it. He smirked.

Until Shonda kneed him in the crotch. The gun fell to the floor as Ian cupped his balls.

Damon scrambled for Ian's gun but accidentally kicked it under the bed. Billie dove for it, one hand reaching into darkness, feeling nothing but dust bunnies and carpet.

Her ribs received a hard kick, and she lost her breath. She groaned and flipped onto her back.

Ian loomed over her. He bent down to retrieve the weapon she'd stupidly brought but was suddenly met with a fist to his cheek.

He went over like a felled tree.

Shonda called out, "Got 'em!" She held up both weapons with pinching fingers. "I hate guns."

"Me too," Billie groaned.

Damon grabbed them both from Shonda and aimed them at Ian, whose nostrils were now rimmed in blood.

"Should've brought Dunphy," said Damon, peering over the muzzle.

"Hold him steady," Billie told him. She dug into Ian's pocket and took out his truck keys. She removed his wallet from his back pocket and slid out all the cash, all six hundred dollars. She handed both those things to Shonda.

"You're not stealing my truck," Ian growled.

Damon knocked him out cold with the butt of one of the guns.

"There's a chop shop in Paterson that can help you," Billie said. "I'll give you the address. Do not use your Torn Cross connections. Take my gun with you, and give it to a guy named Lenny. Tell him thanks but no thanks."

"If Colfer catches you, you're dead," Damon said to her.

"Likewise," she told him while she dug around in her own pockets. "You know what else I also found in my center console? Zip ties and duct tape."

"You're outfitted like a serial killer," Damon said.

"Bind him."

Damon nodded then got to work securing Ian to the bed. After that, he went outside to get Ian's truck.

Shonda stood as far away from Ian as she could and trembled. "He touched me."

"If it makes you feel better, he's going to prison."

"It doesn't." Shonda sighed, but she sounded a hair's breadth from a breakdown.

Billie gestured toward the passed-out Ian. "You told Neil that Colfer had Starla's diamond in his possession this whole time, but that couldn't be. Otherwise, Ian wouldn't be here trying to kill us for it."

"I panicked," Shonda said, clearly offended by Billie's accusation. "So I lied. It got Neil to focus his murderous rage on someone else."

"So whoever Jasmine was talking to on the phone–"

"She never mentioned Colfer's name. She just said, 'I know who has the diamond, and when I get it, we'll have our proof.' Then I listened to her podcast episode about Starla Wells. It wasn't hard to make the connection. I had simply used it to my advantage."

"Doesn't explain how Ian knew," said Billie.

"Well, I didn't tell him," said Shonda.

"Damon?"

Shonda cocked her brows as if to say, "Are you insane?" She pushed the curtain aside to glance outside, probably checking to see if Damon was on his way back. "I don't know if I can disappear forever. I love Damon." It didn't sound as if it was Billie she was trying to convince.

"I get it," said Billie.

"I doubt you do," she bit back. "What would a nice Jewish girl like you know about my relationship?"

"You fell for Damon because he was dangerous. Or maybe because he made dangerous things seem safe. He's good with his hands and with guns. Your life has been unpredictable and unfair, and it's nice to be with a person who sheds light on the shadows."

Shonda stared at her. "I guess you sorta do get it."

"Colfer Dryden wants you dead, but he's lazy. Likes immediate payout. Run off with Damon, and if things get stale, go your own way, but always check your back."

Shonda nodded just as Damon returned. He jerked his chin at Billie. "That address?"

Billie scribbled it on the notepad on the nightstand and gave it to him. He slipped it into his pocket.

"Wipe your prints off Ian's gun and leave it," Billie said. "Take the one I brought."

Damon nodded. "Thanks for all your help," he said before holding out his hand for Shonda.

She stared at his palm for a moment before taking it.

Billie shut the door, slipped on a pair of latex gloves, and dialed 9-1-1 from the room phone. "There's been some kind of incident at the Bridgeview Lodge. I saw one of those gang members there. Room 10." She hung up. Then she texted Malley from her own phone. *Break in the case at Bridgeview Lodge.*

She could hear Ian's muffled cries through the tape. She didn't stick around and wait for the cops to show. She parked across the street and watched the action while pressing an ice pack to her torso.

And yet she felt amazing.

CHAPTER FIFTY-ONE

When Billie arrived home that night, the house was dark except for the glow of the television screen flashing across Gramps's still form. He had fallen asleep in the recliner. An opened can of seltzer, its bubbles still popping inside the aluminum, was miraculously still clutched in his hand.

She knew that she should wake him, send him off to bed, only he looked too peaceful to disturb. So Billie plucked the afghan from the sofa, a patchwork of oranges and browns that her great-grandma had knitted in the seventies, and draped it over him.

Billie then hauled herself up to her attic bedroom. She fumbled for the cord in the darkness, swatting it with her hand twice before grabbing it and pulling hard.

The light shone, and a voice from behind her said, "I see you've let the caged birds free."

Billie bit back a cry and stumbled into the banister, wincing when the railing hit her bruised skin. She spun around just as Aaron stepped toward her, his lips quirked in a half smile.

She almost should have expected him, except he hadn't sneaked into her bedroom since they were in high school. She felt nostalgic and also a little peeved.

Billie rubbed gingerly at her side. "Can't you text me a heads-up like a normal person?"

"And ruin the surprise? This is more fun."

"You missed a crazy night." She kicked off her shoes and shimmied out of her coat. She eased onto the edge of her bed with exhaustion. He stood over her then. He had changed his clothes from when she had last seen him at the *Malta Club*. He was now wearing a Prussian-blue button-down shirt, and he smelled like aftershave and spearmint.

He had showered and dressed up to come over.

Billie was pretty sure she reeked like sweat and whatever mildewy aroma permeated the Bridgeview. She rose from the bed, thinking she should at least change out of her shirt, spritz on a body spray that David had gotten her from the mall, but Aaron disagreed. He gently pushed her back down.

He put his hands on either side of her and crawled onto the bed, forcing Billie onto her back. She didn't stop him. "Easy," she said. "I'm a little banged up."

"I can't imagine the other guy," joked Aaron as his weight fell on top of her. His belt buckle pressed slightly into her hip. His pupils were as large as buttons.

He brushed a strand of dark-blond hair off her eye. "I'm sorry about before. At the club. I was worried for my brother, and I was a bastard to you."

"I haven't exactly been Little Miss Sunshine to you either."

"No, but I deserve it." He swallowed, and his Adam's apple bobbed. "I really want us to make it."

She pushed herself up slightly to her elbows. "Then you need to stay here. My family needs me, and if you want to be with me, then I need to know you're going to be around. For a long time. Otherwise, what's the point of us?"

That caught him off guard. He hadn't expected her to be quite so blunt, except she wasn't finished. She traced the fleshy line on his neck. "How did you get that scar?"

He pressed his hand over hers. "I was double-crossed. The deal went south, and I nearly died. And when I came home, after a long stint in the hospital, my father said, 'Shame about the job.'"

"Your dad's a dick," she said.

Aaron laughed softly. "He is, but he made me who I am. And sometimes, I even like that guy."

"Yeah," she whispered. "I like that guy too. When he's nice and helping me out, not threatening to kill two innocent people."

"I wasn't going to take out Damon and Shonda, you know."

"You *were* going to serve them up to your dad." She stared into his eyes. In the light of her bedroom, they shone like amber. She shifted slightly under him.

"I would do anything to protect Matty," he said. "Even if it's the wrong thing."

Billie thought she might understand him in that way. She would do anything to protect David, even if that meant risking her life so Neil Goff could uncover a lost diamond.

"How is Matty, by the way?" she asked.

Aaron leaned down and ghosted his lips over her neck.

Her breath hitched.

"Home," he said. "Apparently, the police found Ian Dryden tied up in a hotel room at the Bridgeview, wearing Jasmine's earring. They let Matty go." He nibbled on her ear.

"How fortunate."

"Indeed," he said, his voice husky. "Guess the BCDB got Jasmine's killer."

"Possibly," she said.

He stared at her. "You mean, you're not sure it was Ian?"

"I'll be sure when I hear a confession," she said.

"You could've been killed." He was serious then, pressing his thumb to her chin, tilting her face so that she would have to look at him. "I like you in one piece." Then he added softly, "I really don't want to lose you again."

She wrapped her hand around his neck and brought him in close for a kiss. She didn't want to lose him either.

When Billie awoke the next morning, Aaron was already dressed and sitting in the chair she used as a dirty-clothes hamper. Her T-shirt and jeans had been neatly folded and left on top of the armoire. He was leaning forward with his hands on his knees. "I gotta sneak out."

Billie grabbed her cell phone from the nightstand and squinted at the time. Shit. It was late. "You should have left an hour ago."

"I know," he said. "But I wasn't in any rush. I like it here with you."

She pushed herself up and kicked her feet over the side of the bed. She rubbed sleep from her eyes and blinked furiously to bring moisture to her contact lenses, which were dry like dust. "We'll do the usual plan," she said.

Aaron smiled. "It never let us down before."

Billie gingerly shrugged on her bathrobe, still sore from the kick to her ribs, and crept down the attic stairs. She opened the door and poked her head into the hallway. Sounds flowed from the kitchen. Cabinet doors opening and closing. The coffee pot percolating. Gramps's gruff voice. She gestured for Aaron to follow her downstairs and into the foyer. They stepped quickly but quietly, two burglars desperate for a clean getaway. All that was missing were striped outfits and burlap sacks of money.

She pushed Aaron toward the front door while she darted into the kitchen. She stretched her arms over her head, winced, and said loudly enough to cover the sounds of the lock being turned, "Good morning, family!"

Gramps sat at the kitchen table in his T-shirt and pajama bottoms, but his eyes were narrowed and disbelieving. Shari was also there, sipping her coffee, smiling vacantly.

"What's gotten into you?" Gramps asked just as a person yelped from the foyer.

Oh no.

Then David's voice. "Oh, shit, man. Sorry."

Gramps scrambled to his feet and ducked out of the kitchen. Billie closed her eyes for one second of reprieve and went after him.

Aaron stood awkwardly near the hall closet, his hand pressed delicately to his eye.

"What's going on?" Gramps asked.

"I hit Aaron with the door," said David, looking apologetic in his dirty scrubs. "I was coming in as he was going out."

Gramps whirled on Billie. "Oh, really?" Then, darkly, he said, "I should've known something was up! You and your big stretches and loud greeting."

Aaron stood there helpless, his eye swelling.

"He needs to put a cold compress on that," Shari said from the hallway.

"I'm all right, Mrs Levine. I was just going," said Aaron.

"You hear that? He was leaving." Gramps opened the front door and gestured wildly – as if he was presenting a duke at court – for Aaron to go. "Well, let's give the young man room to exit."

Aaron attempted to kiss Billie's cheek but then must've thought better of it. He mumbled to her, "I'll call you later."

"The hell you will," said Gramps.

Billie turned on her grandpa. "Are you for real?"

Gramps pointed his finger through the window to Aaron's retreating figure. "He's gonna get you killed."

"How?"

"His father!" he yelled.

"I can handle the Goffs," she said, but it sounded weak, as if she didn't believe it herself.

"I know you were at the Bridgeview last night," Gramps said, practically spitting in anger. "You don't think I hear things?"

"Blech," said David. "That is not a clean place for a hookup."

"I wasn't there for that," she said in a disgusted voice. "I busted Ian Dryden."

"You almost got killed," Gramps retorted.

Shari's eyes went wide.

"I didn't," she emphasized to her mom. "I was fine." To Gramps, she said, "I'm an adult."

"I'm your superior," Gramps said. "I can fire you."

"You wouldn't dare!"

"Try me!"

"Okay, okay," David said, wedging his body between them. "I think we all need a breather."

Gramps threw up his hands in disgust and trudged up the stairs. "I'll see you later."

David called up to his back, "Don't leave the house today. Billie and I have an appointment."

"We do?" she said.

He cast a quick glance at their mother before he looked at Billie and mouthed, "Safe Horizons."

Billie sighed. The afterglow of her romp had been worn bare, like a scratched-off lottery ticket.

CHAPTER FIFTY-TWO

A woman whose name tag read Barb and who introduced herself as the resident liaison escorted Billie and David around the Safe Horizons campus (her word).

Barb was probably their mother's age, but she looked far younger. She had graying blond hair that fell in waves down her back. She wore bohemian-style clothes and clunky turquoise jewelry and smelled like rose perfume.

Billie liked her even if she was, in essence, a real estate agent.

"This is our dining room." Barb held her arm out, her bangle bracelets sliding down her wrist, as if showcasing the space on *The Price Is Right*.

It was set up exactly as it had been in the photo on the website, with several round tables covered in white tablecloths and red napkins. Bud vases holding single red roses adorned each table. There was classical music and a waitstaff. If Billie hadn't known better, she would have thought she was on a cruise.

Normally, the website pictures never matched reality, but in this case, they did. It should've made Billie happy, but her heart simply sank.

David smiled, but he did so painfully. He also knew they would never be able to afford this place. What were they doing here?

Barb led them down a cream-colored hallway with beatific art on the walls. "The residents paint the canvases," she explained.

"You have art classes?" asked David.

"Oh, yes," Barb said. "And music appreciation. We do cooking too. Pottery. Yoga is very beneficial."

Now the word "campus" made sense. It wasn't a memory center or assisted-living facility. It was a fun college for old people.

Billie's cell phone buzzed with a text from Tasha Nichols. Billie slowed her pace to check the message.

FYI. Wake for Tommy Russo tonight at Rizzo's in Northvale. Some friends and I are going to pay respects. For Jasmine.

It was no vigil, but it was thoughtful. Only Billie wasn't anxious to attend. Catholic wakes made her uneasy; she blamed the open casket.

"Keep up, Billie," said David as they rounded a corner and passed a common room in which several residents, some in wheelchairs, some at tables, were surrounded by staff in pink scrubs hovering over them. Billie was reminded of Louise caring for Roxie Russo.

This seemed like a rich person's game.

Barb smiled and called to a petite woman whose hair looked recently coiffed, "Mrs Wong, you look beautiful."

The woman smiled and patted her hair. "Friday is my beauty parlor day."

Today was Saturday.

Billie turned to Barb. "You have a salon?"

"Oh, yes," said Barb. "They work wonders there. Color. Cut. And a shave."

Finally, she led them down a hallway. Barb unwound a key from her neck and unlocked a door. She held it open and insisted Billie and David go in first.

"This room has a small kitchen, but based on what you told me about your mother, she would be in our Cottage wing. Those rooms only have a sink and fridge. We don't allow Cottage residents to have access to a stove, for obvious reasons. But other than that, the rooms would be the same."

It was a model room, she explained. The bed was made with a heavy duvet. A plasma TV hung on one wall. A small café-style table and chairs were set up in front of a bay window, covered in gauzy curtains. A bouquet of real tulips had been placed on the table. *Tulips in November.*

The bathroom was probably as large as Billie's attic bedroom. It boasted a granite counter and a rain shower.

"Our mother doesn't remember to bathe too often," Billie said, feeling slightly unsettled by the admission, as if she shouldn't be airing Shari's dirty laundry to a stranger.

But Barb simply nodded. She dealt with this all the time. "Our staff is trained to help."

Billie wondered if her mom would be willing to let a stranger see her naked.

Barb must've noticed Billie's worry. "It's weird for our residents at first, but they adapt. We treat them like family, and the socialization helps a lot. So many of our residents were used to being left alone in front of the television like children."

David cringed at that.

"Which we understand," Barb added quickly. "It's difficult to care for an ailing adult. Alzheimer's is a ruthless disease, and I don't just mean for the person who has it. The family suffers the most. We lose the people we've known our whole lives."

Billie's eyes began to burn. She dug a knuckle into her eye socket and cleared her throat. "When we spoke on the phone, you said there was a Medicaid option."

Barb waved them into the hallway. "Let's head to the garden."

Of course, the garden.

David and Billie followed Barb through French doors and onto a stone patio. It was cold outside, but Billie noted large heaters standing like sentinels next to benches. "Outdoor air is so important to our well-being," said Barb. "We wouldn't want to deny that to our residents simply because it's getting cold."

Billie agreed.

They sat on a bench made of expensive plastic boards. A plaque read, "Donated in Memory of Ellie Winslow."

It was warm with the heater.

Barb took the vinyl folder from under her arm and opened it. She handed David the brochure and clicked a pen, circling numbers. "Unfortunately, this facility doesn't accept Medicaid."

Billie sank lower into the bench.

"What's the cost?" asked David, looking as if he already regretted asking.

"The rent for our Cottage rooms starts at $6,975," said Barb.

Billie's voice pitched. "A month?"

Barb nodded then gestured around at the heaters, the exquisite garden, the residents sitting with wool blankets on their laps, staff members offering hot chocolate. "It's a first-rate facility."

"We don't have that kind of money," said David.

Understatement of the millennium.

"I understand," Barb said.

"I don't think you do," David said hotly. "We love our mother just as much as anyone else who can afford this place. I work in a subacute and rehab facility. I know what it's like to see patients bear the brunt of inadequate staffing. We can't put her in a place like that."

Barb nodded along.

"But we also can't take care of her the way she needs," he went on. "We have to work. It's an impossible choice." He bent over and ran his hands through his hair, and Billie could see how consumed by guilt he was.

David had another opportunity to start fresh with Matty, but how was he expected to work, date, and take care of Shari? To live his life. How was Billie to do the same?

And yet how did they shuck off the responsibility of caring for their mother? The woman who had birthed them and raised them. Who loved them despite their flaws.

She was their *mom*.

It *was* an impossible choice.

"What about the day program?" Barb said, flipping through her folder until she found another brochure. "It's done through our sister site, but it's very good and a hundred percent covered by Medicaid. A van would pick her up in the morning, bring her to the facility. She could do art, pottery, crafts. Same as here. She'd get lunch, and then they would transport her home around four."

David brightened. "That sounds like a solution." He closed his eyes and said wistfully, "I could work the day shift again."

"That would be nice," said Billie cautiously, waiting for the catch.

"There's just one hiccup," Barb said.

And there it was.

"We have a waiting list. A long one. However, priority usually goes to the younger patients because of the severity."

Small miracle.

"If you want, I can submit your paperwork for that," Barb said kindly.

Billie and David glanced at each other, nodded, and then said to Barb, "Yes. Do it."

They all rose to their feet and shook hands, and David and Billie walked to the parking lot alone, neither of them saying anything.

Finally David said to her, "Maybe everything will work out."

Billie stole another glance at Safe Horizons and nodded, but she couldn't find her voice to agree with him. The truth was, she just didn't know what the future would be like, and there was no sense in making predictions.

It could all change in an instant.

CHAPTER FIFTY-THREE

Billie and David returned home, relieved and exhausted in equal measure. While he went to his room to play video games, she went into the kitchen to talk to her grandfather.

Gramps was sitting at the kitchen table with the newspaper out in front of him, reading glasses perched on the tip of his nose, but his eyes were staring blankly at the wall.

She liked that he still read the paper. She liked that she had never found him swiping mindlessly through his cell phone, looking at memes.

She leaned against the doorframe. "Truce?"

Gramps harrumphed. "We're not at war."

"Aren't we though, sometimes?"

He harrumphed again.

But Billie knew from experience that he couldn't stay mad at her. She was, after all, his favorite granddaughter. His *only* granddaughter, but still his favorite.

"Will I expect to see Mr Aaron Goff around here more often?" he asked.

"Not with that attitude," she joked. The truth was she didn't know what she was doing with Aaron. She knew that she loved him, but that wasn't always enough.

She decided to change the subject. "How's Ken doing?" she asked.

"He died," said Gramps.

"What?"

He rubbed at the jowly skin around his chin. "The hospital

called this morning. He passed in his sleep." He smiled sadly. "I was gonna see him today. Guess he saved me the trip."

She pushed off the door molding and wrapped her arms around Gramps's shoulders. "I'm so sorry."

He patted her as if she needed the comforting. "Nothing to be sorry for. Ken was never going to live a long life. If the booze didn't get him..." His voice trailed off.

But it wasn't the booze that killed him. Billie got to him first.

Gramps rubbed at his eyes and then pushed himself away from the table. He got to his feet. "I gotta call Rothman's Funeral Home," he said. "When Ken was still a beat cop, he had made arrangements in case he was ever shot—" His voice broke. He cleared his throat. "Shot in the line of duty. The hospital is sending him there, but I gotta make sure everything is up to his standards." He tried to sound strong, but he was failing. Billie could hear it in his voice. He was devastated.

He'd lost his best friend.

"Do you want help?" She took out her phone and held it up. "I can call *Nagel*'s."

"Nah," he said. "I gotta tell the guys myself. They'll want to hear it from me."

"All right." She felt so helpless. There had to be something she could do.

Gramps sniffled. "He didn't have any family, not really. Just a nephew in AC who didn't give a rat's ass about him." Gramps's eyes sparkled with tears, and Billie found herself on the verge of weeping. "He wasn't a bad guy," he said.

"I know," she said, sniffling.

"He really wasn't." Gramps broke into sobs.

Billie hugged him again. Then David entered the kitchen and asked, "What's going on?"

"Ken died," Billie said through tears.

David nodded, took two steps toward them, and enveloped them in a giant hug.

* * *

Billie sat on the couch with her mother and stared blankly at the television screen while David got ready for work.

They were watching *Stormy Weather* on the Soap Opera Network. It might've been a repeat. Even Billie wasn't sure anymore. Not that she could be bothered to pay attention. She simply stared ahead, her eyes blurry, her brain heavy with death.

"Remember when you used to watch this with me when you were a little girl?" Shari said suddenly. "You used to annoy me with questions."

Billie turned to her mother. For a moment, she was speechless. A pleasant spark had bloomed in her chest. "You remember that?"

"Yes," Shari said with a smile. She turned her attention back to the television. "But I forgot what's happening now in the story."

"If it makes you feel better, I don't know either." Billie snuggled into her mom and rested her head on Shari's shoulder. "I *think* Harold just found out that he has a secret love child."

"Ooh," said her mom. "He's my favorite character."

"He is?" Billie asked, surprised.

"He has the best storylines. Also he would do anything for his kids. He would never leave them. Not like your father."

Billie laughed despite herself. "Yeah. Dad sucks."

David came down the stairs, dressed in scrubs, with his hair gelled. "I'm off to work. I'll see you tomorrow."

"Bye, honey," Shari said.

David gave Billie a surprised look. Billie shrugged. Today might've been a bad day for Gramps, but it was becoming a good day for Shari.

As David headed out the door, Billie's cell phone buzzed from a number out of the BCDB. She got up and excused herself to take the call.

"Levine Investigations," she said with an eye still on her mom.

"Billie, it's Malley."

"Oh, hey," she said brightly, hoping he had forgiven her for that ambush outside the *Wagon*. It boded well that he was, at least, returning her call.

"So you were right. If Starla didn't come from money, she certainly knew how to find it."

Billie heard voices in the background. Other phones were ringing. A cacophony of office noises.

"There was an incident linking Starla to Paul Russo," Malley continued.

"Which incident?"

"On the index card that the girl had," he said impatiently. "Starla reported a black eye to 9-1-1 in–"

"December of 1990," finished Billie as she took her phone into the kitchen to grab a pen and paper.

"So," he said, "apparently, the patrolman who wrote down the report claims that Starla didn't want to press charges."

"All right. Did the patrolman write down who hit her?"

"No," Malley said, clearly irked. "Because she wouldn't give him a name, so I tracked him down. He's a sergeant now if you can believe it." Malley huffed. "Anyway, Starla Wells had been assaulted at Paul Russo's home, and Russo pressured some higher-up to make this report disappear."

"Were Starla Wells and Paul Russo having an affair?" Billie asked breathlessly.

"Don't go jumping to conclusions," he said.

"Because she was transgender?" asked Billie.

"That's not why," he said.

"Then what?"

"It took a lot of phone calls to the tech nerds in the department, but one of them managed to track down that shell corporation on the money order you texted me."

"Let me guess. It was owned by Paul Russo," she said, satisfied.

"No," he said, even more satisfied. "The Donovans."

"Roxie's family," she cooed. She gasped as her synapses fired. "Starla Wells was born Claude Donovan."

"It's a good guess. We would've never made this connection thirty years ago. As far as we could tell, Paul and Starla would've never crossed paths."

"And now?" she asked.

"We'll consult the cold-case squad. We'll need to see if we can pull DNA."

Billie deflated. That wasn't the turn of events she had been expecting since it hardly seemed immediate. "What if Paul Russo murdered Starla *and* Jasmine?"

"We're holding Ian Dryden on suspicion of Jasmine's murder," Malley said.

"Is he talking?"

"What do you think? Anyway, what's Russo's motive?"

"They were sleeping together," Billie reiterated. "He didn't want his wife to know."

"Gotta prove it."

Billie sucked on her lower lip. She could still hear her mom's soap opera playing in the living room. "It took thirty years," Reginald said, "but I'm glad to know the truth about my son."

"Huh–"

"Huh what?" Malley huffed.

What if Jasmine was also hit at the Russo residence? The black eye. The one Nuri said Jasmine tried to hide with makeup, the one Tommy also claimed to not know anything about.

"Levine?" Malley said.

"Paul Russo has to talk," she said.

"We're gonna bring him in after the wake."

"He's just going to get a lawyer," she said, frustrated. "He won't tell you anything."

"We'll worry about it. We know what we're doing. Anyway, stay clear of the whole clan."

"But I'm headed to Tommy's wake tonight."

"Billie," he warned.

"What? I'm bringing my mom. I can't cause trouble with my mom there."

Malley grunted. If he didn't believe her, he didn't say. But he didn't believe her.

She popped her head back into the living room and said to Shari, "Do you own anything black?"

CHAPTER FIFTY-FOUR

Billie and Shari drove to the Rizzo Funeral Home in Northvale, a brown building with a rectangular portico and lush green grass. A flagpole sat in the center of the lawn, surrounded by mulch and colorful mums. A shovel was stuck in the ground as if left mid-job.

The place resembled an elementary school more than a mortuary, an observation Shari noted.

"Is this a school?" she said.

"No, Ma. It's a funeral home," Billie reminded her.

"Oh no, who died?"

"Tommy Russo. A client. No one you knew."

Shari breathed a sigh of relief.

They were both dressed in somber shades. Shari wore black pants and a gray sweater, and Billie was wearing a black dress that had once been part of a witchy Halloween costume. Either way, they cleaned up well for a wake.

Billie had even done her mother's hair in a low bun and offered her a swipe of pink lipstick. The whole effect took five years off Shari's face.

Billie leaned into her mother. "You don't have to talk to anyone if you don't want to."

Shari nodded numbly.

Inside, the funeral parlor was staged like an old lady's living room. There was lush, dark carpeting and floral sofas, brass-tinged coffee tables that held little plastic holders for prayer cards, and watercolors in gilded frames on the walls. And doors. Lots of doors with easels out front showcasing giant photos of the deceased.

Most of the faces were weathered, belonging to people who had lived long lives; only Tommy's appeared as if it could've been from his high school yearbook. He'd been so healthy then – dark eyes and hair to match. A sly smirk. Tan skin. He could've done anything, could've been anyone, but he couldn't stay away from the drugs.

Billie's chest ached.

A young man in a drab suit sat behind a desk. He looked up at Billie and her mom and smiled with thin lips. It seemed like a look he had practiced – one that was pleasant but not too pleasant. Friendly but sympathetic. Kind but not perky. "How can I direct you?"

Billie pointed to Tommy's portrait. She knew where she had to go; she just couldn't bring herself to go in there yet.

Billie didn't do well at wakes, too comfortable with the Jewish system of burying the dead within twenty-four hours.

The man rose from his chair and pointed a slender hand toward the room in the back. "Suite 110."

Billie nodded and steeled herself. Just like she didn't like hospitals, she didn't like funeral parlors.

But at least in a hospital, one stood a chance.

She was glad to have her mom with her.

Billie opened the door, and Shari entered the suite first. It was a massive room, similar in size to a hotel ballroom. Rows of maroon chairs were set up, the front rows filled with the bottoms of older women.

At the head of the room was the coffin. A giant mahogany box sat with its lid open to reveal Tommy Russo. Just a kid.

Billie swallowed phlegm to moisten her throat. Her feet felt cemented in place. Her mom glanced around, spotted all the people, and hunched her shoulders as if trying to disappear. "Can I wait with the man in the suit?"

She meant the lobby. "I don't know, Ma," said Billie,

thinking about how easy it would be for Shari to slip outside and disappear down the busy road.

"I can stay with her."

Billie glanced over at Tommy's roommate, Glenn Peters, who hovered awkwardly by the coatrack. He was wearing a gray sports jacket and a red tie. He looked as uncomfortable as she felt.

"Hey," she said.

He nodded in greeting. "I paid my condolences, but I, um, don't know what else to do."

"It was nice that you came," said Billie.

Glenn leaned toward her a little bit in order to keep his voice low but still be heard. "He looks so different. I mean, I know it's makeup and everything, but he could've looked like that all the time. He could've been clean." Glenn must have also been thinking of his sister.

"I know exactly what you mean." She squinted and glanced at the mourners huddled near the coffin.

She spotted Paul Russo right away, wearing an outrageously expensive suit, and next to him another man with the same white hair and eyes.

"That's Tommy's dad," said Glenn, following her gaze. He tilted his chin at a woman, tall and slender, with long, dark hair, exquisitely dressed in a Chanel suit. She could've been a cast member on the *Real Housewives of New Jersey*. "And his mom." She held a tissue to her nose and was sobbing loudly, but it sounded like a performance.

"Anyway," Glenn said, "I feel like I should stay for the prayer part, but I don't know what to do with myself. So if you want me to wait with your mom, I can."

Billie nodded. "That would be great. Thank you." She turned to her mother. "This is Glenn. He's a friend. He's going to sit with you in the lobby. All right? You can't leave." She turned to Glenn and lowered her voice. "She has Alzheimer's."

"Got it." Glenn offered his elbow, and Shari took it. She looked relieved as he escorted her outside the room.

Not for the first time, Billie felt like crying. She hadn't known Tommy well, not like Glenn. She only knew the drug addict. But she couldn't help but think that if he had stayed clean, Tommy could've had a cool roommate, an awesome girlfriend, and a great life.

He had none of that now.

Billie waited in line to offer her condolences.

Tommy's mother held out a cold hand for Billie to shake. Her eyes were dry, but her voice was wobbly. "Thank you for coming."

"I'm so sorry for your loss," Billie said automatically, but the whole ordeal felt dramatized.

She shook various mourners' hands, repeating the same line over and over again.

Then she stopped at Paul Russo. His eyes widened. He was clearly surprised to see her. Of course he was. He was hoping to be done with her.

"I came to pay my respects," she said. "I really am sorry that I wasn't able to figure out who killed Jasmine."

He pumped her hand.

"Or Starla Wells."

Paul Russo blanched.

Got you.

"Well, thanks for coming," he said quickly, curt and dismissive. "The priest will be here soon to preside. I imagine you don't wish to stay for that."

"Why would you assume that?"

Paul Russo's face reddened. His Adam's apple bobbed. "I didn't–"

Billie leaned in close and whispered, "I know what you did."

He immediately stiffened. *Got you again.*

She smiled smugly and made her departure. On her way to the lobby to get her mom, she passed Tasha Nichols, Nuri O'Brien, and a bunch of other girls from the Safety Brigade, all dressed in black leggings and dark, oversized sweaters.

Billie caught Tasha's eye and jerked her chin. Tasha walked over with a dubious look.

"I think I have a big theory about Starla Wells and Jasmine," Billie said. "Is your Sleuth Squad interested?"

Tasha raised a brow. "Perhaps. Let's see what you got first."

"Stay tuned." Billie said goodbye to the girls and Glenn before collecting her mom.

"Are we leaving?" asked Shari. "I have to use the bathroom."

Billie led her mom down the hall to where a placard hung above a door that read "Ladies' Lounge."

Shari used to say that one should always judge a place by the cleanliness of its restrooms, and this place was spotless. There was even a sitting area with a plush sofa and starlight mints in a bowl. This was where they found Louise sitting while Roxie Russo washed her hands at the sink. She was dressed in a black suit and dress flats. Her white hair was coiled in an elegant bun and fastened with a sparkly clip. She wore rings on all her fingers and a brooch with a clear center gem surrounded by a circle of emeralds.

"Do you need help?" Billie asked her mom.

"I don't think so," said Shari.

Louise observed Shari as she went into the stall. "How's she doing today?"

"Pretty good, considering," said Billie, briefly forgetting that she *was* at a funeral home.

"We take the victories when we can get them," Louise said as she rose from the couch to offer Roxie a paper towel.

And that was when Billie noticed how the light hit Roxie's brooch. Billie stared at the huge gem, cut with precision to resemble ice.

Roxie asked Louise, "Who are we here for again?"

"Tommy," Louise said slowly. "Your nephew."

"Oh," Roxie said, her voice almost like a baby's. "How sad. My brother died, but we didn't have a funeral."

Louise patted Roxie's hand now, softly. "No?"

"My mother wouldn't let us," she said. "Poor Claude. I don't remember where he's buried."

Billie's brain felt like a rocky shore, all the waves crashing at once. She smiled gently. "Mrs Russo, that brooch is stunning."

Roxie brightened. "It's a family heirloom. My grandmother gave it to my brother, but then he died, and it was lost for a little while, but then I got it back." Her voice sounded as if it was coming from a faraway place.

Louise cut in, "We were so worried that Tommy had sold it off, but we found it, didn't we, Miss Roxie?" She turned to Billie. "It was tucked away in a secret little compartment under the molding. Stumbled upon the opening while vacuuming. Jasmine must've hid it there to keep it safe. Wasn't that kind of her? Although why she didn't tell me…I would've insisted Mr Russo add it to the safe deposit box."

"Because, Louise," said Billie, dropping the pretense, "that's an eight-carat diamond in that brooch."

"Is it now?" Louise said, her smile faltering.

"Have you ever heard the name Starla Wells?" Billie asked.

"I don't think so," Louise said thoughtfully.

"But you have. Right? Mrs Russo?" Billie asked. "You told Jasmine about your brother, didn't you? That Claude became Starla?"

The toilet flushed, and Shari emerged. She went to wash her hands. The water ran, and Shari said, "I want to go now."

"One sec, Ma." Billie turned back to Roxie. "You gave Jasmine a black eye."

"Now why would she do a thing like that?" Louise asked.

"Jasmine had taken the brooch and squirreled it away in the wall. And when Roxie couldn't find it, she lashed out at Jasmine and punched her because that brooch meant a lot to Roxie."

Roxie cried, "It was a family heirloom! Grandmother said it was for the first-born, but Claude was dead to us, you see? He was gone, replaced by this whore. The diamond was meant for me. A precious gem. Nothing else like it in the world, so I took it back." She stared down at her hands, gnarled and arthritic. "There had been so much blood."

"Miss Roxie!" Louise cried. "What are you saying?"

"Paul shouldn't have given it to her, but he said he owed her for a job."

"The arson," said Billie. "Paul had her burn down the *Lucky Lous* as revenge against the Torn Crosses for seizing his olive oil shipment. And in return, he let her keep the diamond. He couldn't have known that Roxie would kill to get it back."

Roxie began to pace frantically around the bathroom. She roughly grabbed Louise's sleeve. "Paul said that I couldn't wear it on my finger because Colfer would know what I did, so I had it made into this brooch." She swiped at her blouse. "It's beautiful, isn't it?"

Louise paled. "Oh, my word."

Billie leaned into Louise and whispered, "It's not possible that Mrs Russo also killed Jasmine, not in her condition, but it makes sense that Paul did to cover up Roxie's crime."

Louise covered her mouth with her hand.

"Say nothing to him. I'm going to call the cops, all right? Just pretend everything is normal."

Louise nodded silently while Billie gently led her mom from the restroom and ushered her down the hall. Billie was walking so fast her mom couldn't keep up.

"I gotta make a call," Billie said to Shari as they exited the funeral home and made their way to the car, which was parked on the far side of the lot. The choice of spot was now a regrettable decision, as the sun had all but disappeared.

"It's dark," said Shari as she huddled in her coat.

Billie unlocked the passenger's-side door and eased her mom into the seat.

"We'll leave in a minute," she told Shari. She closed the door and dialed Detective Malley. He didn't answer, so she left a message.

She spoke rapidly into the phone. "Roxie Russo is wearing the missing diamond because it's a family heirloom! Roxane Russo killed Starla Wells. She admitted it in the ladies' room." She felt so proud of herself. "Oh, it's Billie, by the way, and I'm at Rizzo's in Northvale. Send a car or whatever you do when someone guilty of murder is discovered by a twenty-four year-old PI. Boo-yah."

She ended the call with smug satisfaction.

Roxane Russo had killed Starla Wells, and Paul killed Jasmine Flores to cover it up.

She knew it.

She just knew it.

She opened the passenger's-side door and said to her mom, "We need to sit tight. You want me to put on the radio?"

But Shari shook her head.

"Are you hungry? I could go back and steal that bowl of mints from the bathroom."

Again, Shari shook her head. Then she pointed behind Billie and said, "Olive oil shyster."

"Huh?" Billie whipped around. Standing in front of the car was Paul Russo, and he wasn't alone. Beside him was Colfer Dryden.

CHAPTER FIFTY-FIVE

"Well, well, well," Colfer said with a slick grin. "If it isn't my favorite Jewish-American bitch."

He was dressed in dirty jeans and a collared shirt. He wore a sturdy canvas jacket, the kind she'd seen on construction workers. His hair was gray and close-cropped. He had a thick beard, and his cheeks were pockmarked by old acne scars. He looked like his son, Ian, just older and meaner. And harder.

Paul Russo glanced over his shoulder. Billie could see the anxiety rolling off him in waves. He growled, "Get rid of her."

"What about the old lady?" Colfer jerked his chin toward Shari, who sat frozen in the car.

"Take her too," said Paul. "No witnesses. You'll deal with the nurse later. I can't have any of this come back to me."

Louise? "Help!" Billie cried and was immediately hit so hard she fell to the asphalt. Her ears rang. A drop of blood began making its descent down her cheek.

Colfer lifted her off the ground and slapped a hand across her mouth. She tasted axle grease on his skin. She squirmed, and he tightened his grip. She tried to shake him loose, but he hissed at Paul, "You don't think this won't come back on me? My boy's already in the slammer for a hit I didn't order."

Billie stopped moving.

Colfer tilted his head toward the back of the lot, where a nondescript blue sedan was parked in darkness. "Pop the trunk," he barked.

Paul hit a button on a key fob. The trunk lid opened.

Colfer dragged Billie toward the car.

Inside the trunk, she spied plastic zip ties and duct tape. The tools of a serial killer.

"After what you did to Ian," he cooed into her ear, "I'm going to enjoy this."

Paul Russo checked nervously behind him. "I thought you'd bring a van."

"Vans are too sinister. This is less conspicuous."

"Hurry up," Paul hissed.

Colfer said, "Tape her mouth."

Paul huffed, but he obliged, pulling a gray piece of tape off the roll. When Colfer moved his hand away from Billie's mouth, she cried, "Russo has Starla's diamond!"

Paul moved to spread the duct tape over her lips, but Colfer jerked Billie out of the way.

"You lyin'?" he whispered into her ear. "Because I will kill you."

"His wife is wearing it right now. I saw her in the bathroom."

Colfer eyed the funeral parlor's front door as if weighing his options. "Maybe I'll go check."

"No," Paul barked. "Be smart, Colfer. This is a stall tactic. You have to get rid of her. Someone's gonna see."

"Police are on their way," Billie said. "I called Malley. Told him that Paul Russo paid Starla Wells to burn down the *Lucky Lous* as revenge against the Torn Crosses for stealing his olive oil shipment. And as payment, he gave Starla the Donovan family heirloom."

"She's lying!" Paul glanced back at Rizzo's and then at Colfer. He lowered his voice and repeated, "She's lying. I had nothing to do with the fire. Neil did." His eyes flitted around, grasping for something to reel in Colfer, settling on anti-Semitism. "You know Jews. They're liars. They protect their own."

Billie stared at Colfer. "You sure about that? You wanna take that chance?"

Colfer considered that for a second before he tossed her to the ground and lunged for Paul.

Billie scrambled to her feet and ran to her mother, but Paul snatched her by the wrist, tugging her toward the sedan. "We had a deal."

"Deal's over," said Colfer. "You owe me more than what we agreed upon."

Billie had one more ace up her sleeve. "Call it even, since the Torn Crosses stole your latest olive oil shipment with Tommy's inside knowledge."

Paul growled at Colfer, "I knew it was you."

Colfer laughed. "She's playing us both." He laughed again, almost savagely. Then he narrowed his eyes at Paul and withdrew a gun from his waistband.

Billie tried to wrestle her hand back, but Paul's grip only tightened.

"Put that away," Paul begged. "Someone will see."

"Did you kill Starla?"

"No."

"I don't believe you." Colfer cocked the gun and pointed it at Paul.

Billie teetered as far from the muzzle as she could.

People began filtering out of the funeral parlor, including Roxie and Louise.

"He's telling the truth," Billie said quickly. "Paul didn't kill Starla. Roxie did."

Paul whispered, "She just wanted her ring back."

Colfer kept his gun aimed at Paul. "I loved that club. I loved that woman. She was the diamond. You get that?"

"Colfer, there are witnesses," Billie warned.

Just then, Colfer went down. He cried out and dropped the gun. Paul Russo dove for it, releasing Billie, who kicked the gun out of the way. It skidded across the parking lot like a stone skipping across the surface of a lake.

Shari Levine stood over Colfer, holding the shovel that had

been stuck in the mulch outside the funeral parlor. The edge was tipped in Colfer's blood. "Don't you touch my daughter!" she screamed at him.

He pressed a hand to his wound.

A black SUV sped into the parking lot, its lights flashing.

The truck hadn't even properly stopped before Malley flung open the door and jumped out with his Glock drawn.

Paul Russo's hands went up. So did Colfer Dryden's.

Billie called to Malley, "Am I still more trouble than I'm worth?"

He shook his head as if he found the whole situation exasperating. But he was smiling.

Billie was leaning against a patrol car while Detective Richards was jotting down notes.

She crossed her arms and watched as a paramedic took Shari's blood pressure. The lights from the bus illuminated the entire parking lot. The sky was that shade of blue that was so dark it was nearly black. There wasn't a star to be seen.

Malley was inside, taking a statement from Louise. Several mourners stood outside, watching the chaos, including Tasha and some Sleuth Squad members, who huddled in their coats, too curious to go inside where it was warm. The true-crime junkies needed their fix.

A woman in uniform was tagging the shovel Shari had used to take down Colfer.

Billie gestured toward her mother and said to Richards, "She saved me, y'know?"

Richards tapped his pen against his notebook. "She's your mom. That's her job."

Billie smiled sadly to herself. "She's still good at it."

"You all right?" he asked.

Billie wiped away the tears and cleared her throat. The adrenaline was wearing off. "So, you think Paul Russo killed

Jasmine Flores? I mean, it makes sense, right? He must've killed her to keep it quiet. She knew everything."

Richards considered that. "We have Ian Dryden in custody for Jasmine's murder."

"But Paul–"

"Claims he was on a business trip in Sicily. We'll check it out."

"Oh," she said. "It couldn't have been Roxie. Doesn't seem likely."

Richards shrugged. "I really can't be talking about this stuff with you."

She gave him a look.

"A nurse was with her most of the time," Richards said. "Just doesn't seem likely. She may not even go down for Starla. Not in her condition."

"Paul will though. Right? Accessory after the fact or whatever?"

Richards laughed softly and continued to scribble. "Or whatever." He grew serious. "Listen, you did good, kid, but we're pretty confident that it was Ian. He wanted Tommy dead. He just got to the girl first." He cast a look at Shari. "When your mom's all checked out, you can take her home. Sit tight."

Billie nodded and thumbed through her phone to waste time until she felt eyes on her. Glancing up, she spotted Nuri O'Brien watching her.

Sleeves pushed up, Nuri's tattoo was on full display. *Murder Girls suspect everyone.*

Perhaps it was time that Billie did the same.

CHAPTER FIFTY-SIX

That evening, Billie maniacally clicked a pen while sitting at the kitchen table, surrounded by her laptop, cell phone, and notebook. The pen eventually fell apart in her hand.

"Office supplies don't grow on trees, you know. And that kid at Staples has it out for me," said Gramps as he headed toward the fridge with a stack of papers tucked into his armpit. He retrieved a bottle of beer and twisted off the cap with the hem of his shirt.

"You returned an opened box of dollar highlighters," said Billie. "What was he supposed to do about that?"

"They were *dry*. Stand by your product." Plopping into the chair next to her, Gramps set the papers on the table and said, "What's with the anxiety?" His eyes jumped from the dismembered pen to her cell phone screen, which displayed a portfolio of tattoo art. "You thinking of getting one?" He took a swig from the bottle.

"A hamsa," she said, pointing to a patch of bare skin on her wrist. She gave him a furtive smile. "To match Aaron's."

Gramps spat out the beer. Droplets landed on her notebook, blotting the ink.

Snatching it away, she patted it dry with her sleeve. "Jesus, I was freaking kidding."

He grabbed a napkin and wiped at his chin. "Not funny. Never funny."

"Yeesh. Calm down." Billie blew out a breath. "So what happened at Ken's?"

"I went into his safe." He looked guilty.

"You gonna spend those gimels?" she asked, half kidding, while staring at her poor penmanship and a name – Crystal Dean.

"I might need them to pay the property taxes," he said through sips. "Ken left me his house."

"What? He left you his place?" She pointed toward the window. "The one around the block?"

Gramps nodded at the stack of documents he had dropped onto the table. "That's a copy of his last will and testament. What's his is now mine, and all the crap it entails."

For a moment, Billie sat back in her chair, staring dumbfounded at the wall. In this real estate market, even Ken's dump of a house could fetch nearly $400,000. Shari could live comfortably at Safe Horizons for several years. Unfortunately, it wasn't Billie's inheritance to milk.

"What are you going to do?" she asked Gramps.

He pressed the cold beer bottle to his forehead as if trying to relieve a headache. "I don't know. I can't think about it now. The hospital released Ken's body to the funeral home. I have an appointment there tomorrow afternoon. He made arrangements for cremation, but I still gotta go and talk to the guy about a service." He glanced her way.

"You want me to come with you?" she asked.

"If you don't mind."

"Course not."

Gramps tilted Billie's little notebook toward him and downed the rest of his beer. "Crystal Dean. Colfer's alibi, huh?"

"Yeah," said Billie. "This case still feels off. I'm trying to figure something out. At Rizzo's, when Paul and Colfer had me cornered–" Gramps grumbled "–Colfer said something about a hit he didn't order. Then at the Bridgeview–"

"Again, when you were cornered," Gramps interjected.

"*Ian*," Billie continued, ignoring that comment, "said 'I want the diamond the Spanish girl had.' How would he know that

Jasmine had Starla's ring? Colfer didn't know that. Tommy hadn't known that Jasmine had found the diamond. Someone must've told Ian that it still existed somewhere."

"He could've assumed she was holding out on him," said Gramps.

"Ian's an imbecile. He moved against his father, thinking there was a big payday coming his way." Billie dropped her head and stared at the kitchen table. "What isn't adding up?"

Gramps gestured to the notebook with his beer bottle. "You think this Crystal Dean is a clue?"

Billie shrugged helplessly. "What do you know about her?"

Gramps got up from the table and rinsed the now-empty bottle. He set it in the recycling bin by the door and stared outside into the dark. "Not much. Gang groupie. Trailer-park trash. Colfer bedded a lot of girls like that."

"Yeah," she whispered, an idea forming. "Trailer-park trash." She hurriedly gathered her things. "What time is your appointment tomorrow at Rothman's?"

"One o'clock," said Gramps, turning his attention from the window to her. "Why?"

"I'll make it. I just gotta stop at Kentwell tomorrow morning for a meeting." She would definitely want a Safety Brigade escort. "We'll talk later about the shiva, too, after I make a call to the tattoo parlor."

She awkwardly gripped her laptop and notebook while scrolling through her phone before pressing it to her ear.

"I swear, Belinda, if you get a matching tattoo, I will–"

She shushed him. "I'm looking for an artist who covers up botched tattoos. – Yes, I'll hold."

"Belinda," warned Gramps.

But she was already in the hallway, heading up to her room. A plan was beginning to form.

CHAPTER FIFTY-SEVEN

Billie arrived late to the meeting on purpose because she wanted to make an entrance. Also she'd had to wait for Rebecca to walk from her post at the Safety Brigade office to Billie's car in the visitor lot.

Rebecca was carrying a notebook and had a lot to say about her duties at the Safety Brigade. She was a faucet, left on and flooding the sink.

Billie opened the door to the conference room with a to-go cup from the *Ugly Mug* in her hand and a slight spring in her step.

Rebecca took a seat at the table, pressing the notebook to her chest, holding it tight like a shield. Meanwhile, Tasha Nichols stood in the front, nearest to the chalkboard, dressed in a white shirt and slim tie. She clearly took her presidential duties very seriously. Billie was banking on that.

"You're late," Tasha said.

The table was surrounded by young female faces including that of Nuri O'Brien, who looked like she hadn't slept in days.

"It'll be worth it, I swear," Billie sang, her voice loud and exuberant. "Good morning, Sleuth Squad. I've gathered you all here today to discuss a case. And not just any case but *the* case. Starla Wells."

Tasha crossed her arms and sighed. "We know how it went down. We were at the wake, remember?"

Billie dropped her bag to the table and marched toward the chalkboard, edging Tasha slightly out of the way.

The sunlight streamed through the windows as if it too was dying to bear witness. It would not be disappointed.

Billie grabbed the eraser and swiped it across the chalkboard, obliterating notes and cross-references. Tasha cried out. Several girls gasped.

"Trust me," Billie said with a wink.

She plucked a piece of chalk from the ledge and began to write down names.

Roxie Russo.

Tommy Russo.

Paul Russo.

Louise. *Poor Louise. She was fine but out of a job.*

Starla Wells/Claude Donovan

Ian Dryden

But, then:

Felicia Jann-Smith

Bex

There was another name to add, but not until the end.

Tasha narrowed her gaze at the board. "What are you playing at?"

"Hear me out." Billie turned to the girls and squared her shoulders. It was time for serious business. Clearing her throat, she said, "I realize now that many of you are aware that Roxane Russo, née Donovan, killed her sister, Starla Wells, in order to steal back a family heirloom that she claimed was rightfully hers. Did Roxie kill Jasmine Flores? Unlikely. So who did?"

"Ian Dryden," Tasha said as if Billie was an idiot.

Billie turned to her. "The problem with this case is that from the very beginning, Jasmine wasn't truthful." She pressed the chalk to the board. "First and foremost, Jasmine Flores did not become interested in the Starla Wells murder until episode fifteen of her podcast, adorably entitled, 'Wells, Wells, Wells,' which dropped in January. That was after she and Tommy had been dating for a few months, having gotten together at a Halloween party last year." Billie pointed to Tommy's name on the chalkboard. Then she pointed to Louise's name. "Roxie's nurse said that Jasmine was a kind girl who spent time with Roxie. After all, Roxie was her boyfriend's ailing aunt, and Jasmine wanted to make a good impression on the judgmental Paul Russo, who thought the girl was only after Tommy's money. Perhaps Jasmine was patient with Roxie as she listened to her ramblings about jewels and long-lost brothers and, eventually, a stabbing that she had gotten away with."

"Where are you going with this?" Nuri asked.

Billie tapped the chalk to the board. "Suddenly, Jasmine brings her friends – the Sleuth Squad – this interesting cold case. A case from the nineties that no one had heard about before."

"So?" Nuri said. "We learn about old cases all the time from the internet."

"I had to do a lot of digging to find any information on Starla Wells. The internet did not giveth like it did for the Golden State Killer or the Boston Strangler. No book has been written about Starla. No interviews. How would Jasmine have even stumbled upon this case? Unless her boyfriend's aunt told her."

"Fine," Tasha said, annoyed. "What difference does it make if Jasmine learned about the murder from Roxane Russo or from the internet?"

"Doesn't it bother you that Jasmine brought you a murder she already knew the ending to?" asked Billie, knowing it did, in fact, bother Tasha. "Why didn't she tell you the whole story? That Starla was transgender? That Starla was born Claude Donovan? That she was the in-law of Paul Russo? That's a big deal. Why not share this with her Sleuth Squad sisters from the beginning?"

The girls murmured. Billie was right. A Sleuth Squad could not operate on secrecy and omission.

"She must've had her reasons," Tasha said, speaking above the din, but Billie could see that this was getting to her.

"She did have her reasons, and I bet you know what they

were." Billie sipped from her coffee cup for effect. She circled Felicia Jann-Smith's name in several blue loops.

"Who's that?" asked one of the girls.

"Ms Jann-Smith is a literary agent for the Gilded Spine Agency. She specializes in true-crime stories, and Jasmine was her newest client."

"So Jaz told this woman about Starla Wells?" asked a girl in a pink sweater.

"She did," Billie said. "They had a contract. Ms Jann-Smith had plans to sell Jasmine's book at auction once it was completed. She sent me an email last night confirming this. According to the agent, Jasmine's story could retrieve an advance worth six figures. A college kid helped solve a decades-old murder, and the villain of the story is the wife of bazillionaire Paul Russo."

"A college kid? But *we* all did it," said one of the girls. "The Sleuth Squad."

"That's right," Billie said almost patronizingly. "But Jasmine didn't want to share the byline, or at least not right away. She wanted to solve the murder on her own with a gentle nod to you all. She dated a drug addict. She went undercover. She took the risks."

Tasha scoffed.

Billie turned to her. "And it pissed you off."

Tasha opened her mouth, but no words came out.

So Billie continued. "I checked with the Safety Brigade office. Rebecca?" Billie pointed to the girl in the corner.

She raised her hand as if answering a question in a lecture.

"You work at the Safety Brigade, don't you?"

"That's right," she said in a small voice.

"Speak up," said Billie.

"Yes, yes I do."

"Did Jasmine use the app, requesting an escort?"

"Yes," she said. "But it was so early, and no one was available. The bylaws dictate that if someone needs an escort and no one's around, the on-call volunteer must go, and they must log it in."

"Is Jasmine's name logged?"

"No."

"Why is that?"

Billie stared at Tasha Nichols, who was sputtering like a broken fountain. "I–I–"

Billie said to Tasha, "Jasmine had been stalked by Ian Dryden, and she felt unsafe, so she asked for an escort. Tasha, you were on call that morning. You came and walked Jasmine to her car in the Kentwell lot, but you didn't tell the police that, and they didn't think to check."

The girls murmured. Why hadn't she said anything?

"We had a fight," Tasha said loudly. "You're right. I was pissed about the book and the agent and how she sold us out."

"And you didn't think to mention this?" asked one of the girls.

"It didn't look good for me," she said. "But I swear I didn't hurt her. I was just angry. And she knew it. We had words. That's it. Then she went off to her car."

No one looked convinced.

"I *swear.*"

"What did you fight about?" Billie asked.

"It happened like you said. Jasmine solved the Starla Wells case. She didn't give me specifics, and she wouldn't say who murdered Starla, but she did say that she knew where the diamond was hidden, and it was going to prove everything. Everyone would learn what happened." Then, for emphasis, she added, "In *her* book."

"Everyone was going to know," Billie repeated. "Eventually."

"I didn't *kill* her. I would never." Tasha looked around the room imploringly. "You have to believe me."

"I believe you," Billie said.

"What?" Tasha said, clearly surprised. "You do?"

"Yes, and I will tell you why. Rebecca?"

Rebecca flipped open the notebook. "A freshman whose boyfriend got violent called for an escort to the gym, and Tasha went. That was recorded in the log."

"And what time?"

"Nine."

"So it was unlikely that Tasha beat Jasmine in the head with a pipe, lifted her into the trunk of her car, and went off to escort a girl to the gym without blood evidence on her," Billie said.

Tasha pointed adamantly at the chalkboard. "Of course. Like I said. I would never hurt her."

"I'm not done." Billie picked up the chalk and drew a line from Ian's name to Jasmine's. And then another line to a still-empty spot.

"I'm not following," said a girl.

"Just wait. It gets better. So Tasha did escort Jasmine to her car. But when Jasmine went on the app and asked for an escort, the app sent a blast to all Safety Brigade officers, and that included–" Billie filled in the empty space "–Nuri O'Brien."

"What?" Nuri rose from her seat, but Rebecca pushed her down.

"Jasmine had been avoiding you," Billie continued. "Something you left out but that I was able to piece together from the lovely agent, who said Jasmine had flippantly promised her best friend a piece of the action. Tommy's aunt had a ton of jewelry. What was the big deal about stealing a brooch from a woman with Alzheimer's? Until Jasmine realized what she was sitting on. That this story, this crime, was her *I'll Be Gone in the Dark*. But she couldn't fence a famous stone like that. And there went Nuri's payout. Her windfall. The money she needed to promote her podcast. Hell, with that kind of money, she could start a whole podcasting network."

"That's ridiculous," said Nuri. "Jasmine never told me she had changed her mind."

"She didn't have to; you overheard her and Tasha arguing. You knew the diamond would end up with the police. So you followed Jasmine to the Percy Street Parking Garage. She often went on Tuesdays to retrieve Tommy. You *had* to talk some sense into her. This was a diamond worth half a mil – probably more now with inflation – that could help you. Jasmine was already rich. She didn't need the money. But she wouldn't listen, so you had to stop her. You hit her over the head with a pipe you found."

"That's ridiculous," said Nuri with a snarl. She lifted her lithe arms to address the audience. "Tommy was a known junkie. He hung out there with lowlifes like him."

"Tommy wasn't there that morning. He was sleeping in his car after helping the Torn Crosses steal containers from his uncle's latest shipment. You know about the Torn Crosses, right? After all, you're a member."

The room exploded. Billie waved down the roar.

"It took me a bit, but then I figured out what was bothering me. Ian Dryden knew that Jasmine had died knowing the whereabouts of an eight-carat diamond when no one else did. Not his father, Colfer, who thought Neil Goff had stolen it off Starla's corpse. Not Tommy. Not even the cops. Only Ian was certain that Jasmine had hidden it somewhere. What did you tell him, Nuri, for him to slash my tires? Corner me at the Bridgeview? That I was on the right track? That it was only a matter of time before I located it?"

"I don't even know him," Nuri said, but the facade was crumbling.

"Sure you do. He's your half brother. Took five minutes of digging to discover that Crystal Dean is your mom. Crystal from Moonachie who was one of Colfer's many side pieces. She got pregnant in 2001, had you, and a few years later married Sean O'Brien, who legally adopted you as a toddler."

Tasha cursed.

Nuri folded her arms defensively. "So what? Doesn't make me a Torn Cross."

"This is where I prove your guilt by association." Billie circled another name on the chalkboard – Bex. To the girls, she said, "Bex is a tattoo artist in Bergenfield." She turned to Nuri. "You referred me to the tattoo parlor, remember? I fudged some things and told the receptionist that I wanted to cover up a crude tattoo of a gang symbol from a misspent youth and asked for the best in the biz. She kindly put me in touch with Bex, who texted me some of her work." Billie took out her phone and opened an image. She held it in front of the girls. Everyone but Nuri leaned over in their chairs to get a better look. "Here's the 'before.' Note the torn cross above a row of skulls. Awful, right? Now look at the 'after.'" Billie swiped left to the image of MGSE written in a Gaelic font within a green clover. "Same skin. Nuri's skin to be exact."

Tasha roughly grabbed Nuri's arm and pushed up her sleeve.

"That 'before' photo could be anyone," said Nuri as she snatched back her hand.

"Bex will testify in court that it's yours," said Billie. "And the prosecutor will argue that after you killed Jasmine, you panicked and called Ian. He hefted Jasmine's body into the trunk. He thought to wipe everything down. It was a good spot. It's where Tommy went to get high. No one would suspect you. The BCDB didn't. They didn't even look into your background because they already had Tommy and Matty Goff as their prime suspects. You weren't even a blip on the radar. Until me.

"*Sneaky* of me, wasn't it?" Billie grinned. "You might've gotten out of the Torn Crosses, but you didn't get far."

Nuri's eyes bounced from Billie to Tasha to the exit. She bolted from her chair and flung open the door, but Malley was waiting outside with Richards. Richards snagged her and read Nuri her rights.

The girls then filed out to make statements.

Malley laid a fatherly hand on Billie's shoulder. "You did good. Looking into that agent and tattoo artist, that was smart.

Good detective work. But I think we need to talk about getting you a real investigative gig. One with steady pay; one that is safe. Let me talk to my friend."

Billie exhaled and watched as Nuri was led away. "I'll think about it."

CHAPTER FIFTY-EIGHT

Nagel's was crowded. Every graying and balding head in Bergen County stopped by to pay their respects and sit shiva with Gramps. It didn't look like a somber occasion since there was more laughter than tears.

Gramps had reluctantly dipped into Ken's blood money to pay for the spread. Good Jewish deli wasn't cheap. Platters of pastrami and Swiss cheese, seeded rye, and spicy mustard sat on a table in the far back. Bernice made her rounds with the coffee carafe while Gramps presided over his congregation with stories about him and Ken during basic training and then, later, their most infamous collars back when they had been on the force.

Billie sat across from Nicole and Calvin in her usual corner booth and shifted uncomfortably in a brown corduroy skirt and cardigan set. Her lipstick matched the vinyl cushions. She was completely overdressed for *Nagel's*, but it was for a nice occasion.

She checked her watch.

Calvin was wearing a blue dress shirt and tie. His dark hair had been perfectly edged at the temples. Billie smiled to herself, imagining him going to the barber and asking for the group-date special. He seemed like a real down-to-earth guy. No red flags that Billie could spot, and she had excellent creep radar.

Billie checked the time again.

"It's early," Nicole assured her.

"Right." Billie sipped from the water glass, leaving a smudge of lip color behind.

"So Nicole says that you're a private investigator," Calvin began. "That's really interesting."

"It can be," Billie said. "I just solved a big case, and I'm going to be working part-time for an investigative firm."

"That's amazing," Calvin said.

"Thanks." She was happy about the turn of events, even a little relieved. What insanity could she get up to working in an office?

"Billie is really savvy," said Nicole. "Toughest girl I know."

Billie grinned but dismissed that comment with a wave. Then she thought better of it. "You know what? I'm not gonna disagree with you."

Calvin laughed.

Billie liked him already.

Nicole turned around and watched as Gramps hugged one of his cop buddies. Softly, she said, "How's your grandfather holding up?" To Calvin, she added, "His friend recently died."

"Oh, I'm sorry," said Calvin. "Old age?"

"Yes. Let's go with that," said Aaron as he slid into the booth on Billie's side. "Sorry I'm late." He was dressed in dark denim jeans and a green button-down shirt that made his eyes pop like emeralds. He smelled like bergamot and soap.

"It's fine," said Billie quietly, taking another sip of water.

"You're not late," Nicole said reassuringly. "We were early. This is Calvin. Calvin, Aaron Goff."

Aaron rose from his seat and shook Calvin's hand.

Bernice came by and asked if they wanted to hear the specials.

"We're expecting two more," Aaron told Bernice. "Can you come back in a bit?"

"Take your time, honey," said Bernice as she sauntered away.

"My brother and his boyfriend are joining us," Aaron explained to Calvin.

"That boyfriend being your brother," Calvin said to Billie.

"Yes," she confirmed. "Sorry for the ambush."

Laughing, Calvin lifted his water glass. "I don't mind. I'm an extrovert."

"He handles students' complaints with the empathy of a rabbi," Nicole added.

"Sounds like a good gig," said Aaron.

Calvin turned to Aaron. "What do you do?"

Billie waited for Aaron to say something like import/export or the old cliché, sanitation. Instead, he just shrugged. "I'm in between jobs at the moment. Got any leads?"

"Not in my department at Kentwell," said Calvin, "But I'll keep my ears open. You got a degree?"

"No," Aaron said. "But I could go back to school."

Billie chuckled. Aaron gave her a look. "Oh, you're serious," she said.

Aaron didn't respond to that, but his mouth quirked into a slight smile. He opened the menu. "The Reuben is excellent."

Calvin's gaze trailed down the long list of deli foods. "I'm definitely having a cup of matzoh ball soup."

Nicole's eyes sought Billie's, and she raised her brows.

So far, the date wasn't a disaster, but it was early yet.

Billie leaned into Aaron and whispered, "Where were you before? I thought we were driving here together." After Billie had dropped her mom off with Mrs Rodriguez, Aaron had sent a cryptic text: *Meet you there. Something came up.*

"I had to make an important meeting."

Billie's heart sank. "Never mind." Her voice came out harsh and louder than she intended. "Meeting" probably meant that he had been shaking someone down for money. Or worse.

"Billie–" he began.

But she smiled broadly and phonily. "So who's up for half sours?"

Billie's cell phone rang in her purse, the high-pitched default tone. She glanced at it, mortified. "Sorry, it's just if my mom–"

Nicole waved that away. "It's fine. We get it."

Calvin gestured to his phone on the table. "I keep mine out in case my little brother needs me."

Billie exhaled then glanced at the text message from David. *Mom got into the Safe Horizons day program! She starts Monday. No more waitlist. Couldn't wait to tell you! See you in a few.*

Billie grinned. Her chest felt warm and tingly.

How did this even happen?

"Good news?" Aaron asked, trying to sound sly, but she heard it, an undercurrent of pride.

"Yes," Billie said, surprised as she glanced at Aaron. "*Someone* pulled strings to get my mom into this program." Billie grabbed Aaron's hand under the table and squeezed. He flushed. "So half sours and knishes?" she asked.

"Yeah," said Calvin. "And blintzes. I've never tried those."

"You won't be disappointed," Aaron said, but he was staring at Billie as he said it.

Billie raised her hand to flag down Bernice just as Matty and David walked through the door to hoots and hollers from the back of the deli. She heard Gramps cackling, "Ken lost his pants! He handcuffed the perp in his drawers," before wiping a tear from his cheek.

She slid over to make room for David, who asked quietly, "Everything okay?"

"Yeah," responded Billie. Nicole playfully nudged Calvin with her shoulder. Aaron laughed at something Matty said. "Everything is exactly as it should be."

ACKNOWLEDGEMENTS

Writing may be a solo endeavor, but publishing is not. There are so many people I would like to thank for helping Billie Levine see the light of print.

First, thank you to my agent Liza Fleissig for her tenacity and unwavering support. She has championed my work at every pitch meeting and to every editor. I am incredibly lucky that her foresight is what landed me at Datura Books. She is a force, and I am in awe of her every day.

I am also eternally grateful to my editor and publisher Eleanor Teasdale who read my Jewish, East Coast Veronica Mars and immediately envisioned it as her lead title to a new venture. I am beyond humbled by your faith in me and my writing, and I truly feel like the luckiest author in the world.

A huge thank you to the most impressive publishing assistant in the biz – Desola Coker – who graciously lets me clog up her inbox with random book recommendations, panicky emails, and just general what's goin' ons. One day we will hang and get that boba tea.

And thank you to Bryon, Caroline, Amy, and everyone else at Datura who supports and champions Billie.

I wouldn't be here without the love of my writing crew: Katrina Monroe, my wife in another life, who pushes me to explore my characters in deeper and more meaningful ways; Katie Moretti, whose publishing wisdom is worth its weight in million dollar advances; and Elizabeth Buhmann who happily reads every draft and gives me a bulleted list of things to fix. You are my sisters.

Props to Jill who makes sure my Jewish references and jokes have broader appeal than to just me, and also for checking my grammar.

I want to give a shout-out to my husband Bob, for his love and encouragement, and to my children who aren't impressed by anything I do. You all keep me grounded, and I love you for it.

Lastly, I want to thank my New Jersey brethren who have read this book, and I hope there are many of you. Please forgive any mistakes I've made regarding how long it actually takes to drive from Teaneck to Hackensack in traffic. For egregious errors in geography, please don't hesitate to contact me. Otherwise, let's just say we *fuhgeddaboudit*.